...N KURLAND

"[Kurland] consistently
delivers the kind of stories
readers dream about."
—The Oakland Press

THE MAGE'S DAUGHTER

A Novel of the Nine Kingdoms

**BERKLEY
SENSATION**

$7.99 U.S.
$8.99 CAN

S ▷ EAN

ISBN 978-0-425-25483-7

9 780425 254837

5 0 7 9 9

"I dare you to read a Kurland story and not enjoy it!"
—*Heartland Critiques*

**Praise for the novels of *New York Times*
bestselling author Lynn Kurland**

Princess of the Sword

"Beautifully written, with an intricately detailed society born
of Ms. Kurland's remarkable imagination."
—*Romance Reviews Today*

"An intelligent, involving tale full of love and adventure."
—*All About Romance*

The Mage's Daughter

"*The Mage's Daughter*, like its predecessor, *Star of the Morning*, is the best work Lynn Kurland has ever done. I can't recommend this book highly enough." —*Fresh Fiction*

"I couldn't put the book down . . . The fantasy world, drawn so
beautifully, is too wonderful to miss any of it . . . Brilliant!"
—*ParaNormal Romance*

"This is a terrific romantic fantasy. Lynn Kurland provides a
fabulous . . . tale that sets the stage for an incredible finish."
—*Midwest Book Review*

Star of the Morning

"Terrific . . . Lynn Kurland provides fantasy readers with a
delightful quest tale starring likable heroes."
—*Midwest Book Review*

"A superbly crafted, sweetly romantic tale of adventure and
magic." —*Booklist*

Lynn Kurland

THE MAGE'S DAUGHTER

BERKLEY SENSATION, NEW YORK

THE BERKLEY PUBLISHING GROUP
Published by the Penguin Group
Penguin Group (USA) Inc.
375 Hudson Street, New York, New York 10014, USA

Penguin Group (Canada), 90 Eglinton Avenue East, Suite 700, Toronto, Ontario M4P 2Y3, Canada
(a division of Pearson Penguin Canada Inc.) • Penguin Books Ltd., 80 Strand, London WC2R 0RL,
England • Penguin Ireland, 25 St. Stephen's Green, Dublin 2, Ireland (a division of Penguin
Books Ltd.) • Penguin Group (Australia), 707 Collins Street, Melbourne, Victoria 3008, Australia
(a division of Pearson Australia Group Pty. Ltd.) • Penguin Books India Pvt. Ltd., 11 Community
Centre, Panchsheel Park, New Delhi—110 017, India • Penguin Group (NZ), 67 Apollo Drive,
Rosedale, Auckland 0632, New Zealand (a division of Pearson New Zealand Ltd.) • Penguin Books,
Rosebank Office Park, 181 Jan Smuts Avenue, Parktown North 2193, South Africa • Penguin China,
B7 Jaiming Center, 27 East Third Ring Road North, Chaoyang District, Beijing 100020, China

Penguin Books Ltd., Registered Offices: 80 Strand, London WC2R 0RL, England

This is a work of fiction. Names, characters, places, and incidents either are the product of the author's
imagination or are used fictitiously, and any resemblance to actual persons, living or dead, business
establishments, events, or locales is entirely coincidental. The publisher does not have any control over
and does not assume any responsibility for author or third-party websites or their content.

THE MAGE'S DAUGHTER

A Berkley Sensation Book / published by arrangement with the author

PUBLISHING HISTORY
Berkley Sensation trade paperback edition / January 2008
Berkley Sensation mass-market edition / December 2012

Copyright © 2008 by Lynn Curland.
Excerpt from *Dreamspinner* by Lynn Kurland copyright © 2012 by Kurland Book Productions, Inc.
Cover art by Dan Craig.
Cover design by George Long.
Map illustration copyright © Tara Larsen Chang.
Interior text design by Kristin del Rosario.

ISBN: 978-0-425-25483-7

BERKLEY SENSATION®
Berkley Sensation Books are published by The Berkley Publishing Group,
a division of Penguin Group (USA) Inc.,
375 Hudson Street, New York, New York 10014.
BERKLEY SENSATION® is a registered trademark of Penguin Group (USA) Inc.
The "B" design is a trademark of Penguin Group (USA) Inc.

PRINTED IN THE UNITED STATES OF AMERICA

10 9 8 7 6 5 4 3 2 1

ALWAYS LEARNING   **PEARSON**

The MAGE'S DAUGHTER

Prologue

❧

Winter's chill hung in the air like thousands of polished silver shards, poised to fall soundlessly to the ground.

A young woman stood in the midst of that chill, heedless of its potential to harm her, and motionless, as if simply breathing in and out was all she could manage. She remained there for quite some time, fighting visibly to keep herself upright. In time, she took a careful step forward, only to rest again, still breathing raggedly, still adding to the frost.

Nicholas, lord of Lismòr, stood at the edge of the enclosed courtyard and shivered in the brutal cold. He spared a fond thought for the hot fire that burned in his solar not fifty paces behind him but knew there was no hope of enjoying it anytime soon. The fire would burn itself out before the young woman before him agreed to give up her current pursuit and come inside.

It had taken her the whole of the morning to get herself dressed and out of her bedchamber. The remainder of the day had been spent shuffling step by painful step out to the courtyard. She had refused a crutch of any sort, vowing that she would keep herself on her feet without aid or not at all. That she had managed it for any length of time said much about her strength of will. Nicholas suspected, however, that her will would not—no matter its strength—be able to see her across the distance left before her. Enough was enough. He strode out into the courtyard and stopped next to her.

"Morgan," he said quietly, "you must come in."

She didn't answer him. Perhaps she didn't have the strength for it.

"Please, my dear," he added.

She bowed her head. For several moments, she simply stood there and trembled. Then she held out her hand.

It trembled as well.

Nicholas ignored it and lifted her easily in his arms.

"You'll drop me, old man," she gasped weakly.

"I might, if you weighed as much as a half-empty sack of flour," Nicholas said grimly. "But as you do not, I'll manage, despite my creaking knees."

He carried her easily out of the courtyard and back along the cloister until he reached his solar. His page opened the door as he approached. He walked inside and crossed the chamber to set Morgan down in a chair near the hearth. He put more wood on the fire, then turned to look at his charge.

She clutched her cloak tightly to her throat and stared unseeing into the distance.

"Run and fetch wine, William," Nicholas said quietly to his serving lad. "And whatever sort of soup Cook has on the fire."

"Of course, my lord," William said and ran off quickly.

Nicholas took off his cloak and cast himself down in the chair facing Morgan. He leaned back and watched as she stared at horrors he could not see. He supposed he had some idea of what they were, for he had seen the shadows of them. They had been dreams of darkness and evil.

He did not envy her those dreams.

He looked up as William brought a tray of food and set it on a small table in front of Morgan. Nicholas dismissed the lad to a comfortable stool in the corner, then reached for wine. He poured it into the rustic pewter cups he'd begun to use after Morgan had dropped one too many of his glass goblets and refused to drink from them further. He hadn't cared about the glass, of course, but she had, so he'd humored her.

"Morgan," he said, "have some wine." He paused. "Morgan?"

She turned her head to look at him, but it was several moments before he could tell that she saw him.

"My lord?" she rasped.

"Drink, my dear," he said, reaching over and pressing the cup into her hands. "It will do you good."

She looked down at the cup as if she'd never seen one before and had no idea what to do with it. Finally, she seemed to come to terms with what it was. She bent her head and managed to bring the cup up far enough to drink from it. She set it down carefully on the tray, then leaned her head back against the chair and closed her eyes. Within moments, she was asleep.

Nicholas sipped his own wine as he watched her. Her weariness was to be expected. Poisons fashioned by the black mage of Wychweald were generally fatal, and Morgan had ingested more than was polite. It had taken all his skill as a healer, and all his strength as something more than a healer, to counteract the poison's effect. Even then, he hadn't been completely certain that she would survive—no matter what he had hoped at first.

She had, though she'd remained abed for over a fortnight, too weak to move. She had spoken to him eventually, but not past conversing on the most rudimentary of subjects. She hadn't asked him why she found herself at Lismòr, not hundreds of leagues away at the palace of Tor Neroche where she'd been attacked. She hadn't asked him who had healed her. She hadn't expressed any interest at all in what she was going to do in the future.

He put on a good face whilst she was awake, but now that she slept, he could admit to himself what he'd been unwilling to before: she was terribly hurt. She was infirm, brittle, almost transparent. He wondered if she would ever completely heal.

He sighed deeply. There was no more he could do for her that night. He put his hands on his knees. "William," he called softly, "help me with the doors, won't you?"

The lad jumped up and opened the door. Nicholas set aside the table, then lifted Morgan into his arms. She didn't stir as he carried her out of the solar into the frigid night air, nor did she rouse when he and William took off her cloak and boots and put her to bed.

"More herbs, my lord?" William asked uneasily.

Nicholas shook his head. "We're past herbs now, lad. Light the fire, would you? I'll sit with her yet awhile. You go on to bed."

"Thank you, my lord."

Nicholas sat in a chair at the foot of Morgan's bed and watched her by the glow of hearthfire and candles. Either she would draw on her own strength to heal or she wouldn't. All he could do was watch and hope.

There was nothing else to try.

One

Tor Neroche was under siege.

Miach of Neroche stood at his window and stared down into the courtyard below, contemplating the truth of that. It had been a brutal, unrelenting assault on the front gates for the previous fortnight. Now, though, it was only the latecomers who were rushing into the courtyard, come in their finery to witness the nuptials of Adhémar, king of Neroche, to the lovely and very demanding Adaira of Penrhyn.

The inside of the palace showed just how thorough the onslaught had been. There was hardly a scrap of floor within that was not covered by some sort of servant, pile of luggage, or minor noble wishing he had either come sooner or with more money to bribe the Mistress of the Wardrobe into giving him a decent place to sleep. Miach had found himself grateful, for a change, that he was Adhémar's brother; at least he had a bed.

Unfortunately, even with his ties to the throne, he didn't completely escape Mistress Wardrobe's forbidding frowns or her charms of ward made against him when she thought he couldn't see her. Obviously he had alarmed her at some point in the past. But he alarmed most of the servants simply by virtue of who he was and what he did, so perhaps there was no point in trying to determine where he had run afoul of her ire.

For all he knew, she was unsatisfied with the deference he showed the king.

Adhémar no doubt shared that sentiment.

Miach sighed deeply, then turned away from the spectacle below. He was heartily sick of watching his brother prepare to wed when he had other things to be doing and other places to be going.

He sat down in front of his fire and closed his eyes. At least he could be seeing to his business whilst he waited for Adhémar to see to his. He stilled his mind and briefly examined his spells of defense on the northern border. Finding them unchanged from earlier that morning, he hesitated, then decided there was no harm in seeing to something of a more personal nature. He cast his mind farther in search of the essence of a certain woman. It was something he'd discovered he could do during the past month whilst he'd been about the taxing business of ignoring the wedding preparations going on downstairs.

He mentally roamed over the mountains, down and across the vast plains of Neroche to the south, then farther still across the sea to the Island of Melksham.

He let out the breath he hadn't realized he'd been holding. Morgan was still alive on that island, just as she had been for the past month. He was tempted to see if he couldn't have a more complete idea of how she fared, what she was doing, what she was thinking, but that seemed too invasive somehow. It was enough to know that she lived still.

He'd had moments when he'd feared she wouldn't.

He opened his eyes, then jumped a little in surprise. His brother Cathar sat across from him, watching him gravely. Miach rubbed his hands over his face.

"How long have you been there?" he asked.

"About an hour," Cathar said, holding out a mug of ale. "You were very far away."

"I was working," Miach said. "Mostly." He accepted the ale and downed it gratefully. "Is there something useful happening downstairs, or just more of the same?"

"The ceremony should begin soon, actually," Cathar said. "I came to fetch you."

"Finally," Miach said in disgust.

"Well, you know Adhémar couldn't resist delaying things a bit longer, just to see how many people he could annoy."

"He's succeeded, at least with me. I'm ready to have the torture over with so I can go."

"Go?" Cathar echoed, a smile playing around the corners of his mouth. "Go where?"

Miach eyed his brother. "You know where."

"To Melksham, to see about Morgan," Cathar said. "Aye, I knew. I'm just wondering if Adhémar will allow you to."

Miach opened his mouth to protest, but Cathar interrupted him with a laugh.

"I'm provoking you," he said. "I know 'tis only good taste that has kept you here this long." He finished his ale and set the cup down. "Is your lady well?"

"She lives still," Miach said. "I can tell nothing more than that."

"No word from her?"

"I didn't expect any, actually."

"At least none you'd want to hear," Cathar agreed. He put his hands on his knees and rose. "So, you'll be polite during the wedding, then be off to Melksham. Do you have a plan for when you arrive?"

Miach set his cup aside, then rose and followed his brother across the chamber. "I thought I would just fall on my knees and blurt out an apology."

Cathar whistled softly. "I imagine you'll need to get past the point where she wants to arrange all of her blades artistically in your gut before you attempt that."

Miach would have argued, but he feared Cathar was right. He would be fortunate indeed if Morgan ever spoke to him again.

"What of what you'll leave behind?" Cathar asked as they made their way down the twisting tower stairs. "What of the realm's defenses?"

"I don't have to be here to see to them," Miach said, "but you knew that already. As for anything else—" He shrugged. "I'm working on it."

Cathar only grunted.

Miach walked with his brother through the marble-paved hallways, lit by dozens of glittering lamps and flanked, of course, by piles of luggage that hadn't found homes yet. At least he wouldn't have to trip over those much longer. A few more hours, then he would be on his way.

He paused at the doors to the great hall. They were open and the tables laid for the wedding feast. Miach looked above the massive hearth at the back of the hall. In times past, the Sword of Angesand had hung there, protected from theft by its own magic, waiting for the right hand to come wield it.

The sword was no longer there.

Miach didn't particularly like to think on why not.

The Wielders of the Sword of Angesand will come, out of magic, out of obscurity, and out of darkness . . .

He dragged his hand through his hair as he turned away from the hall and those words. He had thought, half a year earlier, that he might need the power of the Sword of Angesand to aid him in besting Lothar of Wychweald, the black mage to the north. He'd sent Adhémar off on a search for a wielder for that sword, then followed along a pair of months later to find out why his brother hadn't returned. It had been then, on the day when he'd found his brother, that he'd first laid eyes on Morgan of Melksham.

And lost his heart.

He had traveled with her for a month, come to love her more with each day that passed, and dreaded with equal fervor the moment when he would have to admit to her that he wasn't Miach the simple farmer, as he had led her to believe, but Mochriadhemiach, the archmage of Neroche. It might not have mattered so much who he was except for her loathing of magic in general and mages in particular.

She'd discovered his identity—and that he believed her to be one of the prophesied wielders of the Sword of Angesand—at a most inopportune moment. Her anger had been so great, she had taken that magical sword, brought it down against that very table at the back of the hall, and splintered it into a thousand pieces. She'd fled, encountered Lothar of Wychweald, then drunk poison he'd given her before Miach had been able to catch up with her. He had had no choice but to send her unconscious self back to Melksham to heal whilst he remained behind and attempted to see to the tatters of the realm.

But the tatters were mended, for the moment, and he would

make do without the Sword of Angesand. He would also allow himself a pair of days to travel south and attend to the matters of his heart.

"Miach, should you have changed clothes, perhaps?"

Miach looked at Cathar, trussed up uncomfortably in his finest court clothes, and shrugged. "Adhémar told me not to stand out."

"But black, Miach," Cathar protested. "Could you not have donned something less forbidding? You have six brothers, you know. Surely you could have found something in one of our closets."

"The rest of you don't dress any better than I do," Miach said, "save Rigaud, and I wouldn't wear anything he owns. This way I'll fade into the background, which will please Adhémar the most."

Cathar frowned thoughtfully. "Can't say I wouldn't rather be less conspicuous myself. All right, let's be about it."

Miach took a fortifying breath, then followed his brother into the chapel.

There were so many people inside, there was scarce room for him to squeeze through them to reach the front. He looked over the company as he did so. There was the usual royalty from neighboring nations, ambassadors where the royalty could not be troubled, as well as the odd assortment of dwarves, wizards, and an adventurous elf or two. And a quartet of mercenaries.

Miach smiled at those last lads as he took his place at the end of the line of his brothers. They were Morgan's companions; two men, a dwarf, and a lad who had hoped for adventure but gotten quite a bit more than he'd bargained for. They had remained at the palace as his guests over the past month, waiting with him for tidings of Morgan's condition.

Could he be blamed if he'd asked more than a respectable amount of questions about their dealings with her? He'd had her company for less than a month, long enough to learn to love her, but not nearly long enough to know her as he would have liked. Their tales of her everyday doings had been a balm to his heart. He'd been equally willing to listen to tales of her skill with a sword; those had come as no surprise to him. After all, she had studied with Scrymgeour Weger.

Weger's fame as a swordmaster was widespread and sober-

ing. Graduates of his tower at Gobhann couldn't be called as-
sassins, but they were certainly men for whom anything but
swords had ceased to exist. Ostensibly Morgan had gone there
to improve her swordplay, but Miach suspected the true reason
she'd sought the solace of Weger's tower was because Weger
shunned anything to do with magic or mages.

"Did you bring anything to eat?"

Miach looked at his next eldest brother, Turah, who was
standing on his left. "What?"

"I'm hungry and I suspect this will take all day," Turah said
with a gusty sigh. "I should have brought a stone. I could have
at least been sharpening my knife."

Miach held out his hand and a sharpening stone appeared.
Turah looked at it, then laughed.

"I don't dare. But," he said, taking the stone and tucking it
into a pocket, "I'll use it later. You couldn't conjure up a chair
for me as well, could you?"

"Too conspicuous," Miach said, though he supposed there
might come a time when he would wish for the same thing.

He waited for the proceedings to begin, but apparently the
heralds were waiting for Adhémar to see one last time to his
hair. He clasped his hands behind his back and silently recited
all the shapechanging spells he knew. He knew scores, which
passed the time pleasantly, but he finished and still nothing
was happening save guests shifting in their seats and a few
unfortunate souls succumbing to fits of coughing.

He turned his mind to reciting silently spells of reconstruc-
tion, where a change could be made and fixed for a predeter-
mined amount of time. That took quite some time as well, for
he knew many. He was then forced to move on to changes of
essence, where a thing's true nature was affected in a way that
rendered it permanently transformed. Those spells were few
and immensely complicated. Though reciting them mentally
kept him awake, it didn't hurry Adhémar along.

He had finally resorted to inventing new ways to induce
warts and other disfigurements upon his brother the king when
the heralds and musicians finally arrived to trumpet the im-
pending arrival of that king and his bride. After another handful
of minutes, Adhémar finally came ambling down the aisle, re-
splendent in his finest court clothes and wearing a very large hat

with an even larger plume of feathers. Miach thought the toes of his brother's shoes were overlong and curled overmuch, but what did he know? If he ever managed to wed, he would wear boots.

Adaira, the eldest princess of Penrhyn, swept down the aisle a few minutes later in her own bit of finery, sporting an even taller plume on her hat than Adhémar's. There was a bit of jostling between bride and groom as they attempted to find the best spot for being seen there in front of the priest, then they settled down for what would no doubt be a very lengthy and detailed recounting of dowries, exploits, and other flattering items necessary for the occasion.

"You're yawning."

He looked at Turah, who was watching him with a smirk. "It's keeping me awake."

Turah smiled and elbowed him companionably, then turned back to watch the spectacle. Miach did as well, but he suspected that given the fact that the priest was still heaping praise upon Adhémar's already swelled head and hadn't even managed to mention the word marriage, he was going to be there awhile. Perhaps no one would notice if he let his mind continue to wander.

He wandered mentally down that well-worn track across the plains of Neroche, and over the sea to Melksham. This time, he thought that perhaps it wasn't inappropriate to be a bit more thorough in his search. He could at least see what Morgan was doing. He let his mind brush over the walls of the university at Lismòr and seek out where she was no doubt walking in the morning sunshine—

Except she wasn't.

He froze, his breath catching. He searched through all the buildings that made up the university and orphanage, but found nothing.

But it couldn't be. He was certain she'd been on Melksham Island that morning. He'd felt her presence, faint but definite. Of course he hadn't tried to determine the condition of her health, but he'd assumed she was at least still alive.

He swept over the land surrounding Lismòr, but found no sense of her. He cast his mind about in ever larger sweeps over the whole island, but found . . . nothing.

"Miach!"

He came back to himself to find both Turah and Cathar shaking him.

"Miach, you're screaming," Cathar said urgently. "Stop it!"

Miach realized that the entire collection of souls come to witness Adhémar's wedding was watching him with astonishment and alarm. Well, except Adhémar, who was glaring at him as if his fondest wish was to take his sword and plunge it into Miach's chest.

Miach shook off his brothers' hands. "I can't find her. I can't feel her anymore." He backed away from them. "I must go."

"You will not," Adhémar said in a commanding voice. "You will remain where you are until I am wed. If you do not, I'll . . ." He seemed to be searching for an appropriately dire threat. He drew the Sword of Neroche with a flourish, came close to removing his betrothed's hat, and then pointed that sword threateningly at Miach. "I'll see you hanged!"

"You'd like to think you could," Miach said shortly.

"Then I'll see you replaced!" Adhémar spluttered.

Miach didn't bother replying. He pushed his way through Adhémar's guests, then ran out of the chapel, through the passageways, and up to the tower chamber.

He didn't have many personal things, hardly enough to fill up half the wardrobe that sat in a corner near the cot he occasionally used when he had no choice but to sleep, so he didn't bother with gear for himself. He did dig around in his armoire for a particular knife, which he stuck in his belt, and a particular ring, which he shoved into his boot. He turned toward the door and found his way blocked by Morgan's companions.

"Miach?" Paien of Allerdale said, his visage blanched. "What has befallen Morgan? Well, more than what's already . . ."

"I don't know," Miach said, trying to ignore his own distress. "I don't know, but I'll find out. Perhaps 'tis merely my unease that speaks."

They didn't look convinced.

He wasn't either.

"I'll send word," Miach promised, "once I know more. Will you wait for me here?"

Paien looked at his comrades, then back at Miach. "Aye, we will. Perhaps Prince Cathar will vouch for us while you're gone."

Miach nodded. "Tell him I asked it of him if he hesitates, though I don't imagine he will."

He shook hands all around, bid them farewell, then pushed through them and ran down the stairs. He slipped through a particular door and walked out onto the battlements. He leapt up onto the parapet wall and gathered his thoughts—

"Damn you, Miach," Adhémar thundered suddenly from behind him, "I vow this time—"

Miach dove off the wall and whispered a spell of shapechanging as he fell. In the next heartbeat, he was beating dragon wings against the air and rising toward the tops of the castle walls. Adhémar was standing on the parapet, waving his sword in a fury and cursing himself hoarse.

Miach couldn't stop himself. He spewed out a blast of fire that no doubt singed more than Adhémar's feathered hat, then rose high into the sky and sped south.

It was sunset before he reached the Island of Melksham. He circled the university, then swooped down and landed in the innermost courtyard next to the fountain. He shook off his dragon's shape, then hunched over with his hands on his knees and sucked in desperately needed breaths. It was bitterly cold, something he hadn't noticed as he'd been flying. He wanted a hot fire and something to drink, but he could wait for both until he had found out what had befallen his love. He took a final breath, then heaved himself upright so he could look about and get his bearings.

Nicholas, the lord of Lismòr, stood not twenty paces away with his hand on the arm of an overanxious archer. Miach froze, realizing only then that that archer was but one of two dozen with their arrows pointed at him.

Nicholas pushed the lead archer's bow down so the arrow pointed at the ground instead of at Miach's heart. The other archers followed suit.

"William, dismiss the guard for me, then you may go to your rest," Nicholas said to the lad standing at his elbow. "I can see to this whelp myself."

"As you will, my lord," William said. He made Nicholas a bow and turned to see to the guard.

Miach watched the guardsmen walk away, most looking uneasily over their shoulders at him as they did so. He waited until
they had all gone, then crossed the courtyard to where Nicholas
stood. "What befell Morgan?" he asked without preamble.

Nicholas frowned. "What do you mean?"

"I lost my sense of her," Miach said impatiently. "What
befell her?"

"You've made good use of your new skill, haven't you?"
Nicholas said, sounding pleased.

"Aye, and that is the only reason I remained at Tor Neroche
until now, which you knew," Miach said evenly. "Your Grace,
I left my brother's wedding before they had even finished list-
ing his many marvelous accomplishments, terrified that I
would come too late and find my lady dead. Is she?"

Nicholas looked at him in surprise. "Well, of course not."

Miach rubbed his hands over his face. It was either that or
weep. The relief that washed over him was so great, he almost
had to sit down.

Nicholas clapped him on the shoulder. "Come have a drink
with me and I'll tell you all."

Miach nodded silently, then followed Nicholas across the
courtyard and into what he assumed was one of Nicholas's
private chambers.

It was a luxurious solar, with finely wrought tapestries on
the walls and heavy rugs on the floor. A fire burned cheerily in
the massive hearth set into the far wall. Miach sat down gratefully, then accepted a cup of ale, which he drank in one long
pull. He set the cup down on the table in front of him, then
looked at Lismòr's lord.

"Where is she? If she's alive, why can't I feel her?"

Nicholas smiled. "The answer to both is Weger's tower."

Miach blinked, just certain he'd heard the older man
awrong. "What?"

"She's in Gobhann," Nicholas said. "I took her there myself, actually."

"You did *what*?"

Nicholas laughed. "I understand your surprise, believe me.
I thought it a very poor idea as well, but she wouldn't listen to
me. She's very determined, you know."

Miach could hardly believe his ears. He had expected to

find Morgan very ill. Indeed, as he'd flown he'd repeated silently all the spells he'd learned over the past pair of fortnights,
spells that he was certain would drive out whatever lingering
poison Nicholas hadn't been able to see to. He'd actually tried
to prepare himself to find that she had died.

But he hadn't expected this.

"I tried to convince her 'twas too early to leave Lismòr,"
Nicholas remarked, sipping brandy from a delicate goblet,
"but she refused to listen to my pleas. She would have made
the journey herself if I hadn't insisted on taking her. As it was,
I dragged the whole thing out for a solid se'nnight—and
earned more than my share of curses as a result." He smiled.
"It may comfort you to know that she's found her tongue, at
least."

"Oh, vastly," Miach managed. He shook his head in disbelief. "I shouldn't be surprised, but I am. Of all places, why
there?"

"Why do you think?"

Miach sighed. "Because she wants nothing to do with
magic in general and mages in particular." He paused. "Or is it
that she wants nothing to do with a particular mage?"

"I imagine that was part of it," Nicholas said. "I suspect
she's also running from her dreams."

"Poor gel," Miach said quietly. He sat for quite a while,
looking at a tapestry of a battle scene on the wall across from
him, then made his decision. He would find Morgan, apologize, then change them both into evening mist and waft over
the walls before Weger could kill him. He looked at Nicholas.
"My thanks for the tidings, my lord. I'll go now."

"Go?" Nicholas echoed. "Go where?"

"To Gobhann."

Nicholas looked at him with a smile. "You'll need a sword,
my lad. Do you have one?"

Miach patted himself, then shrugged. "Apparently not. I'll
just conjure one up when I get inside the gates. Besides, I'll
only be inside long enough to find Morgan and convince her to
leave with me. If worse comes to worst, I'll bind Weger with a
few spells so we might walk out the front gate."

"Do you think so?"

Miach looked at him sharply. "I think, Your Grace, that I

can manage to control Scrymgeour Weger for as long as necessary, no matter his reputation for fierceness. Don't you?"

"Well, you certainly could," Nicholas said slowly, "if Gobhann weren't a magic sink."

Miach heard the words, but it took a moment for the meaning of them to register. He blinked in surprise. "Gobhann is a *what*?"

"'Tis a magic sink," Nicholas said.

Miach found that his mouth was hanging open. Worse still, he wasn't sure when it had fallen open. "That's impossible," he began.

"It isn't, which you well know. There are places enough in this world where magic is nothing but a fond memory. It shouldn't surprise you, actually, that Weger would choose such a place for his home. He's not overly fond of mages, is he?"

"So rumor has it," Miach said faintly. A magic sink? Of all the things he had expected to hear in Nicholas's solar, that was the last. Just what in the hell was he supposed to do now?

He was so tired, so damned relieved to find that Morgan was still alive, and so floored by what he'd just learned, he was tempted to laugh. He rubbed his hands over his face and settled for a handful of rather vile curses instead, lest Nicholas think him mad.

And perhaps he was, given that he was actually considering going inside the place.

"That is why you couldn't feel Morgan any longer," Nicholas continued, as if they spoke of nothing more remarkable than the ten months of rain Chagailt saw each year. "She has entered Weger's gates and no magic in the Nine Kingdoms, nor all of it combined, will reach inside there and gain a sense of her. Nor will it bring her out. If you go to fetch her, you'll go as a mere man. And if I were you, I would be more worried about how I was going to get myself back out Weger's gates than how I was going to convince Morgan to leave with me."

Words suddenly failed him. That wasn't a common occurrence, and he found it almost as unsettling as the tidings he'd just learned. And just how was he supposed to maintain the defenses of the kingdom of Neroche when he would be required to check his magic at the door?

"You could just leave her there, I suppose," Nicholas mused.

"I can't," Miach said without hesitation. "And it has nothing to do with her destiny, or her magic, which she refuses to acknowledge, or that I want to keep her safe at Tor Neroche. Even if it isn't with me, she deserves a life in the sunshine." He paused. "Don't you think?"

"I do, but I imagine she won't." He smiled. "But you don't expect anything else."

Miach shook his head. "I'm not under any illusions."

"And you aren't going after her from a misguided sense of guilt, are you?" Nicholas asked.

Miach managed a wry smile. "It is love, Your Grace, that motivates me, not guilt."

"I thought as much," Nicholas said, sounding satisfied. "Now, let's consider the realities of your visit. How is your swordplay?"

"Not as bad as you might think," Miach said.

"Without your magic?"

Miach pursed his lips. "Aye, startlingly enough."

"Then perhaps you should have a decent meal, a good night's sleep, and be on your way first thing. Perhaps your task is to meet her as just a man, not a mage. But do it quickly, for you cannot leave the realm untended. And you cannot ask another to do it in your stead."

"Trust me," Miach said with a deep sigh, "I never forget that." He reached down and pulled the ring out of his boot and the knife that matched the Sword of Angesand from his belt. He handed them both to the lord of Lismòr.

"Keep those for me, Your Grace, if you will. I'll return for them after I've convinced Morgan to come back with me."

"You're optimistic."

"Always," Miach said gamely.

"You'll need to be. Now, go find a meal," Nicholas said. "It may be the last decent one you have for some time to come."

Miach suspected he might be right.

Several hours later, he lay in Morgan's bed, trying to sleep and finding it impossible. First, there was the difficulty of being in a place where Morgan had been but a handful of days earlier. Then there was the problem of wondering if Morgan would even speak to him. And if she did, what good would it do him if he wouldn't get back out Weger's gates?

And finally, how was he to leave the realm's spells of defense unattended while he went about satisfying his own desires?

He supposed he might manage to shore things up with an uncommon amount of magic and hope it would last until he could see to it again.

He sighed deeply. He had already put his foot to the path before him and he would not turn back. A few days of his being inside Gobhann would not leave Neroche in ruins. Perhaps most men didn't leave Gobhann easily once they'd entered it, but he wasn't most men.

Aye, he would, for once, lay aside his duty for a few days and see to the matters of his heart.

Surely no ill would come of it.

Two

Morgan of Melksham stood in the long, high-ceilinged gathering hall that stretched along the seaward side of Weger's tower and stared down at the water below. The sea was never calm here, on the northwest side of the island, though she had wondered over the years if it churned with an especial fierceness near Weger's keep simply to terrify the novices.

It was a well-known fact that the only way to leave Weger's tower alive was through the front gates, the only ones who left through the front gates were those who bore his mark, and the only way to earn his mark was to complete his training. Where the others went was a matter of conjecture. Rumor had it that the failures were tossed off Gobhann's parapet into the water below. Morgan had never paid all that much attention to how those who hadn't survived their initiation year had been dispatched except to be glad she hadn't needed to put up with their poor swordplay any longer.

Unfortunately, considering the abysmal condition of her own sword skill at present, it was not inconceivable that she would meet her own end in some uncomfortable way very soon.

She pulled her cloak closer around her and shivered. She was cold, and it had nothing to do with the chill in Weger's gathering chamber or the bitter draft that seemed to find its way through the cracks in the mortar surrounding the windows. She felt tired and weak and very ill. It was a wonder Weger had overlooked those flaws and let her inside the keep.

Then again, Weger let quite a few people in. Whether or not they remained was another thing entirely. The first test alone spelled doom for most. Either one of Weger's fiercer students or Odo the gatekeeper would assault the hopeful swordsman just as he was relaxing and thinking himself quite clever to have made it inside the front gate. Morgan remembered vividly her own initiation successfully overcome so many years ago.

Yesterday, though, had been something entirely different. She'd managed to shuffle inside the gates, just after dawn and just barely. It had taken all her strength to merely stand there and draw in breath. Master Odo had raised his sword, but lowered it immediately in surprise. Morgan had felt for the sword she'd borrowed from Nicholas only to realize she'd left it in the wagon. She'd looked at Odo in consternation, received the same sort of look in return, then watched him resheath his sword. He had barked at her to follow him.

She'd tried not to notice that he'd taken the pace of a man escorting his aging and infirm granny to her last meal.

In time, and after scores of appalling pauses to catch her breath and at least a dozen other skirmishes waved off by Odo, she had gained the upper levels of the keep. She'd come out into the topmost courtyard—at sunset no less—by sheer willpower alone.

She had waited for the final challenge to come from whomever the honor belonged to that day and wondered what in the hell she was going to do without a sword. She had supposed she might manage to remove one from someone else and use it to save her own neck, but before she could identify a likely victim to burglarize, Weger himself had come to stand in front of her. She had opened her mouth to speak, then felt herself pitch forward.

She'd woken in her accustomed chamber, the one she'd enjoyed after she'd earned a place in Weger's closest circle, to find a roaring fire burning in the hearth and a luxurious pile of blankets laid atop her—things she had certainly never enjoyed before. She couldn't credit Weger for wanting to coddle her.

Pity was not a part of him, nor was compassion. Perhaps he wanted her fully conscious so she would remember the humiliation of being booted from Gobhann like a particularly vile bit of refuse.

The booting hadn't happened yet that morning. The only soul she'd seen had been Weger's page, a fearless lad named Stephen. Stephen had brought her breakfast, then frowned fiercely at her a pair of hours later when she'd insisted that she would at least leave her bed and seek out the gathering chamber. He'd followed her there, muttering dire warnings under his breath. She'd finally sent him away with a curse, but she hadn't been so distracted that she hadn't seen the look of concern he'd worn as he'd run off.

Perhaps she looked as bad as she felt.

The door behind her opened. She looked over her shoulder and found that Stephen had brought her yet more to eat. He shot her an arch look, then headed purposefully for the far end of the chamber. She gathered up the tattered remnants of her strength and shuffled toward the hearth. She passed bookshelves full of treatises on war and benches and chairs empty of soldiers. Any soul deserving of a place on any of those seats was outside working.

She refused to think about the fact that it was exhausting just to think about joining them.

She noticed, once she felt like she could stop watching her feet so she didn't fall, that Stephen had placed a cushion on one of the chairs nearest the fire and was busily plumping it.

"Sit here," he commanded.

"Absolutely not," she said, drawing herself up.

"Weger ordered it be brought—"

"Then let him place his delicate arse upon it," Morgan snapped, panting as she finally managed to reach the chair opposite the one Stephen was hovering over. She collapsed onto it with a groan. "I need no such pampering."

"But—"

"Cushions," Morgan said in disgust. "What next? Lace at my wrists?"

A pointed clearing of a manly throat made her realize that she and Stephen were not alone. She watched as Weger made himself comfortable on that recently fluffed cushion.

"Quite lovely, Stephen," he said. "Thank you. You're dismissed."

Morgan tried not to flush as Scrymgeour Weger folded his arms over his chest and looked at her. Perhaps at another time she could have dared an insult, then drawn her sword to defend herself against his ire. Now, it was all she could do to draw breath and hope he'd forgotten what she'd just said.

He nodded toward the substantial meal sitting on the table in front of her. "Eat that."

She thought it best to distract him with a little obedience. The food was nothing compared to what she'd eaten at Lismòr, but at least it was hot. It took her an inordinate amount of time to work her way through even a small portion of what was set before her, but given that such was the condition of all the things she did, she supposed it didn't merit any special notice.

When she had eaten all she could, she sat back. She didn't dare even hold a cup of wine. She'd had too many slip through her fingers and land on the floor at Lismòr to trust herself.

Finally, when she knew she could put it off no longer, she looked at Weger. He didn't appear to be preparing to rid himself of her, but then again, with him, one never knew.

There were quite a few things one didn't know about him, beginning with his age. He might have seen thirty-five, perhaps forty winters, though there was no frost in his dark hair. He had the look of a professional soldier about him, muscled but lithe, hardened by years of swordplay, spare in his movements and economical in his speech. His face was too craggy to have been called handsome—not that she supposed anyone would have applied such a term to him. He was formidable and for that she had admired him from the start. But young? She didn't think she could say that. His eyes showed that he had seen more than a young man could have.

"What befell you?" he asked.

She had known that question would come, but she found she was unprepared for it just the same. What to tell him that wouldn't result in him hurrying off to find a sharp sword to use on her? Weger shunned all things magical and disparaged thoroughly anyone who had dealings with it. What would he say when he learned that not only had she carried a magical knife with her all the way through Neroche, she had destroyed a legendary blade that had hung on the wall in the palace of Tor Neroche for centuries and fallen in love with the archmage of the realm?

Well, the last she might be forgiven for not admitting, for she wasn't sure she loved him at all. In fact, given the way he'd betrayed her with lies and subterfuge, she thought she just might hate him.

"Well?"

She wrenched her thoughts back to the question at hand. "I was poisoned," she croaked.

"By whom?"

She cleared her throat. "Lothar of Wychweald."

One of his eyebrows went up in surprise. "Indeed. Where did you encounter him?"

"Tor Neroche."

The other eyebrow joined the first. "Why were you all the way up there?"

He would wonder that. She had a deathly fear of boats that he had taunted her about more than once. "I was delivering something to the king of Neroche on behalf of Nicholas of Lismòr."

"Ah," he said, nodding wisely. "You couldn't refuse that quest, given who'd asked you to take it on."

"I owe Lord Nicholas much," she agreed.

"So you do." He considered her for quite some time. "I'm surprised any of the Neroche lads allowed Lothar inside their gates."

"I don't think they knew he was there," she said. "I certainly had no idea who he was until after I'd drunk what he'd offered me." She paused. "I was in haste."

She didn't think she could be blamed for leaving out the fact that she'd been leaving the great hall in haste because she'd just taken the Sword of Angesand and slammed it against the king's table, splintering it into innumerable pieces with more than just her strength of arm.

"That was a very stupid thing to do," Weger remarked.

She blinked, then realized he'd been talking about drinking Lothar's brew. "Aye," she managed. "I know that now."

"Why did he choose you to attack?"

"I think I was in the wrong place at the wrong time."

He grunted. "I daresay. Well, who healed you? He must have been powerful. Not many survive Lothar's poisons."

"I'm not sure who it was," she admitted reluctantly. "It might have been Nicholas of Lismòr."

It was also possible that it could have been another more magically inclined sort of man. The sort of man one might have found puttering about as archmage of some realm or another.

Possibly.

"But who brought you to Lismòr, if you were in Tor Neroche?"

"I'm not sure of that either," she said, but in this at least she had her suspicions. Miach had no doubt changed himself into some dastardly creature straight from her nightmares, clutched her in his deadly talons, and carried her back to Lismòr to drop her off where he might be troubled with her no longer. Perhaps he had healed her as an afterthought.

She didn't care to speculate.

Weger studied her for several more eternal moments. "Did you come here to hide?"

She patted herself for a weapon, but her borrowed sword was in Nicholas's wagon and the rest of her gear was keeping her own sword company somewhere at Tor Neroche. The best she could manage was a butter knife. She fingered it purposefully.

"I don't hide," she said.

And that was true. She'd never hidden before and she wasn't hiding presently. What she was doing could quite properly be termed a regrouping, not a scurrying inside a place where she could avoid the unpleasant dreams of magic that had plagued her since she'd first touched Nicholas of Lismòr's blade—and her even more unpleasant associations with a certain mage.

"I came to regain my strength," she said firmly. "I will pay you for the privilege, of course."

He blinked in surprise. "Well, of course you won't. And that wasn't what I was after. I just want to be sure you aren't running from something you should be facing." He looked at her closely. "But I don't imagine you run, do you?"

"Nay," she lied.

He grunted at her. "I suspect there's a great deal more to the tale than you've told me, but you can relate the rest after you've recovered. That will be repayment enough for all the coddling you're having."

Morgan nodded, but she thought the price very high indeed.

"I'm interested in what you thought of the palace," he continued, slapping his knees and rising, "but I'll have that later as well. For now you'll eat, sleep, and work when I tell you to, but not until. You'll regain your strength in time."

"Thank you, my lord," she said gratefully.

He started to walk away, then paused. "There's a new aspirant coming up the way," he said, turning to look at her. "You might enjoy watching his final challenge."

Morgan nodded, grateful for something to do. There was nothing more delicious than watching a man who had entered Weger's tower with an overly optimistic appraisal of his skills be reduced to tears by the gauntlet he'd run on his way to the uppermost level.

Of course, she hadn't wept on her first day.

Today, though, she wasn't at all sure that she wouldn't weep just trying to get there to watch. It was all she could do to convince herself that she actually could get up out of her chair. It took several tries, but she finally heaved herself to her feet. Weger caught her by the arm before she overbalanced and went sprawling into the fire, then held on to her until she managed to get her legs steady beneath her.

"You're exceedingly lucky to be alive," he said grimly.

"Aye," she managed. "I think so too."

"You need to rest."

"Later."

He grunted at her. "Very well. You may come watch, but then it's back to bed with you." He took her arm and walked her over to the door, then left her there.

Morgan clutched the door frame until she caught her breath, then left the hall and shut the door behind her. She put her hand on the wall and started down the passageway. It was more of an effort than she wanted to admit to limp toward the end that opened into the uppermost courtyard.

She wondered, as she shuffled along, if Weger had built the place, or inherited it, or pilfered it. The whole fortress rested between two enormous towers of rock, looking as if it had

simply grown spontaneously from the stone. There were courtyards on many levels, open to the air and reached by stairs cut
into rocky outcroppings. It was magnificent, in a stern, unyielding kind of way.

But best of all, there was no magic within the walls. Morgan had believed that previously because rumor had said as
much. She knew the truth of it now because she had whispered
a spell that morning in the privacy of her own chamber and had
it drop into the silence like a rock dropping into a bottomless
well.

She had been vastly relieved.

She stopped at the end of the passageway, sheltering herself from the worst of the stiff sea breeze that blew through
Weger's tower almost without ceasing. Normally she would
have strided out into it and enjoyed its fierceness, but today
she was past striding, and she feared the wind would blow her
away.

She heard the fighting before she saw it. She looked out
into the courtyard and saw a few of the older students gathered
there, waiting to watch the carnage. There wasn't much in the
way of entertainment at Gobhann, but the thrashing of a potential novice provided some, at least.

Jeers and abuse accompanied the new lad as he fought his
way up the stairs. Morgan almost smiled. It was cheering to
listen to the same sort of mistreatment of a lesser swordsman
by his betters that she had offered during her previous, lengthy
stay at Gobhann.

Soon the taunts faded away and all that was left was the
ring of swords and the grunts of men at their work. Morgan
tried to get a glimpse of who was fighting, but Weger was in
her way. He finally looked over his shoulder, saw her, and
stepped aside so she could see. She expected to find a man of
decent mettle in the process of being reduced to pleading for
mercy.

Instead, not fifty paces away from her, stood none other
than Mochriadhemiach of Neroche.

The bloody archmage of the realm.

She was so surprised, her knees almost gave way. Fortunately, there was a wall handy and she was able to lean against

it and keep herself upright. She could hardly believe her eyes, but they at least were functioning as they should. She gaped at Miach and wondered what in the *hell* he was thinking to come inside a place where his magic was going to be completely useless . . . and given that his magic was the only thing to keep his sword skill from being called nonexistent, he was truly in trouble.

Well, perhaps that was a bit harsh. She studied him dispassionately for quite some time and had to admit that while he might not be besting his opponent, he was at least holding his own—and his opponent was very, very good.

And then, quite quickly, he wasn't holding his own anymore.

Morgan watched him stand there with his arms down at his sides, his sword point down against the stone, his chest heaving.

She didn't want to watch him anymore. Unfortunately, she couldn't make herself look away. Just the sight of him was like cool, soothing rain after endless weeks of unbearable heat. She closed her eyes briefly, swallowed hard, then had to look again.

He was beautiful. She'd forgotten, in those days of haze and pain, just how handsome he was. His features were perfectly proportioned, his form no doubt the envy of every man in the keep, and his bearing regal. And there was something more about him, something that simmered under the surface of his very polished appearance, something quite lethal. Whatever else he was, he was a very dangerous man. Perhaps he was less roughened about the edges than the other men standing in a circle around him, but he was just as perilous.

And his eyes were still that palest of blues.

She was interrupted in her lusting—an alarming thought in and of itself—by Weger backing up to stand in front of her. He blocked her view, but she thought that perhaps she should be grateful for that.

"What do you think?" he asked over his shoulder.

"Throw him off the parapet," Morgan wheezed.

Weger grunted, then strode out into the courtyard. He nodded for his student to move, then took up that lad's place. For the briefest of moments, Morgan felt sorry for Miach. It wouldn't have surprised her to see Weger take him on at that point, just to humble him a bit more. But Weger only folded his arms across his chest and looked at Miach.

Eye to eye, if anyone was curious.

Morgan reminded herself that she hated Miach of Neroche. He had lied to her, led her unwittingly to a fate she had never wanted, then revealed himself as who and what he was only because he'd had no choice. He had allowed her to fall in love with him, passing himself off as a simple farmer, when he knew that he was most definitely not and he *knew* how she felt about mages. He had obviously abandoned her at Lismòr without once returning to see if she lived or not.

There was the difficulty of wondering why he found himself standing not thirty paces in front of her at present, but that was something she would work out later, when she was more herself.

"Who are you?" Weger demanded. "Your name, before I cut it from you."

Miach didn't flinch and he most certainly didn't cower. Morgan watched him incline his head in a marginally deferential way.

"You could call me Miach," he said quietly.

Weger stared at him for so long that even Morgan began to grow a little uncomfortable. Miach, however, merely stood there and let Weger study him all he liked.

Well, whatever else could be said about the fool, it had to be conceded that he didn't lack courage.

Finally, Weger shrugged. "As you will. Why are you here?"

Miach only hesitated slightly. "For sword skill, my lord."

Weger grunted. "Obviously, since you have none of your own. What will you give me in return?"

Morgan held her breath. No one earned Weger's mark without giving something dear in return. Some brought gold, or family heirlooms, or offered to stay on afterward and see to other menial tasks in the keep for a certain period of time. She had remained in his tower as a swordmaster as her payment. But Miach?

She suspected what he would have to offer would be things Weger would never want.

"I will give you whatever you ask," Miach said finally.

Weger considered for an absurdly long period of time before he nodded. "Paul, show our new lad here his luxurious accommodations. Work begins at dawn tomorrow."

Miach bowed low, then bowed to Paul as well.

But he looked about the courtyard, as if he searched for something in particular. Morgan jerked backward into the shadows. She wasn't at all sure that Miach wouldn't be able to hear her heart pounding from where she stood, though she was fairly certain he wouldn't be able to see her. She was too far in darkness for that.

He looked worried. Perhaps he feared he would never escape back out Weger's gates. Perhaps he worried he wouldn't make it past the first se'nnight. She couldn't imagine that he was worried he hadn't seen her.

He left in the keeping of the novices' mentor. Morgan watched him until he'd disappeared out of sight, then jumped at the feel of Weger's hand on her arm.

"Morgan, go to bed," he said shortly. "You're of absolutely no use to anyone if you can't keep yourself on your feet."

She was surprised enough at him calling her by her name, something he had never done, to allow him to pull her toward the hallway that would eventually lead to her chamber. His usual term for her was *woman* or *wench* or simply a grunt in her direction. Perhaps he was more concerned about her than she'd suspected.

She let him escort her to her chamber itself and didn't argue when Stephen caught up with them, bearing yet more food.

She also didn't argue when Weger stood in her doorway and glared at her until she finished as much of her supper as he determined she should.

"Now sleep, wench," he ordered, then slammed her door shut.

Morgan sat on the edge of the bed and sighed. She would sleep, just as soon as she allowed herself to wonder about a few things.

Miach had to have known his magic would be useless inside Gobhann, hadn't he? If he hadn't, he surely would have felt it the moment he stepped beyond the gate.

Yet he had continued on through his initiation challenges just the same.

She couldn't bring herself to believe he had come for her, but she could think of no other reason. The question was why. All he'd ever wanted from her had been her hand on the Sword of Angesand, but since that sword was now gone, her usefulness to him should have disappeared as well.

Had he come to censure her for her actions? If so, then why had he waited until she'd come inside Gobhann? He could have come south at any time and shouted at her.

But he hadn't. He hadn't shouted at her, not even after she'd destroyed a sword that had been in his family for generations. He'd just looked at her with pity in his eyes, as if he had known what she'd suffered and wished he hadn't been a part of it.

She decided abruptly that she didn't care why he was there. She had her own life to live, a life that did not include magic, finger-waggling, or an archmage who had no sword skill.

She put herself to bed before she had to think on it any longer.

Three

Miach sat on a stool in what could be generously termed a cell and wondered what in the hell he'd been thinking to come anywhere near Gobhann.

He was without magic, without a sighting of Morgan, and without even so much as a dab of horse liniment to use in rubbing out the knots he could feel all through his back thanks to Weger's brutal and relentless training regimen. He'd spent the previous three days training with the sword from dawn until well past sunset. The only respite from swordplay had been those pauses several times during the day when he'd been invited to run up the stairs from the base of the keep to its parapet and back down again to improve his stamina.

And he'd entered Weger's gates willingly?

He was beginning to wonder if he'd lost his mind.

It wasn't that he was unaccustomed to physical work. He did stir himself to go out to the lists now and then. He tended his own horse, cut his own meat, shoved his brothers out of his way as the occasion arose.

But this was something else entirely.

It had begun the moment he'd set foot inside Weger's gates. He'd had the luxury of but a handful of heartbeats to accustom himself to having his magic snuffed out as if it had been a particularly offensive candle before he'd been assaulted by the gatekeeper. He had passed that first test easily only because he'd been expecting the like and he'd been prepared for it. The successive challenges had been increasingly difficult, but he'd expected that as well.

He hadn't shown as well as he would have liked, but he'd been distracted by all the looking about he'd done to see if Morgan was there. He hadn't expected Morgan to be engaging in any swordplay, but he had assumed he would at least see her.

He hadn't—not even in the uppermost circle where he'd come face-to-face with Scrymgeour Weger himself. *That* had truly been a moment worth recording in the annals of the histories of the archmages of Neroche. He'd wondered, absently, what Cathar would have said if he'd been watching. Nothing polite, no doubt.

He bowed his head and tried to stretch his aching shoulders. Well, at least he had the comfort of not finding himself immediately thrown back out the gates, or over the walls, or whatever Weger did with those completely unworthy of his time. That he'd been allowed to stay had been flattering, but it hadn't solved any of his more pressing problems, the first being that he still had no idea if Morgan was truly inside the keep or not.

He had to know. Soon. The realm could not wait.

He rose and drew his cloak around him as he left his cell. He would have to search while he was at liberty to do something besides hoist a sword. At least he'd had the good sense to wear black to Adhémar's wedding. It allowed him to be less conspicuous whilst he did a bit of spying to see if Morgan was indeed inside the keep.

He walked along silently, then paused at the entrance to the common dining chamber. He listened for several moments, but heard nothing useful so he continued on. He wandered through passageways, up several staircases, and along the edges of the courtyards. Unfortunately, he seemed to be the only one fool enough not to make the best use of dark by sleeping.

He finally stopped in the uppermost courtyard where he'd encountered Scrymgeour Weger. It was empty, as empty as every other place he'd been that night.

Or, perhaps not.

He spun around, his sword halfway from its sheath, only to

come face-to-face with Weger himself. He resheathed his sword and nodded to the lord of Gobhann. He bowed for good measure, but Weger didn't acknowledge it. He was merely still, as if he'd been made of stone.

Miach supposed that was how he intimidated—though he wondered why the man bothered. Surely rumors of his sword skill were enough to terrify all but those too stupid to realize their peril. Miach was not that sort of lad and he understood the danger quite well. He didn't flinch as Weger regarded him impassively, but he was tensed and ready for any sort of assault.

Weger turned suddenly and started across the courtyard. "Follow me," he threw over his shoulder.

Miach supposed he had no choice. He followed, but warily. Was Weger going to throw him off the parapet? Miach supposed he wouldn't find it an easy task, nor was Miach particularly worried about the descent. Surely the tower's dampening influence did not extend past the walls. If nothing else, he would change himself into a hawk, or a breeze, or a bit of dew as he fell and regroup when he landed.

Weger led him over to the far wall of the upper courtyard enclosure and opened a gate that Miach hadn't noticed before. Miach followed him through it and out onto another flat space that couldn't have been called a courtyard, but couldn't truly have been anything else. It was here that Weger stopped.

Miach considered a quick spell, but rejected the idea immediately. The deadness of the ground he stood on was testament enough that he was still within the sphere of Weger's influence. He clasped his hands behind his back and looked at Gobhann's lord expectantly.

Weger fished about in a pocket, then held out a key.

Miach took it automatically. Well, better a key in his hand than a knife between his ribs.

"Thank you," he said. "I think." He looked at the key, then back at Weger. "What's it to?"

Weger pointed to his left, to a set of stairs cut into the sheer side of a cliff. They wound upward at an alarming angle before disappearing into the darkness above. Miach looked at Weger.

"I don't understand."

"There's a chamber up there," Weger said.

"And you think I should use it?"

Weger looked at him coolly. "Don't you have things to see to . . . my lord Archmage?"

Miach knew he shouldn't have been surprised, but he was. "Ah," he began.

Weger nodded sharply toward the stairs. "Your magic will work within that chamber."

Miach blinked. "It will?"

Weger glared at him. "Can you do nothing but ask stupid questions?"

"I didn't expect this," Miach said honestly. "I'm off balance."

"I daresay," Weger grunted. "Well, whatever else you do, don't lose that key. It's the only one I have."

Miach wasn't one to indulge in overly enthusiastic displays of gratitude, but he was tempted to drop to his knees and kiss Weger's scuffed boots. But since he suspected Weger would kick him off the side of the keep if he did so, he settled for a silent sigh of relief. He could stay long enough to do what was necessary to find Morgan.

He made Weger a very low bow. "Thank you, my lord."

"Why are you really here?" Weger asked, folding his arms over his chest. "It cannot be simply for the swordplay."

"Can't it?"

"Why would it be?" Weger asked. "Surely your magic makes up for your substantial lack of skill."

Miach didn't bother taking offense. He also didn't bother revealing his real reason for coming inside Gobhann. He was quite sure if Weger knew that he'd come for Morgan, he would do all in his power to remind her of her distaste for magic . . . and mages. Nay, it was best to keep his true motives a secret until he had no choice but to reveal them.

He shrugged with a casualness he most certainly didn't feel. "I lost something."

"And you think you'll find this missing thing here?"

"I might."

Weger grunted. "Well, if what you're missing is sword skill, then perhaps you've come to the right place."

Miach smiled. "If I don't find that here, the fault will be entirely mine."

"Aye, it will." Weger nodded toward the stairs. "Best be about your labors, then."

Miach started toward the stairs, then paused and turned back around. "A question, my lord."

"Pray, make it an intelligent one."

Miach smiled briefly. "How did you know who I was?"

Weger looked at him with disgust. "Think you I only heed the affairs of my keep?"

"Well," Miach said nonplussed, "it isn't as if my face is on the money."

"Nay, but you look like your brother, the king, and his face *is*. And I've heard that the youngest brother's swordplay is better than any of the other brats rampaging about in the hallowed halls of Tor Neroche—though that doesn't say much about the quality of your swordmaster, does it?"

"My father would have been offended," Miach said with a small smile.

Weger only grunted. "I also know the names of all the Neroche lads. *Miach* is quite a bit closer to Mochriadhemiach than it is to Cathar now, isn't it?"

Miach nodded, acknowledging the point. "I usually give that name accompanied by a little spell of insignificance. Not possible here, though, is it?"

"Apparently not. Now, take the bloody key and go do what you do so I can sleep peacefully at night."

"Do you ever go up there?" Miach asked.

The look Weger shot him made him smile in spite of himself.

"I suppose not," he said. He inclined his head. "My thanks, my lord."

Weger walked away. "Training begins at dawn," he threw over his shoulder. "Don't be late."

Miach supposed he didn't dare. He watched Weger go, then turned to look at the stairs. He allowed himself a moment of profound relief before he climbed up them, ignoring the sheer drop to his right. He did look a time or two, simply because the moon was out and he couldn't help himself. A man would fall off the steps and land hundreds of feet down on rocks that would break him instantly into innumerable pieces. And he had the sinking feeling that the air was just as dead magically there on those rocks as it was where he stood.

Best to be careful, then.

He finally reached a doorway cut into the rock. He fitted the key into the lock and entered the chamber. He staggered as his magic returned to him with a rush. It took a moment or two before he managed to lock the door behind him. He leaned back against it and slid down until he was sitting on the floor.

He closed his eyes and set to work checking the spells of defense that he had set all along the borders of Neroche. They were all intact save for the strange erosion he had noticed several months earlier, as if their underpinnings were being washed away by a tide he could not see. It was the usual amount of damage, though, and he corrected it without complaint.

As an afterthought, he examined the borders of Riamh, Lothar's land to the north. He set spells of ward along Riamh's border with Wychweald, promising himself a good apology to his cousin King Stefan later, when he had the time for it.

He came back to himself to find the chamber just as dark as it had been when he'd entered it and bitterly cold. He had no idea how much time had passed, but it had to have been a decent amount because he was stiff. He rose with a groan and stretched out his back.

He was, again, considerably grateful for the key.

He wrapped his cloak around himself, then let himself out of the chamber. The wind hit him so hard, he staggered and caught himself against the rock face to his right. He took a moment to accustom himself to his lack of magic and the howling wind, then locked the tower chamber door, pocketed the key, and went down the stairs.

If Weger had any idea of the gift he'd given away . . .

He froze on the bottom step as he realized that the shadows to his right contained more than a body might reasonably expect. A dark shape detached itself from the overhang and walked out into the courtyard. Miach looked at Weger in surprise.

"Did I need a guard?"

"Keeper, more like," Weger said. "I'll lose interest soon, no doubt. You keep that bastard from Wychweald at bay, though, so consider this repayment."

"I will."

"But don't think it will win you any lenience during the days," Weger said, frowning fiercely. "You're naught but flesh here, mage. My sword is sharp and my patience for pampered princes nonexistent. You'll earn whatever you take away: a mark or your final resting place on the rocks below."

And with that, he turned on his heel and strode away. Miach watched him, openmouthed. He stood there for several minutes until the preposterousness of the slander dissipated enough for him to move. Pampered? It was so far from the reality of his life, he could scarce begin to address it. His days were spent seeing to nothing but the defenses of the realm, an endlessly grinding task that left him with no time to do anything but eat when he remembered to, train with his sword when he dared, and snatch a few short hours of sleep each night when he could stay awake no longer.

He shut his mouth and started across the courtyard. The brisk wind blew some bit of perspective back into his poor, fogged mind. Perhaps there was some truth to Weger's charge after all. He remembered vividly Morgan's reaction to her first sight of Tor Neroche. It had been clear to him at that moment how accustomed he was to the immensity and grandeur of the palace, a place he had taken for granted from birth. He had lived his entire life, save a year he preferred not to think on overmuch, dividing his time between the grandeur of Tor Neroche and the sweeping beauty of the palace of Chagailt. He worked hard, true, but he did it in spectacular surroundings.

None of that mattered at Gobhann, obviously. He suspected that Weger was serious: either he would take away a mark or he would find himself flung off the walls.

All the more reason to work on his swordplay.

And perhaps whilst he was doing that, he might actually manage to find the woman he hoped was within Gobhann's dreadful walls.

He walked through the gate and across Weger's uppermost courtyard. He was so intent on reaching his bed that he almost ploughed a lad over before he realized what he was doing. He grasped the boy by the arms to steady him.

"Sorry," he said automatically.

The lad jerked himself away and almost went sprawling.

The hood fell back away from his face as he struggled to keep his feet.

Or her feet, rather.

Miach closed his eyes briefly, then reached out again to take Morgan by the arms. She held him off, swayed for a moment or two, then stumbled away.

"Morgan," he said, "wait."

He started after her only to find someone else in the way.

"I'll see to her," Weger said.

Miach stepped back. He was so astonished by how frail Morgan was, he could do nothing but watch as Weger took her by the arm and walked her off into the shadows.

"Why are you out of bed, woman?" Weger growled. "I told you to stay there until I gave you leave to move."

"I can decide when I'll leave my own bed, thank you very much," Morgan snapped.

Miach started to follow them, then caught a full view of the warning look Weger threw him. He stopped immediately, then merely stood there and watched them walk away together. Weger was clucking over Morgan like an anxious hen and Morgan was, unsurprisingly, having none of it. He would have smiled at the thought of someone else being subjected to her stubbornness, but he was suddenly far too envious of Weger's position in Morgan's life to smile. He was no nursemaid, to be sure, but he would have given much to have been the one to tend her.

He was giving much, as it happened.

He looked thoughtfully after them and considered the look Weger had given him. Rather too possessive for a man whose only interest in Morgan was her sword skill, to his mind.

Damnation, what next?

He watched until he could see them no longer, then turned and made his way back down to his frigid cell. Dawn would come sooner than he cared for and there would be the task of swordplay to keep him from thinking too much. He felt a little unsteady as he walked into his chamber and shut the door behind him.

Morgan was alive and he had seen her with his own eyes. It was a start.

A pity she was just as displeased to see him as he'd feared she would be.

Four

Morgan dreamed.

She stood in the great hall of Tor Neroche and stared up at the Sword of Angesand hanging over the fireplace. It sang a song of Camanaë, a beautiful song that wove itself in and out of her thoughts until she became part of it. She reached up and the sword leapt off the wall and into her hand as if it had been waiting for her to come call it.

And then someone spoke her name.

She turned around. There on the other side of the table stood Mochriadhemiach of Neroche. She wanted to walk around and throw herself into his arms, then she remembered that he had lied to her about who he was and what he wanted from her—which was, as it happened, her hand on the sword she held.

A great anger welled up in her. It raged through her with a sound of rushing wind, white hot in its fierceness, leaving her blind to all but her fury. Miach had lied to her. He had called her love.

She lifted the sword—

And brought it down with all her strength against the lord's table before her.

The blade splintered, shattered, sparked as it disintegrated into thousands of shards and bits that floated through the air before her like snow.

Morgan stared at the haft of the sword, that beautiful hilt that was worked with a tracery of leaves and flowers, and could not believe what she had just done. She looked over the table, but Miach no longer stood there.

In his place was Gair of Ceangail, the black mage who had slain his entire family with a single act of arrogance . . .

Morgan woke with a gasp. She wasn't supposed to dream inside Gobhann. She certainly wasn't supposed to dream about black mages and other mages and swords she had once held that were now no more.

She forced herself out of bed, shaking as she did so. She dressed, but it took her far longer than it should have. Her hands trembled so badly when she tried to drink tea that it splashed all over the floor. She set the cup down and sat on the edge of her bed until she thought she could get herself across the room. She would drink later, when she'd regained control of her frenzied imagination.

Her dream was an aberration. Gobhann was a safe place for her. As long as she was within its walls she had no magic, no terrible dreams, nothing to fear. Her unwelcome and hopefully solitary nightmare had no doubt come because she'd been in bed too long.

She'd been there since she'd seen Miach in the upper courtyard a se'nnight ago. She'd had too much time to think about things she should have avoided, too much time to listen to her blood sloshing languidly through her veins, and far too much time to wonder how it was that Miach of Neroche managed to say her name differently from anyone else.

In a small, private way that made her want to curl up next to him as if he were a merry fire and she in desperate need of his warmth.

She would have given herself a good shake, but she feared that would land her back in bed, so she contented herself with a selection of curses chosen for their ability to drive foolish thoughts from her head. She shut her door behind her with a bang, then squeaked in surprise as something slid along the wall toward her.

She had to take several deep breaths when she realized it

had only been a sword that had tipped her way. She picked it up and looked at it.

It was plain and unadorned, but light—obviously made for her strength of arm. She drew it partway from the sheath. It was lethally sharp and obviously freshly forged. She would have wept, but she was too tired. Truly Weger had done more for her than she deserved.

She resheathed the sword and considered briefly using it as a cane, but that was an appalling thought, so she carried it and vowed to not use it that way unless she simply had no other choice.

She made her way out to the courtyard, assuming that since Weger had left a sword for her, he intended that she use it. She paused on the edge of his training circle. He was working with someone she would have found nothing more than a marginally worthy opponent two months ago, but now found simply exhausting to watch. She wondered, briefly, if she would ever regain her strength enough to be what she once was.

Weger noticed her and held off his student. He resheathed his sword and strode across the courtyard to her.

"You found your new blade."

"I did, my lord," she said with a nod. "It was very generous and I thank you for it."

He nodded toward the stairs. "Come with me. You'll train someone today."

"A novice?" she asked, following him with as much spring in her step as she could muster—which wasn't much. She was better than she had been, though. Perhaps lying abed had been more useful than she'd thought.

"Nay, he's not a novice," Weger said. "He's passed the first four levels, and quickly too. In fact, only one other soul has ever progressed at such a pace."

Morgan watched her feet so she wouldn't trip and land upon her lovely sword. "Who was that?"

"You, of course," Weger said. "You don't think I'd completely insult you, do you?"

"You'd be justified in it."

"Nay, gel, you can still best half the lads in the keep even now. But try not to indulge in any womanly swooning whilst you're about this labor. It wouldn't be good for morale."

She nodded and followed him to the next courtyard down. It was, as it happened, the one with the most sunshine. It was also the most protected, sheltered as it was from the sea air by the upper levels of the castle. She was unwholesomely grateful for the warmth—she who in another life had preferred the cold, cruel wind that drove all but the most hardy indoors. But now she was not herself and the wind threatened to steal not only her breath but her strength as well. A bit of light exercise in the sunshine was welcome indeed.

"As I said before, this lad has some skill, but nothing to match yours," Weger said. "Even in your weak condition, you should be able to keep the upper hand easily."

Morgan nodded, let him take her cloak and scabbard, then took her sword in her hand and moved out from behind him to face her student.

It was Miach.

"Begin," Weger commanded.

Morgan raised her sword only because Weger had trained her too well to obey without question. "We'll s-start with ri-right-handed sweeps," she said automatically, stammering in spite of herself.

But she swung amiss on the first attempt. Miach's reflexes were, fortunately for him, far quicker than hers. He caught her blade with his and stopped it from slicing across his face. She was so startled by that, she almost dropped her sword.

Weger made a sound of disgust.

Morgan took a better grip on her sword, then began again. Miach did nothing more than follow her movements faithfully, as if he truly sought to learn something new. She remembered suddenly a conversation she'd overheard in a tavern near Tor Neroche. The men behind her had been discussing the archmage of Neroche.

He can outride the king, outfight Cathar the Fierce, weave melodies in the wind that would shame Nemed the Fair, and do all these other things that normal men couldn't do even if they had magic—and the archmage can do all these things in spite of his magic.

She realized that though she had fought alongside Miach in a skirmish or two, she had never fought against him. It was obvious by the way he was engaging her that he was far beyond needing to learn what she was supposed to be teaching him.

Why was he in Gobhann?

"Come on, woman," Weger said impatiently, "pour some energy into seeing to this whelp."

Morgan had to rest for a moment. "I'm trying."

"Try harder," Weger growled. "Dredge up your irritation for something. Perhaps pampered lads who've never done a decent day's work in their lives. Nay, here's something else: mages. Think on how much you loathe them, those prissy, finger-waggling meddlers who tamper with lives and kingdoms and scores of other things they shouldn't."

Prissy? Morgan looked at Miach and was forced to admit that of all the things he might be, prissy was not one.

Weger continued on with his list of things mages befouled, but Morgan could hardly pay attention to it, much less muster up any enthusiasm for it. She found that she couldn't look Miach in the eye either. Every time she did, she faltered.

Damn him to hell, why had he come?

"Morgan, be about it!"

She raised her sword and attacked Miach, but she was weak and clumsy. Perhaps Weger was the one who should be damned. Why was he goading her so? It wasn't possible he knew who Miach was.

Was it?

"Bloody hell," Miach exclaimed, flinching suddenly.

Morgan looked at his arm and saw the rent there in his sleeve—and the slice across his arm under the rent. Her sword fell from her hand and landed with a clang against the stone under her feet. "I'm so sorry," she said, embarrassed beyond belief.

Miach shook his head. "My fault. I was in your way."

The arm of his tunic was rapidly growing wet. Weger stepped around her and examined the wound. She watched in consternation as Weger borrowed a marginally clean rag from another student and cinched it tight around Miach's arm.

"Have that seen to," Weger commanded.

Miach nodded and resheathed his sword. "I'll return as soon as I have."

"Miach," Morgan began weakly.

"'Twas an accident, no more." He smiled at her. "Not to worry."

She would have tried to apologize again, but he shook his head quickly. He put his hand briefly on her shoulder as he passed her. She turned and watched him walk across the courtyard and lope easily down the stairs.

Weger picked up her sword, resheathed it, and handed it to his page.

"Stephen, take that back to her chamber and see food provided for her."

"Of course, my lord."

Weger draped her cloak around her shoulders. "I provoked you prematurely," was all he said before he turned and walked away.

Morgan watched numbly as the handful of other men who had been watching followed Weger up the stairs. She stood there and blinked against the faint light from the winter sun. She had never once in her long and illustrious career at Gobhann cut another soul accidentally. She had never, as it happened, cut someone intentionally. It had been a matter of pride with her, that she should be careful and skilled enough to have full control over her blade at all times.

She turned and made her way slowly over to the wall, leaned on it until she'd caught her breath, then started to shuffle along it, using it like a cane to steady herself.

She wished she'd had her sword.

She spent the evening in front of the fire in Weger's gathering chamber. She couldn't bring herself to go to bed. She'd slept the afternoon away and found herself troubled not by dreams of destroying legendary swords, but by dreams of bad swordplay. She had fought opponent after opponent but managed to cut every last bloody one of them.

Sleep, apparently, was not what she needed at present.

She excused herself to escape the food Weger was trying to force on her and managed to walk all the way to the door and out into the passageway without stopping. She wasn't going to examine how long it took to catch her breath after she'd closed the door behind her.

She was, she supposed, very fortunate to be alive.

She made her way out to the courtyard, then stood on the edge of it and let the wind blow across her face. She stood there for quite some time, grateful for an empty place where she could wheeze with abandon. Unfortunately, it wasn't empty for long. She pulled back into the shadows at the sight of someone striding across the courtyard with a truly appalling display of energy.

She realized immediately that it was Miach. And just where did he think he was off to at this time of night in such haste?

Before she could think better of it, she followed him across the upper yard and through the gate set into the far wall—though she did it at a much slower pace. She came out eventually into a smallish, flat place that was even more inhospitable than the courtyard inside the walls. The wind was blowing a gale and it cut through her as if she wore nothing at all. The only means of escape was a staircase, cut into the side of the mountain. She looked up and saw a black figure near its top.

What was he doing up there?

She supposed that if she'd had any sense at all, she would have turned around and gone straight to bed. No doubt Stephen had left some species of delicate tea there by her bedside to tempt her. It might actually still be warm if she hurried.

She decided that it could wait. She walked carefully across the courtyard and paused in front of the steps. She stood there for quite some time, trying to judge whether or not she could manage them. They weren't necessarily narrow, but they were very steep, very uneven, and they were flanked by rough rock on one side and on the other . . . well, nothing at all.

She climbed five steps before she had to stop and rest. It was madness. She should have crawled back down those five steps, congratulated herself on a show of wit, then hurried as quickly as possible back to her chamber.

Instead, she continued to climb. Perhaps Miach couldn't tend his arm himself and she could be of some use. 'Twas a certainty he would never ask for aid freely, so perhaps she should simply demand that he allow her to see to it.

All for the good of the realm, of course, nothing more.

She climbed for hours. Well, perhaps it wasn't hours, but it felt like it. The weather was terrible, the wind frightening in its ferocity, and her own form simply unequal to the task of climbing more than a handful of steps at a time before having to rest again. She reached the top at last, drenched and freezing and firmly convinced she'd lost her mind. She would never, ever climb those steps again.

She remained where she was for quite some time, struggling to breathe in enough air to satisfy her burning lungs.

Eventually, she looked at the door and saw the keyhole there. That did her no good given that she had no key, nor any useful tools to use in besting such a simple lock. As an afterthought, she pushed on the door.

To her surprise, it gave way.

She peered inside. It was a smallish sort of chamber, boasting not even so much as a chair. There was certainly no hearth for keeping a body warm, nor any windows for allowing a body to see what the weather was doing. She knew all this thanks to the soft, warm glow that came from a ball of werelight that hovered near the ceiling.

Werelight?

Miach sat cross-legged on the floor in the middle of the chamber, silent and unmoving. Morgan took a step inside to investigate both him and his light, then gasped as magic slammed into her like a wave. Her own magic. Magic she had never wanted, had desperately tried to deny having, and would have cut from her if she'd been able.

The door slammed shut as she fell back against it, which she supposed saved her from a tumble down the stairs. She closed her eyes as she drowned in dreams and spells and things she shouldn't have known anything about.

No wonder Miach came here.

She was curious how he'd found the place, but decided that was something she didn't need to know. She stumbled past him and managed to get herself down onto the floor without too much trouble. She leaned against the wall facing him and watched him.

He didn't look much worse for the wear of his wounded arm, but he did look tired. She wondered how long it was he spent each night in such a terrible place, doing whatever it was archmages did. For all she knew, he was simply snoozing.

Then again, perhaps not. Though the room was bitterly cold, there seemed to be some sort of heat coming from him. Was he making magic? She supposed that was possible. It was also possible that he was using enormous amounts of energy to list all the ways he could do damage to the hearts of foolish mercenaries. She wouldn't have been surprised.

She studied him as he sat there, and collected her former loathing of him like spoils from a particularly plentiful battlefield.

First, he'd allowed her to believe he was a simple farmer, not the archmage of the realm. He had also allowed her to believe that his brother was a bumbling oaf, not the king of Neroche—though perhaps she couldn't lay her eagerness to believe that at Miach's feet. She'd been more than happy to call Adhémar an insufferable prig. All he had to do was open his mouth to convince everyone within earshot that they were better off far away.

Miach was nothing like his brother. He was a plainspoken, easily amused man who seemed perfectly content to tromp about in his boots doing good. Who would have thought he was the most powerful mage in Neroche? She certainly hadn't.

Not that it excused him. He should have told her who he was and *what* he was. That he hadn't was something she thought she might never be able to forgive him for.

He sighed suddenly, then rubbed his face with his hands. He looked around him blearily and his gaze fell on her. He looked so surprised, she almost smiled.

Almost.

She quickly reminded herself that she had good reason to hate him.

There was a flash of something across his face—relief, perhaps. It was gone as quickly as it had come, and he assumed a more careful expression. He stretched out his legs and rubbed them absently as he looked at her. "Morgan," he croaked, then he cleared his throat. "Morgan, how long have you been here?"

"I don't know," she said. "And I didn't come to visit, I came to see about your arm."

"Oh," he said, putting his hand over it, "that. 'Tis but a scratch."

"I doubt that. Let me see it."

"Nay."

She patted herself for a knife but found, distressingly, that she still didn't have one to hand. Her new sword was lying on her bed, else she would have used that. She settled for a fierce frown. "Let me see it, damn you."

He smiled at her as if she amused him somehow, then sobered abruptly when he caught sight of her glare. He sighed and pulled up the sleeve of his tunic to reveal a terrible slice across his arm that had been sewn together with ugly, hasty stitches. Morgan swallowed, hard.

"I'm so sorry," she whispered.

He shook his head. "It was an accident."

Morgan saw the prints of five fingers burned into his flesh above the new cut. Those were prints she was responsible for. She'd given them to him another time when she'd healed his arm with magic of her own.

She attempted another swallow. She wasn't entirely successful.

"I could try to see to that," she ventured.

He pulled his sleeve back down. "I'm fine. It will heal. Besides, now that you're here, I'd rather talk—"

She flung herself to her feet in a sudden panic. She didn't want to talk. She didn't want to know what he wanted from her that would have nothing to do with her sword skill and everything to do with her magic. If he wouldn't let her see to his arm, the most sensible thing she could do was flee.

"I have to go," she said, holding on to the wall as the chamber spun violently around her.

His hands were immediately on her arms. She didn't want to rely on him, but she had no choice. She allowed him to hold on to her until she thought she could step away from him and not land on her face.

"I am well," she managed.

He said nothing.

She realized he was looking at her, but she couldn't identify the expression. She didn't want to identify it. Coming to check on him had been monumentally stupid. The farther away from him she managed to get herself, the better off she would be.

She found, suddenly, that he was draping his cloak around

her shoulders. He fastened it under her chin, then stepped back.

"You need to be abed," he said quietly.

"I don't need your cloak—"

"You're welcome," he said with a smile. "Give it back to me later."

Morgan didn't want it. She didn't want something that smelled like Miach, like sweet earth and sunshine and mountain air blowing through the pines. She didn't like the warmth or knowing that he was giving up something for her comfort.

But before she could protest, she found herself shepherded out of the tower chamber and crowded onto the landing with him as he locked the door behind him. She did her best to ignore the fact that she was half a foot from being in his arms.

She also tried to ignore the fact that losing the magic she'd felt inside had drained her more than she'd dreamed it could. She was cold and weary and heartsick.

"I'll go first," Miach said, putting the key into a pocket and stepping down a step. "I'm afraid I can't block much of the wind."

She could only nod with a jerk and pray she wouldn't find herself blown off the side of the mountain.

Miach paused. "I could carry you."

"I'm fine," she said quickly.

And she was, for half a dozen steps. Then she found that her legs were shaking so badly, she could hardly stand. Miach took her hands and put them on his shoulders.

"Climb on my back," he said.

"Nay," she gasped, "you'll kill us both."

"I could run down the steps with you and miss nary a one." He shot her a quick smile, then patted her hands on his shoulders. "Put your arms around my neck, gel, and climb on."

Morgan was quite sure she'd never done anything like it in her life. Praying she wouldn't send them both plunging to their deaths, she put her arms around his neck and let him lift her onto his back. She pressed her face against his hair and hoped she would live to see the courtyard again.

She was never going up these dreadful stairs again.

Fortunately for them both, Miach was as surefooted as he'd claimed to be. It didn't take but a handful of minutes before he was letting her slide down to her feet. Morgan clutched his shoulders and rested her face against his back until she thought she could stand on her own.

She released him, then stepped away. She felt herself begin to fall, but an arm was there for her to reach for. She grasped it, only to find that the owner of that arm wasn't Miach.

It was Weger.

Morgan blinked in surprise. "Where did you come from?"

"Guard duty," he said mildly.

Morgan let him pull her away. She looked at Miach. He only made her a low, formal-looking bow.

"A good night to you then," he said, as if she'd been a grand lady.

Weger tugged on her. She stumbled away with him because he left her no choice in the matter. She walked until they reached the gate, then looked back over her shoulder. Miach was standing where she'd left him, watching her. Moonlight shone down on him, a lethal, polished bit of business dressed all in black.

She had to look back in front of her, or risk going sprawling. She concentrated on putting one foot in front of the other until Weger had her standing in front of her own door. She looked up at him, trying to breathe evenly.

"I went to see about his arm."

Weger grunted, then opened her door for her. "Stephen brought you tea. Finish it before it grows cold."

"He only wants me for his war," Morgan blurted out.

Weger stared at her for several minutes in silence, then he shrugged. "And what man with two wits to rub together *wouldn't* want you for his war?"

Morgan couldn't exactly tell him that the kind of thing Miach wanted her for had little to do with sword skill and everything to do with the magic she might or might not possess.

Nay, Weger wouldn't understand at all.

"Go to bed," Weger said, nodding into her chamber, "before your womanly thoughts overwhelm what good sense you used to have. I don't want to see you tomorrow. Stephen will bring you food."

Morgan nodded, went inside, then heard the door close behind her. She went to stand in front of that terribly luxurious fire. It was surely nothing Miach would enjoy. Novices didn't even have braziers to warm themselves by. She stood in front of her own fire until she was warm enough to take off her cloak. It was only then that she realized she was still wearing Miach's as well. He would be cold.

She blew out her breath, then folded his cloak and set it upon a stool near the fire. She drank her tea, then went to bed before she had to think on anything she didn't care to.

What man with two wits to rub together wouldn't *want you for his war?*

Weger had a point. After all, wasn't that why she had spent many years training? She'd fully intended to be the kind of mercenary lords would pay exorbitant sums to have at their disposal. Why wouldn't the king of Neroche—or his archmage, for that matter—want her to wield a magical sword for him?

Unfortunately, she hadn't given a damn what the king of Neroche wanted, but she had found herself caring very much what his archmage had wanted from her.

And that hadn't had a bloody thing to do with swords or swordplay.

She would have thrown up her hands in disgust, but she was too tired. She settled for a weak snort. If *she'd* had two wits to rub together, she wouldn't have given Miach another thought, but she would have agreed last fall to wield the Sword of Angesand because it was a very famous sword and any swordsman worth his mettle never passed up the chance to wield a very famous sword.

A pity she'd smashed it to bits.

She rolled over with a fierce frown and a vicious curse.

Miach. Magic. The fate of the realm and her heart.

Terrible subjects, all.

Five

Miach sat in the lower dining hall, nursing a mug of ale and trying to look inconspicuous. He couldn't say there were many who lingered after supper, but there were a few and he thought it best to outlast them before he made for the tower. He hadn't had anyone mention that it was odd he seemed to enjoy climbing stairs to nowhere, but there was no sense in pressing his luck.

Another se'nnight had marched on. He had passed four more of Weger's levels, to the disgust of many of the men there and the outright anger of many more. He supposed he had to admit, with as much objectivity as he could muster, that he had earned his advancements. He'd driven himself into the ground from dawn well past dusk, training with his assigned masters as long as they would humor him, then finding other equally obsessed souls to cross swords with after his masters had gone to supper.

He had good reason. If he reached the upper levels, he could train where Morgan might be loitering. Not that she would be overfond of seeing him, but perhaps he could wear her down, like the Sruth that was nothing but a modest stream at its head but eventually cut its way through the mountains of Cnàmh-lus.

Unfortunately, he suspected Morgan was made of sterner

stuff than even those granite peaks and it might take more time to cut through her defenses than even he had to hand.

He turned away from that thought. He had to believe that at some point she would be willing to talk to him. She hadn't wanted to the week before, but perhaps she'd been feeling particularly ill and had had little patience for pleasantries.

That, he could believe. He'd been shocked at how frail she'd felt as he'd lifted her onto his back and carried her down the stairs. 'Twas no wonder Weger was forever sending her back to bed. Miach wondered how she managed to heft a sword.

He also wondered, now that he had the luxury of thinking on it, why the hell Weger had forced her to face him—and goaded her so terribly whilst she'd been at it. Had Weger been purposely trying to remind Morgan of her aversion to mages or had it been something else entirely? The man seemed to be very possessive where Morgan was concerned, far beyond what a swordmaster should have allowed himself to have for even a treasured pupil.

He bowed his head and rubbed the back of his neck. There was nothing to be done about it at present. He hadn't seen Morgan since the night in the tower chamber, which worried him. Had the exertion of the climb set her back in her recovery? He supposed that if something truly dire had happened to her, Weger would have summoned him. Perhaps someone had had the good sense to shackle her to her bed where she might rest.

Weger didn't seem to need any, though. Miach had found him at the bottom of the steps every night, standing in what poor shelter the mountain provided. Weger had consistently brushed off his thanks. Miach had wondered, in the odd moment when he'd been free of some physical task, why it was that Weger had aided him by means of the tower chamber key. Surely he had to know that Miach was there for more than just sword skill. Perhaps he merely thought it would be good sport to watch Miach try to convince Morgan to leave with him . . . and fail repeatedly.

He pulled himself away from his unproductive speculation. He had no idea what Weger thought and no desire to find out. His task was to gain access to the upper courtyard where he could see Morgan. Now, what he needed to do was see to his spells so he could go to bed.

He looked about the dining hall to judge its emptiness. It was free of diners, save a lone man sitting at a table in a darkened corner, watching him.

Miach sighed lightly. That was Searbhe, another in a rather substantial string of enemies he'd managed to make over the past fortnight. There had been abundant grumbling over his progress from many and outright cursing from many more when he was within earshot. Searbhe was one of the more vocal of the lot. He let no opportunity pass to complain about the obvious partiality Miach seemed to enjoy from Weger. Miach never dignified that accusation with a reply. It was ridiculous, especially since Weger had nothing at all to do with his progress; any advancements he made were determined by the men who trained him.

Miach would have ignored Searbhe entirely, but there was something about him that just wasn't right. He claimed to be from Iomallach, which Miach knew was a lie. Miach knew the ambassador from Iomallach well; Searbhe did not have his accent.

He supposed if he were to choose a far-flung locale that would be unfamiliar to most, he would have chosen such a place, but why did Searbhe find that necessary? It was odd to make such a point of feigning to be from an area he wasn't.

Unless he had something quite significant to hide.

Miach considered it for a moment or two, then shook his head and drained his ale. Searbhe was irritating simply because he made a point of heckling Miach every chance he had. Miach could shrug that aside easily enough. Growing up with six brothers had made him impervious to needling. Whatever other mischief Searbhe was about just couldn't be all that interesting.

Miach set his cup aside and rose. He couldn't wait the other man out and he doubted Searbhe had the wherewithal to be interested in what Miach did at night. He left the dining hall and wandered the passageways briefly before he started up the stairs toward the upper levels.

He heard the sound of a footfall behind him and stopped. He continued on, then stopped again. Perhaps he had been too hasty in dismissing Searbhe's interest in him. He pretended to fix something in his boot, then continued on, running up the stairs. He burst out onto the uppermost courtyard and turned, pulling his sword free of its sheath as he did so.

He managed to meet Searbhe's blade before it cleaved his head in twain, but it was a near thing. He fought off the man's assault, though, with more ease than he would have expected. Perhaps Miach's time at Gobhann had not been wasted.

And then Searbhe struck him suddenly with the flat of his blade directly over the slice on his arm. Pain flashed through him and his left arm went numb.

"Damn you," Miach gasped.

Searbhe said nothing but continued a very brutal assault. Miach wished absently that he hadn't spent most of the day training. He was tired and tiring more by the moment. He kept his left arm close to his body and fought with his right hand alone. Searbhe, of course, continued with two-handed swings, relentlessly pushing Miach back across the courtyard.

Miach fought until he was so weary, he wondered how he might lift his arm again. He knew that Searbhe had struck him twice more on the arm, but he honestly couldn't remember at what points during the skirmish that had happened. He realized, though, that if he didn't do something soon, he wouldn't be walking away in one piece.

He feinted to one side, then knocked the sword out of Searbhe's hands when he let his guard down. He put the point of his sword to Searbhe's throat before the other man could lean down and snatch up his sword.

"Be done," Miach suggested, his chest heaving.

"I'm not finished with you," Searbhe spat.

Miach tapped Searbhe under the chin. "You should be."

"You won't leave here alive, whoreson," Searbhe hissed.

"We'll see, I suppose," Miach said with a shrug. He removed his sword from Searbhe's throat and kicked the man's sword over to him.

Searbhe bent to retrieve it, then flung himself at Miach, the knife in his hand flashing in the moonlight. Miach caught Searbhe's wrist and saved himself a skewering.

"Enough," Weger commanded, stepping out from the shadows behind them.

Miach shoved Searbhe backward. "You'll find I don't take kindly to threats."

"And you'll find I mean mine," Searbhe warned.

Miach rested his sword against his shoulder and stared at Searbhe until he turned away with a curse and walked off.

Miach watched him go, then looked at Weger. "An interesting lad, that one."

"We have all sorts of rabble come through here," Weger said offhandedly. "You're proof enough of that, I suppose."

Miach only smiled, unoffended. "No doubt. Now, if you'll excuse me, my lord, I'm off to see to some business." He made Weger a bow and walked away.

Weger caught up with him immediately. "I wonder," he said, "given the nature of your business, why you're here and not closer to home."

"I'm looking for something."

"So you said, but I'm wondering what the truth is."

"I didn't lie before," Miach said mildly.

"You weren't completely frank either, and you'll regret that cheek when I take over your training," Weger growled. "Now, give me the truth. What are you here for?"

Miach supposed there was little reason in denying it any longer, given that Weger likely already had his suspicions. "I'm here for Morgan."

Weger nodded knowingly. "I thought so—and I can't blame you. You couldn't ask for a better swordsman."

"I don't want her for her sword skill."

Weger came to an abrupt halt. He turned to look at Miach with his mouth hanging open. Miach supposed that Weger wasn't surprised often, but he looked it then.

"Then what *do* you want her for?" Weger asked.

"With all due respect, my lord, that is none of your business."

Weger looked at him in astonishment for another moment or two, then his expression hardened. "I see."

"So you do." Miach smiled wearily. "If you don't mind, my lord, I'll be about my affairs. Dawn comes early."

Weger only grunted at him. Miach continued on his way across the courtyard. He found, to his surprise, that Weger was walking next to him. Well, at least he wasn't cursing him or sticking him with a handy blade. Perhaps he was simply looking for something appropriately crushing to say.

Miach paused at the bottom of the mountainside stairs and watched Weger study him for a moment or two.

"You won't have her," Weger said finally.

And with that, he turned and walked away.

Miach was tempted to list all the reasons he hoped Weger was wrong, but decided it wasn't useful. All he could do was see to his business quickly and go to bed so he could pass another level on the morrow. He wouldn't be able to convince Morgan to come with him until he could see her more often than simply by chance.

He waited for a bit just to make sure no one else was following him, but saw no one. He turned and took the steps three at a time until he reached the tower chamber. He paused at the door, but couldn't hear anything but the roar of the ocean below and the shrieking of the wind. Perhaps that was enough for the moment. He locked himself inside and went about his business as quickly as possible.

He had no idea how much time had passed before he came back to himself, nor did he want to know. He was simply grateful that the damage done to his spells was no worse than usual. He rubbed his hands over his face and fought the urge to simply lie down on the floor and succumb to sleep. His arm was on fire and he felt an unsettling tingle run through him every time he moved.

Obviously, another trip to the apothecary was called for.

He left the chamber, locked it behind him, then made his way wearily down the stairs. Perhaps if he managed a cup full of useful herbs and a decent night's sleep, he might have the energy tomorrow night to do more than just repair what was being damaged on Neroche's northernmost borders. The slippage of his spells hadn't increased, but it was steady. That didn't bother him as much as that the mischief didn't bear Lothar's mark.

What in the hell was going on in the realm?

He cursed his way down the remainder of the stairs. He was torn, as seemed to be his state of late, between duty and his heart. There would come a time, he feared, when he would not have the luxury of seeing to both. He would have to go—sooner rather than later.

But he couldn't leave without Morgan.

He almost ploughed her over before he realized she was sitting on the bottom step. He came to a teetering halt on the step above her, caught himself on the rock wall, then slipped past her. She was sound asleep, in spite of the bitter cold. He would have put his cloak around her, but she was already wearing it. He wasn't sure how to take that, so he thought he might do well to not take it at all. She was cold, nothing more.

She was also guarding the steps.

Or she would have been if she hadn't been asleep.

He squatted down in front of her. A wave of fever again washed over him. He cursed silently. His arm had been better until Searbhe had gone at it. He could feel his fingers again, but the wound throbbed persistently. Damn it anyway. He permitted himself a shiver, then turned his attentions to the sight of the woman sitting in front of him.

She was no less beautiful than she had ever been, but she was gaunt. Even sleep could not take away the dark smudges under her eyes or the hollows of her cheeks. She had always had slender fingers, but her hands now clasped in her lap were bony. They were the hands of an old woman, sick unto death, not the hands of a woman who had the whole of her life to look forward to.

He would repay Lothar for that, when he had the chance.

For now, perhaps the best thing he could do was see Morgan to bed. He would do so quickly, before Weger had the chance. He put his hands over hers gently. She sat up with a start, then focused on him.

She looked at him, mute, for quite some time. That she did so, instead of leaping to her feet and drawing her sword, gave him more hope than he'd had in weeks.

"Thank you," he said, the wind blowing his words away as if they'd been nothing.

She struggled to her feet, then clutched the rock until she was steady. "'Tis for the good of the realm," she said, pushing past him.

He wasn't surprised by that. He had fully expected that

winning her forgiveness would be difficult. But the fact that she'd come to guard him—even if it was just for the sake of the realm—was a promising sign, to his mind. Perhaps he might even manage part of an apology before she bolted herself inside her bedchamber.

He caught up with her in a single stride, then walked next to her without saying anything else. He would have offered her his arm, but he knew she wouldn't take it. He did, however, manage to reach the gate first and open it for her. She didn't look at him as she shuffled through it. Miach pulled the gate to behind him and walked with her across the courtyard. He waited until they were in the shelter of a passageway and the wind had died down far enough for him to be heard before he caught her sleeve.

"Morgan—"

She turned on him. "Why are you here?"

That seemed to be a popular question that night.

He drew her gently under a torch. "I came to talk to you."

She wrapped her arms around herself. "Then talk. Briefly. I'm cold and I want to go to bed."

She was shivering. He wished he had another cloak to put around her. He wished for a hot fire, sweet wine, and hours to explain himself and yet more hours to tell her all the things about her that delighted him and amused him and led him to the realization that he couldn't live without her. Unfortunately, he had none of those things and a very impatient woman standing in front of him.

He reached out and tugged the edges of both their cloaks up closer to her chin. "How are you?" he asked quietly.

"I'm alive," she said flatly. "And surely you didn't come all this way to find that out."

"Not entirely, though that was something I wanted to know." He took a deep breath. "I mostly came to apologize."

She looked at him in disbelief. "You?"

"Surprisingly enough," he said dryly.

"To whom?"

"To you, of course."

Her eyes narrowed. "About what?"

"I have a list."

She leaned against the wall as if she was settled in for a

lengthy conversation. "Where are you going to start?" she asked in a rather chilly tone. "At the point where you first lied to me?"

He looked at her in surprise. "I never lied."

"You never lied," she repeated incredulously. "And allowing me to believe you were someone you were not, telling me that your kin were always angling for a peep inside the palace as if they were peasants, passing yourself off as a simple farmer: all those things were just bits of truth I couldn't recognize?"

He opened his mouth to speak, then shut it. "I don't suppose that could be termed hedging," he said finally.

"I don't suppose it could," she said stiffly.

He sighed. "You're right. I allowed you to believe I was someone I wasn't and I didn't give you the truth when I should have. I apologize for it. I planned to tell you—"

"When? After I'd put my hand to the damned Sword of Angesand and had it blaze with magelight? After you'd used me till there was nothing left?" She looked up at him furiously. "Was that what you planned for me, Miach?"

He realized at that moment that hearing his name from her lips was something he'd missed greatly. He also realized that despite all the thinking he'd done about what he could say to her, there were no easy answers for what he'd done in the fall, no easy way to apologize for not having told her things he should have. He wished, quite intensely, that he'd told her who he was the moment he'd met her.

But if he had, she wouldn't have spoken to him further, so perhaps he couldn't have done anything differently. He could only do his best to make amends at present.

"I wanted to tell you before you saw the Sword of Angesand," he said. "And if you want the entire truth, I didn't want you to wield it at all—"

"Liar," she spat. "Of course you did!"

"I wanted a wielder," he conceded, "but that was before I knew the wielder was *you*. And after I knew that was your destiny, I wanted you anywhere but near that sword."

"I don't believe you," she said bitterly.

"I can't blame you, but it is the truth." He looked at her for a moment or two, then sighed deeply. "Perhaps it won't make my actions in the fall any more palatable to you, but I'd like to explain them if you would humor me by listening."

She glared at him, but she wasn't moving. He took that as tacit agreement.

"I have, whether it is convenient or not, a duty to protect the realm of Neroche," he began slowly. "I found myself in the fall believing that I needed aid in fulfilling that duty. Neroche is under a slow but calculating assault by some species of magic I can't identify. Adhémar has no magic, the Sword of Neroche is nothing but dull steel, and I'm pushed to the limit. I thought if I could find someone to wield the Sword of Angesand, even just to call to its power and add that power to mine, I might purchase myself a bit of time to determine what's undermining my spells."

"Can you not use the Sword of Angesand yourself?" she asked coolly. "Do you lack the power?"

"The sword does not call to me," he said carefully, "and so there is no point in my trying to use it. It doesn't matter how much power I might or might not have. I cannot force the sword to respond to me."

She didn't answer. She wouldn't meet his eyes, but then again, she wasn't walking away or reaching for her sword.

It was progress.

"If Neroche falls," he continued quietly, "there will be nothing standing between Lothar and the rest of the Nine Kingdoms."

"And you're holding the line, is that it?" she asked unwillingly.

"Aye," he said, "I am. And I will not be able to do so indefinitely."

She pursed her lips, but said nothing.

"I think you should also know," he began, "that if the wielder of the Sword of Angesand had been some lad I'd found in a mercenary camp, I would have strapped him to my horse and carried him back to Tor Neroche without a second thought. But the wielder was you, and I knew I couldn't—didn't want to—force you into a destiny you might not want."

"Yet you took me to Tor Neroche just the same."

He met her eyes. "After being attacked twice by the same sort of creatures, I thought that the safest place for you would be within the palace walls. Only the palace didn't turn out to be a safe place at all." He reached out and put his hand on her crossed arms. "I'm sorry, Morgan. I can only tell you that I wanted to talk to you before you saw the sword. Before you fell asleep, didn't I tell you that I had aught to tell you first thing in the morning?"

"Aye," she agreed unwillingly.

"I had planned to tell you everything, but I spent the night and the next day working and lost track of time. You found the sword before I could stop you. I would go back and do that day over again if I could." He took a deep breath. "I would do many days over again, if I could."

She bowed her head and was still for so long, he wondered if she had forgotten he was there.

Then she turned and walked away without saying anything.

Miach leaned against the wall and watched her flee. Well, she didn't flee. She only walked, but it was faster than he'd seen her move in days. Perhaps there was healing happening after all.

He sighed and rubbed his hands over his face. He'd made a beginning at least and she had been willing to listen. She could have simply stuck him and been done with it. His belly was, as it happened, unpierced. He supposed that could be considered a good thing.

His arm pained him suddenly. It pained him almost as much as did his heart.

Regret was a miserable thing.

Scrymgeour Weger watched from the shadows as Morgan walked slowly and unsteadily toward her chamber and the archmage of Neroche turned and walked with equal unsteadiness toward the stairs that led down. He wasn't one to eavesdrop, but he'd found himself trapped without an escape. He'd merely followed the pair across the courtyard so he could brush the mage off and escort Morgan to her chamber himself. He hadn't expected to hear so much, and he was heartily sorry he had.

He leaned back against the wall and considered several things he hadn't before. It was obvious that Morgan knew

Neroche's most powerful finger-waggler far better than she had admitted. That Prince Mochriadhemiach should have wanted to keep company with her was understandable. Not only was Morgan lethal, she was exceptionally beautiful and had wit to match any man Weger had ever met. But magic as well?

Interesting.

And what was that business about the Sword of Angesand? If the Neroche lads thought she was destined to wield it, then her power must be staggering. He couldn't imagine it, though he supposed he wasn't one to judge. It wasn't as if she could have used it within his walls.

But why would an orphaned lass of no consequence find herself in possession of that kind of magic?

She reminded him of someone. He searched back through his memory for quite some time, but decided on nothing useful. She had an elvish look to her, but perhaps that was simply because she was so damned beautiful. Beautiful and deadly. No wonder the archmage of Neroche wanted her and not, as he had put it, for her skill with the sword.

Not that he would have her. Morgan couldn't abide mages.

And since that was the case, Weger supposed it might be wise to keep a few things to himself. She would wonder how he knew so much about anything beyond Gobhann's walls. He would have to tell her why eventually, he supposed, but he would wait for the proper time.

He wasn't surprised, knowing what he knew now, that she had come back to Gobhann. Many came within the gates to escape the magic in their veins. He could remind her of that and offer her the silence of his hall.

He suspected she might be tempted to take it.

He pushed away from the wall and decided to have a final look about. Then he would keep an eye on the mage prince. He hadn't looked particularly steady on his feet, and Weger suspected that had more to do with his arm than with the rejecting blow Morgan had just dealt him.

S_{IX}

Morgan paced the length of the library, feeling rather spry, all things considered. She'd just finished climbing from the lowest gates to the uppermost courtyard without stopping. Well, that wasn't precisely true. She'd had to stop at the top of every staircase, but it hadn't been several times on each as she'd been forced to the previous se'nnight. She also ignored the fact that the feat had taken her the better part of the afternoon. She almost believed that she might someday feel again as she had before.

Well, at least her form might feel as it once had. She despaired of her heart ever recovering.

Damn Miach of Neroche to hell and back.

She turned and looked out the window at the roiling sea below her. She wasn't quite sure what she should think about the apology he'd offered the night before. She supposed it wasn't every day that the archmage of Neroche expressed regret to a no-name shieldmaiden—after having come inside Gobhann to do so, no less.

She turned away from the window. Perhaps she would do better not to think on any of it overmuch. It could only lead to thinking on things she couldn't understand . . . or remedy.

Perhaps that was how Miach felt as well. There were some things that simply couldn't be undone, no matter how many prettily spoken apologies were offered.

"Morgan."

She looked up to find Weger standing in the doorway. "Aye, my lord?"

"Come with me," he said urgently. "Now."

He turned away. Morgan hurried across the chamber, then struggled to keep up with his swift strides. She felt better, but not that much better. She paused first in the middle of the courtyard, then at the gate to catch her breath. Weger cursed her every time she stopped, but she simply couldn't go any faster. He continued on through the gate in the wall and to the stairs that led up to Miach's tower. She had to stop at the bottom of them and lean over until the stitch in her side eased enough to allow her to straighten. Then she looked up at Weger.

"I can't climb these again."

"You have no choice," he said. "Hurry."

She would have told him absolutely not, but there was something in his eye that told her he wouldn't accept anything but her acquiescence. She took a deep breath, put aside her unease, and started to climb. She'd only managed a handful of stairs before she stumbled and had to clutch the hem of Weger's tunic to keep from falling off the side and plunging to her death. The sun hadn't fully set yet and she could see very well just exactly what lay beneath her. Three hundred feet down and nothing but jagged rocks as a landing place.

Weger cursed and grabbed her hand to pull her along after him. Morgan didn't dare ask what he wanted, nor did she have breath for asking why he was so concerned that she visit a place where magic was possible.

He shoved the key into the lock, then pushed her inside the chamber. She staggered as magic ran through her like a fever. Weger lit a torch and jammed it into a sconce.

"Look," he said.

Morgan did, then understood why Weger had been in such terrible haste.

Miach was lying on the floor, still as death. He was barechested, but not shivering. There were red streaks trailing up his arm toward his shoulder, like claw marks from some terrible beast. She stepped over him, then dropped to her knees next to him and put her hand on his face. He was on fire, the fool. She closed her eyes briefly. What had he been thinking?

"He fell senseless earlier," Weger said grimly. "He was calling for you in his fevered dreams, so I brought him here and came to fetch you."

Morgan ran her fingers over the red streaks on Miach's arm. She supposed she could open the stitches, draw forth the pus, and then treat him with herbs. She could brew tea, perhaps, and hope that it counteracted the infection. She had learned how in the infirmary below during her first month at Gobhann. But that would take time.

Miach obviously did not have the luxury of time.

"And just what is it, my lord," she said, her mouth appallingly dry, "that you intend me to do for him that the apothecary cannot?"

"I assume he had good reason to call your name instead of Master John's."

She closed her eyes briefly. Aye, he'd had good reason, indeed. She knew what would heal Miach, heal him instantly so he would wake to himself, whole. And if she used that knowledge, Weger would know just what she was capable of—and then he would throw her off the walls. But if she didn't do something for Miach quickly, he would die. She couldn't let that happen, no matter the cost to her personally.

She took a deep breath. "I have a little magic," she said, spitting out the words as quickly as possible. "I never asked for it and I don't want it." She paused, then looked up at Weger. No sense in not seeing the extent of his disgust.

He was, however, merely leaning back against the door with his arms folded over his chest, watching her without expression. His hand was comfortably far from his sword hilt. "Can you heal him with that magic?"

Morgan felt a little winded. "I think so."

He studied her for another moment or two. "I daresay you have quite a tale to tell to the right listener."

"I suspect, my lord, that the right listener would not be you."

"You might be surprised." He gestured toward Miach. "Do what you can then, woman. I'll avert my eyes."

Morgan couldn't even manage a smile. For one thing, she wasn't at all sure that Weger wouldn't finish her off when he saw her use a spell and find it responsive to the magic in her veins. And secondly, she wasn't sure Miach would live.

He burned with a terrible heat, but he didn't thrash about. Perhaps he had no more strength for thrashing. Perhaps he was closer to death than she feared. She took his hand, then reached out to smooth his hair back from his brow.

She searched through dreams and words spoken for anything that might help her. She considered the spell of healing that Adhémar had once given her. She could still see the results of that on Miach's arm: five fingerprints were indelibly burned into his flesh. But that spell had only healed a slice in Miach's flesh; it had done nothing for infection. How was she to see to that?

Before she panicked truly, she began to hear words in her head. She couldn't understand them at first, but once she did, she immediately understood how they might be used in drawing out poisons.

Had Miach used that spell to heal her? This voice was not his, but she had no time to determine whose it was. It was enough to have the words there in her mind, ready for her use. She put her fingers over Miach's wound and repeated the spell faithfully.

She hadn't but breathed the last word when he suddenly jerked his arm away and sat up with a start.

"Ouch, damn you—" he began. Then he apparently realized who was holding on to him. He smiled. "Morgan."

Then his smile faded and he went very still.

Morgan understood. She watched him look at her for several heartbeats, his eyes wide with surprise. Then he slowly turned his head and looked up at Weger, who was still leaning against the door. Weger's expression was, as usual, inscrutable. He tossed Miach a fresh black tunic and a key.

"There you are," he said. "Work begins at dawn. You look fit for it now."

Miach leapt to his feet. "Thank you, my lord."

Morgan was not so swift to rise. She had to use Miach's freshly healed arm as a means to get up. "My lord—" she began.

Weger turned, his hand on the door latch. "We'll speak later." He shot Miach a look. "Don't keep her here all evening. She needs sleep."

And with that, he left the chamber, slamming the door behind him.

Miach looked down at his arm. Morgan looked as well. Five new fingerprints had joined the first set, only the fresh ones were not as angry looking as the others. Miach smiled at her.

"You're improving."

She ignored that. "Weger brought me here," she said uneasily. "He knew what I could do."

"Perhaps I babbled things I shouldn't have."

She shook her head. "He said you had called for me, nothing more." She paused. "You worried him."

"He only wants me for my magecraft," Miach said lightly. "Because I keep him from being overrun by Lothar's minions."

"How could he not?" she said. She realized, with a start, that she was standing far too close to him for her peace of mind. She backed away and sat down against the wall whilst she could still manage it.

Miach pulled the tunic over his head, then went to lock the door. He returned to sit facing her. "Thank you for my life," he said quietly.

"Aye, well, it was a close thing," she said, far more casually than she felt. "You idiot," she added before she could help herself.

"I beg your pardon?" he said with half a laugh.

"You should have let me see to your arm sooner. You're the bloody archmage of the realm. You have business to see to, business that you can't see to if you're dead!" She glared at him. "Why don't you be about that business so I can go to bed?"

He didn't reply. He simply watched her with a look a duller wench might have termed affection.

"What?" she snapped.

He smiled gravely. "I thought I might try a few more apologies since I have you here."

"What for this time? That you dragged me away from a warm fire?" she asked, desperate to avoid anything more serious. "Aye, you should be sorry for that."

He shook his head. "I'm sorry that you had to find out who I was the way you did—"

"What, with that bloody Sword of Angesand singing in my ears? And the ring? And the knife? You left me there," she said, blurting out what pained her the most. "You left me alone."

She found, to her horror, that tears were streaming down her cheeks.

Miach walked over to her on his knees and reached for her hands. He held them tightly with his. "Morgan, I'm sorry."

She wanted to wipe her face, but he wouldn't release her hands. She settled for trying to rub her eyes against her shoulder. "It doesn't matter now," she managed.

He put a hand under her chin and turned her face toward him. "It *does* matter," he said seriously. "I wish that it had all come about differently." He took her hands with his again. "If I could go back and change things, believe me, I would."

"Why didn't you tell me who you were from the start?" she whispered, looking at him miserably. "In truth?"

"In truth?" He looked down at her hands and rubbed his thumbs over the back of them. "I knew how you felt about mages and I didn't want you to hate me." He looked up. "I suppose it didn't serve me, did it?"

"I don't hate you," was out of her mouth before she could stop herself.

She wanted to take back her words, or add to them, or toss off some sharp remark that would make him rethink his plans to stay at Gobhann, but all she could do was sit there and look at him like the witless tavern wench she had obviously become. Witless and ill. She wondered if she would ever be herself again.

"Well," he said, with a smile, "that's something, at least."

She wanted to run, but she couldn't. She wanted to drive him away, but she couldn't bring herself to do that either. She wished, suddenly, that he was not the archmage and she was not a shieldmaiden full of magic she did not want. If she had met him at a tavern, perhaps things would have been different.

But things were as they were. He was trapped as much by his duty as she was by the nightmares that awaited her outside Weger's gates.

"I'm tired," she said suddenly, pulling her hands away from his. "Please just do what you do so we can be out of this horrible place."

"Morgan—"

"Please, Miach."

He sighed deeply. "As you will." He rose and paced about

the chamber for a moment or two, put his hand briefly on the door, then sighed and came to sit down cross-legged in the middle of the chamber. He looked at her once more for a long moment, then bowed his head.

Morgan looked away as his stillness filled the chamber. Tears coursed down her cheeks until the edge of her cloak was damp. She finally dragged her sleeve across her face and thought surly thoughts until she felt a little more herself.

And then she engaged in much less useful activities. She pulled her cloak and Miach's more closely about her and watched him by the soft light of the torch on the wall. It was foolish, but she couldn't seem to help herself. Never mind that he was not for her. How often did she have the chance to observe him while he was otherwise occupied?

She realized, as she watched him, that she had become far more accustomed to him than she wanted to admit. She knew what the touch of his hand on hers felt like. She knew the music of his laugh and the warmth of his smile. She knew how it felt to be the recipient of his small kindnesses, his gentle teasing, his companionship.

Damn him to hell for them all.

By the time he was finished with whatever it was he did, she was stiff and cross. She clambered clumsily to her feet and glared at him.

He blinked in surprise. "What did I do now?"

She wanted to list a thousand terrible things, but she found she couldn't bring a single bloody one of them to mind. Perhaps she would work on that list later, when she wasn't so distracted by the sight of him.

"'Tis late," she said shortly. "Let's go."

He rose without comment, then followed her toward the door. Werelight floated suddenly over their heads, then the torch went out. She knew it hadn't done so on its own.

"How did you do that?" she asked.

"Years of practice," he said with a smile. "Would you like to learn the spell?"

Nay was on the tip of her tongue, but she found she couldn't quite bring herself to say it. "I am curious," she admitted unwillingly. "But I don't want to learn the spell."

"I won't teach it to you," he said, "but I will show you a few others, if you like."

She nodded.

He said a single word and fire danced again along the top of the torch. "There are, as you might suspect, as many ways to put out fire as there are languages of magic."

Morgan watched and listened as he extinguished and relit the torch half a dozen ways. The last spell sounded familiar. The fire wasn't ruthlessly obliterated, or squelched, or made to disappear; it seemed to smile at her before it gracefully faded to nothing. Morgan looked at him.

"That was a spell of Camanaë," she said in surprise.

"That was a spell of Camanaë," he agreed, looking as if he thoroughly approved of her.

She swallowed, hard. "It was beautiful."

"Well, it is a beautiful magic." He studied her for a moment, then smiled. "Let me try another you might like."

He spoke a trio of words and the fire sprang to life with a beauty so intense, Morgan could hardly look at it. He spoke another handful of words and the fire sparkled away until there was a single, small flash of red. Morgan found that its disappearance left her quite bereft. She blinked, hard, then looked up at him.

"What was that?" she asked.

"Fadaire. 'Tis the magic of the elves of Tòrr Dòrainn."

"Tòrr Dòrainn?" she repeated uneasily.

"Aye," he said softly.

Morgan shivered. She had dreamed of Sarait of Tòrr Dòrainn, but she would fling herself down the steps outside before she thought about why. "That magic was exquisite," she managed, praying Miach wouldn't say anything about those dreams. "How is it you know any of it?

He smiled, a mischievous smile that had her wishing quite suddenly for a chair.

"I know many things I shouldn't, but I am careful with them. The elves there will survive my trespassing."

"You stole the spell?" she asked, surprised.

He tsk-tsked her. "*Stole* is such an ugly word. I might have glanced at the odd book of spells opened conveniently to a page

I needed. 'Tis also possible I once found myself locked in King Sìle's solar and needed something to do to pass the time." He shrugged unrepentantly. "I'm a little vague on the details, truth be told."

She snorted at him. "I imagine you are. So, are those all the pilfered spells you know for ridding yourself of fire, or do you know any more?"

His smile faded. "I know two more, but I'll not use either of them here."

"Why not?"

"Because the first is the magic of Olc. It is . . . evil."

"Do you know much of it?" she asked faintly.

"Aye," he said, though he looked very reluctant to say more. "The other is Caochladh. I don't use that magic without great need, for it changes the essence of a thing. It would change the fire to air, permanently. I would then have to change the air back to fire." He smiled briefly. "Very powerful and very dangerous."

"Then how is it you know any of it?"

"I might have eavesdropped."

She almost smiled. "You didn't."

"I didn't," he agreed. "The spells of Caochladh are taught by a single man at Beinn òrain and only to those who have won the seven rings of mastery—and only then when those souls have proved themselves to be exceptionally discreet."

"And that would be you."

"I may not be many other things, but I am discreet."

"That I can believe," she conceded. "So, how long did it take you to win all these rings of mastery?"

He frowned thoughtfully. "Well, mine was a rather unorthodox journey, so you can't precisely judge the rings by time spent there. I was there in my youth, but I didn't stay long."

"Why not?"

He smiled, looking slightly sheepish. "I missed my mother."

She smiled before she could help herself. "Did you?"

He reached out and pushed a strand of hair back from her face. "I did. She was a wonderful woman and my closest confidant. She was also a damned fine mage. I learned as much from her at home as I ever could have at Beinn òrain. But I did go back later, after I had shouldered my duties. I spent a month showing the masters there what they wanted to see and earned the rings."

"You're not wearing any rings."

He shrugged. "They're languishing in a drawer somewhere. I only wanted them because they were a means to the spells of Caochladh."

"Of course. And this exceptionally choosey man gave them to you?"

"Aye."

She took a deep breath, then let it out slowly. "Who are you?"

"You know who I am."

"I don't understand why you're here."

"Don't you?"

She scowled at him. "You've apologized already. You can go now."

He opened his mouth, then shut it again. He took a deep breath. "I'm not finished here."

"Do you want Weger's mark so badly?"

"It's incidental to what I want."

Morgan didn't think she dared ask him to elaborate. He couldn't have come for her. It just wasn't possible.

He reached out and tugged gently on her braid. "Come on, gel. You should be abed."

Morgan allowed him to usher her out the door because she couldn't think of a good reason to stop him. She walked outside first and gasped in spite of herself at the chill and the darkness that fell over her heart as her magic left her.

Damn the scourge and all its incarnations.

She supposed Miach had locked the door behind him. She couldn't have said for the howl of the wind. She felt him take her hand and didn't protest as he kept hold of it as he led her down the stairs.

She realized he had stopped suddenly only because she had run into him. She looked up and found that he had run into Weger. Weger disentangled her fingers from Miach's, pushed him out of the way, then pulled her off the final step. He tucked her hand in the crook of his arm.

"Dawn," he said to Miach. He looked at Morgan. "I'll see you to your room, Morgan."

Morgan caught sight of Miach's expression. She was certain that his astonishment mirrored her own, but she didn't dare say anything. She walked with Weger across courtyards and through passageways until she stood in front of her own door. Weger opened it for her, then stepped back.

He made her a low bow.

Morgan could scarce believe her eyes.

"You needn't go with him, you know," he said quietly. "You might stay here with me."

And with that, he pushed her inside her room and very quietly shut the door.

Morgan gaped at the door for several minutes until she managed to shut her mouth. She supposed she wouldn't have been any more surprised if Weger had conjured up a fistful of flowers and handed them to her.

She sat down on her bed before she fell there. She reached absently for the tea that was sitting on the little table next to her. It was hot and actually rather tasty. Stephen hard at work again, apparently.

Go with Miach?

Stay with Weger?

She thought about it for the space of five heartbeats, then shook her head. Miach was a fool and Weger . . . well, Weger had obviously taken a blow to the head. Neither of them was serious. She was a rough, unpolished shieldmaiden.

Besides, Miach hadn't exactly offered her anything but an apology. And Weger hadn't offered her anything more than a place to stay.

Unbidden, a vision of elven magic danced before her eyes. She saw its fierce beauty, the spells of Camanaë and their sweetness, all the other things that Miach had shown her, things she never would have seen if she'd never gone into that tower chamber, never agreed to take Nicholas's blade to Tor Neroche, never met a man who patiently fashioned spell after spell so she could look them all over and see what pleased her the most.

Go with Miach and face her dreams. Stay with Weger and live out her life in unrelenting silence.

It was a terrible choice.

One she wasn't sure she could make.

Seven

Miach sat in the tower chamber a se'nnight after Morgan had healed him and wanted nothing so much as to simply lie down and sleep until noon. He wasn't one to shun difficult tasks, but he was willing to admit, without shame, that he might be facing just a bit more than he could adequately surmount.

He'd been invited, the day after Morgan had healed him, to join the lads in the upper courtyard. That he might have managed, but the invitation had come from Weger himself, along with the casually dropped nugget that Weger had decided to take over his training personally.

The torture had begun thereafter before dawn and continued until Gobhann was draped in the lovely colors of twilight. By the time the sun had set each evening, Miach hadn't given a damn what time it was, how lovely the keep looked, or whether or not he'd survived another day. All he'd wanted to do was crawl in bed, but even that hadn't been possible. He'd spent the better part of each night seeing to spells that were now never as he'd left them but hours before. He'd begun to dread the arrival of dawn.

Dawn, however, continued to come. His world had become nothing but swords and spells and wishing that he might, for just a few hours, do something else.

And so he found himself, on that particularly long night after a particularly grueling day, wishing that he could just close his eyes and sleep.

But he couldn't, so he closed his eyes and went about his work. It took him longer than he would have liked, but his spells had begun to shift in a way he could no longer predict. Unless he managed to stop what was eating away at them, he would be shoring them up constantly. He had to determine what was responsible for the assaults and stop it—and that he couldn't do simply sitting in Weger's tower night after night.

He opened his eyes and faced the truth he'd been trying to avoid for days.

He could put off the inevitable for perhaps another se'nnight, but then he would have to go. He didn't particularly want to force Morgan's hand, but he had no choice. The realm could not wait much longer.

He heaved himself to his feet, then left the chamber, locking it behind him. He turned and paused in surprise. Morgan was sitting on the staircase, some twenty steps below him. She had kept watch over him over the past se'nnight, but she had refused to come any farther than the bottom step. Why she'd chosen that terrible perch was a mystery. The wind was biting and it was starting to rain. Miach eased past her and turned to lean toward her.

"Morgan, you've got to get down from here," he shouted.

She looked up at him, then her eyes widened suddenly. "Miach—"

Miach felt himself be flung off the stairs. It was all he could do to grab for the edge of a step and blurt out a spell—and the spell served him not at all. His rapidly numbing fingers were the only thing keeping him from plunging to his death. He swung his foot up on the stairs to try to pull himself up only to have Searbhe kick it back off. The ring of steel was clearly audible above the howl of the wind, but there wasn't a damn thing he could do about it. He could only hang there helplessly and watch Morgan try to save them both.

He'd seen her at her lethal best; she wasn't anywhere near that at present. Fortunately for them both, however, she was proficient enough and Searbhe was not her equal. She finally boxed him on the ear with the flat of her blade, then sent him tumbling down the stairs by means of her foot to his belly.

Miach would have congratulated her on the feat, but he was too busy worrying whether or not his heart would continue to beat long enough for him to get himself back up on the steps. Morgan resheathed her sword, then knelt and grasped him by the wrists. She held on to him until he could hook his leg on the stairs and pull himself back up. She jerked him away from the edge of the stairs and flung him back against the mountainside. He gasped at the pain of sharp rocks digging into his back as she threw herself against him, but he didn't protest. That he was willing to endure such discomfort was indication enough of just how desperate he was to have Morgan in his arms.

He held her tightly and watched the turn of the stairs, waiting for the glint of steel or a change in the shadows. There was nothing, but that wasn't particularly reassuring.

"We need to go," he said against Morgan's ear. "Do you want me to carry you?"

She shook her head as she pulled away from him. "I am well."

She didn't look it, but he wasn't going to argue with her. He took her hand, kept his sword bare in the other, then led her carefully down the steps. He saw nothing, not even in the shadows of the courtyard at the bottom of the staircase. They couldn't have been so fortunate as to have had Searbhe fall to his death.

He resheathed his sword, but kept Morgan's hand in his as they ran across the courtyard, more to keep her on her feet than for any more romantic reason. He was exceptionally grateful she'd had the strength to defend them both, but he could see that she had paid a steep price for it. He opened the gate for her, then shut it behind them with a clang. He ran with her across the inner courtyard until they had reached a passageway where a torch drove away the shadows. Morgan released him, then collapsed back against the wall, gasping for breath.

"I must rest for a moment," she wheezed.

Miach smiled at her. "You have cause. You were magnificent, by the way. I appreciate the gift of my life."

"It was a near thing," she managed.

"Too near," he agreed.

She rested for a moment or two, then pushed away from the wall. "We must tell Weger," she said. "A fair fight is one thing; murder is something else entirely."

"I can't imagine he bothers about assaults until the victims aren't breathing any longer."

"He'll bother about this one."

Miach didn't think so, but he followed her along the passageway just the same until they reached a heavy wooden door. He was absolutely certain Weger wouldn't give a damn who had pushed whom where. It would be better to keep it to themselves and be prepared for a next time.

He stopped Morgan before she put her hand on the latch. "I don't want to say anything about it whilst Searbhe is within earshot," he said quietly.

She looked up at him. "You know something."

"I suspect something," he said. "He's not telling the truth about himself and I find that curious. It may be nothing, but I'm willing to wait him out and see what becomes of it."

"And if he tries to murder you again?"

Miach smiled. "I suppose you'll just have to spend all your time guarding my back, won't you?"

She pursed her lips at him. "I'll think about it."

He didn't argue with her, lest she think on it too long and decide to refuse. He reached around and opened the door for her. "After you."

He followed her inside and looked around with interest. He couldn't say it was a luxurious place, but it was surely more comfortable than anything he'd seen so far. There were bookshelves full of books, numerous well-made chairs, and a very large hearth at one end. The hall was empty except for Weger sitting in front of the fire with Searbhe and another handful of lads he didn't know very well.

"Doesn't he ever sleep?" Miach muttered.

"Weger? Not much, I imagine. You'd think Searbhe would need some now though, wouldn't you? Especially now that he's sporting so many bruises."

Searbhe looked up as they approached. "No novices allowed," he said loudly.

"He is hardly a novice, is he?" Morgan returned sharply.

She stopped behind the chair nearby and looked Searbhe over assessingly. "You're a bit bloodied. Fall down and cut yourself?"

Searbhe got to his feet and loomed over her. "A gust of wind caught me," he said coldly.

"Best stay indoors, then, hadn't you?" she said with a snort.

Miach yanked Morgan out of the way before Searbhe could shove her aside. He glared at Miach, then cursed his way past them and across to the door. Miach watched him leave, then leaned against the back of a chair and watched until the other remaining lads seemed to find his scrutiny uncomfortable and departed for safer ground as well.

Once the chamber was empty, he sat down and tried to make sense of the low arguing that Morgan was doing with Weger. He'd obviously missed quite a bit, because he found they had left pleasantries far behind and were settling for things approaching shouts.

"I know Miach doesn't want him thrown out and I know you won't throw him out, but I think he needs to be watched," Morgan was saying rather heatedly. "I wouldn't put it past him to stab any of us!"

"Searbhe has no desire to harm you or me," Weger disagreed. "'Tis our good archmage that he loathes. I daresay there's a particular reason for it."

"Because Miach has sword skill and Searbhe doesn't?" Morgan asked tartly.

Weger shook his head. "I think Searbhe recognizes him."

"He doesn't look *that* much like Adhémar," Morgan said. "Fortunately. And at least when Miach opens his mouth, all within earshot don't plug their ears."

Miach stroked his lips with his fingers to keep from smiling. Poor Adhémar. Traveling with Morgan in the fall had to have been taxing in the extreme.

Weger pursed his lips at her. "I wasn't thinking the current king of Neroche, actually, though Miach does bear an unfortunate resemblance to him. Our wee mutterer here looks a bit like a pair of his ancestors. I thought at first Symon of Wychweald—"

"Symon of Wychweald?" Morgan interrupted. "Who is that? Is he related to Lothar?"

Weger sighed gustily. "Morgan, do you know *nothing* about the Nine Kingdoms?"

"I've never been interested in anything to do with Wychweald or black mages or things of that sort," Morgan said stiffly. "Nor with anything to do with the rulers of Neroche."

"A little knowledge of the outside world isn't a poor thing," Weger said. "Perhaps you should continue your convalescence here in my library. For tonight, I'll simply tell you that Symon of Wychweald is related to Lothar. He was also the first king of Neroche. How that came about is something you can look up for yourself." Weger shot Miach a look. "I've changed my mind. You look less like Symon than you do Gilraehen the Fey. You have the same pale, spooky eyes he has."

"Thank you," Miach said dryly.

"How would *you* know that?" Morgan asked Weger in surprise.

Miach listened to Weger give Morgan a vague answer about being very well read and wondered silently how Weger could possibly make the comparison he'd just made. He studied Weger, but saw nothing that would have indicated he was anything more than he seemed to be.

Then again, looks often deceived.

"I don't understand why any of it matters," Morgan said. "Even if Searbhe recognizes Miach, why would he care?"

Miach reached for the answer and found it suddenly beneath his fingers. "Because Neroche is at war with Riamh."

"Riamh?" she echoed.

Weger swore in frustration. "History, Morgan. Geography. World affairs. Pick up a book tomorrow."

Morgan buried a curse in her cup.

Miach smiled. "Riamh is not only the name of Lothar's castle, 'tis the name of his realm." He looked at Weger. "Searbhe is kin of Lothar's, isn't he?"

The corner of Weger's mouth tipped up in the slightest of smiles. "My faith in the security of the realm is restored."

"Searbhe of Riamh," Morgan repeated faintly. She looked at Weger in surprise. "How do *you* know who he is?"

Weger hesitated, then sighed. "Because Searbhe is my cousin."

Miach heard Morgan's cup hit the floor. Fortunately for

their boots, the cup was empty. Miach picked it up and set it on the table slowly. He looked at Morgan, but she was staring at Weger with the same sort of look she'd worn when she'd learned who Miach was.

The poor gel.

"Your cousin?" she whispered. "How is that possible?"

Weger leaned forward with his elbows on his knees. "Because as unpleasant a fact as it is, I am Lothar's grandson, many generations removed. Through my mother."

Morgan put her face in her hands.

"I grew up in Riamh," Weger continued impassively, "and did my share of things I regret. To your ancestors, Miach, as it happens. Sorry."

Miach smiled and shrugged.

Morgan lifted her head. Her eyes were wide with shock. "You have *magic*?"

Weger smiled grimly. "Not here."

Morgan shivered so violently, Miach could see it from where he sat. He rose and went to look for a blanket of some sort. He found one wadded up on the end of a bench, shook it out, then walked back to the fire. He draped it over her, then leaned closer on the pretext of tucking it up around her shoulders.

"Are you all right?" he murmured.

"I'm not sure," she said, her teeth chattering.

"Want to go for a walk?"

She took a deep breath, then shook her head. "Not now." She looked up at him bleakly. "Thank you, though."

"The offer stands." He touched her shoulder briefly, then sat down. He rested his boot against hers, felt her press her foot against his so hard it almost hurt, then turned his mind to considering what he'd just learned. The particular properties of Gobhann made sense now. It also explained why Weger knew where the tower chamber was. It didn't explain why Weger had asked Morgan to heal him instead of doing it himself, but perhaps he had a vile sense of humor. That, or he had suspected something about Morgan and wanted to test her. Miach wouldn't have been surprised by either.

"Why did you leave Riamh?" Miach asked.

"Lothar pushed me too far," Weger answered, dragging his attention away from Morgan. "He put my father and my two

younger brothers in his dungeon, let them all rot there until
they went mad, then forced my mother to kill what was left of
them. I tried to fetch them out before that, of course, but I
failed. I hid in the shadows until I was able to retrieve their
bodies and bury them. Then I left. I have no idea if my mother
is still alive or not."

"Does Searbhe know who you are?" Miach asked.

Weger shook his head. "I imagine not. He's much younger
than I am, and I'm quite sure my name is never spoken in
Riamh. Perhaps they've forgotten all about me."

"How old are you?" Miach asked.

"How old do you think I am?" Weger returned, with one
raised eyebrow.

Miach considered Lothar's genealogy, wandered down
through the generations, then paused. There had been a powerful mage from Treunnar who had wed with one of Lothar's
granddaughters . . . and that mage had been slain with his
family by Lothar. Miach would have preferred a few more
details—such as whether or not it had been all the family and
not just a pair of the lads—but he hadn't spent all that much
time memorizing Lothar's generations so the sketchy details
would have to do. He met Weger's gaze. "Your mother is
Eisleine."

Weger looked faintly surprised. "Aye, she is."

"That would make you . . . six hundred and fifty?"

Weger looked at Morgan. "At least he reads, eh?"

Morgan made a noise that sounded a little like a moan.
Miach found her watching them both with an expression he
wasn't sure he wanted to identify. It was either shock or
horror—or both.

Actually, she looked rather ill.

Miach reached out and put his hand on her knee. "Morgan,
perhaps you should go to bed."

"And miss more of these interesting revelations?" she said,
looking as if she would have liked nothing better. "I wouldn't
dare."

Weger leaned over and poured more wine for her. "She's
made of stern stuff; she'll survive. But now that we know who
we all are, I'd like tidings of the Nine Kingdoms. I heard rumors that Adhémar has lost his magic. Tell me of it."

Miach waited until Morgan had drunk some of her wine before he turned back to Weger. He supposed there was no reason not to be frank. In fact, if he hadn't been angling for a proper leave-taking out the front gates with Morgan at his side, he might have felt as if he were chatting amicably with a peer.

So he gave Weger details as thoroughly as he would have given them to Cathar. He told him about Adhémar's loss of magic, about the difficulty with his spells, about his concern that there was something else afoot in the world besides Lothar.

"What of the Sword of Angesand?" Weger asked. "Why don't you use that to do damage with for a bit? Mehar gave me a taste of it one particularly nasty afternoon."

"Did she?" Miach asked with a smile.

Morgan was making choking noises. "You fought *Mehar* of Angesand?" she asked incredulously.

"Of course," Weger said. "A wonderful wench, that one. I daresay you would like her." He looked at Miach. "Why don't you use her sword?"

"He can't," Morgan said. She cleared her throat. "I broke it."

Weger's mouth fell open. "You *what*? That sword is centuries old. It's slathered with magic. Bloody hell, Morgan, it sings!"

"I know!" she exclaimed. "I didn't mean to!"

Weger shook his head. "The bloody Sword of Angesand, Morgan. I can hardly believe it. What a bloody stupid thing to do!"

Morgan glared at Weger. Miach might have believed she was truly angry, but her eyes were very red. He suspected that if he didn't get her out of the gathering hall and out of Weger's sights very soon, she would weep.

"I drove her to it," Miach said pleasantly. He set his cup down on the table with a hearty bang, stood, and pulled Morgan to her feet. "If you'll excuse us, my lord, we'll be off. Morgan needs to be abed."

He didn't wait for Weger to respond. He took Morgan by the arm and pulled her across the hall and out the door before she had the time to protest. He shut the door, then looked down at her.

"Where to?" he asked.

She looked up at him with tears in her eyes. "Thank you."

"You shouldn't weep in front of him," Miach said quietly. "He'll blame me."

"He would have cause," she managed.

"Aye, I daresay he would." He slipped his hand down her arm to lace his fingers with hers. "Where's your bedchamber, gel?"

She nodded toward her right and led him down another passageway to a chamber on a far more lofty level than his own. She stopped at the door, cursed for a moment or two, then looked up at him.

Her expression was very bleak. "I don't want to know anything else about anyone else," she said, her voice catching. "No more souls who should be just soldiers turning into mages."

He put his hands on her shoulders. "I'm sorry, love. I wish I could change things for you."

She pressed her fingers against her eyes. "I can bear no more, Miach. This was too much tonight."

"You'll feel better after a decent night's sleep," Miach said. "Now, does your door have a lock on it?"

"A lock?" she repeated. "Nay, it doesn't. I've never needed one before."

"You need one tonight." He pushed open the door, looked inside, then stepped back. "I'll keep watch."

"You can't mean to stand out here all night," she said in surprise.

"Morgan, there isn't all that much left of the night," he said with a smile. "I'll manage."

"But you'll never be able to stand against Weger if you don't rest."

He turned her around, pushed her inside, then shut the door behind her. He held on to the latch until she stopped tugging and continued to hold on to it until she stopped cursing. Once he was convinced she had conceded the battle, he merely leaned against the door frame and watched the shadows.

He was unsurprised to find Weger emerging from them only moments later. Weger leaned against the opposite side of Morgan's door.

"I want more details," he said without hesitation.

"I imagined you would."

Weger shot him a disgruntled look, then folded his arms

over his chest. "How is it possible that an obviously intelligent but apparently very unmagical girl like Morgan can suddenly destroy a sword forged by Mehar of Angesand—who likely had Gilraehen the Fey standing at her side pouring his own magic into that forging? I would accuse you of lying, but Morgan admitted to it, and I know she doesn't lie."

Miach studied Weger for a moment or two in silence, looked up and down the passageway to judge its emptiness. He saw no reason not to give the man the details he wanted. Perhaps it was time to see if what Nicholas had told him a month ago could be verified by someone else.

"What if her parents were something other than simple, unmagical farmers?" he asked quietly.

Weger frowned deeply. "What do you mean?"

"Does she bear any resemblance to anyone you might have known?" Miach asked.

Weger thought for a moment, then shrugged. "I've always thought her to look a bit elvish, but perhaps that's just my imagination."

"Is it?"

Weger shot him a sharp look, then considered a bit longer. He shook his head, as if he couldn't believe something, then looked at Miach. "She reminds me of Sarait of Tòrr Dòrainn."

Miach forced himself not to react to that. "Did you know Sarait?"

Weger lifted one eyebrow briefly. "As you might imagine, I didn't dine with them often, but I did see her a handful of times. I was with Gair once when we came upon her traveling with her sister Lismòrian." He went suddenly still, then his mouth fell slowly open. "That isn't possible."

Miach waited and said nothing.

"Is Morgan . . . Gair's daughter? Mhorghain?" He pulled back, as if he'd encountered something poisonous right in front of him. "That isn't possible. All the children died at the well."

"So the tale goes," Miach agreed, "but tales are ofttimes wrong."

"What proof do you have?" Weger demanded.

"Nicholas of Diarmailt told me as much. He's been watching over her since Gair opened the well. Or, rather, since the mercenaries who originally took Morgan in left her at his door."

"Nicholas . . ." Weger coughed. "Nicholas of Lismòr? He's the finger-waggler from Diarmailt?"

"The very same."

Weger swore softly. "Does Morgan know?"

"She dreams of Gair, but she clings to the hope that they're naught but nightmares. She doesn't know that I'm sure beyond all doubt."

"The poor gel," Weger said grimly. He rubbed his hands over his face, then looked at Miach. "So, if she chooses you, she faces the burden of her blood and a lifetime of danger because of that blood. If she chooses me, she has peace."

"That sums it up quite well, actually," Miach said.

"I wouldn't raise my hopes overmuch, were I you."

"I'm not."

"I can't stop you from leaving on your own, you know," Weger said conversationally, "right out the front gates."

"In truth?" Miach asked, surprised.

"I wouldn't, usually, but I do have a use for you alive in the north. Consider it my gift."

"I appreciate that, but I'd prefer to leave having accomplished what I came to."

"What, winning Morgan or my mark?"

"Both."

Weger snorted. "Adhémar will howl if you manage either."

"All the more reason to succeed."

Weger smiled faintly. "I like you. A pity I must hate you for what you want to take from me."

"Is Morgan yours for me to take?" Miach asked mildly.

Weger opened his mouth, but shut it suddenly as Morgan's door opened. She pointed the end of her very sharp sword at Miach.

"Go sleep," she said, gesturing with that sword to the bed.

"With you?" Weger asked in astonishment.

She shot him a glare. "Well, of course not *with* me. But he thinks to guard me all night, then attempt to train with you on the morrow. He shut me in my bedchamber!" She shot Miach a glare. "I should stick you for that alone, but I'll accord you the courtesy of a few hours' sleep before I reward you as you deserve."

Miach would have protested, but her hand was trembling badly as she held her sword to his throat, and he supposed discretion suggested that he acquiesce to her demands. Besides, he suspected that if he didn't do what she wanted, she would put him to bed with her sword in his back, then tuck the covers up to his chin. He couldn't deny that the thought of even an hour of sleep was too tempting to resist.

"Besides," Morgan continued, "I was growing increasingly frustrated, being, as I was, *locked inside my chamber*. It was giving me a headache trying to eavesdrop through the door, and my efforts didn't yield a single bloody thing. I'm sure I'll be more successful when I'm out here in the passageway."

Miach exchanged a look with Gobhann's lord over Morgan's head, though he supposed it had been unnecessary. Weger, of all people, wasn't going to talk to Morgan about magic.

He sighed, then went to strip the blankets off Morgan's bed. He returned to the door and wrapped them around her. She looked up at him with wide, haunted eyes, then shut the door in his face.

Miach shucked off his boots and lay down on her bed. He had no trouble hearing the low voices outside Morgan's door. Perhaps he had the advantage of not having to listen to his own cursing whilst he was about it.

"Why is he here, do you suppose?" That was Weger, asking loudly the same bloody question he never seemed to want the answer for.

"I have no idea," Morgan said with a snort.

"Don't you?"

Morgan didn't answer. Miach supposed that if she had nothing to say, then his work was most certainly not done.

But that work had to be done soon. He didn't relish the idea of forcing Morgan's hand, but he had no choice. Even if his duty didn't call, he suspected that he was nearing the end of whatever training Weger was willing to give him. He had to talk to Morgan before Weger threw him out the front gates.

He would take another few days, spend as much time with

her as possible, then tell her what he'd come to say. That he didn't give a damn if she ever picked up another sword, magical or not. He wanted her just for herself.

And then he supposed she would have to choose between him and Weger.

He couldn't say that he was looking forward to knowing what that choice would be.

Eight

❧

A se'nnight later, on a cold, crisp morning, Morgan sat on the ground with her back against the wall in the sunny lower courtyard. She suspected that she had napped, though she couldn't be certain. Things looked no different from how they had the last time she'd managed to peer at what was going on in front of her. She had to admit, just watching it made her want to close her eyes and go back to sleep.

Miach and Weger were training. She supposed that it might have been called instruction, but even to her jaundiced eye it appeared that Miach was more than holding his own. He and Weger were of a height, quite similar in build, and actually quite evenly matched. They almost looked to be of an age, though she tried not to notice that Miach was as desperately handsome as Weger was not. Then again, for a man who was almost seven centuries old, Weger was actually quite well preserved.

As it were.

She shook her head and wondered if there would ever come a time when she would cease to be surprised by those she kept company with. It never would have occurred to her to think that Weger might have possessed magic, though looking back on it now, she could see how it made sense. His hatred for mages was obviously directed at Lothar, who had amply committed acts to deserve it. It was astonishing to think, though, that she had spent so much of her life in the same castle with Lothar's kin.

Things were indeed not as they seemed.

She had passed most of the evenings during the past se'nnight listening to Weger and Miach talk about characters from legend as easily as if they knew them personally—which she supposed they did. She'd learned more about the Nine Kingdoms and their inhabitants than she'd ever wanted to know.

Those evenings had been rather pleasant, truth be told.

She had to admit, quickly lest she be forced to think on it overmuch, that it warmed her heart to watch Weger treat Miach as an equal. Weger seemed to genuinely like him, though there was a strange undercurrent that ran between the two of them— as if there was an unresolved irritation that vexed them equally.

They seemed to be less troubled by it during the days. Perhaps they were distracted by their determination to shadow her at all costs. She would have insisted that they leave her alone, but she couldn't deny that she was more unsettled than she should have been. She would be long in forgetting the terror she'd felt as she'd watched Searbhe fling Miach off those dreadful mountainside steps. It had taken a great deal out of her, both emotionally and physically.

And so she had acquired two sword-bearing nursemaids. She slept in the courtyard during the daytime whilst Miach and Weger trained, and guarded Miach with Weger during the evenings whilst he was at his spells. After another pair of pleasant hours spent in the hall, she forced Miach to sleep a few hours in her bed whilst she and Weger sat outside the door.

She suspected that Weger never slept.

He didn't complain about it, though. Miach complained loudly, but only about her guarding him at night. He didn't want her to watch over him whilst he snoozed comfortably in her bed—his words, not hers—and after the first night, he had flatly refused to do so. She'd finally resorted to tendering a forgiveness for each night that he conceded the battle.

It was a terrible bargain, to be sure.

Especially since she realized that somewhere over the past se'nnight, she had forgiven him all.

It had been impossible not to. Whatever else his faults might have been, he was relentless when he was determined. She still wasn't completely sure why her forgiveness had been so important to him, or what he wanted now that he had it, or why he hadn't left through the front gates. Perhaps he merely remained to see if he could earn Weger's mark.

She couldn't bring herself to even begin to entertain any of the more ridiculous thoughts she'd had in the fall—thoughts of him perhaps having less comradely and more romantic feelings for her.

She turned away from those thoughts with a ruthlessness that made her feel a bit like her old self. Cheered by that, she contented herself with watching Miach execute a very vicious attack. Obviously he had not learned swordplay from Adhémar. Had he been this proficient when he'd come inside Weger's gates, or had he actually increased his skill? If the latter was the case, then he was formidable indeed. She couldn't think of another soul, save herself of course, who had been taken under Weger's wing so quickly.

She watched them for quite some time before she realized she wasn't the only soul taking an interest in their swordplay. Searbhe was standing in the shadows of the wall, watching Weger and Miach coldly. She studied him dispassionately, trying to reconcile his features with Lothar's. In all honesty, she couldn't say they were similar. Then again, when she'd encountered Lothar, she hadn't been at her best, so perhaps she wasn't in a position to judge.

All she knew was that he had no idea they had discussed him in such detail and that he continually hovered at the edge of her field of vision, apparently waiting for a chance to do damage to Miach. That wouldn't happen that day, not with Weger right there. Morgan found that thought somewhat comforting.

She watched Miach for quite a while before she couldn't help but close her eyes. The last thing she remembered was hearing Weger insult Miach in a particularly vile way. Miach's laughter was like sunlight.

She fell asleep smiling.

* * *

She woke, stiff and cold. The sun had disappeared behind clouds and it was starting to rain. She would have considered suggesting a retreat, but she saw that was unnecessary. Miach and Weger had put up their swords.

She would have tried to get to her feet on her own, but Miach was there first, holding down his hands to her. Morgan let him pull her up, but she refused to take his hand.

"I'm not an invalid," she said tartly, clutching her blankets to her chest. "My former state aside."

He smiled. "I know you can walk on your own. I was just looking for an excuse to hold your hand."

"Inside," Weger announced loudly, "before Morgan catches her death from the downpour."

Miach winked at her. "We'd best go before I irritate him so much that he locks us out in the rain."

Weger pursed his lips. "I would let Morgan in. You, however, I would gladly ban from the upper hall if I could. A pity your swordplay is so much improved."

"What you really value me for is my ability to gossip like a lady's maid," Miach remarked, "which needed no improving."

"Aye, well, that too," Weger agreed.

Morgan snorted and walked away from them both. She was concentrating so hard on escaping them and not limping whilst she did so that she didn't realize that she'd run into someone until she looked up and saw Searbhe blocking her way. She stared at him dispassionately.

"You're in my way," she said.

"You're in mine," he returned. "Move."

She started to, then gave him a hearty shove. She had flung off her cloak and reached for her sword only to realize it wasn't there. She would have dodged his descending blade but Miach's was suddenly there in front of her. Searbhe's blade screeched along the length of it, coming to rest at the hilt, uncomfortably close to Miach's face. Miach only shoved Searbhe back and elbowed Morgan out of the way.

"Move," he insisted. He faced Searbhe. "I believe your quarrel is with me."

"So it is," Searbhe said.

"But . . ." Morgan began, but the men ignored her. She

found herself hauled backward by Weger. She glared up at him, but he only shook his head sharply.

"Leave it," he commanded.

"He challenged *me*."

"You were in his way," Weger said, then he dropped his voice. "I suspect that what he truly wants is to slay the archmage of Neroche. Let us see if the archmage has learned enough in the past few se'nnights to avoid it."

Morgan knew there was no point in arguing. Besides, Miach wasn't doing poorly. Indeed, she could admit that not only was he holding his own against Searbhe, he was the far superior swordsman. She was unsurprised to watch him pretend otherwise.

"What is the fool doing?" Weger complained. "Hasn't he paid *any* attention to what I've taught him?"

"He's allowing himself to be underestimated," Morgan said quietly. "He does it constantly."

Weger rolled his eyes. "Ridiculous."

Morgan stood in the rain and watched the very brutal swordfight going on in front of her and found it less ridiculous than terrifying. She realized, with a start, that she cared quite a bit about the outcome. She had no sword and doubted Weger would allow her to borrow his, which left her able to do nothing but hope Miach was in truth holding himself back.

The fight seemed to go on for hours, though she supposed that was only because she marked every meeting of their blades. She decided at that moment that having Miach of Neroche as an enemy would be a very bad thing. She was unwholesomely grateful he was fighting for her. And she was equally as unsettled to find that she was willing to allow him to do the like.

She looked up at Weger. "I think that poison ruined my wits."

He grunted. "It wouldn't surprise me."

Morgan turned back in time to watch Miach catch Searbhe's sword by the hilt and send it flying up in the air. He caught it casually, then pointed both swords at his opponent.

"Are you finished, or would you like a bit more?" Miach asked politely.

"Give me my sword," Searbhe spat.

"You're dangerous with it," Miach remarked. "Mostly to yourself, unfortunately."

Searbhe glared at him, his eyes hot with hate. "I'll see you dead."

Miach shrugged. "I imagine not, but I suppose you'll continue to try." He tossed Searbhe his sword. "There you go, lad. Don't cut yourself."

Searbhe cursed him viciously, then turned and stalked off. Miach stood there with his sword bare in his hand and waited until Searbhe had disappeared up the stairs. Then he turned and came across the courtyard, resheathing his sword as he did so. He pushed his hair back from his face and smiled at Morgan.

"Lunch?"

"You're mad," she said without hesitation. "You provoked him dreadfully."

He only smiled. "I'm pushing him to do something stupid. We'll see, I suppose, if it serves me." He looked at Weger. "My lord?"

"Your swordplay was passable," Weger conceded, "but your taunts only marginally irritating. I expected better from a lad with six brothers."

"I'm tired," Miach conceded.

"It shows. I also think you could have finished him more quickly. Showing off, were you?"

Miach smiled wearily. "Not nearly enough, apparently. I'll work on that as well." He took Morgan's blankets from her. "Let's get out of the rain, woman."

Morgan nodded and followed them up stairways and through passageways to Weger's gathering hall. She set her blankets on a chair by the hall door and walked over to sit down yet again on the chair with the cushion. Neither Miach nor Weger paid her any heed when she complained about it, so she'd given up trying to convince them it was unnecessary.

She sat by the fire, but found she couldn't stay awake. Weger shook her when a late lunch came, but she couldn't manage any enthusiasm for that either. Fighting Searbhe the week before had been more difficult than she wanted to admit.

She sincerely hoped it didn't mean she would never again be herself.

With that unhappy thought to keep her company, she had some wine, then put her head back and succumbed again to slumber.

She woke suddenly, sitting up with a start. The hall was lit only by the fireplace and the chairs near her where Miach and Weger usually sat were empty. At first, she wasn't sure if she was dreaming or awake. Then she looked up and saw Searbhe standing in front of her.

She had the feeling he was all too real.

He drew a knife and leaned closer.

"I see you're alone," he said with a cold smile.

"So I am," she managed.

He opened his mouth, then frowned. "You look like someone I used to know."

"Do I?"

"'Tis impossible, of course, but you look a damn sight like Sarait of Tòrr Dòrainn," he said.

"Interesting," she said faintly. She looked him in the eye, but she was trying to remember if she had any blade loitering within reach. She saw one stuck in Searbhe's belt and decided that would do, if necessary.

"I tried to steal Sarait once." He pointed to a large, ugly scar down the side of his neck. "She gave me this and left me for dead. I can't repay her for the slight, but I can repay you in her stead. I think I'll enjoy it quite a bit."

"Will you indeed?" she said, shifting so she would be able to seize his knife if he struck out at her. She looked up at him. "I'm not surprised she bested you. You're one of Lothar's much lesser sons, aren't you?"

He was momentarily startled and it was that small hesitation that saved her. She jerked the blade from his belt and ducked underneath him, sending chairs crashing as she crawled out of his way. She heaved herself to her feet and spun around to face him.

He drew his sword with a flourish and threw himself at her.

She fought him without any of her usual refinement. It would have been different if she'd had a sword, but she didn't and her body still didn't respond as it once had. She dodged his flashing blade, leapt aside to avoid being stabbed, and did her best to rid him of his sword. She supposed she was fortunate just to avoid being killed.

He flinched suddenly. Morgan saw a knife buried into his shoulder. She guessed it was either Weger's or Miach's, but she didn't take the time to look behind her to see who had thrown it. She jerked it out of Searbhe's flesh and backed up—and into someone.

"Morgan, move," Miach said, snatching what was apparently his knife out of her hand.

She wanted to argue that this was becoming an annoying habit, but she was just too tired. She backed up until she felt a bench hit the back of her knees, then found herself pulled down to sit next to Weger. He looked her over.

"You're better," he noted.

"Aye," she agreed. "But still not whole."

"Nay, Morgan, not that, yet. But you will be. Give it time."

She nodded, then turned back to the fight in front of her. Perhaps Miach had decided that pretending to be less than he was didn't serve him. He was, she had to admit quite objectively, absolutely terrifying. If she'd been crossing swords with him in that mood, she might actually have paused to consider the advisability of engaging him.

Searbhe obviously had no such fears. She would have pointed out his mistake, but she didn't have time. Miach seemed to dredge up another measure of ferocity that left Searbhe stumbling backward in surprise. Miach beat on him until Searbhe had no choice but to merely hold up his sword as a shield. Morgan was almost sure she'd heard him blurt out a prayer of some sort.

Miach knocked the sword out of Searbhe's hands, then caught him under the chin with his fist.

Searbhe's eyes rolled back in his head and he fell to the ground with a loud crash.

Miach stood over him with his sword in his hand and waited for a moment or two. He nudged Searbhe with his foot, but there was no response. He waited a bit more, then resheathed his sword and turned to stride over to her.

He took her by the hands and hauled her up to her feet. "Are you all right?" he demanded.

"Fine," she said, trying to sound more positive than she felt. "Thank you. Debt repaid."

"I stepped outside for just a moment," he said grimly.

"It's hardly your fault," she said.

He shook his head, his mouth tightening. "I shouldn't have left you. Let me walk you back over to the fire." He nodded to Weger. "Excuse us, my lord."

Morgan walked with him, shivering in spite of herself.

"Did he say anything to you?" he asked quietly.

"Nothing interesting," Morgan said. After all, Searbhe had only said that she looked like Sarait of Tòrr Dòrainn; he hadn't said that she looked a *good* deal like her. His words meant nothing. He'd been looking for an excuse to fight her and latched on to the first one he could find.

Surely.

"Someone left a pile of refuse on my floor," Weger said pointedly from the far end of the hall.

Miach sighed. "I'll be back."

She didn't have a chance to say anything to him before he had walked back to join Weger near Searbhe's unconscious form. They discussed something with low voices and sharp gestures. She sat and watched as eventually men came in, bound Searbhe, and took him away. Weger then crossed the chamber and looked down at her.

"You should go lie down," he said mildly.

She shook her head. "Please, nay."

"Why not?" Weger asked. "You're safe now. I'm having Searbhe thrown out the front gates. He won't return inside them. You're safe," he repeated, throwing Miach a look.

Miach stood behind his usual chair with his hands on its back. He shot Weger a warning look, but said nothing.

"Nothing will come inside these gates to harm you," Weger said, apparently preparing to wax rhapsodic about the virtues of his hall. "Truly, you could remain inside these gates and be safe for the rest of your life and enjoy nothing but peace, safety, and absolutely no magic—"

"Oh, enough," Miach said with a curse. He glared furiously

at Weger, then took a deep breath. He turned to Morgan with a substantially softer expression. "I'll go see what becomes of Searbhe when he's outside the gates. I'll return."

She would have stopped him, but he turned and left before she could. She watched him leave the chamber, then looked at Weger.

"What was that was all about?" she asked blankly. "I've never seen him so angry."

Weger shrugged. "Mages are unpredictable. You never know what will set them off. Supper?"

Morgan nodded absently. Why not?

An hour later, she was sitting on the bottom step of that perilous staircase, waiting for Miach. Weger had not come with her. She supposed she couldn't blame him. The wind was blowing a gale and the rain was lashing her unmercifully. If she'd had any sense, she would have gone to bed.

But, as she'd already noted, she had no sense left, so there she sat, huddled in her cloak, guarding a man who needed no guarding. He'd begged her to come inside the tower chamber with him, but she'd refused. She didn't think she could bear the feel of her magic. For that night, at least, she wanted the comforting hush of the magic sink.

To keep herself awake, she considered the benefits of it—and there were many. No magic, no dreams, no wrenching of her heart each time she looked at Miach—

"Morgan?"

She looked up and realized that Miach was standing in front of her. Her heart, as usual, broke a little at the sight of him. She took a deep breath and cursed silently. He'd been too quick about his business. She'd hardly had the time to truly consider all the reasons she would be happier inside Gobhann than out of it.

She put her hands into his and let him pull her to her feet. She looked down at their hands together and found she couldn't pull away. When had it happened, that a man had found the stomach to want to take her hands?

When had she become so soft and pliable that she would want him to?

He put his arm around her. "It's cold, Morgan," he said. "Let me walk you back."

She nodded. She knew she should have pulled away from him, but she couldn't bear to. She had the feeling that he wasn't going to be at Gobhann much longer. How could he? He'd been there over two fortnights already. Surely the realm could not do without him any longer.

Besides, what else did Weger have to teach him? There was only one other person who'd mastered Weger's lessons so quickly—at least in the current century—and that had been she herself. She knew what an aspirant looked like when he was on the verge of being released—

She realized, with a start, that she was standing in front of her chamber. She looked at Miach.

"I don't think I can stay here," she said.

He looked at her in surprise. "At Gobhann?"

She ignored how much relief was coloring his expression. "I meant I don't think I could stay here in this chamber."

He smiled, but it was something of a strained smile. "Of course. You've no need to worry, though. Searbhe won't come inside the gates again."

"What happened to him?" she asked. "I forgot to ask you before you went into the tower."

Miach leaned against the wall under the torch and smiled at her. "He woke, changed himself into a scruffy-looking hawk, and flew off."

Morgan looked up at Miach standing in the soft firelight, his eyes so pale they were almost colorless, his face so handsome she was rendered feeble-minded, and wished for nothing more than to go into his arms and never move again.

But if she left Gobhann, she would be in darkness.

"Morgan?" he said softly.

She shook her head. "I'm fine. Where are you for?"

"I was going back to the upper hall. Weger sent word that he wants to talk."

"Are you going?"

"Why wouldn't I?"

"You were angry with him this afternoon."

Miach smiled. "Aye, but I don't stay that way very long."

"What did Weger say that set you off?"

"I didn't like the picture of Gobhann he painted for you," he said simply. "I also didn't like him trying to convince you to stay here when I want you to come with me."

She swallowed with difficulty. "I see."

He took her hands in his and rubbed his thumbs over the backs of them. "Morgan, I can't promise you safety, or peace, or respite from your dreams, but I can promise you that I will never leave you."

She realized, to her horror, that tears were streaming down her cheeks. She didn't dare wipe them away, lest she draw any more attention to them. She bowed her head and a sob caught her before she could stop it.

"Come with me?" he asked quietly.

She caught her breath and looked up to meet his gaze. She had the feeling he was talking about more than just up the passageway to the gathering hall. "I . . . I don't know."

His smile didn't falter, but it was very grave. "Let's go find a hot fire, gel. It will do you good. You're drenched."

"All right," she managed.

She let him lead her down the passageway, but she could hardly bear it. She didn't want to think that it might be the last time she felt his hand wrapped around hers, or the last time she saw the torchlight on his dark hair, or the last time she found his grave smiles turned on her.

She wasn't sure if she had the strength to face what she knew awaited her outside Weger's gates: magic, dreams, darkness. Miach.

All of that or the stark, unyielding quiet of Weger's tower.

It wasn't a choice she was sure she could make.

Nine

Miach stood at the window in the gathering hall and stared down at the sea churning below him. He had, as it happened, never seen the sea below in the daytime. He'd always been too busy training so that he might have the prize he wanted. He supposed that today might be the last chance he had to reach for it.

A pity he suspected that, despite the easiness of the last few days, the prize didn't want to be won.

He wasn't sure where Morgan was and he didn't dare go look for her. He honestly couldn't remember when she'd left the gathering chamber, though he supposed he'd slept through it. It had been a very long night. It didn't help that his head pained him almost beyond reason. He wondered, absently, if Weger had anything stronger than ale. He would have killed for some of that very potent sour wine from Penrhyn that Adhémar was far too fond of. He sincerely hoped Adaira had brought along a kingly supply.

He didn't dare touch the place on his forehead above his left brow that hurt. It couldn't have been a very large mark, but it burned like hellfire.

It was something he'd accepted during the last watch of the night. Morgan had been sleeping curled up in a chair, no doubt exhausted by the discussion of wizardly minutiae, when Weger had suddenly leaned over and pulled something from the fire. Miach had barely had time to recognize that something as a slim metal rod before Weger had motioned for him to brush the hair back from his forehead.

"Hold still," he'd said casually.

Miach had, only to find himself branded like a heifer.

"Congratulations," Weger had said. "You may leave through the front gates."

"Which way does the sword point?" he'd managed.

"I'm not sure," Weger had said, peering at it. "I'm not a good aim this late at night."

Miach had gaped at him only to watch him toss the iron back in the fire and laugh.

"Ah," had been the only thing he'd found to say.

That had been somewhere near dawn. He'd finally closed his eyes for just a moment, then woken to find that it was after noon and he was alone. Stephen had come in shortly thereafter and set down a hearty meal in front of him.

"Your last one," the lad had said with a gulp. "I think it's over the wall and onto the rocks for you, you poor fool."

Miach had only smiled grimly, then set to with gusto. Over the wall, out the gates; it was the same if he went alone.

The door opened suddenly behind him. Miach didn't dare hope it was Morgan, dressed for travel. He took a deep breath, then turned and looked to see who it might be.

It was Weger, dressed for a usual day's work. Morgan followed him inside. There was, unfortunately, no pack on her back, no cloak around her shoulders.

And she wouldn't meet his eyes.

Miach stood where he was and watched them for several minutes. Weger actually didn't look any happier than he felt. Perhaps Morgan wanted nothing to do with either of them. He supposed that should have consoled him, but somehow it didn't.

Well, there was no sense in delaying the inevitable any longer. He walked across the chamber and stopped in front of Weger. He bowed low to Gobhann's lord.

"My thanks for your many kindnesses."

Weger grunted. "You're welcome. Now, give me back my key."

Miach dug it out of a pocket and handed it to him. "What will you have as my payment?"

"You'll think of something useful," Weger said. "Send it along later. You, however, may go now."

Miach didn't move. He looked pointedly at Weger, but the man didn't acknowledge it. Either he had the wit of a stump or he had no intention of making anything easy. Miach suspected it was the latter and knew he shouldn't have expected anything less.

"I would like to talk to Morgan," he said. "Privately."

"Nay," Weger said, a definite edge to his tone.

Miach found his hand on his sword without knowing quite how it had gotten there. He decided, though, that a swordfight in the gathering hall wouldn't have been wise.

And it wouldn't serve him. If Morgan was going to come with him, she would because she wanted to, not because he had ground Weger under his heel. He glared at Weger, then took a deep breath and turned to Morgan.

"I don't give a damn about the Sword of Angesand," he said in a low voice, "or your magic, or your destiny. I just want you to come out of here—with me."

She looked up at him, mute.

Then she looked away.

"There's your answer," Weger said promptly. "Best be on your way, then. I'm sure you have things to do."

Miach wanted to argue the point, but he supposed there was no use. Perhaps he had been deluding himself. It was clear to him that even though Morgan might have forgiven him, she wasn't interested in leaving with him.

He held out his hand to Weger. "Thank you again, my lord, for the mark."

"You earned it," Weger said. "Fare you well."

Miach looked one more time at Morgan's profile. He hesitated, then spoke. "I love you."

Then he walked out of the room before he had to see the expressions on either of their faces. He closed the door behind him, took a deep breath, and walked wearily down the passageway.

He wandered along the edge of the courtyard, shaking hands with others where appropriate, ignoring slurs elsewhere, then he jogged down the stairs to the lowest level of Weger's tower. He went into the hovel he'd lived in for so long and sat on the stool that listed to one side, much as he had the first few nights he'd been there. He put his face in his hands, carefully, for several minutes and let his hopes dwindle away into nothing.

In truth, he shouldn't have expected anything else. He had wondered there for a few days if Morgan might have changed her mind about him, but apparently he had been mistaken. Her loathing of mages had been clear from the start. He should have accepted that.

He dragged his hand through his hair and sighed deeply. Perhaps it was for the best. After all, what could he offer her? A life of endless peril? Days on end spent waiting for him whilst he saw to the tedious business of being about the realm's defenses, interspersed with hours of life-threatening battles? Would he invite her to sit next to him whilst he stuck his nose in yet another book of spells? Would he force her to be confined in the same country with Adhémar?

Perhaps she had rejected him for that last bit alone.

He sat there for far longer than he should have, but he simply couldn't make himself move. He wasn't one to give in to self-pity, but at the moment he was damned tempted.

He rubbed his hands over his face, cursed, then stood up. He would leave, then return home by the quickest route. Perhaps if he buried himself in the affairs of Neroche, he would be able to forget about the affairs of his heart.

He looked over the chamber a final time, then realized something was on the bed. It was a slim, elegant dagger with a hilt of gold, obviously meant to be tucked cleanly and discreetly down the side of a boot. He drew it forth from its finely tooled sheath and found, to his surprise, that it was covered with runes of the house of Neroche. A kingly gift, to be sure. Miach supposed Adhémar would be intensely jealous and immediately—and loudly—demand that it be his, which Miach supposed Weger somehow knew. It was almost enough to make him smile.

But not quite.

He stuck the knife in his boot, slung his cloak over his shoulders, and left the chamber. He was actually somewhat grateful for the burning in his forehead. It helped ease the ache in his heart.

He walked back through the maze of corridors, then down the final way to the gate, remembering vividly how he'd been assaulted by the gatekeeper that first day. There was a cloaked and hooded figure standing by the gates, no doubt waiting for his own assault. Miach thought to warn the lad, but perhaps there was no point. Anyone fool enough to enter Weger's gates was a fool indeed if he didn't know what he faced.

He opened the front gate himself, then hesitated. He turned and looked back up the way. He was sorely tempted to run back up the stairs, find Morgan, then carry her outside the gates before she realized what he was doing.

But once she was outside the gates, assuming she allowed him to get her that far, her magic would almost match his, her sword skill was superior, and he would be without any means to keep her near him. There was, in the end, no point if she didn't come with him willingly.

He sighed deeply, then turned and walked through the gates and into the sunset.

His magic returned to him in a rush, even more strongly than it ever had in Weger's uppermost tower. He stumbled for several paces, then went down to his knees. He knelt there in the snow and gasped for breath until stars stopped swimming in front of him. He drew his hand over his eyes to try to clear the haze away, then focused on the forest in front of him, just to give himself something to concentrate on besides the almost soul-shattering return of his powers.

It was, he had to admit, a very welcome feeling.

When he thought he could manage it, he heaved himself to his feet. He stood there for a moment or two, took a deep breath, then set off through the snowdrifts piled up against the footings of the castle. It was tempting to turn himself into something with wings and merely fly off, but he decided there was no sense in terrifying anyone looking over the walls. Better to go a mile or two into the forest, then be on his way.

He walked without haste through the woods for half an hour before he realized he was being followed. He was so surprised, he almost stopped. He quickly considered the possibilities and decided that it was most likely Searbhe, come back to finish what he'd started. He continued on, straining to hear the faint sound of a knife hurtling through the air toward his back. He continued to walk for several more minutes as the sun set, then he suddenly melted into twilight mist.

The gasp behind him was immediate. "Miach!"

He wrested himself back into his proper form, then spun around to find that his shadow was none other than Morgan of Melksham, standing thirty paces away from him, gaping at him in astonishment.

He noted that she was dressed for travel. It occurred to him then that she had been the slight lad standing at the gates. He was surprised he hadn't recognized her, but in his defense he had been a little preoccupied.

He wondered what meaning, if any, he should attach to the fact that she had followed him—if she had indeed followed him. Perhaps she had merely chosen to leave Gobhann and her road had conveniently lain with his. Perhaps she'd only called to him because she thought he might have brought along something to eat.

Perhaps he would do well not to think overmuch for the next five minutes.

He made three very quick decisions. He would keep his mouth shut, his hands clasped behind his back where they wouldn't be tempted to clutch her to him, and let her tell him what she was about. He could see from where he stood that she was shivering. He supposed that had more to do with the chill in the air than with nervousness, but it was something he could see to. He took off his cloak, then walked over to where she stood and wrapped it around her. He didn't dare meet her eyes as he fastened the clasp under her chin, lest he see revulsion there.

He was, he decided, a coward.

Admitting it was one of the easier things he'd done in the past month.

"You looked cold," he offered.

"I was. Thank you."

He nodded and clasped his hands behind his back. "Are you," he said, finally, "just out for fresh air?"

She blinked in surprise. "Well, nay," she said. "I thought that perhaps . . . well, I was thinking that you might . . ."

He waited.

She took a deep breath. "I thought perhaps you might need . . . company. Or perhaps someone to guard your back."

He fought the urge to close his eyes in relief. Company or comrade-in-arms. At the moment, he would take either gladly.

"Whatever suits you, Morgan," he said with a smile. He stepped backward and nodded toward the path. "Shall we?"

"Where were you going?"

He rapidly changed his plans. He had intended to return to Tor Neroche, but that would have taken him a grueling day as a dragon and he supposed Morgan would not be amenable to changing her shape. He obviously couldn't ask her to go on any long marches when but half an hour's stroll from Gobhann had seemingly taken its toll on her. Lismòr was a likely spot. She could have a day or two to rest in comfort whilst he determined his final course.

He opened his mouth to suggest that, but found himself interrupted by the very unwelcome sound of a branch cracking under a boot behind him.

He spun around and saw Searbhe standing in the trees some fifty paces from them. He drew his sword with a curse and stepped in front of Morgan. Though it was tempting to do Searbhe in and be rid of the aggravation, he knew he wouldn't. He'd had this same conversation with Weger the night before. Killing a man because he was a fool was not justification enough for murder. Perhaps all Searbhe needed was one last bit of shaming to convince him that a hasty return to Riamh was the best choice to make.

But on the off chance that it wouldn't convince him, Miach decided that lingering in the area wouldn't be wise. He would plunge Searbhe into peaceful insensibility and then he and Morgan would be on their way.

Searbhe started toward them with his sword raised, bellowing a cry that bespoke serious business.

"Can you ride?" Miach said over his shoulder.

"A horse?" Morgan asked.

"Actually, I was thinking about a dragon."

She gasped. *"You?"*

He would have been happy to discuss it further, but Searbhe was, after all, not a completely useless swordsman. Miach pushed Morgan behind him.

"Find a part of the path where it's widest and wait for me there," he said, stepping forward to meet Searbhe.

"I'll kill you this time," Searbhe panted as he swung wildly.

Miach suspected not. He had little trouble keeping the other man at bay, but that was perhaps due to all the effort Searbhe was pouring into a pitiful spell of fettering. Miach engaged him for a moment, but Searbhe wasn't paying any attention to his swordplay, so Miach sighed lightly and propped his sword up on his shoulder. He took hold of the ends of the spell reaching out toward him and gave them a new direction. He stood there and watched as Searbhe's own spell began to wrap itself around him.

Searbhe cursed viciously and batted at the spell wildly until he realized he could stop its assault himself. He did so with a curse, then looked at Miach, his face purple with rage.

"How did you manage that?" he demanded.

Miach pursed his lips. "Did you think I was a village witch's brat, Searbhe?"

Miach ducked to avoid being decapitated by Searbhe's swing, then punched the other man full in the face. He resheathed his sword, waited until Searbhe had shaken off that assault, then looked coolly at the other man.

"Have you had enough *this* time?" Miach asked pointedly.

Searbhe flung himself forward with a curse. Miach kicked Searbhe's sword out of his hands, then caught him under the chin. Searbhe went sprawling. The sound of his head against a rock was loud in the stillness of the evening.

Miach waited, but the other man only groaned. Alive, but not a threat at present. Miach turned toward Morgan. She was standing some fifty paces back down the trail, watching him.

Well, perhaps it was best she knew from the start what she could expect from him.

He slipped into dragonshape as he ran toward her.

Climb on, he said, sending his voice whispering across her mind.

She only hesitated briefly before she flung herself onto his

back and shrieked as he leapt up into the air. Her arms around
his neck made it difficult to breathe, but he decided he would
complain later, when he was certain they both wouldn't die.

He beat his wings against the cold evening air and drove
himself up above the trees. He wished, absently, that he'd
given Morgan reins. She resettled herself several times between his wings and he half feared she would fall off—

"Miach, behind us!" she shouted suddenly.

He looked over his shoulder and swore silently. He vowed to
give her a good apology later for the rough ride, then concentrated on seeing that she lived long enough to enjoy it. He turned
and faced the dragon following him. Searbhe was no better at
shapechanging than he was at his swordplay. Perhaps his head
pained him. Miach could understand that, actually, but he had
no intention of according Searbhe any mercy because of it.

He stripped Searbhe immediately of his spell of protection,
stole his ability to spew out anything but curses, then blasted
him with a gust of fire that singed him from nose to tail. Searbhe
wheeled away with a cry and descended in a cloud of smolder-
ing ruin.

Miach didn't spare him any more thought. Searbhe would
go off and lick his wounds, then no doubt turn for home. Even
if he was tenacious enough to want to continue following them,
he wouldn't find them. Lord Nicholas had his own spells of
concealment, not enough to discourage lads from coming to
study there, but enough to leave any ordinary mage feeling as
if a visit simply wasn't worth his time. Lismòr would be haven
enough for the present.

He drew a spell of invisibility over himself and Morgan,
strong enough to completely cover their passing, and swept up
into the night.

Are you watching? he asked Morgan.

"Are you daft?" she exclaimed. "Of course not!"

*You should. I daresay you've never seen your island from
this vantage point before.*

"I pray I never will again!"

He smiled to himself as he flew along the coast where the
winds made it easier to keep himself aloft. He would never
again take his magic for granted. He would also never take for
granted the woman who was clinging to him and praying aloud.

"What was I thinking to come with you, you shapechanging madman?!" she shouted at one point.

He had no good answer for that. All he knew was that she was holding on to him and not chopping at him with her sword, so perhaps she didn't have all that many regrets.

In time, he saw the faint twinkles of lights at the university. *Pry your eyelids apart, woman, and look where we're going.*

Her grip didn't loosen, but he supposed she braved a look. She was silent, except for a few more shrieking curses, as he spiraled downward and landed in the courtyard.

He resumed his proper form and turned around to catch her by the arms before she landed in an undignified sprawl.

And he stared evenly at the archers in the shadows until they lowered their bows and walked away. Perhaps there would even come a day when he arrived and they only yawned. A body could hope.

He conjured up another cloak and put it around Morgan's shoulders, then hesitated. What he wanted to do was pull her into his arms and keep her there for a handful of lifetimes. He decided, though, that considering he'd just forced her to participate in shapechanging—never mind that the change had been limited to his own shape—anything besides a comradely pat on the shoulders might be daring too much.

He arranged the cloak over her shoulders for a moment or two, then clasped his hands behind his back. Safer there, no doubt.

"I'm sorry I didn't give you much time to think about that," he said quietly.

"Is this what traveling with you will entail?" she said unsteadily. "These appalling dips into magic at every turn?"

He smiled. He was almost certain she'd said the words *traveling with you.* Those words were, to his mind, some of the sweetest he'd ever heard. If Morgan could complain about the possibility of facing his magic quite often, it might mean that she intended to be near him quite often.

"I suppose 'tis possible," he conceded. "Will you survive it?"

"Now is not the time to be asking me that, I daresay," she said crisply. "Not after that last bit of business."

He laughed softly. "It will all seem more palatable when you're sitting next to Lord Nicholas's fire."

"All right," she said, then she looked up at him with a frown as he started across the courtyard. "You know where you're going. Have you been here before?"

"Once," he said. "When I lost my sense of you, I came to ask Nicholas what had happened to you."

"How did you know I would be here?"

He opened his mouth to speak, then shut it. There was no possible way to tell her that without revealing things he wasn't ready to tell her yet. "I just did," he said, finally.

"Then you didn't bring me here at first?" she asked in surprise. "After I . . . drank . . ."

He shook his head. "I didn't, but I beg you not to ask me any more about it. I will tell you everything you want to know, but not tonight. Tonight we need a hot fire, a decent meal, then sleep."

"And Searbhe?"

"He won't find us," he said. "I covered our tracks, so we'll be safe enough here for the moment. He'll lose interest in us long before he manages to stumble upon our whereabouts."

"Safe," she repeated quietly.

He nodded. "I cannot always promise you that, but tonight I think I can. Now," he said with deliberate cheerfulness, "I've gotten us here. It is your duty to win us entry. Let us see if Lismòr's cook can possibly best what delicate edibles I would have found under the snow to put in my stew pot."

She nodded, but said nothing as they walked through the courtyard. She was silent until they reached the heavy wooden door that kept the night and the cold out of Nicholas's solar, then she turned toward him.

"Thank you," she said, looking at his chin.

"For what?" he asked with a smile. "Dragonshape? Providing you with a decent dinner? Singeing Searbhe from stem to stern?"

She smiled faintly. "Nay, not for any of that." She was silent for a few moments, then she took a deep breath and looked up at him. "Peace and safety are uninteresting."

He smiled and took her hand in both his. "I will do my best for those as well, love. And I will compliment you on your bravery—"

"Nay, it wasn't that," she said quickly. "'Twas cowardly,

rather. I couldn't go on without . . . well, never mind that." She took a deep breath. "Thank you for coming to fetch me."

Miach desperately wanted to know what she couldn't go on without, but for all he knew, it was his ability to tell her tales at night to keep her from dreaming.

That was, he supposed, a start.

"Miach?"

"It was my pleasure," he said promptly. He smiled at her. "Truly. Now, see what you can do about supper, would you?"

She nodded, then turned toward the door.

Miach closed his eyes and let out a deep breath, hoping she wouldn't notice the sigh of relief that went along with it.

It didn't matter why she had left Gobhann, what she planned for the future, or if she planned to leave him behind at first light. Well, that would matter a great deal, that last bit, but he wouldn't think about it. He would merely be grateful for the sight of her in some other locale than a cheerless courtyard at Gobhann.

She had come.

He smiled to himself. It was enough for the moment.

Ten

Morgan stood in front of Nicholas's door and lifted her hand to knock. It was an unconscious motion, one she had repeated hundreds of times during her days at Lismòr as a girl and young woman, then dozens more times after she'd left to seek her fortune. She had never, in all those years, dreamed that she would find herself preparing to request entry with a man at her heels.

She had to put her hands on the door to keep herself on her feet. She could safely say that it had been one of the most traumatic days of her life—and it had little to do with the absolute terror of being higher off the ground than a woman could reasonably be expected to find herself.

She'd known Miach would ask her to leave Gobhann with him, known that going with him would mean walking open-eyed into the darkness, known that being too afraid to do the second would leave her watching him walk away from her.

What had surprised her, though, had been to discover that when a heart broke, it actually made a sound.

It had been her heart to break. It had broken as she'd watched Miach leave and found herself too cowardly to stop him. She'd known immediately that she'd made an enormous mistake. It hadn't taken long thereafter for Weger to express the opinion that she really should go follow him.

Of course, Weger had said as much as she'd been halfway out the door, but it had been endorsement enough.

But the relief at catching Miach before he disappeared and the terror of traveling to Lismòr had faded and now she was left with the reality of her life. She was back in a world where nothing was as it had been and she had no idea how to proceed.

She was no longer Morgan the mercenary famous for a disgust of magic and mages that was almost as impressive as her reputation for bringing men to their knees merely by drawing her sword. She was no longer Morgan who dreamed of battles and sieges and Scrymgeour Weger's strictures. She was no longer Morgan who had never intended to become so fond of a man that the mere thought of being without him made it difficult to breathe.

"Fire, Morgan," Miach prompted. "Food. Sleep. In that order."

She looked over her shoulder at him. "Bossy, aren't you?"

He smiled. She almost had to close her eyes against the sight of it. It would have been misery to stay at Gobhann without him; she couldn't say that being away from Gobhann *with* him wouldn't be just as ruinous to her heart. Things were so much simpler in Weger's tower.

Though somewhat less comfortable.

And lacking a certain archmage.

"You think too much." He reached over her shoulder and rapped smartly. "There, I've started you on the right path. The rest is up to you."

She nodded with a jerk. He was right. They were cold, hungry, and tired. Those things could be seen to easily enough.

Besides, he was just Miach; she was just Morgan. He was a decent traveling companion and she was very good with a sword. She could guard his back as he went on whatever business he was about. She could ignore what had gone on between them in another place and time, ignore his magic, ignore hers.

The door was answered by William, Nicholas's page, before she could think any more on it. She peeked inside the solar and found it full of lads sprawled on various rugs and reclining comfortably on luxurious bits of furniture. Nicholas himself was sitting in his accustomed chair, reading from a large manuscript. He looked up, blinked in surprise, then smiled at her.

"Morgan," he said happily. "What a pleasant surprise. Come in, my dear. And I see you've brought a friend."

"Friend?" Miach echoed under his breath.

Morgan elbowed him in the ribs, earned a grunt in response, then turned her attentions back to what was in front of her. "I'm sorry, my lord," she said quickly. "I didn't realize what time it was. We can come back—"

"Of course you won't," Nicholas said, beckoning to her. "William, run and fetch our guests a hearty meal. I imagine they've been traveling for quite some time."

Miach ruffled William's hair as he passed, then nudged her inside. "Don't argue us out of dinner, wench," he whispered.

Morgan glared at him out of habit, but decided he had a point. She propped her sword up in the corner with Miach's, then allowed him to take both cloaks she was wearing and hang them up. She made her way with a minimum of fuss to one of the stools near the hearth and sat down with a grateful sigh. Miach sat down on the stool next to her, so close to her that their knees almost touched. She looked at him quickly, but he only winked at her and held his hands to the fire.

"Better?"

"Much," she agreed.

"Was it worth braving the skies?"

"I'm not sure I can answer that yet in a way you'd want to hear."

He smiled. "I'll provide you with reins the next time."

"Do you actually think there will be a next time?" she asked with a snort.

"I don't know," he said. "Will there?"

She started to tell him there most certainly would not, then shut her mouth. It was probably best not to make any of those sorts of vows when she had no idea whether or not she would be able to keep them. "I suppose that depends on how good supper is," she said weakly.

"I should have let Nicholas know," he said with half a laugh, "though I don't think I need to worry. I have the feeling this meal will be so good you'll be forced to agree to several things that make you uncomfortable."

She scowled. And she hadn't done that the moment she walked out Weger's front gates?

She watched as William soon laid a marvelous meal on a low table in front of them. Miach took a plate, filled it, then handed it to her.

"Eat," he suggested. "Decide about the uncomfortable things later."

She was grateful for the distraction, though she supposed it wouldn't last nearly long enough to keep her from having to think about a very long list of things she would rather avoid.

She managed some of what was indeed a wonderful meal, but found that, after a time, she couldn't concentrate on it. She wasn't one to be distracted by the fairness of any man's face, but there was something about Miach's that rendered her so. It was no wonder that every tavern wench she'd ever watch serve Miach had been so prone to dropping things. He was ridiculously handsome and perhaps for that alone she could have been forgiven for ignoring her supper in favor of watching him.

He ate with gusto, laughed periodically at Nicholas's tale—which she was relieved to find was *not* the Two Swords—and looked genuinely happy to be where he was. Who would have thought that he'd just spent over a month in Gobhann, driving himself past the endurance of any other man she'd ever met just to . . .

Well, she wasn't sure exactly why he'd done it—no matter what he'd claimed.

"Morgan?"

She realized he was watching her and blinked rapidly to clear her eyes. Damnable tears. "What?"

"You're not eating."

She dragged her sleeve across her eyes, then looked at him. "Why did you enter Gobhann?"

"I already told you."

"I know what you told me," she said impatiently. "I want to know the real reason."

He looked at her thoughtfully for a moment, then reached for her plate. He set it down on the floor with his, then pulled her close and put his mouth against her ear.

"I went inside Gobhann because I wanted you to come out of the dark. With me. Because I love you. Because you were made for more than life in that dreadful place." He sat back. "There. All the reasons."

"But the price you paid—"

"Was worth it," he finished without hesitation. "You, Morgan of Melksham, were worth that price." He tucked a strand of hair behind her ear. "Don't you think?"

She didn't dare answer for fear that what would come out would be something akin to a sob. Miach looked at her in surprise, then put his arm around her and pulled her to him. She suspected she should have protested, but she couldn't bring herself to. All she could do was press her face against his shoulder and weep.

It was the stress of her illness, no doubt. It would pass and then she would resume her life as a sensible, sturdy soldier.

But for the moment, she would allow herself the weakness of tears and the luxury of Miach's hand skimming over her hair.

She wasn't sure how long she sat there, weeping silently, drenching him beyond what any man should have had to bear. She didn't pull away and he didn't seem to expect her to. He merely held her close, murmured the occasional soothing word, and stroked her hair.

"Morgan," he whispered finally, "the lads have gone."

She sat back and dragged her sleeve across her eyes. "I'm sorry." She looked at him bleakly. "I'm not a crier."

"You're allowed," he said. "You've had a difficult pair of months."

"I can't carry on like this, though," she said grimly.

"I certainly wish you wouldn't," he said solemnly. "Lord Nicholas will think I drove you to it and then I won't have any dessert."

She looked at him in surprise, then realized he was teasing her. "And here I was going to thank you for your shoulder."

He smiled as he dried her cheeks with the sleeve of his tunic. "You're welcome."

She grunted at him, then pushed herself to her feet, pulling him up with her. She dragged him along after her as she negotiated her way through stray bits of furniture. She embraced Nicholas briefly before she sat down with Miach on a very comfortable sofa.

"Many thanks, my lord, for the meal," she said gratefully. "We needed it."

"Well, your lad seemed to work his way through it well enough, though I'm not so sure about you," Nicholas said with a smile. "You do look better, though. I wouldn't have thought Gobhann would have done you this much good, but I see I was wrong."

"Weger did nothing but feed me and force me to sleep," she admitted. "And it did help, though I'm not completely myself yet. I think a few mornings spent in the lists grinding my *friend* here into the dust will rid me of any lingering malaise."

Nicholas smiled. "Such disrespect, my dear. And after all he went through to bring you home."

"He teases me overmuch. He knows I don't like it, yet he persists." She looked at Miach coolly. "He deserves whatever he has in return."

Miach sat with his ankle propped up on his other knee, looking completely unoffended—and unrepentant. "It is worth all the effort just to watch you pat yourself for whatever dagger you might have to hand. And aye, I likely deserve whatever you toss back my way." He smiled at Nicholas. "Thank you, my lord, for a comfortable place to torment Morgan and an excellent supper to enjoy whilst I was about it."

Nicholas laughed. "Of course, lad. My pleasure." He studied them for a moment or two. "The journey here must not have been overly hard. You don't look particularly weary."

"Actually, we left Gobhann this afternoon," Morgan admitted.

"How did you come so quickly, then?" Nicholas asked in surprise. "Did you run?"

Morgan swallowed with difficulty. "We flew. Well, Miach flew. I . . . didn't."

Nicholas laughed. "Ah, the indignities, Morgan. 'Tis nothing more than you can expect, though, when you travel with a mage."

"I'm beginning to think Miach was repaying me for his month at Gobhann," Morgan said darkly.

"No doubt," Nicholas agreed. He looked at Miach. "So, lad, how did you find Weger's hovel? I won't bother asking Morgan; she'll only enumerate its finer qualities."

Morgan sat back and listened as Miach described for Nicholas in the most unvarnished terms just how dreadful the food was and how brutal the training. He didn't seem overly troubled by any of it, though, nor sorry that he'd been there.

Perhaps it had been worth it to him.

"How did you escape the tower in the end?" Nicholas asked. "Did Morgan open the gate for you or did you fly off the walls?"

"Neither," Miach said slowly.

Morgan waited. She actually hadn't had a chance to think about how Miach had earned his release. Weger had been so busy shoving him out of the gathering room that morning, she had supposed Weger had merely wanted to be rid of him and was letting him leave unharmed and unflung.

Miach looked at her, sighed deeply, then brushed the hair back from his forehead.

There, just above his eyebrow was a bright red sword.

Morgan gaped at it in surprise. It was the very copy of hers, turned just so. She met his eyes, startled. "When did he give you that?"

"Last night. Sometime after we bored you to sleep with a discussion of the trade policies between the dwarves of Durial and the wizards of Beinn òrain."

Morgan reached up to carefully move a stray lock of hair away from the angry wound. "It was fairly given," she said quietly. "You were, and I can say this without reservation, his equal when you left."

He shifted uncomfortably and cleared his throat. "We could debate that, I imagine. All I know is that it's over, and for that I am very grateful. Now stop watching me, woman, lest I blush."

Morgan opened her mouth to comment that his suddenly red eyes left him looking more likely to weep, but he put his hand on her head and turned her to face Nicholas. She looked at Nicholas and shrugged.

"Miach earned that mark," she said quietly. "There is no doubt about that."

Nicholas rubbed his finger over his mouth. "The king of Neroche will have fits over it, I imagine."

Miach grunted. "I'm thinking I'll just keep it to myself."

Nicholas chuckled. "I daresay that is wise. Now, tell me about the rest of your business. Did Weger know who you were?"

"Immediately," Miach admitted, "though he did me the favor of keeping it to himself. He also presented me with a key to a tower just outside his walls where magic is possible."

"Fortunate for you, then," Nicholas said, sounding very surprised.

"Critical," Miach corrected. "It allowed me the luxury of time to convince a certain gel that she was meant for more than a life within those walls."

Morgan felt him tucking hair into her braid. She looked at him and found him watching her with a small smile. She had to look away, before she started up with her cursed tears again.

"And soon you must turn your thoughts to the future," Nicholas said, "but perhaps you could first take a day or two and rest from your labors. Why don't we make it an early night? I'll walk with you to your bedchambers—"

"I imagine Miach has things to see to first," Morgan interrupted. "Is there a quiet spot where he might retreat to work on his spells?"

"Of course," Nicholas said with a smile. "Pull a chair in front of the fire, Mochriadhemiach, and be comfortable. I'll send someone along with something sweet and more wine, lest the labors become too heavy. Morgan, your bedchamber is as it always is. Put your lad in the one down the hall, won't you?"

Morgan nodded, then stood when Nicholas did. "Thank you, my lord, for the safe haven."

He took her face in his hands and smiled at her. "My dear, it doesn't seem like much at all. Just food and a bed. But I'm pleased to be able to provide it." He kissed her cheeks, clapped Miach on the shoulder in passing, then left the solar.

Morgan watched him go, then felt the chamber begin to grow cold as silence descended. She was fine if she was talking, or fighting, or about some other noble labor. It was merely standing and thinking that gave her trouble. She wrapped her arms around herself, then looked at Miach who was still sitting on the sofa.

"I'm cold," she said.

"I'll go build you a fire in your bedchamber—"

"Nay," she said quickly, then she took a deep breath. "Please, Miach. Not yet. Let me stay with you whilst you work."

"Of course, love," he said, rising. He stood in front of her and rubbed her arms for a moment or two, then released her and walked over to toss more wood on the fire.

Morgan walked over unsteadily to sit down in one of the chairs he'd placed in front of the hearth. Miach sat, then captured one of her feet between his boots. "I'll hurry."

"Take all night if you like. I'd prefer it thus, actually."

"Morgan, you have to sleep eventually," he said.

"Do I?" she asked, striving for a light tone. "I think I can avoid it if I work at it."

He sighed, then leaned forward and took her hands in both of his. "I wish I could spare you what troubles you."

"And I wish you could spell me into a dreamless sleep," she whispered. "I don't suppose you have that sort of spell to hand, do you?"

He smiled faintly. "I might."

"Have you ever used it?" she asked in surprise.

"Do you actually want me to admit to that?"

"Was Adhémar involved?"

He laughed. "I'll only say this: there is little point in being a mage if you can't rid yourself now and again of the torment of your eldest brother blathering on endlessly."

"At least you're using your power for good," she managed.

"You cannot pretend not to share the sentiment, if not the execution of the remedy," he said with a smile.

"I'll concede that," she admitted. "He is irritating in the extreme." She looked at him and sighed. "Thank you. I needed the distraction."

"My pleasure. But I will hurry with my business. Whether you want it or not, sleep is what you need."

She nodded, though she didn't exactly agree. She watched him close his eyes, then felt his stillness become a tangible thing in the chamber—that and the power that flowed from him. She watched him for quite some time, somewhat surprised to find that she didn't find it at all strange to be sitting across from a mage without reaching for her sword.

But in time she found that watching his arresting face was no longer enough to block out her unease. It was one thing to say Lismòr was a safe place. It was another thing to realize that it was at Lismòr that she had first begun to dream.

She rose and wandered about Nicholas's chamber. It occurred to her that it had been here that she'd first read something she wished she hadn't. She stopped in front of Nicholas's desk that sat beneath a long, leaded window. She remembered vividly having stood in that exact place in the fall. She'd reached for a book and it had fallen open to a page she hadn't called.

It was there that she'd first read about Gair of Ceangail. Her nightmares had begun soon after, nightmares that had led to her discovering she had magic and to a whole host of other things she hadn't anticipated—

She wondered if more pacing might keep her from thinking any more.

It was worth a try.

She had walked around the room countless times and thrown half a dozen logs on the fire by the time Miach finally opened his eyes and sighed. She could tell immediately that all was not well. She sank down in the chair opposite him.

"What's wrong?" she asked uneasily.

He seemed to consider his words carefully. "Nothing that hasn't been in motion for the past month, but I hear rumors of things that trouble me." He paused. "Creatures, like the ones we saw near Chagailt and near the inn."

"Who is sending them?" she asked. "Who are they coming for?"

"Good questions, both," he said, rubbing his hands over his face and wincing. "I keep forgetting about this."

She leaned forward and brushed his hair off his forehead. "I would make you a poultice for that, but it would heal it—and that would defeat the purpose."

He smiled. "Trust me, the pain is nothing."

She looked at his mark for a moment or two, then met his eyes. "You were at Gobhann too long, weren't you?"

He shook his head. "Nothing has changed substantially in the realm, Morgan, so don't burden yourself with the thought. I was able to do at Gobhann exactly what I could have done at Tor Neroche."

She supposed she had no choice but to believe him. "Well, what will you do now?"

"First, I'll see tomorrow what messages Nicholas has for me. I imagine Paien will have sent word. He and the others were anxious to be going even before I left."

"Are the lads still at Tor Neroche?" she asked in surprise.

"Aye," he said, "I passed many pleasant evenings with them whilst we waited for Adhémar to be about his nuptial madness. We kept ourselves out of his sights by hiding in my tower chamber and discussing your many fine qualities." He smiled. "They are all terribly fond of you."

"They just appreciate my ability to keep them from dying," she said dismissively. "Where is it they want to go now?"

He leaned forward with his elbows on his knees. "I asked them to take the shards of the Sword of Angesand to Durial for me."

She felt a little faint. "I see."

"They wanted to be of some use."

Morgan looked down at her hands for quite some time before she thought she might be able to manage to speak. She lifted her head. "I'm sorry I destroyed it."

He shook his head. "Swords can be reforged—"

"It isn't that," she protested. "I lost control and destroyed something beautiful." She took a deep breath. "I'd never felt such anger. For a moment, I think I almost relished it."

"You had cause, Morgan."

"I was angry, but not for the reason you think."

He put his hands on top of hers. "I can imagine the reason, Morgan. Or at least I flatter myself I can. If the places had been reversed, I wouldn't have been particularly happy to think you wanted me only for my skill with a blade and not for my sweet self. True enough?"

She nodded, but found to her horror that tears were falling on his hands. Her tears. She looked at him miserably.

"I keep telling myself these tears are but the aftereffects of Lothar's poison, but I fear it's just me, turning slowly and inexorably into a tavern wench."

He laughed and released her. "I imagine it's nothing so dire as that. You're tired and you still have healing to accomplish. Let me walk you to your chamber so you can be about it. There will be time enough tomorrow to worry about the rest."

She nodded, then moved out of his way so he could bank

Nicholas's fire. He collected their swords and cloaks, then led them out of Nicholas's solar.

"Miach?" she asked quietly as they walked through the cloister.

"Aye, love."

"Can I be there?" she asked. "When you reforge the sword?"

He smiled down at her. "Of course."

She chewed on her words for a bit before she managed to spew them out. "Can I teach it to sing?"

"Like Catrìona of Croxteth?" he asked. "I imagine you could, if you wanted to."

"I would like to."

"Then you shall."

She nodded and continued on with him until they were standing in front of her door. He opened it, then sent a ball of werelight floating toward the ceiling. He pulled back and smiled.

"All safe."

Safe in the chamber, possibly, but not safe in the darkness that awaited her there. She looked up at him. "Spell me to sleep?"

He winced. "I don't think you're quite that desperate yet. Just trust that you'll be safe enough here. Where is my bed-chamber?"

"'Tis the one at the end of this passageway. That's where Nicholas usually puts visiting royalty."

He blinked, then laughed. "He's teasing me, apparently."

"He's flattering you."

"Perhaps," Miach said with a smile. He looked down at her. "Whatever the case, at least it puts me close enough to you to suit me tonight. I'll sleep with my door open so I'll hear you if you cry out. Unless you'd like me to sleep on your floor."

"The lads would never survive the scandal," she said wearily. "You needn't worry about me. I will be well."

"You will be," he agreed. He shooed her back inside her bedchamber, then spoke a handful of words.

A thin blue line appeared on the floor, stretching from one side of her doorway to the other.

She looked at him. "What is that?"

"A charm of ward, to protect you from any evil. It will

entangle itself around the feet of anyone who crosses your threshold, be he man or mage, and render him immobile. And it will wake me as it does so. Unless," he said, his eyes twinkling, "you want me to sleep on the floor next to your bed. We could hold hands. Very innocent."

She scowled up at him. "Go to bed before the thought overwhelms you."

He laughed then took her face in his hands and kissed the end of her nose. "Going to bed irritated with me will be your salvation, I'm sure. Good night, love. Sweet dreams."

She took a deep breath, then nodded and shut the door. Miach's werelight was still there, glowing softly and lighting her way. She pulled off her boots, shucked off her leggings, and dove beneath a goose-feather duvet fit for a queen without a second thought.

She lay there for quite a while. It helped to look up at the werelight. It reminded her that Miach was watching over her. She didn't want to find that as comforting as she did, but it was impossible not to. In time, her eyes grew heavy. She forcibly pushed away the darkness and the cold and concentrated on the light above her that Miach had given her.

It was the only thing that kept the darkness at bay.

Eleven

Miach sat in the bowels of the university and rubbed the spot between his eyes that had begun to pound. He supposed it was because of the mark over his brow that still burned like hellfire. He wondered absently what Adhémar would say when he saw it. Likely bellow like a stuck boar and then list all the reasons why it had been the height of foolishness. Miach supposed he would have had a point, though looking back on it presently, he could only count it time well spent.

He looked around him blearily, wondering what time it might be, then saw Morgan sitting just around the corner of the worn wooden table from him.

She had fallen asleep with her head against the back of the chair. Her hair was escaping her braid in places and she was swathed in the fur-lined cloak he had conjured up for her the night before.

He shut the book he was reading and allowed himself the pleasure of looking his fill. She was remarkably beautiful, and he was unwholesomely grateful to be looking at her in Lismòr's library.

A throat cleared itself pointedly.

Miach looked at the university's librarian, a dour man named Dominicus, who sat perched like a bird of prey on a tall stool in the corner.

"Are you not finished yet?" Master Dominicus whispered fiercely.

Miach took hold of what patience he had left before it disappeared. It wasn't his habit to be rude to librarians—they did provide him with things he needed after all—but he was tempted. "I am not," he said as pleasantly as possible. "I'll let you know when I am."

"I can't imagine what a soldier needs with books," Master Dominicus added pointedly.

"He's not just a soldier," Morgan said, opening her eyes and turning to look at the man. "He's a very *good* soldier with a very *sharp* blade who I might or might not have seen loitering on the *other* side of the island. I'd let him look at what he wants, if I were you."

Master Dominicus shot Miach a nervous look, then tucked his arms into the sleeves of his robe and remained silent.

Miach smiled at Morgan. "Thank you."

"I live to torment him," she said, hiding a yawn behind her hand. "In fact, I came down here with the express purpose of rescuing you from him before the sun set completely."

"Is it that late?" he asked in surprise.

She nodded solemnly. "You've been down here all day."

"I can't believe I didn't notice you sooner." It was a wonder he hadn't found himself stabbed to death long before now by some testy librarian whilst he'd been about a search for some obscure thing or another.

"I haven't been here all that long. I will say, though, that you were rather involved in your texts. For a mere soldier," she added.

"I appreciate the discretion."

"I imagine you do." She studied him for a moment or two, then shook her head. "Why I ever believed that you were a simple farmer is beyond me."

"You were distracted by my scruffy boots, no doubt," he said with a half smile.

"Well, it isn't as if you're dressed in purple silks," she agreed, "or long velvet robes and a pointy hat."

He laughed in spite of himself. "Nay, I'm not—thankfully. I'll happily limit myself to soldier's gear." He looked at her and deduced by the faint circles under her eyes that she had not had a particularly good night. He pushed aside his book so he could rest his elbows on the table. "So, how may I serve you today? More werelight? Swords? Tales that show the king of Neroche in his least flattering lights?"

She smiled, seemingly in spite of herself. "The latter, assuredly. Start with his most recent humiliation, then work your way backward. You can tell me about your other brothers as well, after you run out of Adhémar's follies."

"I don't know that either of us has the patience for all of them, but I'll give you at least one." He motioned for Morgan to lean forward. "This particular tale begins in the chapel during the beginning of what had promised to be the longest wedding ceremony in the history of the Nine Kingdoms."

"I can only imagine," she muttered.

"No doubt you can. Now, as it happened, Adhémar and his bride-to-be had just taken their places at the front of the chapel and settled in for a glorious recounting of dowries and honors and exploits. I was, as you might imagine, looking for any way possible to keep myself awake, so I let my mind wander south just to see how you fared—"

"Did you?" she interrupted in surprise. "Could you?"

He nodded. "It was something I learned I could do over that first month of your convalescence. I could sense your presence, much like a man might see a candle shining in the dark. Or at least I could, until you went inside Gobhann's gates."

"Which must have been that same morning," she said thoughtfully.

"Aye, it was," he agreed. "When I lost my sense of you, I left Adhémar's wedding at a dead run, and bolted to the parapet where I could throw myself off—"

"Miach!"

"Momentum, Morgan," he said dryly, "not a death wish. I was a dragon within a heartbeat and pulling myself back upward within half a dozen more. Adhémar, as you might imagine, was highly displeased with the interruption I caused and had followed me to tell me so. He was standing on the walls, waving his sword about and demanding that I come closer so he could inflict all manner of bodily harm. Of course, being the dutiful younger brother I am, I obliged him."

"What did you do?" she asked, a smile playing about her mouth.

"I flew up to him, snorted out a bit of fire, and singed off his wedding hat—and a bit more of him, I fear. He was trying madly to put out the flames as I flew over him."

"You'll pay a steep price on your return, I fear," she said with half a laugh.

Miach shrugged. "There isn't much he can do to me, save shout himself hoarse. The thought isn't keeping me awake at night."

She snorted. "I daresay. Now, tell me instead about these other lads of yours. I think I know more than I want to about your eldest brother."

He imagined she did. He settled himself more comfortably, then began his list. "After Adhémar comes Cathar, then Rigaud, Nemed, the twins Mansourah and Turah, then me—"

"The wee babe."

"Aye, if you can believe it."

"I have a hard time," she admitted. "You have old eyes. So, what of these brothers? Which one do you love the most? Which one do you trust the least? Who would you die for without hesitation?"

He smiled, pained. "Those are terrible questions, but I'll answer one or two of them just the same. I would trust Cathar with my life, Turah with my back, and Nemed with a few of my secrets. I would trust Mansourah to take a message for me to another kingdom. I would *only* trust Rigaud to tell me how to dress for a court function."

"I think I remember him," she mused. "He was wearing quite fancy clothes in the great hall. I thought he was the king."

"He would be enormously gratified to hear it. As far as the other question goes—" He shrugged. "I'd give my life for any of them."

"Even Adhémar?"

"Almost without hesitation."

"But you don't trust him."

"Do you truly want the answer to that?" he asked mildly.

"I don't think I need it. That puts you in a difficult position, doesn't it?"

"Very."

She rubbed her arms suddenly. "Oddly enough, I am some-how comforted to think you might be running about behind Adhémar, repairing all the damage he does, rather than him controlling everything on his own."

He smiled. "Thank you. I think."

"It was a compliment." She smiled slightly. "You're fortu-nate to have all those brothers. You must love them."

"Most of them," Miach said. "I have, of course, mixed feel-ings about Adhémar. I daresay Cathar would have made a better ruler, but fate did not decree it thus. And if I don't find what I'm searching for soon, there will be no kingdom for Adhémar to ruin."

"How long have you been doing all this?" she asked.

"Reading in the library?"

"Nay," she said, "what you do. You know." She waggled her fingers at him. "That."

"Fourteen years now. Since my mother died."

She blinked. "But you can't be more than a score and ten."

"A score and eight, actually," he said. "Almost a score and nine."

Her jaw went slack. "You've been the archmage of Neroche since you were *fourteen*? How did that come about?"

He opened his mouth to give his usual response that he was just precocious, but realized immediately that he couldn't hand Morgan such a flippant answer. She would have to know even-tually, so there was no reason not to tell her the truth. Perhaps it would, in some small way, make the past that she had yet to face seem a little easier to bear.

He rested his clasped hands on the table and put on the best smile he could manage. "Well, it all began when I was out rid-ing the borders alone when I was ten-and-three—an arrogant whelp with not enough wit to realize my peril. I was captured by our unpleasant neighbor to the north."

She caught her breath. "Lothar?"

"The very same."

She leaned back against her chair and held up her hands. "Don't tell me any more. I beg you."

"You asked," he pointed out.

"Aye, and if I'd had any idea this was what you were going

to say, I wouldn't have." She considered him for quite some time in silence, then sighed. "I suppose that now you've begun, you had best finish, hadn't you?"

"I had planned to tell you anyway, at some point, so there isn't any reason not to tell you now." He took a deep breath. "I was taken by Lothar because I was too stupid to have taken a guard as I should have. Lothar carried me back to his keep, then threw me into his dungeon where I rotted for an entire year before my parents managed to get me out. My mother died during the attempt. My sire succumbed to his wounds a se'nnight later."

"You were in his dungeon a year," she whispered incredulously.

"Aye."

She reached out and put her hands over his. "How on earth did you bear it?"

"While I was there, or after?"

"Either. Both."

"Hmmm," he said, "well, while I was there is something I don't like to think on overmuch. It was very dark. I think the only reason I didn't go mad was that I'm such a cheerful soul."

She laced her fingers with his. "Miach . . ."

"I continually recited spells, just to pass the time," he continued, looking down at her fingers intertwined with his own. "But the first time I saw light after that year . . ." He took another deep breath. "I thought my eyes would catch fire. And afterward I did my damndest to outrun my demons." He looked at her. "You understand that."

"Aye," she agreed.

"I flew in various shapes when I could, ran in my own shape when I couldn't. And I stretched myself and my power every chance I had so that the next time I met him, I would best him. Only, I didn't fare so well recently. I should have killed him when I saw what he'd done to you." He paused. "I was not thinking clearly."

"It had been a difficult day," she said quietly.

"Aye," he said. He squeezed her hands, then pulled away. "Give me five minutes to read, then we'll go. I am suddenly quite desperate for a bit of air."

"Of course." She paused. "I'm sorry, Miach. About the other. And I'm sorry about your parents."

He shrugged. "It was a long time ago."

"I imagine it doesn't make it any easier," she said. "Now, shall I take the rest of your books back to Master Dominicus and purchase you a bit of peace?"

"Thank you," he said gratefully. He was more than willing to turn his mind to other matters—not that they would be any less grim than what he'd just discussed. At least they wouldn't be quite so personal.

He waited until Morgan had gathered up his books and started toward the librarian before he opened the book Nicholas had given him earlier that morning when he'd knocked on the man's door and asked him for something interesting to read.

He had spent a goodly part of the night before considering the black mages who had the power to affect his spells. Lothar of Wychweald was alive, but Miach was convinced he was not the author of the magic. Wehr of Wrekin was rumored to be dead and even if he wasn't, his power had been so weakened by his last battle decades earlier with Neroche, Miach was positive he was not the man behind the assault. Gair of Ceangail was verifiably dead, so that made him a very unlikely suspect.

There had been other, less powerful men, but he had dismissed them immediately. The magic vexing him was subtle, but substantial. Perhaps he had reason enough to make the journey to Beinn òrain. What good were those seven rings languishing under his old, ratty training clothes if he couldn't have a peep at a few perilous texts now and again?

He looked up and found Morgan arguing in hushed tones with Master Dominicus. She seemed to be enjoying herself, so he took the opportunity to glance briefly at what Nicholas had given him. He was somehow unsurprised to find that the first name that his glance fell upon was Gair of Ceangail.

Gair, the black mage of Ceangail, lived a thousand years before he wooed and wed Sarait, the youngest daughter of Sìle of Tòrr Dòrainn. Her father forbade the match, but Sarait did not heed his warning.

Six sons and a daughter were born to the pair, which softened the king's heart, though Gair never again entered Seanagarra. Sarait visited her father frequently, after she realized Gair's true nature.

Miach let out his breath slowly. Poor Sarait. What a terrible position she had found herself in. He wasn't surprised to learn her father had opposed the marriage. To say Sìle of Tòrr Dòrainn didn't care for mages didn't begin to address his disdain. Weger would have found a friend in that one.

He refused to think about what that might potentially mean for him.

He continued to read, though he already knew what had happened next.

> *Sarait goaded Gair into showing the extent of his power, and he obliged by taking her to a well of evil and vowing to open it, then contain it. Gair demanded that all the children be brought and Sarait, knowing his true nature, feared to leave them behind lest they be without her protection. She sent all her children, save the three eldest, into hiding the moment Gair began his spell.*
>
> *The evil geisered forth and swept over everyone there, though Sarait managed to cover her eldest son from its effects. He told the tale to Gair's kin before he disappeared.*

Miach blinked. Disappeared? He'd always heard that the eldest lad, Keir, had died. And what was that about Gair's kin? He was the son of Eulasaid of Camanaë and Sgath of Ainneamh, though neither the mages of Camanaë nor the elves of Ainneamh would claim him. How had Gair become part of Ceangail?

He sighed and turned the pages on either side of the tale, wondering if he might find anything useful. His gaze fell upon a passage that made him frown in surprise.

> *It was during the 950th year of his reign that Sìle of Tòrr Dòrainn surrendered his throne for a year to his son, Làidir, in consequence of his labors . . .*

Surrendered his throne? Miach stared down at the words for a handful of moments, trying to come to terms with them. He could not imagine Sìle, for any reason, giving up his throne. He imagined that Làidir would only have had the crown if he'd pried it from his father's dead fingers.

He flipped through the pages surrounding that brief mention, but saw nothing more about it. He considered the dates. Sìle was now in the 976th year of his reign . . .

And twenty-six years earlier, Sarait had given birth to her only daughter, Mhorghain.

Had the birth of that wee granddaughter put him in such a state that he would make a piece of magic *that* taxing? He wondered if he might be looking at it awrong, but the dates couldn't be coincidence. Mhorghain had been born and Sìle had set to work. But what would a grandfather make for his grandchild that would cost him so much? And why would his granddaughter require anything so formidable?

Unless that granddaughter had needed protecting.

Miach felt a chill run down his spine. Of course that small gel would have needed protecting. Her sire was Gair of Ceangail.

But fashioning something to protect a small girl when her six brothers were equally in danger from their father's arrogance made no sense. Perhaps the magic had been wrought to guard one of Sìle's own children.

Miach considered them in turn. Sìle's sons, Làidir and Sosar, needed no aid, for they were very powerful and very shrewd. By then, Lismòrian had been dead for almost two centuries. That left Sìle's other four daughters, but Miach dismissed them in turn. Ciatach was wed to Sgur of Ainneamh, Sona was wed to her distant cousin Dileabach, and Alainne had been wed for a thousand years to Murdoch of Meith. That left only Sarait.

Had Sìle made something for Sarait that had put him in bed for a year?

"Finished yet?"

Miach shut the book with a snap and looked at Morgan. "Aye. Just now."

She was watching him with a frown. "You look a little green, my lord."

"I need air," he said, rising. He threw his cloak over his shoulder, picked up Nicholas's book, then pulled Morgan out of the library behind him. He shut the door, took a deep breath, then started up the stairs.

He had to know more about what Sìle had been doing and

exactly what it was the elven king had made. The dates simply couldn't be coincidence.

"Miach?"

He paused and turned to look at Morgan as she stood on the step below him. "Aye?"

"Where are you going?"

"To Nicholas's solar," he said in surprise. "Does that not suit?"

"Nay," she said, "I meant when you leave Lismòr. Where are you going then?"

"Oh," he said, "that. Buidseachd, I think." He smiled. "The schools of wizardry at Beinn òrain." He was also beginning to think he should stop in Tòrr Dòrainn, but perhaps he would keep that to himself a bit longer.

"They'll know who you are there, won't they?"

"Of course." He paused. "Will that bother you?"

"Will I be going with you?" she asked in surprise.

He wasn't sure if she looked pleased or a bit ill. Well, there was no sense in not knowing what she was thinking. "I had hoped you would," he said slowly.

She looked terribly uncomfortable. "People will wonder what you are doing with an ill-mannered shieldmaiden."

"You aren't ill-mannered," he said, "and even if you were, I wouldn't care."

"I don't know why *I* care," she said, putting her shoulders back. "After all, it isn't as if there is anything formal or stated or discussed even . . . um . . . between . . ."

He looked at her in surprise. "Do you *want* there to be anything formal, or stated, or discussed—"

She glared at him and brushed past him to hasten up the stairs. She didn't get far, though, before she had to slow down and merely trudge up them.

Miach watched her go, surprised beyond measure. It was true that he'd come south with the hope that he might somehow begin to convince her that she might, at some point, *want* to join her life to his, but in all honesty, he hadn't held out much hope for it.

He looked up after her and considered. Did she actually want to engage in something more *discussed* with him, or would she draw her sword and skewer him if he dared? He suspected that to avoid that skewering, he would have to tread very carefully.

That he might even venture such a thing was more than he'd hoped for.

Perhaps he would see how much of his attentions she would tolerate, venture a bit of romance, then hope he still had his belly free of any artistically arranged daggers. It might be pleasant for once to attempt to woo a woman who didn't run screaming the other way once she realized exactly who and what he was.

He paused.

He supposed Morgan had already done that.

But she'd come back, in a sense, so perhaps he could indeed venture a few things he might not have dared in the fall. He took the stairs three at a time until he'd caught up with her, then climbed the rest of the stairs at her pace. Perhaps he would talk to her later, when she wasn't ignoring him so thoroughly.

He followed her all the way to Nicholas's solar. She threw him another glare, then opened the door. Miach peered over her shoulder and saw that the lads were gathered for their evening tale. He hardly had a chance to determine what it was before Morgan had shut the door and turned around.

"Let's go to the buttery."

"Why—"

"Because Nicholas is telling the Tale of the Two Swords. If I must hear it again, I will scream."

"What is wrong with the Two Swords?" he asked, even more surprised. "Don't you care for it?"

"There is too bloody much romance in it," she said curtly.

Ah, well, here was the crux of it, apparently. "Don't you like romance?" he ventured.

She looked as though she were trying to decide if she should weep or, as he had earlier predicted, stick him with whatever blade she could lay her hand on. "I don't know," she said briskly.

"I see," he said, though he didn't. He wished, absently, that he had at least one sister. He was very well versed in what constituted courtly behavior and appropriate formal wooing practices, thanks to his father's insistence on many such lectures delivered by a dour man whose only acquaintance with women had likely come from reading about them in a book, but he had absolutely no idea how to proceed with a woman whose first instinct when faced with something that made her uncomfortable was to draw her sword.

Or walk away from him, as she was doing now. "Supper," she said over her shoulder.

Miach caught up to her in one stride, then walked alongside her with his hands clasped behind his back. "So," he began, drawing the word out as long as possible, "what would you think if someone wanted to ply a bit of romance on you?"

She stopped still and looked up at him in astonishment. "On *me*?"

"Of course, on you."

She blinked. "What the hell for?"

He smiled in spite of himself. "For the usual reasons, I imagine."

"Who would be that daft?"

He took a deep breath, then let it out silently. "Well, I would, actually."

Her mouth fell open. *"You?"*

He took a deep breath and reminded himself that he was a prince of Neroche and that there might actually be a woman in the realm who would like to have something formal, or stated, or even discussed with him.

"Aye," he said.

She looked at him for another moment or two in surprise, then sighed and bowed her head. "Miach . . ."

He smiled, though it cost him quite a bit. "A few games of cards," he said. "A bit of time in the lists. A few escapes from dragons bent on incinerating us. Actually, I'm not very good at romance. But I could try. For you." He paused for quite some time. "Unless that doesn't suit."

There, that would do it. She could say him nay, leave with her pride intact, and he would be the one with his heart in shreds. Though he'd already rent his heart when he'd left Gobhann. He wondered, absently, if he'd recently acquired a taste for self-torment. First Gobhann, then Morgan. Where would it end?

Morgan looked down for so long, he began to wonder if

she was trying to think of a way to say him nay without humiliating him. Then again, this was Morgan. She would have humiliated him without thought if he'd merited it.

"Will you sleep in my doorway tonight?" she asked suddenly.

He blinked. "Is that your answer?"

She shrugged and looked away. "It seems as good as any."

He shut his mouth when he realized it was hanging open. Well, that settled that, he supposed. Perhaps he couldn't have asked for anything else. She wanted him to guard her back, just as she'd offered to do for him. Comrade-in-arms. Nothing more. He took a deep breath.

"Of course I will," he said. "If it will ease you."

"Aye," she said, but she wouldn't meet his eyes.

"Supper first?"

She nodded. He walked down the passageway with her and cursed silently. Obviously, he'd grossly overestimated his appeal. Perhaps he should have taken her at her word in Gobhann when she'd reminded him that she had no use for mages. Perhaps he should have realized sooner that she—

Had reached behind his back and taken his hand.

He held his breath as she laced her fingers with his. He was almost cowardly enough not to look at her, but he supposed that whatever he saw in her expression couldn't be any worse than what he'd been through in the past month. He steeled himself for something truly dreadful, then looked at her.

She was watching him gravely.

"What?" he said, a little less enthusiastically than he might have otherwise.

"Aye."

"Aye?" he echoed. "Aye to what? Supper? My sleeping in your doorway? Swords in the lists tomorrow?"

She rolled her eyes. "Nay. Aye, to that other business. Aye to that, damn it."

"Oh," he said, feeling a little like she had just kicked him in the gut. "Romance?"

She glared at him. "I just want it noted that this is *your* idea."

"At the moment, love," he said faintly, "I think I'm quite willing to note anything you'd like me to."

"You're daft," she said, but she smiled at him. "Come on, you impossible man, I need something to eat."

"I think I need something to *drink*."

She pursed her lips and pulled him along with her. He was tempted to laugh, but she truly would have thought him daft, so he merely walked with her and kept his good humor to himself.

He supposed the realities of their future would intrude soon enough, but for the moment he was more than willing to enjoy the fact that Morgan was holding his hand and all her blades were still sheathed.

He would take it for as long as it lasted and be grateful.

Twelve

Morgan dreamed.

A mother walked with her young daughter through a forest, speaking to her in a tongue Morgan understood but couldn't name. A sweet, soothing peace surrounded the pair. Morgan followed them, wanting that peace to envelope her as well.

Soon they came to the edge of a clearing. There was a well there, a well like one might have found in a farm, though this was larger and there was a rough-hewn cap sitting atop it. A man stood next to it, dressed all in black. Morgan knew him: Gair of Ceangail. He had come to uncap the well before him, a well of evil that he had boasted he could control.

Morgan looked around her. She saw lads of various sizes spread out in the glade, all of them older than the girl. She watched the mother, Sarait, leave the girl in the shadows of the trees and walk out to talk to the man.

Morgan knew Sarait wouldn't be able to stop Gair from doing what he intended to do. Only she could, because she knew already what would happen. Without hesitation, she walked out into the clearing and caught Sarait by the sleeve. Sarait turned to look at her.

Morgan blinked in surprise. She felt as though she was looking into a polished mirror.

She would have stopped to consider that, but Gair had already begun to weave his spell of opening. Morgan turned away from Sarait and ran to him.

"I won't let you do this," she said, putting herself in front of him.

He didn't answer her.

Morgan knew the only way to destroy his evil was to destroy him. She wanted a spell of death and one came to her lips as if it had been fashioned for just such a moment. She recoiled at first from its magic, for it was evil, but she knew it had the power to do what she needed.

"I'm not Gair," Gair protested as she began.

She paused and looked at him. "Of course you are. Stop interrupting me."

"Morgan, I'm not Gair!"

Morgan paused, wondering how he knew her name, then shrugged and continued on. Of course he was Gair. She'd seen Gair in her dreams and knew exactly what he looked like.

Morgan listened to him grow increasingly frantic and knew that she was doing the right thing. She had to save the people she loved from his evil.

"Morgan."

She looked to her right. Nicholas was suddenly standing there, watching her with an understanding smile.

"You must stop, my dear."

Morgan looked at him, then back at Gair. "But I must kill him."

"It isn't Gair, my dear. It's Miach."

"It isn't Miach. It's Gair."

"Morgan!" Gair exclaimed.

Morgan took a deep breath to speak the last word of the spell.

Nicholas's hand on her arm distracted her. She looked at him in irritation, but he only smiled.

"Morgan, you're dreaming. You must awake. Trust me."

Morgan didn't want to trust him, but he tugged on her arm. She scowled at him, then turned back to finish her work.

But in Gair's place stood Miach.

* * *

Morgan woke with a start. She realized she was on her feet in the middle of her bedchamber. She was facing Miach, who was also on his feet, wearing a rumpled tunic and hose. His gaze was locked on her and he was unmoving. Power was rolling off him with a heat so intense, she stepped back instinctively. Then she realized that there was a word on the tip of her tongue.

The last word of a spell of death.

She realized in horror that she hadn't been dreaming. She'd been weaving that dreadful spell in truth and she hadn't been trying to use it on Gair; she'd been using it on Miach.

She dropped her spell like a dirty cloth. Miach fell to his knees, gasping for breath. Morgan threw herself down in front of him and flung her arms around him, partly to see if he was still alive and partly because she didn't have the strength to remain on her feet. She had never in her life felt such weariness, not even during her first year in Gobhann when she'd often thought she would simply expire from fatigue.

This was much, much worse.

She bent to look in Miach's face. "Did I hurt you?"

"I'm fine," he wheezed.

He didn't sound fine. He didn't feel fine either. He was trembling, as if he'd been out in the lists for a fortnight without a single rest.

She understood.

He pulled her close and rested his forehead against her shoulder. "Hold on to me," he said hoarsely. "Just for another minute or two."

She put her arms back around his neck and shook right along with him. She knelt there for quite some time, stroking his hair, fighting the urge to break down and weep. Magic was a terrible business, much worse than she'd ever thought.

It should all, she decided firmly, be consigned to the pit of hell.

"What can I do?" she asked him, when she thought she could speak evenly.

"*Don't use that spell on me again* would be my first suggestion," he managed.

She decided that she would be better off to never use any sort of spell again. She sat back on her heels and looked around to see if anyone had watched her try to kill the archmage of Neroche.

Nicholas was sitting on her bed, watching them tranquilly.

"Good morning," he said pleasantly.

Miach grunted, but said nothing. He remained hunched over, breathing raggedly. Morgan moved closer to him and put her arm around his shoulders before she turned to look at Nicholas. It took her only a moment to realize why she was unsurprised to see him there.

"I dreamed you," she said. "You woke me up."

Nicholas shrugged with a small smile. "I heard shouting and came as quickly as I could."

"Shouting?"

"I thought you were having a row. All's well now, though, isn't it?" He stood up and smiled at her. "I'll be in my solar. Come have breakfast when you're ready."

Morgan nodded. She heard him leave and shut the door. Miach groaned and sat back on his heels with his hands on his knees. He looked as if he wanted to do nothing so desperately as to return immediately to bed. "Can I assume you mistook me for another?" he asked faintly.

"I dreamed you were Gair," she whispered. "I thought I was killing him, not you."

"Heaven help me if you truly become angry with me," he said, with a half laugh. He dragged his hands through his hair, then let out a deep, shuddering breath. "Well, that was quite a start to the day."

"How can you jest about this? I could have killed you!" She hesitated. "Could I have?"

He looked at her for a moment, then he shifted to sit with his back against the wall. He patted the place next to him and waited until she had come to sit next to him before he spoke again.

"I suppose you could have," he said, reaching for her hand and taking it in both his own, "for you caught me by surprise. I could have merely thrown the spell back on you, of course, but it would have killed *you*. I had to unravel your spell as quickly as you were weaving it and you had quite a start on me."

She shivered. "What was that?"

"A rather good spell of death, actually." He rubbed his face with one hand, then shook his head sharply, as if he strove to wake. "I don't know where in the hell you learned it. Certainly not from me."

"I don't even know what language that was," she said in a small voice.

"Olc," he supplied. "Lots of nasty things come out of that branch of magic."

"That's one of the languages you wouldn't use to extinguish the torch at Gobhann, isn't it?"

"Aye."

She frowned. "Why do you know the spell?"

"Because I know many unpleasant things," he said. "Whether or not I use them is another thing entirely."

She looked down at his hands wrapped around one of hers and considered several things she hadn't before. "That spell you used on those creatures near Chagailt," she began thoughtfully. She met his gaze. "That wasn't Olc, was it?"

He shook his head. "Nay, love, it wasn't."

"But you're trembling as you were then."

He stroked the back of her hand. "All serious magic is draining, Morgan. The more extensive the magic, the higher the price to be paid. And killing magic does not come without great cost to your soul. Even an unfinished spell," he added.

She shuddered. "I think this is far worse than any battle I've ever fought in. How is it you manage the realm so easily?"

"It isn't done easily," he said with a half smile. "I'm just not one to complain overmuch."

"But how do you bear the magic?" she asked. "How can this be what you face each day?"

He reached up and tucked her hair behind her ear. "Because I grew up knowing there was magic in my veins that I was expected to use," he said gently. "I have never known a day where magic was not part of my life. I would imagine that it is more difficult for those who have their magic come to them when they're older."

"I daresay," she murmured.

"You know, I think perhaps today is not the day to examine that too closely. Let us do as our good Lord Nicholas suggested and join him in his solar. We'll feel more ourselves after a decent meal."

"Is food the answer to everything?"

He laughed. "If it isn't, the question isn't very interesting." He squeezed her hands gently, then heaved himself to his feet. "Shall I wait for you to dress, or wait for you in Lord Nicholas's solar?"

"I'll come find you," she said wearily. "When I think I can manage it."

He squatted down next to her. "Trying to kill me was in retaliation for last night, wasn't it?"

She looked at him in surprise. "What about last night?"

"The romance," he said solemnly.

She gaped at him for a minute, then pointed toward the door. "Get out."

He laughed. "Now you sound more like yourself. Hurry up, wench, lest you come late to table and find I've eaten all your breakfast."

She scowled at him, but he only laughed at her again. He gathered his gear from where he'd slept in the doorway and shut the door behind him. He wasn't, she had to admit after he'd gone, all that steady on his feet.

She couldn't blame him.

She sat where he'd left her until she thought she could stand without falling down, then she had a wash and dug clean clothes from a trunk Nicholas always seemed to keep stocked for her. It took her far longer than it should have because she kept dropping things. She wondered, as she struggled to change her clothes and get her boots on, how it was that Miach managed to do what he did—no matter what he'd said. For herself, all she wanted was a nap.

She left her bedchamber and shuffled wearily around the edge of the courtyard. It seemed to take forever to reach Nicholas's door, but she supposed that came from equal parts weariness and revulsion over the spell she'd used while dreaming. She stood with her hand on the door for several minutes, forced herself to put the morning behind her, then entered the solar.

Miach and Nicholas had their heads together over a stack of books on the low table in front of the sofa. Morgan watched the dark head and the white so close together, poring over a particular page, and found that something inside her heart shifted.

And settled into a place that might have been called home.

She wasn't sure whom she was more grateful to: Nicholas for treating Miach as an equal, or Miach for being so deferential to an old man she loved like a father. What she did know was that when they both looked up from their work, their welcoming expressions made her eyes burn.

Poor fool that she was.

Miach stood and waited for her to come around the end of the sofa. He saw her seated before he resumed his own, as if she had been a fine lady. She didn't feel it. Her hair was still in tangles down her back and her nails were chipped. She would have considered her flaws more diligently, but Miach took her hand and pulled her forward.

"There's breakfast on that table over there," he said, with a knowing look. "Go have some and stop thinking so much about the condition of your hands."

She gaped at him. "How did you know?"

"You were muttering."

She sighed. "Very well." She fetched herself something to eat, then brought a plate back over with her and sat down on the couch. She looked over Miach's shoulder at what lay on the table. "What have you found so far?"

He smiled. "Lord Nicholas has several interesting books squirreled away. I couldn't not nose through them."

Morgan could only imagine what he'd found on Nicholas's shelves. She looked at Nicholas, but he only smiled and handed her a cup of warm wine.

"I promise to make him stop before lunch," Nicholas vowed.

She shook her head. "Don't do it on my account. He can read all day if he likes. I'm happy merely to be somewhere warm and have something decent to drink." Perhaps she could drink herself into a stupor and that would keep her from dreaming any more whilst the sun was up.

She didn't want to think about what the night might bring.

"Is the wine not so delicate at Gobhann?" Nicholas asked with a twinkle in his eye.

"It isn't drinkable," Miach said with a snort, "though one does drink it because the ale is worse. For myself, I'd much rather be here, where the wine is excellent and the company lovely."

"Thank you," Nicholas said modestly.

Miach laughed. "You're quite attractive as well, my lord."

Morgan rolled her eyes as she shoved off her boots and drew her feet up onto the sofa with her. Miach pulled a blanket off the chair opposite him and draped it over her, continuing to carry on his conversation with Nicholas. She found Miach was tucking it under her toes without looking and had to concede that she was uncommonly and unsettlingly comfortable. She ate a wonderful meal, drank delicious wine, then found herself substantially more spent than she should have been.

Miach placed a small cushion against the arm of the sofa farthest from him. "Rest," he suggested.

She supposed it wouldn't hurt, though she had no intention of falling asleep.

She realized she had, though, only because she woke and found herself stretched out on the couch with her feet in Miach's lap. She sat up with a start and looked around her. The table in front of the sofa was burdened with at least twice the number of books it had been the last time she'd seen it, and there were plates and glasses in a pile near those books. Miach was watching her with a grave smile, and Nicholas was nowhere to be found. She dragged her hand through her hair, encountering the same number of tangles she had earlier. She was going to have to find a brush very soon.

"I slept," she said with a yawn.

"Aye, you did," he agreed.

"I didn't dream."

"I hoped you wouldn't."

"Perhaps it was because you were holding my feet."

He smiled. "If only it were that simple, Morgan, I would hold your feet constantly."

"And never accomplish anything else," she said, pulling her feet out of his lap. "But I thank you. I haven't slept so well in weeks." She rested her chin on her knees and studied him. "You must take your turn. Would you trust me to watch over you?"

"Of course," he said, looking surprised, "why wouldn't I?"

"I might truly do you in the next time," she said in a low voice.

He leaned close, so close that she could see all the fractures in his very pale blue eyes. "It was just a nightmare, Morgan. I have them too."

"Do you dream I'm someone I'm not?" she asked lightly. "And want to do me in?"

"I have dreamed of you, but doing you in was never involved."

"I hesitate to ask what was."

"'Tis probably better not to know," he said, sitting back with a smile. He watched her for a moment, then his smile faded. "How are you, in truth?"

She knew exactly what he was talking about. "Terrified," she said frankly. She took a deep breath. "I don't want to go back to Gobhann, but I will admit it was pleasant not to dream whilst I was there." She looked at the books on the table. "Think you there might be answers there?"

He was silent for so long, she had to look at him. He was very still but his eyes were full of pity and no small bit of regret.

"Nay, Morgan," he said quietly, "the answers are not in those books."

She attempted a swallow, but it didn't go very well. "And you would know where they are to be found?"

"Aye."

"Where?" she whispered.

He looked at her for a moment or two in silence, then tapped his forehead. "Here."

She was on her feet without knowing quite how she'd gotten there. She swayed so violently that she almost went sprawling over the table littered with books about things she knew would make her skin crawl.

"Morgan—"

"I have to walk."

She found Miach's hands on her arms, holding her upright. He turned her to face him. "Morgan, you cannot simply will this morning's magic to leave you unaffected. It is too soon to be bolting anywhere—even if it is only from tidings you don't want to hear."

She found, to her horror, that her eyes were full of tears. She couldn't see him standing in front of her, so she felt for his arms.

"Help me with my boots," she pleaded. "I cannot sit here, Miach. I simply cannot. I must at least walk about the cloister. You know why."

He sighed deeply. "Very well."

She held on to his shoulders as he knelt in front of her and put her boots on her feet, then she let him turn her around and help her over to the door. She felt him put her cloak around her shoulders, heard him do the same for himself, then watched him open the door for them both.

It was a bitter, windy day. The breeze found gaps in her cloak and slid its icy fingers through them to chill her even more than her thoughts had. Miach's arm was suddenly around her shoulders, pulling her under the added shelter of his cloak. She wasn't one to lean on a man for strength, but she supposed she could be forgiven it that day. Miach was warm and solid in a world of things that seemed to slip out from under her fingers every time she reached for them. She rested her head against his shoulder, closed her eyes, and thought of nothing as she allowed him to lead her around the covered edge of the courtyard.

It took five turns about the courtyard before she thought she could open her mouth without some horrible, inhuman sound coming out. It took another two before she could actually see something besides a blur of tears. Another handful of times left her almost feeling like herself.

Or what had been herself before she'd laid her hand on a magical knife fashioned by Mehar of Angesand and had her dreams begin.

She turned from that thought as if it had been accompanied by a thousand spells of Olc. She cast about for anything else to concentrate on, anything that had nothing to do with magic or evil or darkness.

She realized, after a time, that Miach was stroking the hand she'd put around his waist. It reminded her of all the times he had held her hand in the past, as if it was something that pleased him.

Why, she couldn't have said. Worse yet, what would others say when they saw him doing such a thing? She looked up to find him studying her. She couldn't even smile. She could only stare at him and wonder what in the hell he was thinking. Romance? To what bloody end? Her hands were rough; her nails were chipped. Her hands were not the sort of hands a man would ask for in any sort of formal sort of business.

No matter what he'd said the night before.

He stopped and turned her to him. "What is it?"

She frowned fiercely at him. It was either that or weep, and she'd had enough of tears for the moment. "I don't understand why you want to . . . well, whatever it is you want to do with me."

"Are you speaking of swords," he asked with a frown, "or something else?"

She tried to muster up a glare, but she couldn't. She found that she could do nothing but look up at him, mute. She feared that if she opened her mouth again, she would simply howl.

He winced, then pulled her close and wrapped his cloak around her. He put his hand behind her head and pressed it against his shoulder.

"You need a distraction, I think, from things that are too serious. Of course," he said lightly, "I am more than willing to oblige you with conversation about other things. Romance is always uppermost in my mind."

"You're daft," she managed.

"Morgan, my love, there is enough of evil and darkness in the world. If a lad and a lass cannot speak of lighthearted things now and again, then the darkness has won."

She felt a sigh come shuddering out of her. "I suppose you're right."

"I am about this. Now, if you're curious why I would like to do something besides face you over blades, I suppose 'tis for the usual reasons."

She hadn't had much time to consider what those might be, but she had a fair idea. She stood still for quite some time before she managed to speak. "So I can be your mistress?" she asked finally, pained.

He froze. "My *what*?"

She looked up at him. "You heard me."

He gaped at her in astonishment for several moments, his mouth working as if he simply couldn't form any useful words. "Do you honestly think," he said finally, "that I would risk my life, my honor, and the safety of not only the realm of Neroche but all the Nine bloody Kingdoms together to fetch you out of Gobhann just so you could be my *mistress*?"

"Sshh," she hissed, nodding toward a pair of students who

were watching them with great interest. She sent them scampering with a glare, then turned back to Miach. "How would I know what you want?"

He looked at her for another long, drawn-out moment, then he bent his head and rested it on her shoulder. He wheezed. Or he might have laughed. In truth, she didn't know which it was. She *did* know, however, that she was on the verge of becoming completely offended by whatever it was he was doing that wasn't nearly as dignified as it should have been.

She finally stomped quite vigorously on his toes.

"Ouch, damn it," he gasped. "What was that for?"

"You were laughing at me."

He fought his smile, without much success. "Morgan, I just never know what you're thinking. And what you were thinking was so far from what I was thinking . . . well, it was either laugh or weep."

"Indeed," she said stiffly.

"Daft wench," he said affectionately, "you can't really believe that is what I want from you."

"I don't know *what* you want. I know what mercenaries mean when they speak of romance and that generally includes a very short bit of business without any entanglements that I never thought was worth my time."

He smoothed his hand over her hair. "I'm surprised you agreed to it with me, then."

"You spoke only of swords and cards," she muttered. "That I thought I could bear." She shot him a dark look. "I have no idea what else it is you expect of your women—"

"I don't have women," he said with a faint smile.

She scowled. "*Potential* women, then. Perhaps you are accustomed to long lines of wenches waiting for you to notice them. Perhaps you . . . er . . ."

"Woo," he supplied helpfully.

She jerked out of his arms. "I'm finished with this conversation."

He laughed and caught her before she managed to escape fully. "Oh, nay," he said, "I'm finding it to be quite enlightening. Let's walk a bit more and talk about just exactly what it is I expect from my women—"

"Miach," she warned.

He smiled and put his arm around her shoulders. "I'll stop provoking you, but I will have the answer to a question. Why do you think most men woo?"

"Because they have no sword skill and need something with which to occupy their time?"

He blinked in surprise, then bent his head and laughed again.

She cursed him, but that didn't seem to intimidate him as it should have.

"It may take me a bit to find a decent reply to that," he said, his eyes watering madly. "Walk with me until I do, won't you?"

She agreed only because walking was better than sitting and thinking. Even walking with Miach, who apparently giggled at everything that amused him, was better than sitting and thinking.

They walked for quite some time before he finally stopped in front of Nicholas's solar and turned her to face him. He took off his cloak, wrapped it around her, then pulled her braid free and fussed with arranging it for a moment or two. Then he met her eyes.

"I have sword skill already," he said with a grave smile, "and no need for things to fill up my days."

She stared at him, mute, for far longer than she should have. "Then why are you about this business of yours?" she asked, finally.

"Because, Morgan, my love, our road is dark and will likely grow darker as we journey down it. If we cannot find a few moments of pleasure and comfort along the way, it will be a grim road indeed. Don't you think?"

"Is that your reason?"

He took her face in his hands. "Nay, love. What I really want is you in my arms as often as possible. This seemed the best way to see to it."

She would have glared at him, but she suspected he was telling the truth.

"Let me woo you, and we'll see how it suits you," he said with a smile. "I'm sure my attentions won't include anything more interesting than sharpening your blades, cleaning your boots, and occasionally brushing your hair. If I'm feeling particularly clever, I might take you out in the lists and allow you to best me."

"Allow?" she repeated incredulously.

He laughed at her and pulled her into his arms. "You're too easy to bait. Let's go inside and we'll work on that very first of all."

She stopped him. "I don't think I can go in," she said, feeling her voice catch in her throat. She managed a very uncomfortable swallow. "There are answers waiting for me in that solar that I can't face quite yet."

"Shall we walk more?"

"Aye, but take your cloak back, then put it around us both. 'Tis foolish, I know, but I feel safer that way."

He nodded, donned his cloak, then drew her under it again. She tried to decide if it was his nearness that soothed her so, or the warmth of his arm around her. She contemplated that for several circles of the courtyard, but came to no decision.

"You won't leave me?" she asked, at one point.

"Nay, love, I won't."

She couldn't ask anything more of him than that.

So she continued to walk in the sunshine. The darkness that awaited her was something she couldn't bring herself to face.

Not even if Miach was there with her.

Thirteen

M iach sat on the floor next to the low table in front of Nicholas's very fine sofa and tried to pay attention to what he was reading. He wasn't having much success, but just the effort gave him something to concentrate on besides what he would have to tell Morgan when she awoke.

He'd finally convinced her, after a score of turns about Lismòr's inner courtyard, to come inside the solar and sit down. He'd built up Nicholas's fire, then suggested she might like to stretch out on the sofa and listen to a story guaranteed to keep her awake. She had agreed, he imagined, only because she'd been so desperate to avoid anything to do with either her dreams or his wooing.

And so he'd told her the enormously fascinating tale of Tharra of Fearann Fàs who had scoured the wastelands east of Beinn òrain for a wife to suit his ugliness. He had hardly gotten Tharra out of the city before Morgan had succumbed to slumber. That had left him with nothing to do but patch his spells and wait for her to wake.

The door opened behind him and Miach looked back over his shoulder to find Lismòr's lord coming inside. Nicholas shut the door behind him and walked silently over to sit in his chair.

"You convinced her to sleep," he noted.

"Finally," Miach said. "She was reluctant."

"I can't say I blame her," Nicholas said, "especially after this morning." He smiled. "You look to have survived your brush with death well enough."

"It was a near thing," Miach admitted. "She's very powerful."

"I daresay. Her strength in many things has come back, though I will admit that there were times during those first few days that I truly feared it wouldn't." He studied Morgan for a few minutes, then nodded. "Aye, she is much improved, even more so after being here such a short time."

"Gobhann is not a good place to heal," Miach said slowly, "though I'll own that Weger did coddle her as much as she would allow, and it did do her some good."

"I don't understand why she loves it there so. It can't be pleasant."

"It isn't," Miach said without hesitation. "It's harsh, unforgiving, and cold as hell. A bit like its lord, actually."

Nicholas smiled. "And how does Weger find himself these days?"

"Relentless." Miach looked at Morgan to judge her depth of sleep, then turned to Nicholas. "I assume you know who he is."

"Aye."

Miach smiled. "And you never said anything to her."

"Would you?" Nicholas asked, raising an eyebrow. "She had to run somewhere when she left Lismòr; I wasn't going to spoil her refuge for her. Besides, if I'd told her, she would have wondered how I knew, and that would have required too many answers I wasn't ready to give."

"You were right not to," Miach said quietly. "Weger admitted his heritage to her a se'nnight before we left Gobhann. It was, as you might imagine, very difficult for her to hear. I don't know what she would have done if you had told her eight years ago."

"She likely would have called me a fool," Nicholas said ruefully, "and gone inside anyway."

"Perhaps," Miach said. "As for Weger, I can understand why he has chosen his current home. He hates Lothar—and perhaps his own magic—with a fierceness that is all the more terrifying because he expresses it so calmly."

"I can't blame him," Nicholas said. "A pity his father was such a fool. I told Smior he was mad to wed Eisleine inside

Riamh instead of bringing her out, but he wouldn't listen. He underestimated Lothar and found himself in Lothar's dungeon as a result. But you can understand how that would happen, can't you?"

Miach shut his mouth when he realized it was hanging open. He wasn't sure if he was more surprised that Nicholas had spoken with Weger's father or that Nicholas knew of his own incarceration in Riamh. "I have no secrets, I see."

"I only know because your mother came to see me whilst you were captive there," Nicholas said mildly.

"My *mother*?" Miach echoed, stunned. "How did she know who you were?"

"Because she was notorious for knowing things she would have been better off not knowing. She tracked me here and came to ask if I knew anything that might help her. You must understand that she was well aware how delicate a balance it was between Lothar keeping you alive and slaying you simply because he could. She was exceptionally powerful, but Lothar is capricious. Smior could have told you that, I suppose." He studied his hands for a moment or two. "There is, I believe, more to besting Lothar and his evil than simply slaying him. Besides, slay him and he has a dozen lads standing behind him to take his place."

"Yngerame should have killed him whilst he had the chance," Miach said grimly.

"I imagine you've talked to Yngerame about that already, haven't you?" Nicholas asked. "He had his reasons for leaving his son alive. He and Symon bound him once, as you well know, even though they knew the spells would not last forever. It wouldn't surprise me if they had foreseen your turn as archmage of Neroche and left Lothar as your challenge—just as Mehar saw Morgan as a wielder of the Sword of Angesand."

"Do you think so?" Miach asked in surprise. "About us both, I mean."

"I am speculating about you," Nicholas said, "though it is a rather educated guess. I've talked to them both about you many times. They are particularly impressed with how you've handled your duties. And as for Morgan, aye, I know that Mehar saw her hand on the sword. She told me so herself."

"Who *don't* you know?" Miach asked in astonishment.

Nicholas smiled. "When you've walked as long on the world's stage as I have, Miach my lad, you'll find that the Nine Kingdoms are not as large as you once thought. You know your share of souls from legend."

"I suppose so," Miach admitted.

Nicholas sobered. "As for Lothar, I imagine there will come a day when you must make the same decision Yngerame and Symon made: either to kill him or to let him live."

"I don't relish the thought," Miach said grimly.

"Neither did they, I imagine," Nicholas said. "But we're moving away from simpler things. Weger's heritage doesn't surprise me, nor does his choice of occupations. And speaking of magic, have you told your lady what she needs to know about hers?"

"You know I haven't." He looked at Lismòr's lord crossly. "Tell me again why I'm the one giving her these tidings and not you?"

"Penance."

Miach would have laughed, but the subject was too serious. "I suppose," he said wearily.

Nicholas smiled. "I'm needling you a bit, lad. You did what you had to in the fall. As for the other, 'tis simple. She will accept the tidings from you because she knows you will tell her the truth. Me, she would discount."

"I don't think so, but I know what you're getting at. I owe her a fair bit of truth and this is as good a place as any to begin. She's been avoiding it, though, as thoroughly as I have. It has been pleasant to remain within your walls and not have to face our future overmuch." He took a deep breath, then let it out slowly. "Thank you for telling me about my mother."

"You're welcome, lad," Nicholas said with a smile. "Some day, when you have a chance, come for a visit and I'll tell you more about her more noteworthy escapades. Desdhemar was a remarkable woman and you're fortunate to have her blood in your veins."

"I know," Miach said quietly.

Nicholas rubbed his hands together suddenly. "Let's speak of less sentimental things. Have you decided what you'll do after you leave here? If you can pry yourself away from my supper table, that is."

Miach smiled. "It will be difficult, I assure you. As for what I'll do, I thought to make a journey to Beinn òrain."

Nicholas nodded. "Wise. They'll have kept a list of anyone who's shown promise of magic over the years. I imagine you'll find several souls there to add to your list. But what of Morgan?"

"I've asked her to come with me."

"And she said you aye?"

Miach had to smile. "I worried there for a bit that she wouldn't, but she agreed in the end. In spite of my magic, no doubt."

"You should stop in Tòrr Dòrainn," Nicholas advised. "But I imagine you've already thought of that."

"Aye, I have," Miach agreed reluctantly. "I have a question or two for Sìle—not that he'll be willing to talk to me."

"He won't have much choice when he realizes that his granddaughter loves you."

Miach smiled briefly. "Do you think she does?"

"I do," Nicholas said, "though it may not serve you much today. I would suggest that you make certain she doesn't have any blades to hand when you tell her what you must. I don't imagine it will go well for you otherwise. I think I'll leave you to it before she wakes." He rose and walked over to the door. He put his hand on the wood, then looked at Miach. "Be careful with her, won't you?"

Miach cleared his throat roughly. It was either that or grow as misty-eyed as Nicholas was.

"Of course, Your Grace," Miach said quietly. "I wouldn't think to do less."

"Which is why I'm trusting you with her," Nicholas said simply. He turned and left the solar, shutting the door softly behind him.

Miach rubbed his hands over his face and wondered how in the hell he was going to manage to spew any of what he needed to say before Morgan turned and bolted. Being the seventh child and only daughter of a black mage so arrogant and so evil that no one spoke his name without loathing was not going to be something that was easy to accept.

Then again, he had a few unsavory characters in his own family tree, so perhaps he would have a few things to tell her eventually to make her feel better.

He sat and stared at her, wanting nothing more than a few more minutes of looking at her in peace. He'd spent weeks at her side without telling her who he was, or what he was, and they had both paid the price. He couldn't do that again. Not now.

He watched her for quite a while before she finally stirred. She opened her eyes, looked at the ceiling for a moment or two, then turned her head and saw him.

She smiled.

It smote him to the heart.

"You're still here," she said.

"Where else would I go?" he asked gravely.

"Oh, I don't know," she said. "You could have flapped off anywhere."

He took her hands in his. "I told you I wouldn't leave."

"So you did," she agreed. She rubbed her free hand over her face. "I didn't mean to sleep."

"You needed it. Perhaps you'll be able to stay awake tonight for a game or two of cards with me. I learned everything I know about cheating from Glines of Balfour."

She smiled. "It won't serve you, given that he taught me as well."

"He taught me different things. He promised that quite faithfully."

She snorted. "And he's too far away for you to do damage to him when you realize he lied to you. But I will indulge you, if you like, just so you'll see the truth of the matter."

He brought her hand to his mouth and kissed it. "Then we'll save that as something to look forward to later." He paused and took a deep breath. "I fear, Morgan, that we can put off the unpleasant no longer."

She closed her eyes briefly, then sat up, pulling her hand from his. "So our days of peace are now ended."

"They need not be," he said. "Truth is that cold, bracing wind you feel ripping through you on the parapet at Gobhann, but it will pass and you will be here again at Lismòr, in this place you love, where you are loved."

Her eyes were unusually bright. "Must you be the one to give me these tidings?" she asked, pained.

"Would you prefer Nicholas?"

"Would I prefer Nicholas?" she echoed. She looked at him in outright shock. "Nicholas of Lismòr? What would *he* know of any of this?"

Miach shrugged with a casualness he most certainly did not feel. "He gave you Mehar's knife and sent you on your quest, didn't he? I daresay he knows more than you might think." That was an understatement, but he wasn't going to elaborate at present.

"I think I prefer you," she said grimly.

That was fortunate, as he doubted Nicholas could be found to question. He nodded. "Do you care to talk while you are sitting down, walking, or flying?"

"Walking," she said without hesitation. "In the exercise yard where no one will see."

Miach decided at that moment that the only thing he had possibly dreaded more than what he had to do in the next hour had been dawn in Lothar's dungeon.

So, he approached it as he had that unenviable task: he kept himself busy. He put Morgan's boots on her, helped her to her feet, fetched her cloak for her, and suggested strongly that she leave her sword behind. He put his hand on the door only to find that she had caught him by the arm.

"Miach, you don't look well."

He took a deep breath, then opened the door. "Air," he said succinctly.

She ducked under his arm and left the solar in front of him. He shut the door behind them, took another deep breath of air that was substantially colder than it had been earlier, then nodded to his left. He started walking only because he needed to be about some useful activity.

Perhaps he was worrying needlessly. It was possible that Morgan would take the tidings very well, look at him the same way after the fact, and not flee for Gobhann.

He felt her slip her hand into his.

"Miach, when did you eat last?"

He looked at her in surprise. "I ate lunch with you. Why?"

"You look green. I don't want you sicking up anything on my boots."

He realized, with a start, that she was teasing him. He might have been impressed if she hadn't looked so green herself. He managed a smile.

"You, wench, are formidable."

"Weger's training."

"Actually, I think 'tis just you," he said, squeezing her hand. "I'm impressed."

"See what you think later," she managed.

He nodded, then walked with her slowly through the maze of passageways out to the yard beyond the inner walls. She seemed content to simply walk and be silent, so he obliged her. After all, 'twas her past they had to discuss. It wasn't his place to push it on her until she was ready.

Well, any more than he had already.

They paced around the perimeter of the yard a handful of times before she stopped. She looked at the ground for several minutes, then looked at him.

"All right," she said. "Tell me."

He started to open his mouth, then had to take a deep breath. "I have spent countless hours thinking on how to begin this, but now I find none is a good place."

"Did you think about it?" she asked in surprise.

"Well, of course. Once I knew what I had to tell you, that is." He paused. "Can you bear this, in truth?"

She looked at him for a moment, then turned and slipped her arms around his waist. Miach wrapped his cloak around her and gathered her close, resting his cheek against her hair.

He thought she might have wept.

He was certain he had.

"If Weger could see us both," he managed eventually.

"He would gouge out his marks," she said darkly.

He shook his head. "Nay, gel, he would understand." He pulled back, wiped her tears from her cheeks, then dragged his sleeve across his own eyes. "We'll weep more later, perhaps in Nicholas's solar where no one will see us."

She nodded, then stepped back. She took his hand. "Very well. I can bear this now."

"Very well." He took her hand and walked along the edge of the yard with her. "Here is how I learned about the things I must tell you. After you left the palace on that fateful evening in the fall, I followed you. Not quickly enough to stop you from drinking Lothar's poison, but quickly enough to catch you as you fell—"

She looked up quickly. "Did you? I didn't know that."

"I should have been there sooner, but Adhémar was bellowing, as you might imagine, and I was forced to silence him. I ran after you, but it was too late. Before I could gather my wits to challenge Lothar, he had disappeared. I couldn't leave you to follow Lothar, yet I knew that I couldn't leave him free within the realm. I was trying to determine the best course, when a white-haired man suddenly appeared in front of me and told me to follow him. I was tempted to kill him and find out who he was after the fact, but he said he could heal you. I was desperate enough to listen to him, but I had no intention of releasing you to him."

"Thank you," she murmured.

He laced his fingers with hers. "Of course. I followed the man out into the kitchen garden only because I thought if we were outside, I might have a better chance of fighting him off. I'll admit now that I was worried. His power was tremendous, and I feared it would take all mine to drive him away. Once we were outside, he instructed me to hand you over, that he had the wherewithal to drive out Lothar's poison. I thought him mad and wasted no time in telling him so."

"Who was he?" she asked.

"He said that he was the wizard king of Diarmailt. His wife was Lismòrian, the sister of Sarait, who was the wife of Gair of Ceangail."

She shivered. "And did you believe him?"

"He knew too much for me not to," Miach said frankly. "It was from him that I learned the tale of Sarait's daughter, Mhorghain."

Morgan stumbled, then caught herself. She took a deep breath. "Go on."

"He told me that he had watched over Mhorghain for years—"

"Why?" she interrupted. "Why would he bother?"

"Because he was Mhorghain's uncle, for one thing. Because Sarait had asked him to watch over her children if something happened to her, for another. The final reason is, it was critical that no one know who Mhorghain was—or where she was."

"But why?" Morgan asked, her voice nothing more than a whisper. "Why would anyone care about her?"

"Because of who she is," Miach said quietly. "Her parentage alone is enough to make her dangerous—and tempting—to many. She is the granddaughter of Sìle of Tòrr Dòrainn through her mother, and the granddaughter of Eulasaid of Camanaë through her father. There are black mages and power-hungry kings who would have given anything to have ensnared her in her youth and turned her to their purposes. Her birthright and her blood make her power immense. Lothar, especially, would have given much to have taken her to Riamh. The reasons for that perhaps do not matter—"

She stopped. "Miach, if you're going to tell me anything, you must tell me everything."

"There are, and I speak from experience," he said seriously, "some things about Lothar's methods of stealing another's power that are better left in the dark where they belong."

She watched him for a handful of moments in silence, then reached up and touched his cheek briefly. "I'm sorry he stole a year of your youth," she said quietly. "I would repay him for it, if I could. And now you must tell me how he does what he does. I think I need to know."

He bowed his head for a moment, then caught her hand and kissed her palm. "Morgan, please—"

"You must, Miach," she said grimly. "I haven't been his prisoner, but I have tasted his brews. I think that entitles me to a few details, don't you?"

Miach dragged a hand through his hair, then caught her hand with his and pulled her along with him. "Now, I'm the one who must walk. And I will tell you what you want to know, but I do it unwillingly and I will give you only the barest of details. Lothar, as you might imagine, takes great pleasure in the terror of his quarry. He has devised ways to feed that fear and drain the terrified mage's power as a result. He never plied his trade on me, but he made certain I saw him do it to enough other fools. If he had captured Mhorghain in her youth, he would have either trained her to use her power for evil without a second thought, or he would have worn her down with terror until she was too weak to fight him. Then he would have taken all her magic and left nothing behind but a husk." He paused. "What was left of her would have been an especially significant trophy to display."

She shivered. "Vile wretch."

"It is who he is. He also bears an especial grudge for all who carry Camanaë blood in their veins. Eulasaid of Camanaë had him thrown out of the schools of wizardry for meddling in things he shouldn't have. He has never forgiven her or any of her descendants for it. And to capture Eulasaid's granddaughter?" Miach took a deep breath. "Irresistible."

She had begun to shake so badly that Miach stopped her. He looked down into her blanched visage, then winced at the tears that streamed down her cheeks.

"So," she said, her voice breaking on the word, "you learned all this about that poor girl. An interesting fireside tale."

He put his hands on her face and wiped away her tears. "Morgan, the tale is yours," he said quietly. "Those aren't dreams you're dreaming, they're memories. You are the woman who inherited power not only from her sire, but elven magic from her mother. Your uncle proves it beyond doubt."

She put her hands over his. "And who is this wizard king who claims to know all this?"

Miach took a deep breath. "His name is Nicholas."

"And he truly saw all this? He watched over . . . her . . . all these years?"

"He watched over *you*," Miach corrected. "He watched over you in secret whilst the mercenaries had the care of you, then he watched over you himself."

She looked at him for a moment in confusion, then realization dawned. Her mouth fell open. "*Nicholas?* Nicholas of *Lismòr*? He is the wizard king of Diarmailt?"

Miach nodded gravely. "He named Lismòr after his lady wife, Lismòrian, who was your aunt. Lismòrian was the eldest of the five daughters of Sìle of Tòrr Dòrainn—"

"Nay," she said hoarsely. "Nay, that isn't possible."

"Morgan—"

She pulled away from him and backed up. "If one more

person I know turns out to be a mage . . ." She shook her head, her eyes wide with shock and grief. "I don't think I can bear it."

"Morgan—"

"Did he bring me here?" she demanded. "Is he a shapechanger as well?"

"Ah—"

She grabbed for his hands and clutched his fingers so hard, he thought she just might break them.

"Teach me the dragonshape."

"Nay," he said faintly, "I'll never get you back out of it."

She pulled on him, starting to run. "Teach me the shapechange, Miach, damn you."

"Morgan—"

"Please," she pleaded. "You know why."

He did.

And he supposed if she wanted to outrun her demons, he wasn't the one to stop her. With any luck, once she'd flown long enough to forget about what she'd learned, he would be able to coax her back into her proper form.

So he ran with her and gave her the spell.

Within the space of a heartbeat, he was rising in the air, chasing after her. He knew he shouldn't have been surprised at the way she'd taken to it, but he supposed he wasn't past it. He chased her through the air, struggling to keep up with her.

Then, as the sun wheeled toward the west, he lost himself in the joy of flight as well and forgot about elves, and wizards, and truths that were hard to bear. He rolled and swooped and dove, feeling Morgan's desperation and fear be replaced by a wild joy that finished stealing what small part of his heart he hadn't already surrendered to her.

The future be damned; he would fly with her as long as she wanted.

And hope that he would be able to convince her to come back to herself when she had finished.

Fourteen

M organ went sprawling onto the frozen ground. She lay still for a moment, trying to assess potential damage. She hadn't broken anything and it was dark enough that probably no one had seen her. Well, except Miach, who was presently turning her over and leaning over her with a hand on either side of her.

"Are you hurt?" he asked, panting.

She shook her head. "I need to work on my landings."

He looked down at her with a wildness in his eyes she'd never seen before yet understood perfectly. There was something about becoming something else, something wild and untameable, even if it was just for a few hours, that left something behind, something that hadn't been there before.

She watched him heave himself up to his feet, then looked up at the sky above her. If someone had told her six months ago that she would blurt out a spell of shapechanging and fling herself up into the air, she would have plunged a knife into his chest without a second thought.

Yet she'd shapechanged without hesitation. She'd propelled herself to impossible heights, then turned and fallen to the earth like an arrow shot from a bow. She'd cried out in a harsh dragon's voice, rolled in the air, and laughed for the sheer joy of it.

And all that time Miach had been there at the tip of her

wing, laughing with her, chasing her, goading her, challenging her to fly ever faster and higher.

If she hadn't loved him before, she would have then.

"Morgan?"

She reached up for the hands he held down to her. She looked at him for a moment once she'd gotten her feet under her, then flung her arms around his neck and hugged him fiercely.

"Thank you," she whispered, blinking hard to stop her tears. "Thank you so much."

"Nay," he said against her ear, "thank you. That was . . ."

"What?"

He laughed a little uneasily. "It was something that tempts me to turn around and do it again."

Unfortunately, she suspected she understood that, as well. She held on to him until she felt like she could stand with any success. The dragon fierceness faded far faster than she had thought it would, leaving her substantially more bereft than she'd ever felt leaving Weger's magical tower. She shivered as she pulled away.

"I'm cold."

"It will pass."

Well, he would certainly know. "I feel as if I've lost a little of myself," she said weakly.

"You left it in the sky," he said with a smile. "Which is, I imagine, why I continue to shapechange. You'll find it again the next time we fly."

"Will there be a next time?" she asked unwillingly.

"You tell me."

She opened her mouth to tell him nay, then realized that she wasn't at all sure she wouldn't do it again. She pursed her lips. "I'm not quite sure how I feel about it."

"Don't decide now," he advised. "Sit by the fire, sip sweet wine, and settle back into yourself. It may take an hour or so before the change leaves you completely."

She nodded, then sighed gratefully as he took off his cloak and wrapped it around her. She felt his hands tremble just the slightest bit as he fastened the clasp at her throat and understood that; she was still not at all steady on her feet. She caught his hands before he drew back, held them between her own, then brought his palms to rest against her cheeks. When she thought she could speak without weeping, she looked at him.

"Thank you for pulling me back out of that," she said finally. "I almost lost myself."

He looked at her solemnly. "I will never let you lose yourself, Morgan. No matter what shape you take, I will always pull you out of it."

"Have you never been tempted to remain a dragon?" she asked.

"Every time I fly," he said with a smile. He took her hand. "Let's go find that fire. It will help with the chill."

She took a deep breath, then nodded. She walked with him back through the inner wall gate. She stumbled several times, though she supposed that came from more than just shapechanging. The truths that she'd heard came back to her in a rush, leaving her far colder than any shapechanging perhaps could have. She shivered all the way to Nicholas's door.

She caught Miach's hand before he managed to get it anywhere near that wood.

"And what do you think of all this?" she asked, desperate to avoid going inside. "Does it bother you?"

He looked at her in surprise. "That you are Mhorghain of Ceangail?"

She nodded.

He put his hands on her shoulders and turned her to him. "I loved you when I believed you were Morgan the mercenary. I loved you when I knew you had Weger's mark on your brow. I love you still, knowing that you're Gair of Ceangail's daughter."

She swallowed. "How can you? Knowing what he did—"

"Because you are not your father any more than I am my brother."

She almost smiled. "In your case, I suppose that's true."

"It's true in your case as well." He leaned against the door and looked down at her. "Morgan, you are Gair's daughter, but you are also Sarait's. Your mother's parents are King Sìle and Queen Brèagha. Your father's parents are Eulasaid of Camanaë and Sgath of Ainneamh, powerful and majestic souls in their own right. I would trust any of them with my life."

"Would you?" she asked, surprised.

"Without hesitation."

"But not Gair."

Miach sighed deeply. "Gair is a mystery I don't know that we'll ever understand completely. I'm not sure why Sarait wed with him, but I don't think he was always as he became. Nicholas might answer that well enough to suit us both. He and Gair were friends for centuries before you were born."

She felt a little light-headed. "I think I need to sit. I'm not sure what disturbs me more: that I'm someone I don't know, or that I shapechanged."

He smiled deeply. "You took to the latter amazingly well. Did you like it?"

"Unfortunately," she said uneasily. "Almost as much as riding. But Weger would . . . well, perhaps Weger wouldn't be surprised."

"I doubt Weger would be surprised by anything," Miach said with a snort, "having likely done all of it himself. Perhaps when we finish our adventures, we'll make a visit to Gobhann. You can tell him all the appalling shapes you've taken and see if he can match them. He won't love you any less for any of it. I know I don't."

Morgan looked up at him. "You use that word easily."

"What word?"

"Love."

"Oddly enough," he said, "I've never used it before. Let's go in."

Morgan looked at him quickly, but he only winked at her. She frowned. "Are you trying to distract me from all these tidings?"

He shook his head. "I'm distracting myself."

"From what?"

"Thoughts of kissing you."

She blinked in surprise. "In truth?"

"Of course, in truth," he said with an exasperated laugh.

"Oh," she said in a very small voice. "I wasn't sure—"

"Go inside, gel," he said, turning her around to face the door, "lest I find myself distracted from my distractions."

She put her hand on the latch. "Miach?"

"Aye?"

She took a deep breath. "I'm not good at this." She paused. "This business of . . . affection."

"I never said you had to love me in return," he said softly. "I just wanted you to let me love you. And before we examine that too closely, let's go in. Just don't look at Nicholas in that way you have that screams there's a mage in the room who needs to have a sword sticking out of his chest. You'll frighten the lads."

"All right," she said, taking a shaky breath. "I'll try."

He opened the door and waited for her to go in. She tucked herself behind him instead and pushed him on ahead. She looked at the floor as Miach led them over to their accustomed places before the fire. She sat down on a chair, then changed her mind. She pulled a stool up in front of Miach's chair and sat down with her back pressed so tightly against his knees, she was certain his feet would fall asleep. She didn't care. She would have sat in his lap if she hadn't been certain she would have shocked all the lads there. She felt him lean forward and put his arms around her shoulders.

"Morgan," Miach whispered against her ear, "it's just Nicholas. Nothing has changed."

"Except the fact that he's a bloody mage," she muttered grimly. "Damn me, but there's no escaping the lot of you."

"Do you want to escape?"

She turned and looked up at him. She was horrified to find that her teeth were chattering and she was very cold. "I'm not sure."

He turned her bodily toward the fire, then rested his elbows on his knees and looked at her. "Hold on to me when you need to. I'll keep you together."

"When will things stop being something other than what I thought they were?"

"Death is the final surprise, I suppose," he said wryly, "so perhaps you'd best steel yourself for a lifetime of this."

She nodded. She looked into the fire for quite some time, taking an unwholesome amount of comfort at having Miach nearby. Unfortunately, it didn't keep her mind from going in circles she couldn't seem to stop.

"If he was the king of Diarmailt," she whispered slowly, "then why isn't he that any longer?"

"When Lismòrian and his sons were slain, he was so grieved that he handed his crown to his nephew and walked out of his city alone, never to be heard from again. That was two hundred years ago."

"Good heavens," she said in surprise. "How old *is* he?"

"I didn't ask," he admitted. "Substantially older than Weger, I imagine. All I do know is that his power was very great and that his love for his lady wife was fodder for bards for centuries."

She looked over her shoulder at Nicholas, telling some tale she knew she would recognize if she had the wherewithal to listen, and wondered how she could have passed so much time with him and not realized what he was. Then again, she'd traveled with Miach for a month and been just as oblivious then. Perhaps she was destined to underestimate the souls around her.

She turned back to Miach. "Did he know who killed his family? He told me that they had been slain, but he never talked about those responsible."

Miach nodded, but quite suddenly he wouldn't meet her eyes. "Aye, he knows. It took quite a while before the truth came out, but he knows."

"Do you know who it was?"

He looked down. "Please don't ask me this question now, Morgan," he said quietly.

"Why n—"

She found that she couldn't finish. She watched the question hang in the air in front of her, unasked, and felt a cold chill descend on her.

It couldn't be.

"Morgan—"

She found that her breath was coming in little gasps. "It can't be—"

Miach only looked at her silently.

She thought she might begin to scream soon. She found herself suddenly hauled up onto Miach's lap. She clapped her hand over her mouth and turned to press her face against his neck. He held her tightly, almost too tightly, as her breath came in gasps. All she could hear, repeating in her head in a howling rush, was what Miach hadn't said.

Gair had killed Nicholas's family.

She put her other arm around Miach's neck and held on,

just to keep herself from splintering into as many pieces as had the Sword of Angesand.

She had no idea how long she sat there until she was able to begin to claw her way out of the swirling hell she'd fallen into without warning, but she began to manage it. The pit was still there, under her feet, but she finally backed away from it far enough to be able to catch her breath. Miach's arms around her relaxed. In time, she realized that he was running his hand over her hair, working it free of her braid. His fingers caught in the tangles, but she didn't complain. The occasional twinge was good. It made her feel as if she had some connection to the world around her.

She finally pulled back far enough to meet his very red eyes. "It was Gair."

Miach closed his eyes briefly. "Aye."

"And yet Nicholas allows me in his hall—"

"You are not Gair," Miach whispered sharply. "Do not, and I mean *do not*, take on your father's sins, Morgan. That is a path that leads to nothing but darkness and evil. And don't cheapen Nicholas's affection for you by thinking he considers you in the least bit responsible. It happened decades before you were born."

She took a deep breath and let it out slowly. "You're right."

"In this, at least, I am." He looked at her seriously. "You became for Nicholas what Gair took away from him: a child to love."

"Do you think so?" she whispered.

"I do." He smiled, then very deliberately leaned forward and kissed the end of her nose.

"You're trying to distract me."

"Is it working?"

She couldn't smile. "Nay."

He pulled her close again. "The last lad is leaving, love. What can I do?"

"Stay with me."

"You know I will."

She pulled back. "Nicholas brought me here after I fell, didn't he?"

"Aye. He was, if I might say it, a most impressive dragon. He fair blinded me with all the gems encrusting his breast."

She wanted to smile, but she couldn't. She heard the door close. She waited until she heard Nicholas settle into his chair before she forced herself to her feet. She waited until Miach had risen as well, then took his hand and a deep breath at the same time.

Her feet were suddenly leaden and it took most of her strength just to force herself to walk across the chamber. She clutched Miach's fingers, then came to an ungainly stop in front of Nicholas.

He didn't look any different. She studied his face, his bright blue eyes, his crown of white hair, and wondered how in the world she ever would have guessed he was who Miach said he was. She tried to swallow, but it didn't help her suddenly parched throat. She felt Miach's other hand come to unobtrusively join the other that she held. His hands were warm, comfortable, *known*.

She took a deep breath. "Are you—" she said, her voice breaking. She didn't bother to wipe away the tears that were streaming down her face. "Are you Nicholas of Diarmailt?"

Nicholas only looked up at her gravely. "Aye, Morgan, I am."

"And who am I?" she managed.

"Mhorghain of Ceangail," he said quietly.

A sob escaped her before she could stop it. It shouldn't have. After all, she'd already heard that from Miach. But somehow there was something final about hearing the same from the man sitting in front of her, the man who had taken her in as a girl and sent her off to Gobhann with tears in his eyes, that made it seem real past any means of denying it.

She felt her way down onto the sofa, then buried her face in her hands and wept. She had assumed she had cried out all her tears, but there was another batch right there for her use.

She wept for the girl who'd been orphaned at six, for her mother who was dead, for the brothers she hadn't had protecting her. She wept for all the nights of bitter chill she'd passed in Weger's tower, trying to dull the pain of no family to call her own.

She wept for Nicholas's kindnesses to her that she'd never been able to accept. She even wept a bit for Miach, who loved her when she did not deserve it and apparently had an inexhaustible supply of patience. She supposed it would serve him well and keep him warm until she had the courage to give him the words he deserved in return.

When she finally came back to herself, she found Nicholas's hand on her head and heard him making soothing noises. Miach's hand was on her back and his foot was resting securely against hers. She dragged her sleeve across her face, then felt a cloth be pressed into her hands. She worked a bit on her face, blew her nose, then took several deep, bracing breaths. She shot Miach a grateful smile, then turned and mustered up a glare for Nicholas.

"You have quite a bit of explaining to do, old man."

"Good heavens, Morgan," Miach said, with an uncomfortable laugh. "Show some respect."

Nicholas only smiled, looking equal parts pleased and relieved. "Nay, this tells me that she has survived the tidings. And as for why I didn't tell you sooner, Morgan, my dear, there are several reasons. Your magic was dormant and I didn't want it awakened until I knew you would have the strength to manage it. And given your legendary distaste for mages, let me also say that if I'd ever told you who *I* was, you would have locked yourself inside Weger's hall and I never would have seen you again."

"As if Weger can even be trusted now," Morgan said darkly. She took a deep breath, then shook her head. "I don't doubt that you are who you say you are, or Miach, or Weger." She looked down at her hands. "I can hardly believe it of myself, though," she said quietly. "It is difficult to find that what I thought was my life has been nothing but a sham."

"Not a sham," Nicholas said gravely. "A preparation." He considered her for a moment. "Would you care for proof?"

She looked up. "What sort?"

Nicholas looked at her for several minutes in silence, then he opened a box on the table at his right and drew out something.

Morgan had no idea what happened to her. One minute she was sitting comfortably on the sofa and the next she was standing in the corner of Nicholas's solar with Miach's arms around her. He held her to him, burying her screams against his shoulder.

In time, she realized that he was singing to her. She had no idea what the words were, but she recognized the tune. Then she realized that she understood the words as well. She stood there for what seemed like hours, listening to him sing against her ear, hearing his voice echoing in his chest, feeling his warmth sink into her darkness.

When she thought she wouldn't shatter, she pulled back and looked up at him.

"What is that song?" she whispered.

"A lullaby of Camanaë," he said, his eyes full of tears. "My mother sang it to me when I would have nightmares as a child."

"Nightmares?" she asked. "What sort?"

"Oh, just your garden variety," he said with half a smile. "Lothar. Dark magic. Creatures from hell chasing me through the passageways of Tor Neroche."

She smiled in spite of herself. "Is that so?"

"It is," he said, smoothing her hair back from her face. "Once my mother was gone, I sang that song quite often to myself."

Morgan closed her eyes briefly. "I don't know how you survived that."

"The same way you'll survive this. You'll run, you'll fly, and you'll weep. And if you want me to, I'll do all three with you."

She nodded, but found she couldn't release him. She was afraid if she did, she would come undone again. It was a truly alarming turn of events. She was a hardened, seasoned mercenary with scores of sieges and battles under her belt, yet all she seemed to be able to do of late was weep and cling to a man as if she couldn't stand up on her own.

Though she had to concede that she had been in truly unprecedented circumstances, so perhaps she could be forgiven that weakness.

"Morgan?"

She shivered. "Aye?"

"Come and sit. Nicholas has put away the ring."

It took quite a while longer, but she finally managed to nod. She let Miach lead her back over to the sofa. She sat down nearest Nicholas and felt Miach settle in next to her. She looked at Nicholas.

"I'm sorry."

Nicholas looked at her gravely. "Nay, my dear, 'tis I who should apologize. I should have warned you. When the mercenaries left you here, they left me the ring as well, but warned me not to show it to you." He paused. "They said it upset you too much."

Morgan took a deep breath. "I think I can bear it now," she said finally.

Nicholas hesitated, then removed the ring from the box and slowly handed it to her.

Morgan took it. It was a flat, square, onyx stone set in a silver metal she supposed was whitened gold or silver. Not silver, perhaps, for it was not tarnished. She took a deep breath. She knew the ring.

She had seen it countless times on her . . . father's hand.

She put her face in her hands and shuddered.

"Morgan?" Nicholas asked quietly.

"I'm fine," she said raggedly. She straightened and blew out what breath she'd managed to suck in. "I'm fine. I think I need to go to bed."

She saw the look Nicholas shot Miach and could imagine the look he received in return.

She handed the ring to Miach. "You keep this."

He blanched. "You want me to wear it?"

"Of course not, but someone has to keep it and it's too big for me." She paused. "Would it bother you?"

He shook his head. "I'll put it in a pocket."

"Do you have the other ring?" she asked. "The one that matches Mehar's knife? I'd like to have it."

"Why?" he asked.

"I'm not sure," she said. She was starting to shake. She wasn't at all sure she wasn't going to be ill very soon. "I think I'm starting a collection."

Miach looked rather alarmed. "I think I should keep it for you a bit longer. Why don't we go for a little walk instead? I think the fresh air might do you some—"

She jumped to her feet before he finished, gave Nicholas the same sort of unremarkable kiss on the cheek she'd given him for years, then bolted for the door. She jerked it open and ran out into the night.

She ran for quite a while, actually.

She came back to herself eventually to find she was running around the perimeter of the outer courtyard, just as she'd done countless times in her youth. Back then she'd been running toward her future.

Now she was running from her past.

She realized, after another long stretch of simply sprinting along the wall in the dark, that she wasn't alone. Miach kept pace with her, just as he had all the times she'd tried to outrun her dreams whilst she'd been traveling north in the fall. He didn't complain, didn't ask her to stop, didn't tell her that she was mad. He just ran with her.

And he held her hair when she finally had to stop, turn, and throw up.

When she'd stopped sobbing and heaving, he put a silver cup in her hand. She rinsed her mouth out with what it contained, spat it out, then looked at the cup he'd given her.

"Where did this come from?" she asked.

"I made it for you just now."

She handed the goblet back to him and dragged her sleeve across her face. "You're handy," she said raggedly.

"Hmmm," was all he said.

She looked at him with the moonlight falling down on him and did what she'd been doing all day. She flung herself at him.

He caught her and wrapped his arms around her. The only difference was she had no more tears to shed. She simply stood there, breathing in and out, and forcing her mind to be still.

"I can bear no more today," she said finally. She looked up at him wearily. "Spell me to sleep?"

"I don't think I'll need to," he said. "You're exhausted. Come sit with me whilst I work, then we'll pretend we're on the road to Neroche and make camp in front of Nicholas's fire. I never finished the enormously entertaining tale of Tharra of Fearann Fàs. It isn't to be missed."

"I'm afraid I'll dream," she admitted.

He considered for a moment. "I don't think you will again, Morgan. Not since you know the truth. But you might freeze, so why don't you come inside with me."

"I may throw up again."

"You won't."

She frowned. "What was in the wine?"

"If you can't tell, perhaps 'tis better for you not to know," he said with a smile. "For all you know, it might even help you sleep."

She didn't think so, but then again, it was Miach making the brew. She watched him toss the cup into thin air and make it disappear. She realized, at that point, that she was no longer startled by anything he did.

And that was possibly the most startling thing of all.

"Oh, nay," he said, grabbing her hand. "Stop thinking, Morgan. It has been an extraordinarily difficult day. I beg you not to add anything more to it."

She frowned at him. "What are you talking about?"

"You looked like you wanted to stab me," he said with a bit of a laugh. "I wasn't sure I'd rid you of all your blades."

"I wasn't thinking about stabbing you. I was just surprised at how accustomed to your magic I've become—and how appallingly wasteful you are. I could have had wine all evening in that cup."

He smiled and pulled her along with him toward the inner gates. "I'll fashion you another later, if you like. Let's go get warm."

She nodded and continued on with him. She found the solar empty when Miach let them in the door and wasn't sure if she was grateful or disappointed. Nicholas was no doubt giving her time to think. She wandered about the chamber as Miach pulled chairs for them in front of the fire, then stopped in front of Nicholas's desk.

Mehar's knife was there and under it was a brief note.

Morgan, you'll need this.

She looked at it for several minutes, then took it and put it in the corner with her sword. She turned and found Miach standing with his hand on the mantel, staring down into the fire.

She crossed the chamber to stand next to him. "Miach?"

He looked at her and blinked. "I'm fine."

"I didn't ask that. What is it?"

He considered for quite some time before he finally sighed and dragged his hand through his hair. "I'm not certain. Something is off. Not in the spells of defense along Neroche's border.

Something else. Or perhaps I'm merely thinking too much." He looked at her. "We need to go."

"I'll get my cloak—"

He caught her by the arm before she pulled away. "Nay, gel, not tonight," he said. "Tomorrow is soon enough. Perhaps after sunset, when we can travel under cover of darkness."

She took a deep breath. "As you will, Miach. If you're certain you want me to come—"

"Well, of course I want you to come," he said, looking surprised. "How will I woo you if you're not with me? Or best you in cards? Or thrash you in the lists—"

"Enough," she said with a scowl. "I understand."

He smiled, embraced her briefly, then allowed her to escape his arms. She stepped away and had to take several deep breaths. It was one thing to talk about going with him all over the Nine Kingdoms; it was another thing entirely to actually do it.

Especially now that she knew things about herself she couldn't deny.

She suddenly didn't want to think about what anyone would say about that, or how she would now have to introduce herself, or in which ways her life had just changed irrevocably in the past twelve hours.

"Morgan?"

She backed him up to his chair, put her hand in the middle of his chest, and shoved. "Give me your boots."

He looked up at her in astonishment. "My what?"

"Boots. Blades. I'll see to them."

He looked at her, openmouthed, then pulled a knife from one of his boots. He handed it to her, then took off his boots and set them by the chair.

Morgan pulled the knife free of the sheath and looked at it, then at Miach. "Beautiful but unmagical," she noted approvingly. "Did Weger give it to you?"

"Aye. 'Tis covered with runes of the house of Neroche. It will send Adhémar into a rage."

"Making it all the more desirable. Get to work, lad. I'm anxious for that tale you promised me."

He caught her hand before she could pick up his boots. "Don't bolt on me, Morgan."

She took a deep breath, then shook her head. "I won't."

He looked at her for another long moment, then nodded. He sat back in his chair and closed his eyes.

She waited until she could see that he was deeply involved in his spells before she took off her own boots, gathered all their blades together and laid them out on the carpet, then fetched gear from a trunk near the door for polishing and sharpening.

She had to keep busy. It made her feel like herself.

She was very afraid that if she stopped, she would find herself falling deeply into a past that would drag her into a darkness she hadn't asked for and didn't want. At least Miach wanted to leave on the morrow. Surely there would be much to do on that journey, many ways to keep herself occupied, and many more opportunities to simply ignore what she'd learned that day. She would be well if she could simply survive the night.

She sat down on the floor in front of the fire and set to work on Miach's boots.

Fifteen

Miach walked through the passageways of Lismòr, on the hunt for a particular gel that he'd somehow lost during the night. That didn't surprise him. Morgan had still been sharpening her sword when he'd finished with his work. He'd understood it; keeping busy kept the demons at bay. But sleep was also a necessity after a certain point, so he'd begged her to lie down next to him and at least try to sleep a little. She had, but reluctantly. He'd begun the tale of Tharra of Fearann Fàs, but had apparently fallen asleep himself before he'd finished it. He had woken to find his blades placed next to him and Morgan gone. He could still sense her within Lismòr's walls, though, so he knew she'd kept her promise.

He wondered how much it had cost her.

Which he would go find out once he'd made another turn about the courtyard and rid himself of his own unease. He blew out his breath. If the assault on his spells in the fall had been a light rain, what was happening presently was a downpour. Only half of what he'd repaired the previous night had still been sound last night.

And still there was something that was covering the kingdom, something that was subtle, but so insidiously evil that even he had to shudder a bit when he faced it.

He dragged his hand through his hair. They would go that

night and see what he could discover. It bothered him not to
have any sense of the creatures that seemed to stalk Morgan,
but perhaps he could do so if he tried a bit harder. It was—or
had been—the burden of Adhémar's kingship to sense fully
what went on in the realm, though his brother had never been
very good at it. Miach had always had a very clear awareness
of his spells and what might have been attacking them, but the
other . . . nay, he hadn't had that gift.

Unless it was used to sense Morgan.

Perhaps he would be wise to stretch himself and see if he
couldn't acquire an impression of what hunted them. He certainly couldn't go all over the realm himself and kill things that
he couldn't sense until they were upon him.

He continued to walk until he was standing in front of the
doorway of the library. He opened the door, then looked inside.

Morgan was there, as he had suspected. She was sitting
at one of the long tables with books spread out in front of
her. Her sword was on that table and she was fingering the
hilt of Mehar's dagger. At least she was holding it without
shuddering—something she wouldn't have done in the fall.
That boded well.

She looked up at the sound of the door shutting behind him.

And she smiled.

It winded him. He managed a polite nod to Master Dominicus, then walked over to sit on the corner of her table.

"Well, don't you look bright-eyed this morning," he said.
"Been at it long?"

"Long enough to irritate Master Dominicus."

Miach smiled. "Did you make off with a valuable tome or
two at some point in the past?"

She shook her head and caressed the hilt of Mehar's knife
lovingly. "He doesn't trust soldiers."

"He would trust us even less if he knew what we were in
addition to that."

She went still.

Ah, so that was it.

Miach swung his leg back and forth idly and suspected that
perhaps yesterday had been too much after all.

Morgan folded her hands on the table, looked at them for

quite a bit longer, then finally sighed and looked up. "I don't mean to be ungrateful . . ."

"Ungrateful?" he echoed, confused. "About what?"

"About all the time you and Nicholas both spent telling me about . . . um . . ."

"The past?" he offered.

She nodded. "Aye. And I'm grateful to you for all the spells you taught me. But . . ." She met his eyes, but seemed unable to speak further.

"But you're not ready to be Mhorghain of Ceangail?" he asked softly.

Her eyes filled with tears. "I'm sorry."

He couldn't blame her. And the last thing he was going to do was force her to accept something she wasn't ready to accept.

He'd learned that lesson already.

He tilted his head to look at her thoughtfully. "Who is it you want to be today? Just Morgan of Melksham?"

"Would you mind?"

"Do you care if I do?"

She was clasping her hands together so tightly, her knuckles had turned white. "I might."

He reached out and put his hand over hers. "You're growing soft, woman. If I'd asked you that question a month ago, you would have stuck me as repayment for the vexation."

She linked her fingers with his. "I don't recognize myself anymore."

He tapped her shin gently with his boot. "I do. You look like Morgan to me and considering that I'm rather fond of her, perhaps you should continue on with her awhile longer. Now, what have you got there in that book?" he asked, pretending great interest in what she was reading.

"Elves," Morgan said glumly, pulling one of her hands away so she could flip the page. "I had no idea there were so many of them or that they had so many adventures." She looked down at the book unhappily. "Weger was right: I am very ignorant of events of the world. I think I could read for months and never know it all."

"No one knows it all," he said. "We'll just muddle through as best we can."

She nodded, but she looked unconvinced. She turned the pages of the very thick book for a moment or two more, then glanced up at him. "Are you ready to go?"

"We'll wait until sunset," he said. "But until then, why don't you put away your books and come train with me? You'll feel more yourself once you've humiliated me in the lists."

"In truth?" she asked, looking as if he'd offered her the crown of Neroche along with an endless supply of extremely skilled guardsmen to go with it.

Well, perhaps not the crown. But the other, aye, that was conceivable.

"I've missed training from dawn to midnight," he said dryly.

"So have I," she said happily, hopping up out of her chair. She stacked the books quickly, shot Master Dominicus a glare, then picked up her sword and smiled. "Let's be about it."

He had to laugh. "After you, my lady."

She didn't even protest the term. She only put on her cloak and walked from the library with a spring in her step that had been missing for quite some time. "You know, I think you'll prove to be a rather formidable opponent." She smiled at him over her shoulder. "I appreciate the distraction."

He was more grateful for it than she, no doubt. He wasn't sure why he thought spending a pair of hours in the lists with her was going to be of any help, but he was nothing if not courageous and he needed a few minutes to think on something besides the affairs of the realm.

He stopped at the edge of Nicholas's outer gardens, tossed his cloak onto a handy bench with hers, then followed her out into the middle of the garden.

"I wonder if this might count as a bit of wooing?" he mused.

"It depends on how well you show, I imagine," she said, loftily.

"Then 'tis a fine line I walk," he said. "If I best you, you'll not want any of my attentions; if I don't best you, you'll not want any of my attentions."

She shrugged. "If you bested me, which you most certainly will never do, I might be amenable to quite a few things. Unfortunately, I'm feeling much better today, so I don't think it will go very well for you."

"Your arrogance, woman, is breathtaking."

"So is my swordplay."

He laughed, "I can hardly wait to see it."

Morgan paused and frowned. "Do you have a ribbon?"

"What color?"

She thought for a moment. "Black," she said finally. "In honor of you."

He produced one from out of the air. She walked over to him and turned around.

"Braid my hair?"

"Unfair," he said, stabbing his sword into the ground. "You're trying to distract me with something I enjoy so I'll be easier on you."

She looked over her shoulder at him. "Do you honestly think I need to resort to that?"

He put his hand on the top of her head and turned her face forward. "I'm teasing you."

"I know."

He braided her hair deftly, tied it at the bottom with his silk ribbon, then turned her around and put his hands on her shoulders.

"And when I best you," he said, fighting his smile, "what prize will I have? Shall you dance with me?"

She blanched. "Dance?"

"Aye. Or perhaps another of any number of other horrifying courtly activities?"

"Do you know any other horrifying courtly activities?" she asked.

He pursed his lips. "Surprisingly enough, I just might. Now, are you woman enough to agree to that, or not?"

She took a deep breath. "Very well."

"And if you best me?"

"I'll think on it." She took several paces backward, unbuckled her swordbelt, then drew her sword and tossed the scabbard aside. "Let's begin."

He smiled at the first crossing of their blades. "You're feeling better."

"Decent food helps. And sleep."

"And the company?"

"Aye. I've always loved Nicholas."

He scowled. "That wasn't who I was talking about."

"I know," she said pleasantly.

She attacked him unmercifully, forcing him back. Then before he could stop her, she had captured his sword between her blade and Mehar's knife.

"I'm happy you're here," she said with a hesitant smile.

It took him a moment or two to recover from that. "You're using your womanly wiles," he protested. "Unfair."

She gave him a mighty shove that sent him stumbling backward. He barely had time to gather his wits about him before she was following that up with yet another ruthless attack.

"Ignore them," she advised.

"That's difficult."

"Be a man."

"That's part of the problem."

She laughed, which undid him almost as much as her admittedly spectacular swordplay. He was forced to work very hard to keep her from completely thrashing him. He had to admit that he was better than he had been and Morgan was not quite where she had been. He supposed that she would recover completely at some point and then he truly would be digging deep for skill that he might not have.

It was a very long morning.

It was well past noon before he finally held up his hand and called peace.

"Do you yield?" she demanded.

"Completely."

"Done, then," she said.

He looked at her and found himself somewhat gratified to find she was breathing as rapidly as he was. He resheathed his sword and walked over to take hers.

"How are you?"

"Wonderful," she said, dragging her sleeve across her forehead. "Thank you for a decent bit of sport. I didn't even have to recite Weger's strictures to keep myself awake."

"I didn't learn any of those," he said with a frown.

"He probably thought you had enough things rattling about in your poor head without his adding to the chaos," she said, sliding Mehar's knife into her boot. "Besides, most of them have to do with spotting mages at great distances so you can avoid them. The rest have to do with how to kill them quickly lest you find yourself unhappily trapped with them."

He smiled wryly. "I'd like to accuse you of exaggerating, but I'm quite sure you aren't."

"'Tis Weger at the helm, after all," she agreed. "I suppose there might be a handful about swordplay tucked in amongst the others."

"I'll ask him to give those to me another time," Miach said. "It likely won't take me very long to learn them."

"Likely not," she said. "What now, my lord?"

"I'll see you fed," Miach said, "then I think it would serve you to have another nap in Nicholas's solar. I'll hold your feet, if you like."

She smiled wearily. "I'll never refuse that offer. I'd also have a bit more of that brew you made me last night. I didn't dream of anything. What was in it?"

He reached out to tug on her braid. "Love and a bit of lavender. A very potent combination."

She looked at him in surprise. "You're daft."

He laughed and took her hand. "Besotted, more like. Now, let's be off to the buttery before you think on that overmuch."

Twenty minutes later he was sitting next to her at a long, rough table, tucking into a lovely bit of stew. He ate heartily, wondering in the back of his mind when they might eat so well again.

He realized, after a time, that Morgan was watching him instead of eating. He turned and smiled at her.

"What is it?"

She leaned her cheek on her fist and studied him. "I was just looking at you."

"Should I be nervous?"

"Nay, there's nothing more to it than that. I've always liked to look at you, truth be told. Even when I thought I didn't like you, I liked to look at you."

"Thank you," he said, finding to his surprise that he was starting to blush. "Not many lassies bother themselves to look at me."

"Why not?" she asked.

"Because I generally encounter women thanks to their fathers' swords in their backs. I daresay what they're looking for is the nearest means of escape." He shrugged. "Most of them don't care for my magic."

"Then it's lucky for me I don't mind it, isn't it?"

He sat back with a smile. "Why, Morgan, I think you might have a few fond feelings for me."

"'Tis possible, but if I were to tell you of them, you'd blush again and where would you be?" She pushed away her bowl. "Let's go. And I'd rather walk than nap, if it's all the same to you."

"As you will," he said. He rose and followed her from the buttery. He watched her out of the corner of his eye and wondered what she was thinking. She seemed very pensive and stopped now and again to look at this building or that passageway, as if she thought she might never see them again. He found her hand and laced his fingers with hers.

"We will come back," he said quietly.

She looked up at him quickly. "You are reading my thoughts, aren't you?"

He shook his head. "Just watching you, as usual."

She walked in silence with him until they reached the outer gates. She nodded to the gatekeeper, then walked with him across the bridge that spanned what looked remarkably like a dry moat. Miach would have walked on, but Morgan stopped him with her hand on his arm.

"I can't see anything in front of me," she said finally. "It is all darkness. Well, except for one thing."

"What?"

She looked up at him. "You."

He pulled her into his arms so quickly, he suspected he'd pulled her off her feet. He hugged her tightly, then set her back down.

"All right," he said briskly, "now *I'm* the one who needs to walk."

"Will it count as wooing?" she asked slowly.

"Are you wooing *me* now?" he asked in surprise.

"I bested you so thoroughly in the lists this morning, I thought it might make you feel better."

He laughed and put his arm around her shoulders. "I think you might be right."

She stopped him. "Do you . . ." she began, then she had to pause. "Do you truly think we'll see it again? Lismòr?"

He wanted to assure her that she didn't need to worry, that they would return, but he couldn't. There were times he left Tor Neroche and wondered if it might be the last time he would see it. He wasn't a grim sort of lad by nature, but the task before him was sobering. Morgan was right to worry.

But as they stood there, he couldn't help but think things would turn out right in the end. Perhaps spring would come in spite of spells and evil and everything that was amiss in the realm. At least on Melksham, things were as they always were. The breeze was light and the smell of the sea something he realized he'd truly enjoyed at Gobhann, in spite of all the work.

"I think we will," he said quietly. He took a deep breath, watched her do the same, then propelled her forward. "We'll return. But let's think on something else for the moment. I'm interested in hearing more about these wooing ideas—"

"Miach!"

He felt Morgan spin him around.

"Draw your sword, you fool!"

He found that her suggestion was unnecessary. Perhaps he should have been impressed that Weger's training had become such a part of him that he was fighting before he was fully conscious of doing so, but he was too unsettled by what he was seeing to spare that any thought.

There were a dozen of them, creatures from nightmares, creatures of the sort he and Morgan had met before. He half wondered if they had simply risen up from the ground. 'Twas a certainty that he hadn't seen them approaching. Then again, he hadn't been watching for them. He had no idea how they would manage to see to them all.

Then he realized that fighting wasn't all he had to worry about.

Morgan was weaving a spell of death—over them all.

"Morgan, stop!" he shouted.

"I can do this—"

He began to undo her words as quickly as she spoke them, pushing himself to keep up with what she was weaving and avoid losing his head at the same time.

He yanked a particularly loathsome thread from her spell and heard her curse him.

"Morgan, you're casting the spell over *all* of us!" he exclaimed as he bumped into her back. "Stop it!"

"I know what I'm doing—"

"You don't," he said, stabbing a troll through the heart. "Just fight and stop the magic!"

"But there are too many of them," she said, saving him from having his head cleaved in twain. "We have to do something."

"I'll see to it."

She stepped aside as he skewered a particularly misshapen creature through the belly. "Then be about it quickly," she suggested.

He had to agree. He was going to have to do something—and soon—or they wouldn't last the day. He fought ferociously and heard Morgan behind him doing the same, but the tide was still coming in swiftly. He took a deep breath and prepared to kill the rest of the beasts with magic. Or he would have if he hadn't been interrupted by a savage roar sounding directly above him.

He jerked Morgan down to crouch next to him and scarcely managed to pull a spell of protection up over them before a glittering dragon swept down from the sky. The dragon covered the field with a fire so hot, Miach began to sweat.

The subsequent screams of their enemies were hard to listen to, and he wasn't unused to the noises of battle.

Soon there wasn't anything left of the trolls but charred remains.

Miach removed his spell, then pushed himself to his feet, pulling Morgan up with him. He glanced heavenward to see the dragon continuing to circle; he would address the identity of that one later. For now, he would see that Morgan didn't fall apart. He cleaned off his sword, resheathed it, then watched Morgan do the same. She turned to him, her eyes huge in her face.

"I didn't think about that spell," she said with a violent shudder. "I wish I'd never heard a word of Olc. It comes far too easily to hand."

He reached out and pulled her into his arms. She was trembling badly. "Unfortunately, my love, the most evil magic is ofttimes the easiest to use." He paused for several moments, debating whether or not to say anything else. He could see, though, that he had no choice. "Morgan," he said quietly, "either you have to stop using your magic entirely, or you have to know what you're doing. If you're going to be Morgan, then you must ignore that other part of yourself. But if you choose to be Mhorghain, then you have no choice but to learn to use your birthright. There may come a time when I cannot undo what you've done."

She looked at him in surprise. "In truth?"

He hesitated, then shrugged. "You do not realize it, perhaps, but your power is immense."

She sighed deeply and rested her forehead against his shoulder. "I should have listened to you."

"Repeat that to yourself several times a day," he said with a smile. "I'm sure it will serve you well."

She pulled back and met his eyes. "I'm too unsettled to give you the response that deserves."

"I know," he said gravely. He looked over her head, then put his hands on her shoulders and turned her around. "There's a distraction for you. Look at that shameless dragon making a final circle. Note the excessive and unnecessary amount of gems on his breast. I imagine his crown was just as overdone. Shocking, isn't it?"

"I fear to say aye, lest something else surprise me," she managed. She paused. "I think I'm less shocked than simply *afraid*. I didn't expect any of this when I first put my hand to Mehar's knife."

"I imagine you didn't," he agreed. "Fear isn't a bad thing, though. It keeps you from doing something you shouldn't," he said as he watched the dragon make lazy, swooping circles in the sky. "It takes courage to learn all the things you *could* do. Credit yourself for that, at least. And there are spells of defense in the other languages of magic. I can teach you those if you like."

"What did you use on those creatures near Chagailt?"

"Wexham," he said. "'Tis the magic that the rulers of Neroche have generally used in their wars. It was a quick and brutal spell, but not evil."

"Is there a difference when it comes to death?" she asked.

"Perhaps not so much for the slain, but there is a great deal of difference for the mage."

She sighed. "I'm surprised you're so cheerful when this is what you face each day."

"Good and evil, my love. Life would be dreary without it."

She put her hands over his, but said nothing.

Miach turned his attention to the dragon who had apparently decided enough was enough. He landed with a flourish some fifty paces away, dazzling them with his treasures. The next moment, the dragon was gone and Nicholas was walking toward them rubbing his hands together.

"That was interesting," he said, looking as if it hadn't displeased him to be useful. "I don't have much call for scorching trolls these days, but I thought you needed an extra pair of hands. Or talons, as it were." He looked about him and his expression grew more serious. "I think we saw to them all, but just in case I suggest a retreat inside the gates." He snapped his fingers and all the corpses were gone. "Wine, children?"

Miach looked at Morgan, then at Nicholas. "Briefly."

Nicholas nodded, then led them back through the gates and to his solar. Miach followed Morgan inside, then watched her as she propped her sword up in the corner as she always did. He noticed, though, that she hesitated as she did it, as if she had some especial thought attached. He supposed he knew what she was thinking, so he made no note of it. He took a seat next to her in front of Nicholas's fire.

Nicholas brought a bottle and three goblets, then made quick work of pouring wine all around.

"So," he said, handing Miach and Morgan their glasses, "what was that, do you think?"

"What's been hunting us all along," Miach said. *Or hunting Morgan, rather,* he thought, but he didn't say as much. He looked at Nicholas and suspected that the old man was thinking the same thing.

"Do you sense any more of them?" Nicholas asked.

Miach cast about the island, but felt nothing. Then again, he hadn't known those were there either. "They are covered by something that eludes me," he admitted unwillingly. "I haven't yet been able to unravel their spell of concealment, though I will say I've never seen its like before. And they saw through my spell of un-noticing—which no one sees through. Well," he amended, "except Morgan."

Nicholas looked at him sharply. "That is odd, isn't it?" He looked at Morgan. "Did you know those brutes were there?"

"Me?" she asked, sounding surprised. "I have no idea. I hadn't considered that I might be able to."

"I think that the next time you encounter these creatures, children, you should both take another moment to see what spell covers them. Perhaps you'll determine why it is they are coming for you."

Miach cursed silently. "I hadn't thought about it before, but I suspect 'tis our magic that has drawn them here. I wasn't careful at Gobhann and neither of us has been so here. The shapechanging alone could have been enough to do it. And I think that before we somehow draw more of them to your home, Your Majesty, we should be on our way."

Nicholas smiled at him. "That sort of deference, lad, might have earned you a pair of saddlebags packed by my cook, but I imagine you won't be traveling on horseback, will you?"

"I think we must fly," Miach conceded, "but I can erase those tracks easily enough. No one will sense our passing, or the magic that made the shapechanging happen."

"Devious," Nicholas remarked.

"I learned the art from Lothar," Miach said dryly. "I can hide quite a few things, but I'll limit it to just our shapechanging for the moment." He looked at Morgan. "We'll make for Angesand first and beg a meal from Hearn. We'll gather tidings, then head east." He rose. "My thanks, Your Grace, for the refuge. We needed it."

Nicholas rose as well. He embraced Morgan, then put his hand on Miach's shoulder. "I would tell you to be careful, but you are that already." He smiled at them both. "I'll expect you back at some point."

Miach put on a cheerful smile, watched Morgan and Nicholas do the same thing, then thanked Nicholas again and led Morgan from the solar.

She was quiet as they walked through the maze of passageways and through the outer yard. In fact, she didn't look at him until they were standing outside Lismòr's gates.

"I would like to come back here again," she said quietly.

"I know, love."

She took a deep breath, then put her shoulders back. "What shape?"

He considered briefly. "Hawk until we reach Bere, I think, lest we draw any attention to ourselves. Then we'll change to dragons over the ocean and not worry about being conspicuous. We'll be to Hearn's by morning if we hurry, in time for breakfast and a bit of sweet water."

"I'll follow you."

Within moments, they were wheeling toward the east. He covered them as they went with a spell of un-noticing and counted on that being enough.

He didn't want to think about what might happen if it wasn't.

Sixteen

The sun had barely begun to rise when Morgan found herself once again in her own form, lying in a drift of snow. The only thing she could say for herself was that at least she was flopping onto softer landing spots. She lay there for a minute, then clambered out of the snow with a curse only to have to lean over with her hands on her knees until she caught her breath. Miach pulled her up and hugged her so tightly that she squeaked.

"Leave me my dignity, would you?" she managed.

"Impossible," he said, holding her close and smiling down at her. "I love you."

"Because I'll shapechange with you?" she asked crossly.

"Because you're fearless," he said. "And you make a very lovely dragon."

She rolled her eyes and pulled out of his arms. "Let's go find something to eat before all that dragon fierceness goes to your head and withers your wits."

"I imagine 'tis a bit late for that," he said, catching her hand. "Let's make haste and see if Hearn still has something on the fire."

She walked with him out of the woods and saw that they were farther from the castle than she'd suspected. She looked uneasily at the stretch of plain. The only good thing she could say about it was at least if there were things coming for them, they would be able to see them coming.

"Don't worry," Miach said quietly.

She blew stray wisps of hair out of her eyes. "Miach, we can't tell when they're coming, we don't know who's sending them, and we always find ourselves outnumbered when they attack. Tell me what about that *shouldn't* worry me?"

"Our magic is stronger," he said simply. "And we don't use it for ill."

"Honestly, Miach, I don't think those creatures care what you do with your magic—and I doubt they even know I have any." She shivered. "Magic. What was I thinking?"

"Unfortunately, I don't think you had much choice." He squeezed her hand. "Let's run. Hearn's walls will provide some bit of safety."

"I hate to bring this inside his gates," she said in a low voice.

"I've hidden our tracks. And we won't stay long."

She nodded, but she was no more at ease than she had been before.

She ran with him across the plain toward the castle in the distance. It was Aherin, the home of the lords of Angesand and their very remarkable horses. She had been there in the fall with Miach, hoping to find a way to get herself to Tor Neroche that didn't involve walking for hundreds of leagues. Miach had sweetened one of Hearn's wells and she had put in a few hours with Hearn's garrison lads and that had earned them enough horses for their entire company. She supposed, now that she had the luxury of thinking about it, that Hearn had given them the horses because he'd known who Miach was.

"He didn't."

Morgan looked at Miach in surprise as she slowed to a walk. "Stop that."

He smiled. "I'm not peering into your head, Morgan. I was thinking on the last time we were here and how you had done the heavier labor. I looked at you and gathered you were thinking the same thing. And I will tell you now, Hearn did not give us those horses because of me. He did it for you. I hardly did anything."

"It took you *four* days to do hardly anything?" she echoed in surprise.

He shrugged unrepentantly. "It was completely self-serving on my part. I wanted an extra day or two alone with a certain lovely mercenary and I was fully prepared to drag things out in order to have them."

"You didn't."

"Well," he amended, "I did do *some* work. I could have sweetened that well with a single piece of magic, but I didn't want anyone to know I'd done it—and Hearn wanted the enchantment to last a thousand years. It took a fair bit of effort, but I did it *very* slowly. I'll tell you all about it if we manage to win ourselves a nap in that same loft. For now, let us make haste. I don't remember having any supper last night."

She supposed it wouldn't serve her to point out that he hadn't wanted to stop for supper. She merely walked with him through the village and up the way to the keep. He stopped with her at the gate and inclined his head to the guardsman posted there.

"We're here to see his lordship, if you please."

The guardsman looked at him doubtfully. "And who'm I to say has come?"

"Miach and Morgan. He'll know the names."

The guard shot them one last look of distrust, motioned for his fellows to train arrows on them, then walked off shaking his head. Morgan hoped Hearn would let them in. She didn't want to think about what she might be eating if he didn't.

Hearn himself appeared at the gate within minutes. He looked at them in surprise, then looked behind them. "Where are your mounts?" he asked.

Morgan suppressed a smile. How like a lord of Angesand to inquire first about horseflesh.

"Our mounts are safely tucked away at Tor Neroche," Miach reassured him. "We, on the other hand, are rather unsafely in the sights of a few unsavory characters. We're here to beg a few hours of sleep."

Hearn looked at him assessingly. "Not long enough to work on my other well?"

"Not now, unfortunately," Miach said. "But I will return and see to it another time."

Hearn nodded toward the keep. "Come and eat with me first, then you'll sleep the day away if you like. You both look weary. But first I'll know more about why you left your horses behind in the mountains. Surely it would have been easier to ride than walk." He looked at Morgan. "Was it your idea to leave them behind, Mistress Morgan?"

"Nay, my lord," she said honestly.

Hearn looked over her head at Miach. "It was your brother's doing, wasn't it?"

"Not entirely," Miach said with a grave smile. "I bear some responsibility for it."

Hearn grunted at him, then looked at Morgan. "That lad walking next to you irritated you and you fled without your horse, didn't you? Or did he finally tell you who he was and it angered you so that you fled without your horse?" He shot Miach a dark look. "The material point being you are without your horses."

Morgan smiled up at him. "I am very sure they are being taken care of as befits their kingly status. And as for Miach, aye, I now know who he is."

"Did you beat the truth out of him, or just threaten him with your sword until he burst into tears and confessed everything?"

Morgan laughed in spite of herself. "Actually, neither. He lied about himself all the way to Tor Neroche, then he was forced to admit to me who he was at a most unfortunate moment. He's been attempting to put himself back in my good graces ever since."

Hearn looked briefly over her head at Miach who walked on her other side. "A daunting task, no doubt. So, Mistress Morgan, how has he attempted that? Did he actually pick up a sword and try to impress you with it?"

"In a manner of speaking," Morgan agreed.

"I think I might have to see that to believe it," Hearn said with a snort.

Morgan listened to Miach and Hearn begin a discussion of what was more useful, magic or blades, which lasted until they had reached the great hall and were sitting down to an eminently edible breakfast. Then they turned to discussing Adhémar's potential offenses. As she listened, she found herself not a little surprised at how comfortable she felt. For so many years her world had been limited to Lismòr and Nicholas, Gobhann and Weger. Perhaps her heart had grown to include her companions, Paien, Camid, and Glines, but even then she supposed she'd always held herself aloof.

It had taken Miach of Neroche, with his small smiles and relentless affection, to make her see that her heart could include so many more good, honest people.

"I think she likes you," Hearn said loudly.

Morgan realized with a start that she was watching Miach and he and Hearn were watching her.

She pointedly ignored them and had laughter as her reward. Miach tapped the side of her boot with his and winked at her. She glared at him briefly, then turned her attention back to her meal. Miach and Hearn ceased to tease her, but found many other things to feed their mirth. Miach laughed more than Morgan had heard him laugh in days. She wasn't sure what it was about Aherin that made him so lighthearted.

Perhaps there was something in the water.

An hour later, she was crawling up toward the hayloft in Hearn's stables, a hayloft that kings despaired of sleeping in. She knew this because Miach had told her as much in the fall. It was no less an honor this time than it had been before, but she was almost too tired to appreciate it.

By the time she had yawned her way to the top, Miach had already spread out the blankets Hearn had given them.

Side by side and a substantial distance apart, as it happened.

She stood on the top rung of the ladder and frowned. "Why so far apart?"

"Because," he said, looking as if he were trying very hard not to laugh yet again, "the last time we were in this loft, you almost stabbed me for merely trying to hold your hand."

"I did not," she said stiffly, which earned her a bit of a grin that he apparently couldn't stifle. She scowled at him. "I was very rude to you then. I apologize. And I want you to know that I've marked all the times you've laughed at me this morning and I'll repay you for them properly when I have the energy. For now, stop being ridiculous and come share this blanket with me."

"Ridiculous?"

"Well, aye, ridiculous," she said. "You'd think I had plans to ravish you—Miach!"

One moment she was standing on the ladder, the next she found herself sprawled in the hay. She lay there for a moment or two, surprised beyond measure. Then she sat up and looked at him.

He looked as surprised as she felt.

She felt her eyes narrow of their own accord. She got to her knees and very deliberately unbuckled her swordbelt. She set it aside.

"You'll regret that," she said seriously.

He took off his sword quickly and tossed it behind him. "I imagine I won't, but—"

She flung herself at him. She realized immediately that she would not best him. He was far stronger than she was and far cannier than she would have expected. She did her best, almost rolled them both off the edge of the loft, and tried various other things that should have earned her at least a grunt from him. It occurred to her, at some point during that brief skirmish, that Miach had grown up as the youngest of seven brothers and that he likely had participated in all sorts of wrestles.

She had never stood a chance.

Far too quickly, she found herself pinned in the hay by a grinning fool.

Well, for a moment at least. His grin faded abruptly and he looked at her with an expression she couldn't quite identify. It wasn't horror, or distaste—it certainly wasn't embarrassment for having bruised her dignity. Before she could decide what it was, he had heaved himself to his feet. He shook himself off like a dog, sending hay flying all over her.

"Stop it, damn you," she spluttered.

He reached over and pulled her up. He brushed the hay off her shoulders and back, then paused.

"You'd better do the rest," he said, sounding rather uncomfortable.

Morgan shook herself off, then turned and frowned at him. "Well?" she demanded. "What have you to say for yourself?"

He reached out and picked hay from her hair. "I apologize?"

"You're mad."

"I might be," he agreed. He smiled at her ruefully. "My mother would have been appalled by my lack of chivalry."

"Then why did you do it? Surely this isn't on your list of appropriate wooing activities."

He laughed. "I daresay not, but it was either that or ravish you and I thought it the lesser of two things I shouldn't do. And I want you to concede that the ravishing was your idea—"

She put her hand over his mouth. "You should have stopped with the apology."

He kissed her palm, then took her hand away. "Very well. I'll admit that both the throwing and the ravishing were my ideas. I apologize. I was looking for a distraction."

"You're daft," she said with a scowl.

"And you're beautiful," he said, tilting his head to look at her fondly. "I'm having a hard time concentrating on anything but you."

She sighed. "I think I understand that, at least. I should be thinking of sieges and swordplay and how to better my own, yet all I can think of is when I might next be in your arms." She met his eyes. "Along with, heaven help me, a few other things."

He closed his eyes briefly, then looked at her.

She almost had to sit down.

"A prince of the house of Neroche does not kiss a princess of the house of Tòrr Dòrainn without wooing her properly first," he said, through somewhat gritted teeth.

She looked at him in surprise. "Is that written down somewhere?"

"I just made it up."

"You're an idiot."

His mouth worked for a moment or two, then he hung his head and laughed. "I'm not," he said, looking at her from under his absurdly long eyelashes. "I'm trying to save my sanity. I vow, Morgan, if I start kissing you, it's entirely possible I won't be able to stop. I would prefer to be in a place where someone else's spells were keeping us safe so when I wasn't able to stop kissing you, at least I wouldn't be responsible for seeing us dead thanks to my preoccupation with other things." He paused. "Put simply."

She removed a particularly long piece of straw from where

it stood out from his tunic like the blade of a sword. "And if you were Miach the farmer instead of . . . well, that other business of yours? What then?"

"If I were Miach the simple farmer and you Morgan the simple village gel, we would have been wed an hour after I first clapped eyes on you and we would be right now taking advantage of this luxurious hayloft to do far more than just kiss."

She looked at him, then realized what he meant. "Oh," she managed, with an alarming amount of breathlessness. "I see."

"So you do. Unfortunately, we are who we are and I'm still trying to keep my wits about me. So, despite all the other things I would prefer to be doing, I must allow that sleep is what we need most." He smiled at her. "Come with me?"

Morgan couldn't muster up anything inconsequential to say. All she wanted to do was stick her fingers in her ears and see if she could clean them out.

Had he said *wed*?

She sat down next to him on that very fine blanket, then squeaked as he pulled her back to lie beside him. He turned on his side, propped his head up on his hand, and smiled at her. Then a frown creased his brow. She reached up to smooth it away before she thought better of it, then curled her fingers into her palm and put her hand back down at her side where it couldn't do anything else untoward.

"Morgan, what is it?"

She swallowed, hard. "Did you say *wed*?"

"Well, of course *wed*. What else?"

She took a deep breath. "I didn't think . . . I mean, I wasn't sure . . ."

He smiled, looking slightly pained. "Morgan, why else would I woo you, if not to wed you? Why else would I have Mehar's betrothal ring digging a hole in my ankle if not to give it to you at the appropriate time?"

"Oh," she said, quietly. "I see."

"Of course, there are a few things standing in our way," he admitted. "Putting the realm to rights. Convincing you to say me aye. Securing the appropriate permission from elven grandfathers."

Morgan swallowed, rather unsuccessfully, actually. "Elven grandfathers?"

"You have one, my love, and he will be quite opinionated about you when he learns you're alive."

"I wish you were but a simple farmer," she whispered. "I wish I was nothing but a witless village wench. It would be so much easier."

"You don't really wish that," he said, "do you?"

"At this moment? Aye. In all the other moments?" She paused, then shook her head. "Nay. I wouldn't change you, not even for that. Nor me, I suppose. A bit of peace would be nice, though, wouldn't it?"

"We'll have it, eventually. And we'll steal what bits of it we can on the way. For now, you should sleep whilst you may. We'll be hard-pressed to find much more of that on our road, I imagine. I'll go keep watch."

He kissed her cheek, then sat up and crawled over to sit on the edge of the hayloft.

She watched him for quite some time, contemplating the turns her life had taken that she never would have expected. The last time she'd been in Hearn's hayloft with Miach, she hadn't known who he was or what he was capable of—and she hadn't known the same about herself. He'd been a farmer and she a shieldmaiden.

But now he was the archmage of Neroche and she a witless tavern wench after all, for all she seemed able to do was seek out ways to keep her arms around him. And when she didn't have her arms around him, she was begrudging herself the separation and wondering how soon she might yet again put her arms around him.

Pitiful.

She tried to sleep, truly she did. It was impossible. There was too much light and Miach was too close to her to resist. She finally gave in, crawled over on her knees, and sat down behind him. She hesitated, then put her arms around his waist and put her cheek against his back.

He put his hands over hers, but said nothing.

"What are you thinking?" she asked, finally.

"About when I first loved you," he said.

She blinked, hard. "Is that so," she managed. "Not the realm?"

"I thought enough about the realm whilst we flew. I'm permitting myself a few minutes of more pleasant reflection."

"Hmmm," she managed. She chewed on her words for quite a long time. "So," she said, finally, "when was that happy occasion you were thinking on?"

"The first time I saw you," he said. "You were standing at the edge of a clearing near an inn just outside Istaur. I thought I'd never seen anyone so perilously beautiful." He laced his fingers with hers. "Then that next day, when you woke and looked at me as if you would have liked to kill me—well"—he laughed a bit—"then I knew I was in trouble."

She smiled in spite of herself. "You're brave."

"And you are easy to love," he said. He squeezed her hands briefly. "I became more besotted with every day that passed, not that you would have noticed."

"Oh," she said softly, "I wondered."

"Well, I should have told you what I felt, but I couldn't until I told you who I was and by the time I was ready to tell you who I was, it was too late and I feared you would never forgive me."

"I forgave you."

"A monumental occasion for which I am very grateful," he said honestly. "Now, what of you? When did you first love me?"

"Chagailt," she said without hesitation, then she froze. It took her quite a while to catch her breath. "I suppose I can't deny it any longer, can I?"

He squeezed her hand. "I won't press you," he said, though he sounded rather hoarse.

She rested her cheek against his back. "Actually, I think it might have been before that. You were so kind to me—especially when I didn't deserve it. You held my hand, you distracted me with tales, you watched me whilst I slept. At Chagailt, we were in the library and you lay in front of the fire and looked up at me as if you thought I was worth your notice. I'd never had a man look at me as you did—and you do—as if he . . ."

"Loved you?"

"Aye," she said quietly. "And by the time we reached Tor

Neroche, I wanted very much for you to mean something with those looks."

He shifted so he could face her. "Did you?"

She nodded, then she looked down at her hands. "I knew that I was not fine enough for such a place, but I told myself that didn't matter because you were but a farmer yourself."

He winced. "Oh, Morgan—"

She shook her head. "'Tis in the past, but when I discovered your true identity, what distressed me the most was to think you wanted me—as you guessed at Lismòr—simply to wield the Sword of Angesand, not that you wanted simply me. I had convinced myself by the time I reached Gobhann that I had rid myself of any feelings for you. Then I saw you in the courtyard and it was . . ." She smiled. "It was like rain after a drought. I think it was then that I knew, deep down, that I couldn't go on without you. That is why I left Gobhann, in spite of what I knew I would face. Because I couldn't imagine my life without you in it."

He looked at her gravely for a moment or two, then he leaned forward and kissed her.

Morgan almost fell off the loft.

It wasn't that she hadn't been kissed before. Nicholas had kissed her several times in a fatherly way on the cheek, or on the top of her head. This was something entirely different.

Miach's lips were whisper-soft against hers, but he might as well have stabbed a dagger into her heart for as much as his lips against hers surprised her. He lifted his head, looked at her with stormy eyes, then slid his hand under her hair, pulled her closer to him, and kissed her again.

Just long enough to make her realize it had been a very bad idea indeed.

"Oh," she managed as he lifted his head to look at her. "This isn't good."

"I told you so."

"Aye, well, you were right," she said crossly. "That doesn't solve the problem, does it?"

He smiled at her. "I daresay we should stop whilst we can."

"Do you think so?"

He took a deep breath, then pulled her closer. "Of course not."

He bent his head and kissed her for quite some time. By the time he stopped, she thought she might manage to fall off the edge of the loft all on her own.

"Well?" he asked.

"Words fail me."

He laughed and kissed her quickly. "I understand, believe me." His smile faded. "I want you to wed me, Morgan. I must ask Sìle first, then I'll ask you. But that is what I want."

"I suppose I'll think about what I'll say," she managed, feeling rather flushed.

His eyes widened briefly, then he laughed. "You do that."

She reached out and touched his face. "Perhaps you should shore up your strength against that day. Go sleep."

"I don't think I can after that."

She found it impossible not to smile, just a bit. "I don't think I can either, but you at least should try." She rose unsteadily to her feet, then went to stretch out on the blanket. She leaned up on her elbow and patted the place next to her. "Sleep," she said firmly. "I'll keep watch."

He hesitated, then came to lie down next to her. He drew her arm over his waist. "For an hour, but no more. We dare not stay long here."

"You're more worried than you let on."

"I am," he agreed with a sigh. "It concerns me that we were found so easily on Melksham. It worries me to stop here and possibly draw something inside Hearn's gates, though I have spent a great deal of energy making certain we are hidden." He paused for quite some time. "I worry that I might not be able to protect you. I would fly you to Tòrr Dòrainn right now on my back, but I'm too damned tired. That and I fear that somehow my magic might be sensed in spite of how I've tried to hide it. It concerns me that we might be drawing those creatures to us without using any magic at all. What I want is for us to disappear for a few days so I can find answers."

"How can I help you?"

"It is enough that you are here with me," he said quietly. "I can see to the rest."

"I can guard you, at least," she said. "If something comes, I'll wake you." She looked into his very red, very pale eyes.

"And the horses will alert us to anything untoward, don't you think?"

He sighed. "They would. And Hearn has his own breed of magic. I imagine we'll be safe enough. But we must leave before sunset. We'll be to Tòrr Dòrainn by sunset tomorrow if we fly hard."

"Please let us eat here before we go," Morgan groaned. "I don't think I can eat anything raw."

Miach laughed. "I'll remember that."

She looked at him by the light filtering in through a high window and found that she was unwholesomely glad to be where she was. She could have been sitting in an austere, cheerless chamber in Gobhann. Instead, she was in a hayloft kings had despaired of ever sleeping in and she was with a man who said he loved her.

It was so much more than she had ever expected, standing there in Gobhann, watching him from the shadows.

She found he was smiling at her. "What is it?" she asked.

He shook his head. "I'm begrudging myself sleep."

"But why?"

"Because you're here to look at."

"I can move—"

He pulled her down and wrapped his arms around her. "I'll manage to sleep somehow. Why don't you bore me with something you learned about all those adventurous elves. I'm sure that will put me right to sleep."

She smiled. "I sense a distinct lack of respect in you."

"We'll keep that to ourselves. Besides, I'm teasing. Who did you read about?"

"Tachartas of Tòrr Dòrainn," she said, settling her head more comfortably on his shoulder. "Do you know him?"

"I know *of* him, but not any particulars. Enlighten me."

She did, until she felt his breathing deepen. He twitched a time or two, then slept deeply. Morgan waited several more minutes, then carefully disentangled herself from his arms and sat up. She simply watched him for quite some time.

Perhaps he did love her after all. She supposed stranger things had happened. Mages earning Weger's mark. Shield-maidens finding out they were actually elves. That sort of thing. Perhaps it wasn't unthinkable to find that a man could love her.

She reached for the other blanket, spread it over him, then hesitated. She considered kissing him, then decided against it. It was too tempting, he was too tired, and she supposed if she started, she might not be able to stop.

Weger would have been appalled.

She crawled over to the edge of the hayloft and sat where she could swing her legs off the edge. She tried, rather unsuccessfully, to think about something besides the man behind her. It was terrible, actually, to think on how much she'd come to depend on him. She couldn't bring herself to think about how much she loved him. And whilst she was about the labor of trying to avoid thinking about either of those two things, a thought came at her from out of nowhere.

What if something happened to him?

She was rather grateful to be sitting down, all things considered, though that didn't help with her inability to catch her breath. She recited handfuls of Weger's strictures, but found no comfort in them. She bowed her head.

Love was a terrible thing.

She hoped she wasn't making a terrible mistake indulging in it.

Seventeen

Miach woke and instantly knew that he'd slept longer than he should have. The shadows were different in the loft. He also felt almost human instead of feeling pushed so hard and so long that he hardly recognized himself. He enjoyed the sensation for a moment or two before he sat up and saw Morgan sitting next to him, watching him silently.

"You let me sleep too much," he chided gently.

"You needed it," she said. "And it wasn't that much. Well," she amended, "it was, but you looked so tired I didn't have the heart to wake you."

He dragged his hands through his hair. "I'll admit I appreciate it. How have you wiled away the hours?"

"Watching you. Talking to Hearn. Watching you a bit more."

"And what did you think?"

"Hearn was very interesting."

He blinked, then laughed. "You're a heartless wench."

"Hmmm," was all she said.

He looked at her and saw immediately that something was amiss. Her expression was very grave. And she was sitting rather far away from him, all things considered. She made no move to come any closer.

He found himself, suddenly, rather unwilling to ask her

why—on the off chance she'd changed her mind for some reason.

A coward, that's what he was.

But he'd known that before, so it came as no great surprise to him at the moment. He took a deep breath. "We should go," he said.

She nodded and went to gather up her gear. He collected his own things, then followed her down the ladder. He was relieved to see that it wasn't as late as he'd thought it to be. They would still have time to have something to eat, then be on their way before much more of the day passed. He turned around and found Morgan standing there in the passageway between the rows of stalls, wearing the most unsure expression he'd ever seen on her face.

"What is it?" he asked in surprise.

A single tear trailed down her cheek. "I don't know if I can do this."

He found that apparently there was enough of his heart to still be shredded. He took a deep breath. "What do you mean?"

"I've never cared what happened to anyone else," she said grimly. "It wouldn't have bothered me if they died. And now . . . now, look at me!"

He clasped his hands behind his back. "Is it not what you want?" he asked. He paused. "Am I not what you want?"

Her eyes widened. "I never said that."

"Then what are you saying?" he ventured.

She glared at him. "I'm saying that if you take foolish chances with your life and leave me alone as a result of them, I'll . . . well, I'll take my blade to you myself and finish anything anyone else leaves of you!"

Miach found it in him to smile.

"This isn't amusing," she snapped.

He looked at her for a moment in silence, then he slowly held open his arms. She cursed, then took two steps forward and flung herself against him. She wrapped her arms around his neck and held on tightly.

"Of course you're what I want," she whispered fiercely. "Just be careful with yourself, damn it."

He held her close and closed his eyes. It was unwholesome, that sense of relief that rushed over him. "I will be," he promised.

"I've never cared about anyone like this before," she said, her voice catching. "It's worse than any magic ever could be."

"Is it worth it?" he asked carefully.

"I don't know," she said, her voice muffled against his shoulder.

Her answer might have worried him if she hadn't been holding on to him so tightly. He supposed he could safely assume she didn't mean what she was saying.

"I think you love me," he murmured.

She pulled back far enough to look at him. "What does it matter if I lose you?"

"You're not going to lose me. Why would anything happen to me when I have you to guard my back?"

She sighed. "There is that, I suppose."

"Would you like a distraction from these troubling thoughts?"

"A distraction?" she echoed. "What sort?"

"This sort."

He tipped her face up and kissed her. He kissed her for far longer than he should have, but rather chastely, all things considered. By the time he lifted his head, he supposed he would still be able to walk steadily. He wiped away her tears, then kissed her once more.

"Let's go," he whispered. "We'll beg something quick to eat from Hearn and be on our way."

She took a deep breath and nodded. "Aye."

He put his arm around her shoulders and led her out of the stables. He wasn't going to say as much, but he shared her concern for his safety—and hers. He'd already come far too close to losing her to Lothar, losing her to Searbhe at Gobhann, losing her to creatures he couldn't have foreseen at Lismòr. That didn't begin to address the magic he might not be there to defend her against.

He wondered briefly if that was what had driven Sìle of Tòrr Dòrainn.

He left the stables with Morgan to find Hearn leaning

against the wall, looking up at the late-afternoon sky. Hearn saw them, then pushed away from the wall and smiled.

"Finished?"

"With what?" Morgan asked.

"I came to wake you both. I found you, um, otherwise occupied."

Miach could feel Morgan's blush from where he stood. He smiled. "I can't seem to help myself," he said easily.

Hearn looked at him sternly from under bushy eyebrows. "I think you'd better help yourself, lad, unless you have something akin to a wedding in mind."

"I do," Miach said easily, "if she'll say me aye."

Hearn looked at Morgan. "Well?"

"I'm thinking about it," Morgan conceded.

Miach smiled as she slipped her hand into his, then looked at Hearn. "I need a message or two sent. Have you a lad who might be willing?"

"I'll see it done, and I'll see you fed before I send you on your way, but I've also a few tidings for you. I've already given them to Mistress Morgan, but I'll repeat them for you."

Miach nodded, though he supposed by the grim look Morgan was now wearing, they wouldn't be tidings he would particularly want to hear.

He walked with Morgan into Hearn's hall and found that a meal had already been prepared for them. He ate with Morgan and listened to Hearn tell of what he'd heard. He was unfortunately unsurprised to find the tales revolved around terrible creatures that killed without any reason and moved on to kill again.

"At least that's the rumor," Hearn added. He looked about him, then leaned in. "I can't speak for every victim, but from what I can gather, those as were killed had magic." He paused. "Camanaë-style magic."

Miach heard Morgan gasp. It hid his own quite handily.

"And what do you suspect?" Miach asked.

Hearn shrugged. "I only know tidings from horses that come through my gates. But they're honest animals, for the most part. What they've witnessed distresses them. Those beasts roaming about are nothing like they've witnessed before."

Miach sighed. "I'm working on discovering who's sending them. I'll see them stopped."

"If anyone can, 'tis you, lad. Now, something for a message?"

"Please."

Miach watched Hearn walk off to look for quill and paper, then nursed his ale and considered the messages he needed to send. It took him only a few minutes to scribble down something for Cathar and something else for Paien of Allerdale. His brother would need to know what was happening in the realm, and Paien needed to know 'twas time to take the shards of the Sword of Angesand to Durial. He folded the sheaves, then handed them to Hearn. Hearn frowned.

"Aren't you going to seal them?"

"No one will bother to open them."

Hearn smiled briefly. "Handy, aren't you?"

"You've no idea," Morgan said wryly.

Miach smiled at her, then pushed back his ale. "Thank you, my lord, for the refuge. We needed it."

"'Tis here for you any time you need it," Hearn said, rising. "I'll walk you to the front gates, then you can be on your way. Unless there's anything else I can do for you?"

Miach shook his head. "We have what we need for the journey, but I appreciate the offer."

Hearn nodded, then walked through the courtyard and down to the gates with them. Miach thanked him again, watched Morgan embrace him warmly, then he took a deep breath and looked at her.

"Ready?"

"Aye."

He thanked Hearn one last time, then took Morgan's hand and walked through the gates with her. The sun was setting, which troubled him somehow. It bothered him enough to not be able to sense what was coming at them; not being able to see it either was doubly unsettling.

"Miach, you didn't send that missive to Adhémar," Morgan said quietly.

He dragged his attention back to her. "I wanted the tidings reported accurately," he said.

She looked at him in shock. "But surely Adhémar wouldn't stoop so low."

"He has before. 'Tis better this way. Cathar will pretend he heard tidings in the lists and Adhémar will believe him."

"I knew there was a reason I didn't like him," she muttered.

He smiled grimly, but said no more. It was a sorry state of affairs when king and archmage couldn't meet on common ground. Part of it was his fault; he had no patience for idiocy and his brother the king was full of that. The rest of it was Adhémar's fault for not treating him like a man full grown and trusting him with anything serious. So, they didn't speak of demanding things and the realm marched on as best it could.

Actually not, at present, but that wasn't Adhémar's doing.

He paused after they had left the last house in the village behind them, then looked over the plain.

"I think we should cross this," he said slowly, "then take wing in the forest."

"How far is it to Tòrr Dòrainn?"

"At least a fortnight on horseback," Miach said. "The road leads past Ainneamh and up into the mountains. It is not difficult for the first se'nnight, but it is as it progresses. I think it better not to attempt to run. It will take too long and leave us too exposed. We'll take wing in that far forest there."

"As you will, Miach."

He squeezed her hand and walked into the twilight.

And into the middle of hell.

They were suddenly surrounded by a score of the creatures he had come to expect. He was so shocked, he almost lost his head before he managed to draw his sword. Damn it, it just wasn't possible that they could have sensed him and Morgan. He'd hidden their tracks completely. Not even Lothar would have been able to find them.

Unless they were coming for Morgan and he should have been hiding her very essence instead of her magic.

He fought, heard Morgan fighting behind him, and considered what sort of spell he dared use. He didn't want to draw every fiend in Neroche down to Angesand, yet he saw no way to prevail without aid.

Before he could give it the thought it deserved, horsemen

poured out from the village. They encircled the trolls, then attacked. He backed up against Morgan, hard.

"No magic," he said quickly.

"Aye," she said, then she swore.

Miach saw her fighting a hideous creature that was half again as tall as she was. Miach pulled Weger's knife from his boot and flung it into the creature's eye. It paused, shook its head, then slowly fell backward and crashed to the ground.

The remainder of the battle was bloody, but mercifully brief. It wasn't a quarter of an hour later that all their enemies lay lifeless on the ground. Miach hunched over with his hands on his thighs and sucked in ragged breaths until he thought he could straighten and not puke. He heaved himself upright and stumbled over to where Morgan was looking at the carnage, breathing equally as raggedly.

"How did they find us?" she asked him.

He wanted to tell her that it was their shapechanging magic. After all, it was the only magic they'd used in the past twelve hours. Well, save that spell of insignificance he'd put on those missives, but surely that hadn't called to them so quickly.

He looked at Morgan helplessly. "I don't like not to have all the answers, but in this instance, I seem to have none. I've snuck into Riamh and walked past Lothar himself without being noticed. I have no idea why these creatures see through the way I'm hiding us. Unless there is something in our blood that draws them. I haven't hid that."

She looked at him for quite a while in silence. "Is it me . . ." She cleared her throat. "Do I attract them? Because of . . ."

"Merely who you are?" he asked very quietly. "I will admit that the thought has occurred to me. You've been at every attack except the one on Adhémar before I sent him south. Those creatures had the same stench of evil about them, but they were not so gruesome looking as these lads. As for the rest of the attacks—" He shrugged. "I think there is something to them searching out Camanaë blood, but I fear there is more to it than that, for I bear that blood as well." He paused. "I just don't know."

"What now, then?"

"We'll make for Tòrr Dòrainn without any magic. And

I'll completely hide any traces of our essences, not just our magic."

"What's our other choice?"

"Retreat to Tor Neroche—"

"Nay," she said immediately. "I won't run, and neither will you." She paused. "Do you think we should seek them out?"

He looked about him for a moment, then sighed deeply. "I've considered it, but I think it won't serve us. We could go all over Neroche and look, but since we haven't sensed them before, I can't imagine we'll sense them in the future. And that doesn't solve the problem of where they're coming from."

"It doesn't, but it also doesn't do anything to stop these creatures from killing innocent villagers."

"If there was anything I could do differently, I would. I think our only choice is to continue on and be quick. But we will still stop in Tòrr Dòrainn." He had to. If that talisman did indeed exist and it would do anything at all to help him keep Morgan safe, he would have it if he had to pry it from the king of Tòrr Dòrainn's cold, dead fingers.

"We'll run, then," she said firmly. "I'm much more myself today. I'll manage."

She was better than she had been, but plainly not herself. Miach started to say as much, but she shook her head.

"I will manage," she said. "Have a look at these lads. I'll go thank Hearn for the aid."

Miach didn't protest. He cleaned his sword on the snow and resheathed it, then went to fetch his knife. He pulled it from the creature's eye, then froze as he reached out for a bit of the troll's tunic to use in cleaning that blade. He frowned. What the lad was wearing was less a tunic and more some sort of leathery flesh. He rubbed snow carefully on his knife, then stuck it back into his boot before he squatted down to have a closer look at what he'd killed.

The troll was covered with some sort of webbish magic. It was a part of him in the same way the tunic was, only rather less cloth and more flesh. Miach tried without success to unravel the spell. Every time he thought he had hold of it, it slipped away from him.

Much like his spells of defense, he realized with a start.

He had to stand up only because if he'd remained squatting,

he would have fallen over from surprise. He stood there, looking down, and finding that things were not at all as he'd suspected they were.

Whatever was sending the creatures before him was also undermining his spells. He would have staked his life on that.

But it wasn't Lothar. This magic was different, less crude, less showy.

Somehow more evil.

Miach looked up into the darkening sky and wondered. He considered again his list of black mages, but could credit none of them with something this devious. Devious and slippery and impossible to take hold of. It was like nothing he'd ever seen before.

He had to find out what was causing it before there was nothing left of the realm.

He dragged his hand through his hair, then turned back to the west. Morgan was standing with Hearn, talking earnestly. Actually, she was shaking her head vigorously every time Hearn said anything. Miach left his mystery behind and walked over to them.

Hearn turned to him as he approached. "I told your lady here that I've a pair of horses with wings on their feet. You'll take them—despite her resistance."

"I cannot guarantee their safety," Miach said without hesitation.

Hearn looked at the fallen for a moment or two, then looked at Miach. "If these sorts of beasts fill the land, I won't have any horses anyway, will I? Send the mounts back when you've finished, or bring them back yourselves when you have a chance. They will fly for you, if you ask it."

Miach bowed his head. Horses would mean nothing less than the difference between success and failure. He blew out his breath and looked at Hearn. "How do I begin to thank you for this?"

"Name your firstborn son after me."

Miach managed a laugh. "We just might."

Hearn looked at Morgan from under his bushy eyebrows. "You're bested, gel, admit it. Give in graciously."

Morgan sighed. "A wise warrior knows when to surrender and bow to the superior man."

"So as that warrior pretends to bow, he can pluck the knife from his boot and do a little damage to that superior man, is that it?" Hearn asked with a snort.

She laughed a little. "Aye, my lord, so it goes. But I thank you. We've yet to come to your hall that we don't leave with horses."

"A terrible habit," Hearn said. "Can't imagine why I keep spoiling you two." He winked at Miach, then turned and walked off, calling orders to his men to tidy the battlefield.

Miach watched him go, then turned to Morgan. "This is a gift that can never be repaid. We'll make good time and be able to do so without magic." He looked at her. "Can you kindle a fire?"

"I've managed to survive by less lofty means than you, my lord," she said archly. "I'll see you don't freeze at night. I can also, if you can believe it, hunt."

"Then what shall I do? Knit?"

"I suppose you'll think of something." She smiled, but it faded quickly. "I hate to ride these good beasts into danger."

"We'll vanish into the mountains and no one will be the wiser. They will be safe enough."

He stood with Morgan until the horses arrived, stocked with gear, and looking ready to run. Hearn took their reins and handed one set to Miach and the other to Morgan.

"Unremarkable looking," Hearn said, "but very fleet, stout-hearted, and loyal. I've told them of your plight. They're prepared to aid you as they may."

"Their names?" Morgan asked, stroking the black on the right.

"Fleòd for Miach and Luath for you. Send them off when you've no more need of them. They'll find their way home."

"Thank you, my lord," Miach said, with feeling. "In truth, we cannot thank you enough."

"I have another well awaiting your pleasure," Hearn said cheerfully. "After you wed my Morgan here, you can come honeymoon in my loft. Work on my well during the day and on my namesake during the night. If you manage to win this gel, of course."

Miach smiled in spite of himself. "I'll see what I can do about the latter that I might manage the former."

Hearn nodded, then turned and boosted Morgan up into Luath's saddle. Miach shook the lord of Angesand's hand, then took Fleòd's reins and mounted. Hearn looked at them both.

"Fare you well," he said. "And be *careful*."

Miach supposed he wasn't merely concerned about the horses. He nodded to Hearn, looked at Morgan, then urged his horse forward. Luath followed along without hesitation. Miach waited until he and Morgan were out of earshot before he pulled up and looked at her.

"I hate to run the horses in the dark, but I fear even more not doing so," he said quietly.

"Don't you think they know where they're going?"

He nodded. "Aye."

"Let's fly, then."

They rode through the night. Miach had considered stopping to rest several times during that journey, but his mount had only flicked his ears back at him as if to call him mad and continued on without hesitation.

But now, even he had begun to feel the need of a brief respite. As dawn was breaking, he reined Fleòd in and looked at Morgan, who had done the same.

"How are you?"

"Exhausted," she admitted. "I'm not sure I'll ever walk again."

He smiled wearily. "I suspect the horses could go on for quite a bit longer, but perhaps they'll have pity on us." He nodded toward a beautiful, clear stream. "Let's see how that tastes."

She looked about her, then frowned. "Where are we?"

He swung down and walked in front of Luath to hold up his hands for her. "Chagailt is to the northwest, through that forest."

She landed, swayed, then steadied herself. "Then perhaps we shouldn't stop," she said anxiously. "Not after what happened to us in that forest the last time."

Miach considered. "This is the forest south of Chagailt, not the one to the west of it, but I understand your concern. The horses need to be watered, though, if only for a few minutes. A quarter hour won't matter."

"Very well," she said, but she loosened her sword in its sheath.

Miach led the horses to the stream and let them drink. He felt Morgan come up beside him and put her arm around him. He gathered her close and rested his cheek against her hair, then closed his eyes and was grateful for ground beneath him that didn't move.

"Miach?"

"Aye, love."

"About these creatures," she began slowly. "There's a part of me that fears there may come a time when we won't best them." She looked up at him. "I'm not happy thinking that, and I don't doubt our skill . . ." She shrugged helplessly. "Even a superior warrior finds himself bested at least once." She paused. "It is usually his last battle—for obvious reasons."

"I don't believe we'll fail."

She looked off into the distance for a minute, then turned to him. "What of Searbhe?"

Miach nodded. "I wondered about him. I looked for his presence on Melksham one night at Lismòr and didn't sense him. But I am not as adept at that sort of thing as I would like to be. I want to believe he ran home to Riamh, but I don't know."

She frowned. "Then you don't think he's responsible for any of this?"

"I don't."

"I think that doesn't reassure me."

"I daresay it shouldn't," he said grimly. He looked around them, then put his hand briefly on her shoulder. "We'll hurry."

She nodded.

But she didn't look any more at ease than he was.

They would water the horses, then continue on. If nothing else, perhaps they could outrun whatever might be seeking them.

He didn't want to think on what it would mean if they couldn't.

Eighteen

✦

Morgan opened her eyes and saw daylight streaming down through trees around her. Though the sight was beautiful, the fact that it was day and not night bothered her. She remained still and tried to determine why. The last thing she remembered was Miach saying that he felt safe enough to camp under the eaves of Sìle's forest. She had no recollection of getting down off her horse and rolling up in very cozy blankets. Perhaps a se'nnight with hardly any sleep had been more taxing than she'd wanted to admit.

She wasn't one to complain about the harshness of any given journey, but the one they'd just made had been grueling. They'd ridden almost without ceasing from Hearn's keep, though not always at a gallop and certainly with much less speed as they made their way through the mountains. Miach had estimated they would reach Tòrr Dòrainn in a fortnight. They had made it in eight days, eight terrible, endless days. They hadn't seen anything untoward. Then again, they hadn't exactly stopped long enough to see much of anything at all. She'd finally resorted to memorizing the spells Miach taught her to keep herself awake in the saddle.

Or, rather, she had for the first pair of days until she found she remembered most of the spells on her own.

She was still trying to come to terms with that.

Miach had then presented her with the choice of learning more difficult spells of Camanaë or beginning her study of Fadaire. She chose the latter because she sensed that it amused him to know he was giving her something he shouldn't know anything about. She'd asked him, at one point, how he'd learned those spells in truth. He'd said that, in addition to truly finding himself locked in King Sìle's solar one night, one of Sìle's grandsons had been particularly susceptible to bribery and that the masters at Beinn òrain really should keep better locks on their more perilous elvish texts. He did point out to her that he'd picked the lock on that particular book without any magic so they wouldn't know who'd been at it.

She rather liked him for that, all things considered.

And so she'd learned what he taught her, a bit because it pleased him, but mostly because she was afraid not to. She told herself that the spells were nothing more than strictures, not unlike what she had learned at Weger's. She suspected that as long as she considered them only that, she could bear to learn them.

Heaven help her if she ever had to use any of them.

She rolled over onto her belly and rested her chin on her fists where she could look at Miach sitting on a blanket, resting his forearms on his bent knees. He tossed a stick onto the fire, then smiled at her.

She smiled back, because she simply couldn't help herself. She'd known from their journey north in the fall that Miach was a decent traveling companion, but this trip had been different. Perhaps it had been because she'd allowed herself to accept the small considerations he gave her as a matter of course. She'd stopped telling him she didn't need help off her horse, that she could fetch her own water, that the cloak she had was sufficient to keep her warm and he could keep his. He was determined to treat her as something delicate and fine; she'd given up trying to convince him that she was anything else.

And she'd come to rely on finding him there when she woke from whatever brief sleep she'd had, on seeing him riding beside her, on having him tell her all manner of tales to keep her awake.

But what she'd come to realize perhaps most profoundly

over the past eight days was that there was a depth of resilience to Miach that she'd never expected to find in anyone besides herself. She suspected that even when she had reached the limits of her endurance, Miach would be able to continue on. She didn't want to find that comforting, but she couldn't help it.

"Interesting thoughts?" he asked.

She shook her head. "Just kind ones about you. I won't repeat them, lest you blush, but I will tell you that you let me sleep too long. You should have taken a turn."

He shrugged. "I'll sleep in Seanagarra whilst you're about the arduous task of meeting all your relatives."

She ignored the flicker of unease that ran through her. "We aren't close, are we?"

He smiled. "Not particularly. We've just passed the eastern border of Ainneamh. Seanagarra is half a day's easy ride farther east still—or a full day's quick walk."

"But I thought Tòrr Dòrainn was part of Ainneamh."

"A story perpetrated by the wishful-thinking elves of Ainneamh," he said dryly. "Despite rumors to the contrary, it has always been its own country and we are right on its border. I fear, though, that we may reach the palace sooner than you'd care to. The horses seem determined to see us there."

She twisted around to look behind her. There stood Fleòd and Luath, apparently quite ready to be going. She looked back at Miach. "Do you think they're following Hearn's instructions?"

"I imagine they are," he said, "though I suspect it isn't entirely altruistic on Hearn's part. He just wants us back safely so we can see to his well and his garrison."

"Would you mind?" she asked. "Going back again?"

"To Aherin?" he asked in surprise. "Of course not. Things seem to improve each time we do. This time you didn't look at me once as if you wanted to stab me—though you did almost roll me out of the loft onto the floor."

"You threw me in the hay."

He laughed softly. "And so I did. I promise I won't the next time we find ourselves there." He smiled. "May that day come swiftly."

She nodded, then watched him turn back to his contemplation of the fire. She waited for him to speak again, but he seemed content to merely sit there and watch the flames. He looked impossibly tired and she could understand. He'd stayed awake many times when he'd allowed her to sleep. Perhaps what he needed was to sleep for a pair of hours in that elvish palace up the way before they moved on. Surely spending any more time than that in a place where she would most certainly not find any relatives would be unnecessary.

Actually, maybe it would be best if they just continued on. She could ride behind Miach on Fleòd and hold on to him whilst he slept.

That sounded reasonable.

"Miach?"

He reached out and put his hand on her head without looking at her. "Aye?"

"I think we should keep going," she said, cursing herself for the tremble in her voice. "The realm calls, doesn't it?"

"I have business here as well, Morgan," he said, amused. "A day or two won't hurt."

Perhaps it wouldn't hurt him, but she couldn't say the same for herself. It wasn't every day she rode into an elven palace and presented herself to an elvish king as a long-lost granddaughter. That she should have the cheek to even consider such a thing was appalling. That she should intend to do the like and have the outcome be agreeable was yet more far-fetched. She would have begun to seriously doubt herself, but Miach and Nicholas were both so certain . . . and then there were her dreams.

Difficult to deny the last.

She felt Miach's hand under her chin. He lifted her face up. "Don't worry."

She didn't bother to deny it. "I don't like not knowing what to expect."

"Which is why you're so comfortable with me," he said dryly.

"At least I know that given the choice, you'll waggle your fingers—though you have resisted admirably over the past se'nnight. I have no idea what to expect from . . . well, from this business in front of us." She found that her mouth was suddenly and quite appallingly dry. "I think we should just keep going."

"You won't regret this." He smiled down at her. "Trust me."

"Do I have a choice?" she asked crossly.

"It seems to have worked out well enough for you in the past, wouldn't you say? Nay," he said quickly with a half laugh, "don't answer that. Instead, how would you like a brief distraction before we pack up and go?"

"What sort?" she asked, finding it in her to smile.

"The sort that I like best," he said with an answering smile.

"Cards? Swords?"

"Absolutely not," he said, leaning toward her.

Morgan closed her eyes.

But the kiss never came.

Morgan opened her eyes, ready to complain, then realized why Miach wasn't moving.

There was a sword at his throat.

She looked up and saw that they were surrounded by a half dozen men. Miach straightened gingerly, then held up his hands.

"I have no blade," he said easily.

The man holding the sword snorted. "As if you needed one, Prince Mochriadhemiach. Just remember I could slit your throat before you could spew out a spell."

"Perhaps you could try, Dionadair, but my magic does not require any spewing," Miach said evenly, "so slitting my throat would not serve you."

Morgan blinked. She'd never heard anyone call Miach *prince* before. She had grown so accustomed to thinking of him as simply Miach that it was unpleasantly surprising.

She wondered, uneasily, what else would come as an unpleasant surprise.

She watched Miach sit perfectly still until the elf named Dionadair removed the sword from his throat. He rose without haste, then held down his hand. Morgan took it and scrambled to her feet with far less grace. She didn't have a chance to say anything before Miach had quickly pulled her hood over her face and drawn her behind him.

Morgan was tempted to protest, but she supposed he had good reason for what he did. She was tempted to run and fling herself on that very fleet Angesand steed, but she supposed Miach knew that. He kept his hand on her arm until she took a deep breath and forced herself to relax. Then he squeezed her

arm briefly and released her. She turned around so they stood
back to back. At least she would make certain he didn't find a
blade plunged into his heart.

Unfortunately, turning around didn't accomplish much past
giving her a decent look at the men guarding her. She was rather
glad her face was in shadow. It saved her from embarrassing
herself by gaping at what were easily the most beautiful men
she had ever seen—beautiful and terrible and glittering, as if
they were come recently out of a dream. No wonder Miach was
so mesmerizing to look at. Obviously whatever elven blood he
possessed had come to the fore in him.

She paused. Did she look like that? To be sure, she hadn't
spent much time looking into a polished glass—indeed, she
couldn't remember the last time she had—but she was fairly
sure that she hadn't seen anything in herself that came close to
resembling the beauty she was looking at.

She leaned back against Miach and fought the urge to weep
in appreciation.

"Why are you inside King Sìle's borders, Prince Archmage?" Dionadair asked coldly.

"I'm bringing His Majesty something he lost," Miach said.

"Give it to me and I'll see it delivered."

"I fear I cannot," Miach said calmly. "His Majesty can do
with me what he wishes after the fact, but I will deliver this to
him in person. With or without your escort, Dionadair," he
added.

"Is that so?" Dionadair said scornfully.

"Would you care to test it?"

Morgan had the presence of mind to note that Miach had
that same edge to his voice that he'd used with Searbhe at
Gobhann. Perhaps these elves would do well to heed it.

Then again, perhaps these lads didn't care. She couldn't
imagine anyone daring to mar their perfection with any sort of
blade.

Dionadair grunted finally. "Very well. We'll see you there."

It wasn't an enthusiastically made offer, but perhaps she
and Miach could expect no more. Morgan realized she'd been
holding her breath only because she managed to let it out. She
straightened and decided that her sword could remain safely in
its sheath.

Then she realized her sword was over by the fire.

Truly, it had been a very trying year so far.

"We have Angesand steeds that need stabling," Miach said. "You know what sorts of tales they'll bear if they aren't treated properly."

A pair of the guardsmen abruptly deserted them to hasten over to the horses, where they stopped and made appreciative noises. Morgan watched another guardsman pick up their gear—including her sword—and carry it off. That left only three elves to escort them. Morgan supposed that if things deteriorated too quickly, she and Miach could easily see to them—swords or no swords.

Though she suspected that wouldn't be the best way to introduce herself to the court.

Miach turned around and looked at her. "Follow my lead, I beg you," he whispered.

"That wasn't exactly a friendly welcome," she whispered back. "They don't seem happy to see us."

"They're not happy to see *me*."

She frowned at him. "Why is it I'm beginning to think there are things we should have discussed before?"

"Because you're as intelligent as you are beautiful. Just trust me."

It was too late to do anything else. She tried to take his hand but he shot her a warning look. She scowled at him, but she supposed he knew best. She suspected she would have something to say about it later, though, when they weren't being observed so intently.

The day marched on. They were allowed to drink from streams as they crossed them, permitted to forage in their saddlebags for the last crusts of bread they possessed, then led ever farther into a pine forest.

A forest like unto nothing she'd ever seen before.

She was beginning to feel even more like a provincial miss than she had when she'd first caught sight of Tor Neroche, terrible and impenetrable, so many months ago. As with that palace, here all she could do was stare, openmouthed, at what she saw.

The trees were laden with sparkling snow, the ground covered in a soft blanket of white that was clearer and more beautiful than she'd ever seen. The path was a dark brown, bare and easily trod, as if something otherworldly kept the snow away from it. She'd seen snow before, and walked in forests before, but here somehow everything was draped in some sort of shimmering magic that made it appear as if it had somehow just been thought of. The colors of needle and bark were so rich, she was tempted to just stand still and drink them in until she'd satisfied herself. The magic that made them so was exquisite.

It was also unsettlingly familiar.

In time, the deep pine-filled woods gave way to leafier, more musical trees. Morgan had scarce managed to decide if she understood the song or not before the trees parted and she saw the palace of Seanagarra.

She stumbled.

Miach caught her, steadied her, then released her. They continued on. At least Morgan thought she continued on. She felt like she was walking into a dream. It reminded her more of Chagailt than Tor Neroche, but even then, the comparison did not do Seanagarra justice. It shimmered with an enchantment that was so beautiful, so mesmerizing, so bewitching that she could not look away. She tried to find Miach's hand, but he wouldn't take hers. She tried to look at him, but she couldn't see him for the haze clouding her vision.

"Miach, please," she whispered hoarsely. "I can't wake up."

She felt his arm go around her shoulders immediately. He pulled her close.

"'Tis Sìle's glamour," he whispered in her ear.

"Do you see it?"

"Oh, aye," he said ruefully. "Try not to heed it. It will pass once we reach his hall."

Morgan nodded. She closed her eyes and let Miach keep her from falling on her face. It was better that way. She could still hear the shimmer of magic singing around her, but at least she didn't have to look at it anymore.

It seemed to her that a great deal of time had passed, but perhaps not before Miach squeezed her shoulders, then released her. Morgan looked around her and found that they were inside the gates of the palace and it was sunset.

She walked with Miach over polished stone floors, through

hallways covered with beautiful murals of gardens and forests, and finally to a set of heavy wooden doors that soared up into darkness above them that seemed to go forever and be filled with twinkling stars.

The doors opened. Morgan took a deep breath, then continued on with Miach into what she assumed was Sìle's formal audience chamber. The floor was a pale marble, as were the pillars holding up an intricately carved ceiling. Morgan looked down to the end of the hall and saw the enormous throne there, carved of burnished dark wood.

A man, white-haired and majestic, sat on that throne. Morgan saw the substantial gold crown upon his head and supposed that it could only be Sìle. He was leaning back on his seat, tapping his foot impatiently, as if he'd been interrupted on his way to supper and wanted to have his duty over with so he might continue on to it.

The guards stopped them some twenty paces away from where the king sat, then stepped away, leaving her to stand there with just Miach. Miach made Sìle a very low bow. Morgan curtseyed awkwardly, just because she thought she should. She wished, absently, that she'd made a better job of it. The king's expression was thunderous.

"Well?" he demanded. "What do *you* want?"

Miach bowed again. "Thank you, Your Majesty, for allowing us to come so far with such a distinguished guard. As always, your graciousness is legend—"

"Oh, be done with that," Sìle snapped. "I don't like mages, which you well know, Prince Mochriadhemiach, and I don't like unexpected guests. Why are you here? Tell me quickly before my soup grows cold."

Miach bowed yet again. Morgan was tempted to tell him to stop, but she knew nothing of the niceties that elves required. Perhaps Miach would have a backache before the audience was finished. He started to speak, but he was interrupted.

"He says he brought you something you lost, Your Grace," Dionadair put in loudly. "I can't imagine what that would be."

"Neither can I," Sìle growled. "Well? What is it? And who is that filthy urchin you have there?"

Morgan ran into Miach's hand before she realized he had put it out to stop her. She supposed it wouldn't serve her to fling her knife at the king, and she also suspected that she did look like a filthy urchin. She took a step backward and watched as Miach clasped his hands behind his back and made Sìle yet another low bow. He straightened.

"Your Grace," he said slowly, "there is no easy way to prepare you for this."

"Prepare me for what?" Sìle demanded. "If you've wasted my time, *boy*, I vow you'll suffer for it."

Morgan watched Miach as he turned to stand in front of her.

"Ready?" he whispered.

She closed her eyes briefly. "Don't leave me."

"I won't. Here we go." He carefully lifted her hood away from her face and set it back off her head onto her shoulders. Then he stepped aside.

Sìle's gasp echoed in the hall.

Morgan watched as the king shot to his feet, then stumbled down the handful of steps from the dais to the floor. She was tempted to turn and flee, but she had passed much sterner tests than this.

And she supposed Miach might just catch her before she gained the hall doors. He was rather fast, all things considered.

She watched Sìle as he came to stand next to Miach, his face full of astonishment and disbelief. She kept her back straight, her chin raised, and let him look his fill.

She supposed that while he was about it, she might as well have her own look. He was no less handsome than any other elf she'd ever seen, though his face was lined slightly and his hair was white as snow. His eyes were green, the color of hers actually, and currently wide with shock. He gaped at her and fumbled for something to lean on. Miach put his shoulder conveniently within reach and Sìle clamped a hand on it.

"It can't be . . . it isn't . . ." Sìle looked at Miach, apparently at a loss for words.

"It's not Sarait," Miach said quietly.

Sìle took a ragged breath. "Then who?"

"'Tis Mhorghain, Your Majesty," Miach said quietly.

"Mhorghain," Sìle repeated, almost soundlessly. "Little Mhorghain." He looked at Miach. "But how is that possible? Keir said no one had survived."

Miach shrugged just the slightest bit. "Either Keir didn't

see her, or he didn't want anyone to know she had escaped. But this *is* Mhorghain, Your Majesty. Beyond all doubt."

Morgan listened to them call her a name that she'd never had used on her and found that somehow, she didn't mind it. Especially the way Miach said it—as if her name was a treasure he only shared with those who might appreciate it. She looked at Sìle and saw, to her complete surprise, that his eyes were welling up with tears.

"You look so much like Sarait," he said in disbelief. "For a moment there, I thought you *were* Sarait."

She cleared her throat. "Is that so, my liege?"

Sìle took a hesitant step toward her. He wasn't quite as tall as Miach so she wasn't forced to look up as far. He stopped a handsbreadth away and stared at her in amazement. Then he hesitantly reached out and touched her face.

"Mhorghain," he whispered in awe.

Morgan couldn't find anything useful to say, so she remained silent.

"Dionadair," Sìle said, not taking his eyes from her, "go fetch the queen. Make haste, lad!"

Morgan looked at Miach, but he only shook his head just the slightest bit and took several steps backward. She had just begun to consider how she might protest that when she was distracted by the arrival of several more elves inside the hall. She was accustomed to immediately assessing the number and kind of potential enemies, but her skills were seemingly out of reach at present. She supposed there might have been fifteen elves; there might have been more. All she knew was that the sight of so many of them was almost too much for her.

Sìle reached for a woman whose hair was as dark as his was white and pulled her close to him. "Are you seeing what I'm seeing, Brèagha?" he asked.

The woman looked at Morgan and her eyes filled with tears. "I am, husband."

Morgan would have smiled or attempted to dredge up her very rusty manners and use them, but she wasn't feeling precisely herself at the moment. She would have given anything to have clapped Sìle on the back in a friendly gesture of camaraderie, nodded briskly to the rest, and bolted for the door.

And damn that Miach of Neroche if he wasn't standing well away from the press, looking perfectly at ease.

She glared at him, then turned back to the dozen—she found the wit to manage that tally after all—souls who seemed determined to greet her as if she were long-lost kin they had despaired of ever seeing again.

Which she now supposed she might well be.

They were touchy, these elves. They seemed determined to embrace her and pat her and press her hand. She did her best to be polite, but after the journey she'd had and all the worry she'd endured, she wasn't sure how much longer she could keep a pleasant expression on her face.

"Come," Sìle boomed suddenly, "you'll sit next to me and eat. You're terribly thin. You'll tell me where you've been hiding—who hid you, by the way?"

"Nicholas of . . . Diarmailt," she managed. Even saying it sounded strange. She wanted him to be just Nicholas of Lismòr. She wanted Miach to be just that handsome lad with the mark on his brow and the unwholesome habit of muttering spells at the odd moment. She didn't want anyone to be who they weren't supposed to be.

She didn't want to be Mhorghain.

She was beginning to suspect she'd made a terrible mistake.

"Those damned mages," Sìle grumbled, drawing her hand through his arm and pulling her toward the open doors to the right of his throne. "He should have sent word."

"He was trying to keep me safe," Morgan protested. "As was my lord Mochriadhemiach, whom we're leaving behind."

"Eh?" Sìle said, pausing. "Oh, the mage. He can eat with the garrison."

Morgan dug her heels in. "But you can't—"

"Husband," Brèagha said, stopping Sìle at the door, "offer the young prince of Neroche your hospitality."

Sìle scowled. "I don't like him."

"You would like it even less if he were to seek refuge with Ehrne because you were rude to him."

Morgan watched Sìle consider that, then nod to his wife. "He may stay the night. But he'll still eat with the garrison."

Morgan looked frantically for Miach, but he was only leaning negligently against Sìle's throne, watching her with a grave smile. She shot him a look that bespoke significant retribution, then found herself suddenly besieged on all sides by elves wanting to see to her comfort. Before she could send them all off to do something more constructive, she was taken over by her grandmother and a pair of aunts. She was led into what she supposed was the dining hall and a place was made for her on Sìle's right, a place liberated because a tall, very handsome elf was displaced.

Morgan looked up at him as he pulled out her chair. "Who are you?" she asked.

"Làidir," he said with a low bow. "I'm Sìle's eldest."

"I didn't know Sìle had sons," she managed.

He smiled. "No one ever talks about us. We're not nearly as pretty as the girls."

"But you're beautiful," Morgan blurted out.

He put his hand briefly on her shoulder. "You've a discriminating eye, obviously." He looked at her for a minute, then smiled. "You look so much like your mother, 'tis almost a little unsettling. But it eases my heart. Now, sit, niece, and enjoy your meal. I'll go see to your escort."

"Thank you," she said gratefully. She sat down next to the king of Tòrr Dòrainn and felt more uncomfortable and conspicuous than she ever had before in her life. She wondered if she should kill Miach sooner rather than later for having handed her over without protest.

She realized that the queen had come to sit on her right hand. She put her hand over Morgan's.

"Eat, darling," she said with a smile. "I'll show you to your chamber soon. I imagine a good night's rest will make things easier to bear in the morning."

Morgan nodded gratefully. "Thank you, Your Majesty."

Brèagha only smiled and motioned for a page to pour Morgan wine.

"Now," Sìle said, turning and fixing her with a purposeful stare, "I'm ready to hear your tale. Begin at the beginning, won't you?"

Morgan had a long drink of wine, pushed aside thoughts of murdering a certain archmage, then began where she thought she should.

She had the feeling it was going to be a very long evening.

Nineteen

Miach sat on the steps leading up to Sìle's throne and sighed deeply. He would have given much for someplace to put his head down. He didn't expect to wind up in the dungeon, but he would have settled happily for it at the moment. Then again, considering the look on Sìle's face when he'd seen Morgan, he might just find himself sleeping—albeit briefly—in a decent chamber.

He rubbed his hands over his face then jumped in surprise. Sìle's heir, Làidir, stood there in front of him, staring down at him with an expression that was somehow less than welcoming.

Miach sighed lightly. Perhaps he'd pilfered one too many spells on his last visit.

He rose and made Làidir a bow. "Your Highness," he said deferentially. "A pleasure, as always."

"I have a question or two for you, Prince Mochriad-hemiach," Làidir said without preamble. "Over supper, in the kitchens."

"It would be an honor."

Làidir didn't move. "Some might consider that location to be an insult."

"Are you trying to insult me?" Miach asked mildly.

Làidir studied him for a minute. "Perhaps."

Miach smiled. "Food is food, Your Highness. The closer it is to the fire, the hotter. Besides, I've never been in Seanagarra's kitchen."

"But you've been in several other chambers here, haven't you?"

Miach clasped his hands behind his back. "Prince Làidir, if there's something you wish to say to me, please be blunt. I'm in need of food and sleep, not games."

Làidir stared at him for a minute or two in silence, then nodded abruptly toward a door at the other end of the hallway. "I'll be frank with you over supper."

Miach followed him willingly. At least he was being fed. He supposed he couldn't ask for much more than that.

Elves were, as Adhémar would have said, impossible creatures. They were intensely private, fiercely loyal to those of their ilk, and generally antagonistic to anyone who wasn't an elf. The elves of Tòrr Dòrainn were substantially more aloof than the elves of Ainneamh. Sìle had a particular aversion to mages, which Miach supposed he could understand, considering how many of his descendants he'd lost to them.

It didn't bode well for him, actually.

He followed Làidir along corridors and down stairs until they reached the kitchens. Miach sat down within sight of the fire and soon was applying himself to a marvelous meal. He heaped lavish praise on the head cook's head and was rewarded with almost more than he could eat.

And all through the meal, Làidir merely sat across from him at the table and watched him. Miach thought about reminding Làidir that they were kin—Màire of Meith, Làidir's sister Alainne's youngest daughter, was his grandmother several generations removed—but he supposed that wouldn't improve things any, so he kept that to himself.

He finally put his knife and fork on his plate and pushed it aside. He had a final drink of a very fine, dark ale, then looked at Làidir.

"Thank you. That was most welcome."

Làidir nodded, but didn't smile. "How is it you came to be Princess Mhorghain's escort here?"

Miach gave a serving girl a smile as she refilled his cup, then he turned back to Làidir. "I was very fortunate to be in the right place at the right time—"

"That isn't an answer," Làidir interrupted severely.

"It would be," Miach said evenly, "if you'd let me finish."

Làidir's mouth tightened briefly, then he nodded curtly. "Very well. Go on."

Miach supposed he must be curious indeed if he was willing to submit to that sort of rudeness. He leaned forward with his elbows on the table. "I had been off looking for my brother in the fall and found Mhorghain traveling in a company with him."

"I heard a rumor that Adhémar lost his power," Làidir said, "and that you sent him on a quest to look for a wielder for that sword of Queen Mehar's you have hanging in your hall. I also heard that the sword was destroyed."

Miach blinked at that. "How did you hear that?"

"I travel a fair amount," Làidir said with a faint pursing of his lips. "One does what one must to keep busy, and inns are the best place for reliable gossip." He sipped his ale. "Who broke the sword? I heard it was a wench. Some witless girl you picked up in your travels?"

Tidings traveled swiftly, apparently. Miach didn't particularly want to tell Làidir anything, but perhaps it was best he knew before he insulted Morgan and found himself skewered because of it. He wrapped his hands around his cup. "It was Mhorghain."

Làidir choked. Miach couldn't take any enjoyment in it, though Morgan likely would have. It took quite a while for Sìle's heir to recover.

"Impossible," he gasped.

"I watched her do it," Miach said calmly. "'Tis my fault, of course. I neglected to tell her who I was as we traveled together, and she was justifiably angry with me when she learned the truth." He smiled deprecatingly. "She has a particular aversion to mages."

"A girl with sense," Làidir said grimly. He nursed his own ale for a few minutes, then shook his head. "I don't understand why she didn't come home sooner." He shot Miach a look. "Was she being held against her will?"

"Nothing so dire," Miach said. "She simply didn't know

who she was. Nicholas of Diarmailt had watched over her for years—"

"Why didn't King Nicholas tell her who she was? She could have been living her life in peace and safety here!"

Peace and safety. Miach grimaced. Would those words never cease to torment him? It was best Làidir never know the import of them. Miach wouldn't have put it past him to use them himself.

"And where is the former king of Diarmailt?" Làidir continued angrily.

"Your *brother-in-law*," Miach said pointedly, "is safely and anonymously running the university at Lismòr."

"On Melksham?" Làidir asked, stunned. He sat back in surprise. "I hadn't considered that, though I should have. He had said he planned to leave his crown to his nephew, but I never thought he would lower himself to dwelling in such a rustic place." He cursed briefly. "Why didn't he send word when he found Mhorghain? How old was she when he took her in? What has she been doing until now?"

"You know," Miach said, "these really are questions you should be putting to your niece. I will warn you, however, that she considers Nicholas something of a father. You would do well not to disparage him."

"I wouldn't," Làidir grumbled. "Mage though he is, he at least treated Lismòrian as he should have."

That was an understatement, or so the tales went, for Nicholas's adoration of his lady wife had been legendary.

"As for why King Nicholas didn't send word," Miach continued, "I think he wanted to shield Mhorghain from her memories—at least at first. Then I think he thought it best to keep her ignorant so she would be safely hidden from those who might want her dead." He looked at Làidir. "Wise, don't you agree?"

"I think he took a great deal on himself," Làidir said stiffly.

Mentioning that Sarait had asked for Nicholas to watch over Morgan was probably something else better kept to himself. Miach only inclined his head. "Argue with him over that when next you meet. And as you well know, there's nothing you can do to change what's gone before. All you can do is be grateful for what you have now."

"Of course," Làidir said. "And since she'll now be fine with us, you may be on your way tomorrow."

"I'll go when Mhorghain asks me to."

Làidir frowned fiercely. "The only reason you want to stay is so you can make clandestine forays into places you shouldn't go."

"I would like a peep into your father's library, if possible," Miach admitted. "I'm looking for something I think I might find there."

"Is that all you're here for? Books?"

Miach considered. It wasn't that Làidir wasn't trustworthy, it was just that his duty was to be where Sìle could not and bring back details the king never could have gleaned on his own. Whatever he told Làidir would go straight to Sìle's ear. He would have to choose his words carefully.

"I would like," he began slowly, "to reassure your father that I only have Mhorghain's best interests at heart."

"To what end?" Làidir asked.

Miach looked at him evenly. "I imagine you'll divine that on your own if you think about it long enough."

Làidir looked at him blankly for a moment, then his mouth fell open. "You cannot be serious."

Miach only watched him. Perhaps that training at Weger's had actually been of more use than he'd hoped. He was able to watch Làidir spluttering like a teakettle without feeling the need to respond. He simply sat and waited for the other man to wear himself out.

"You cannot be serious," Làidir repeated. He stood and looked down his nose at Miach. "My father will never give her to such a one as you."

Miach lifted one shoulder negligently. "I am a prince, just as you are."

"As if you could begin to compare Neroche to Tòrr Dòrainn!"

"Perhaps not, but you forget that elvish blood runs through my veins, just as it does yours," Miach said, "and not just from Ainneamh. I claim kinship with Màire of Meith, whose mother, if memory serves, is your sister. So perhaps I am not so unworthy as you might think."

Làidir leaned his hands on the table and glared. "If you

think," he began in a low, dangerous voice, "that my father will give another of his children to a *mage*, no matter what parentage you would *like* to claim, then you are as foolish as you are brash. We will not lose another of our family to your ilk."

Miach wondered why in the hell he'd expected this to turn out any other way. He'd anticipated resistance to the idea of his wedding Morgan, of course, but in the back of his mind, he'd held out the hope that the resistance would be bested eventually. Obviously he'd been too long in Weger's tower and his wits had rotted.

"I loved Sarait," Làidir said, "but she was blinded by her heart."

Miach blinked at the non sequitur. "I beg your pardon?"

"Sarait loved Gair, at first," Làidir said with a fair amount of distaste. "Gair courted her and flattered her and convinced her he was other than he was. More's the pity that my father didn't destroy the bastard when he first set foot in Seanagarra. Believe me when I tell you that he won't make *that* mistake again."

"You underestimate Mhorghain—"

"And you underestimate your peril," Làidir snapped. He shoved his chair out of the way and strode angrily from the kitchens.

Miach looked at his cup of ale and considered. He couldn't imagine Sìle actually doing him in, or being able to. He supposed he wouldn't have put it past Làidir to try. Làidir seemed to be nurturing an especially virulent hatred for Gair in particular and mages in general. It was an intense hatred indeed, if it had been burning this brightly for twenty years.

He pushed away his cup, thanked the cook for a memorable meal, then made his way from the kitchens. A page was waiting at the bottom of the steps to show him to his accommodations. He wondered if he might be sleeping in the dungeon after all.

He was slightly relieved to be shown a chamber not in the cellar. It had to have been Queen Brèagha's doing. She, at least, didn't seem to mind him. Of course, that had been before he had arrived with her granddaughter's name on his lips, but there was nothing to be done about that now.

His gear was there, as well as water for washing and clean clothes. He desperately wanted to cast himself down and sleep for a se'nnight, but he had things to see to before he could. He had to check on his spells, and he needed to know how Morgan was faring.

He unbuckled his swordbelt, laid his sword on the bed, and left the chamber. He wandered through passageways briefly, but saw nothing of Morgan. Well, it was still early and he suspected she was still being interrogated over supper. He would see to his business, then venture to the dining hall. Perhaps Sìle would be more reasonable after he'd had something to eat.

He continued to wander until he found himself in an enormous private garden. He walked through it until it flowed into the forest. There was a bench there, in a little corner that seemed to be free of the full strength of Sìle's glamour. Miach sat with a sigh, closed his eyes, and set to work.

Things were not so dire as they had been, though perhaps it only seemed thus because he was bone weary. He patched until he simply could do no more. It cost him much to hide his tracks, but he didn't hurry that along. He would be more thorough in the morning. If he didn't sleep for a few hours, he wouldn't manage even that.

He opened his eyes, then started in surprise.

Morgan was leaning against a tree not ten paces away, watching him. Actually, she was glaring at him.

He rose and walked over to her. "Morgan, my love," he said, reaching out to pull her into his arms, "what a pleasure."

"Ha," she said with a snort. "Don't you *Morgan, my love* me, you coward. You threw me to the wolves!"

"I was being unobtrusive."

"So unobtrusive that you were invisible?" she said tartly.

"I thought it wise. Actually, I had supper with Sìle's heir." He smiled down at her. "It never hurts to flatter the relatives, you know."

She didn't answer. She only put her arms around him and held on tightly. "It will not matter," she said, her voice muffled against his shoulder. "The king doesn't like mages."

"Then you should get on quite well with him, shouldn't you?"

"I've changed my mind—at least about a few mages. I don't think he ever will." She looked up at him. "He spent most of the evening warning me about you. I didn't like it."

He smiled. "Then I suggest you distract yourself by remembering the look on the king of Tòrr Dòrainn's face when he first saw you. You have brought him—and the rest of his court—great joy today. His desire to take over your life will ease as time passes."

"Ha," she said crossly. "You didn't hear him. He plans on remedying my lack of proper education, disabusing me of the notion that swords are an acceptable weapon for elvish princesses, and preventing me from gallivanting any farther through the Nine Kingdoms with the youngest prince of Neroche. His words, not mine. I don't think he has any intention of listening to anything you might want to say to him."

Miach smiled ruefully. "Nay, I imagine he doesn't."

"Tell me again why we are here?" she said sternly.

"Because I thought it wise to give your grandfather a chance to have you near him for a day or two before I tell him I plan to take you from him."

"See?" she said in irritation. "There it is again. A grandfather I never knew trying to dictate to me what I can and cannot do. I am *not* his to give or take."

He took her hand and led her along the paths that led under Sìle's most beautiful trees. "Morgan, you deserve to be courted and won as befits a princess of Tòrr Dòrainn. A prince of the house of Neroche does not—"

"You'd best not be inventing this on the spot," she warned.

He smiled. "In this case, I'm not. A prince does not wed a princess without observing certain formalities."

"Rubbish," she said with a snort. "What formalities?"

He brought her hand to his mouth and kissed it. "I have a list, but you may not want to hear it now, especially since I haven't done so well with formalities so far. Aside from the fact that we didn't have a proper introduction, I haven't sent you gifts, or composed poems and lays to your beauty—"

"Nay, you lied to me about who you were, beguiled me with spells in your tower at Gobhann, then convinced me to shapechange. I will admit that you did give me quite a lovely silver cup at Lismòr, but then you took it away moments later."

He took her face in his hands and smiled at her. "See? I've much to remedy."

"Miach—"

He kissed her softly. "Part of my wooing you properly involves my presenting my suit formally to your grandfather. I

think before I do that, you should let Sìle shower you with all
the affection he was never able to before. Enjoy the company
of Queen Brèagha and your aunts. Give me time to nose about
in his library, then I'll talk to him. I don't imagine he'll have
any illusions about what I want. And when he says me nay,
then you'll decide what to do."

"He won't say you nay."

"Oh, he will," Miach said. "He will tell you, no doubt, that
the house of Neroche is not as distinguished as the house of
Tòrr Dòrainn. Then he will point out that I am but the youngest
of that house."

She rolled her eyes. "You're the bloody archmage of
Neroche, for pity's sake!"

"That is not an asset in your grandfather's eyes."

"Miach, he will *not* tell me who I will wed," she said. "And
I don't care about any of that courtly business." She opened her
mouth to say more, then apparently thought better of it. She
looked up at him. "Does it matter to you?"

He tucked a stray strand of hair behind her ear. "What matters to me is that when you come to live with me in Tor
Neroche, you feel as though I had the wit to earn the approval
of your family. If some asp-tongued countess taunts you with
a list of a score of things her lord did to win her, I'd like you
to have an even longer list to give back. You are Sìle's granddaughter and because of that, you deserve to be properly
courted."

"I don't suppose tossing me in the hay counts."

He laughed. "I don't think it does. I'll think of a few more
appropriate activities."

She rested her head against his shoulder. "All right. How
long must we stay?"

"Another pair of days," he said. "I'll make good use of the
time. Sìle's library is extensive and I'll find plenty to do there."

She sighed. "Will you at least kiss me good night every
evening?"

He smiled. "I think that's a requirement."

She put her arms around his neck. "Then do it properly,
won't you?"

He bent his head to do just that, but found himself interrupted by a noise. It wasn't precisely a roar, but it was close.

"What are *you* doing?" a voice thundered from their left.

Miach stepped away from Morgan in spite of himself. He turned and made Sìle a low bow.

"Nothing," he said, feeling as guilty as a lad of ten summers who'd been caught with his hand in his father's coffers.

"Why are you here instead of the stables where I ordered you to be put?"

"He was seeing to his spells," Morgan said. "Spells that keep Lothar at bay, as it happens."

Sìle looked at her from under bushy eyebrows. "We wouldn't need to worry about Lothar if it hadn't been for Yngerame of Wychweald siring him. The same Yngerame that this whelp claims as sire generations ago."

Miach clasped his hands behind his back and decided that it would be unwise to remind Sìle that Yngerame was his grandson-in-law.

"Actually, I believe he was seeing to far more than his spells," Sìle continued, sounding highly displeased.

"He was walking me to my chamber—"

"'Tisn't his place," Sìle growled. "In fact, I daresay his place is anywhere you aren't." He took her by the arm and pulled her away. "Come away before he feels too comfortable near you."

Morgan dug her heels in. "Your Majesty, I am very grateful for your hospitality and your kindness to me tonight. That said, I will *not* listen to you disparage a man who has never been anything but kind to me."

Sìle paused, then tugged at her again. "I'll thank the youngest prince of Neroche properly tomorrow and send him on his way with fine gifts."

"Nay—"

"Aye—"

"Your Majesty, I insist—"

"Mhorghain, you need someone to help you make these sorts of distinctions. We never, *ever* have dealings with mages. They're not our sort of people."

Miach watched Morgan shoot him a glare over her shoulder. He held up his hands in surrender. She cursed him rather thoroughly, which seemed to please Sìle, then allowed the king of Tòrr Dòrainn to escort her from the garden.

Miach could hear her cursing all the way back to the house.

He bowed his head and laughed, then shook his head as his mirth faded. She'd have more to say to him on the morrow, no doubt.

He made his way back to the very luxurious chamber he'd been given, stripped, then crawled between the silken sheets. He looked up at the ceiling and considered.

He would spend the morning in Sìle's library and see if he couldn't discover the truth about the talisman he suspected Sìle had made for Sarait. Perhaps he would also stumble upon something that might help him in his current quest.

Aye, he would do what he could, give Morgan a day or two to come to know her family, then they would be on their way.

He touched the mark on his forehead and reminded himself he was indeed not the least of the sons of Anghmar of Neroche, though that was surely not a sentiment Sìle of Tòrr Dòrainn would agree with. It wouldn't matter to Morgan, perhaps.

But it mattered to him.

He had been serious about Morgan having a very long list of things he had done to properly win her—and that list couldn't include swords, or perilous journeys into darkness, or marks over the brow. It was a little late for formal introductions and handsome gifts and long, drawn-out negotiations between royal houses, but he would, at some point, see what he could do about a few more traditional things.

Perhaps when he was certain he would have a kingdom to take her back to.

He spared a final thought for his spells, then checked the spell of un-noticing he'd woven beneath Sìle's own spells of protection. It would serve for the next few hours.

He closed his eyes, then opened them again. He considered for quite some time, then drew a spiderweb-like spell over himself. It would wake him if anyone came or if anyone tried to lay a spell on him.

He felt for Morgan's bedchamber, then laid the same sort of spell across her door. It would disappear when she woke, so she wouldn't know it had been there.

But he would.

Just in case.

He rolled over and fell into an uneasy sleep.

Twenty

Morgan stood in the chamber she'd been given and looked down at herself. She had been scrubbed from head to toe, dressed in clothing so fine she hardly dared move, and coiffed so her hair somehow fell over her shoulders and down her back in fat, loose curls. She would have preferred to have had her hair braided so it didn't get in her way, but she hadn't dared say anything to the serving girl whilst she'd been about her work and she hadn't dared touch the miracle that girl had wrought after the girl had finished.

Her gown was no less awe-inspiring than her hair. It was a long, flowing bit of business in white with pointed sleeves hanging down to the tips of her fingers. The fabric whispered something magical as she moved, but she couldn't understand what that something was and she feared to inquire too closely. She held up her hand to see if the material would sing a bit more, then caught sight of her nails. They'd been trimmed and buffed and polished until they resembled something that might have belonged to a woman whose most taxing endeavor was stitchery, not swordplay.

Astonishing.

She turned and looked at her bed. Her sword lay there alongside Mehar's knife. Well, she obviously couldn't take it with her, but she hesitated to leave it behind. She looked

around her, then shrugged and slid the blade under the bed.
Perhaps only the serving girls would look there and they would
have no use for what they found.

She fingered Mehar's knife for quite some time. There certainly wasn't a good place for that on her person. Instead of her
sturdy boots, she was wearing dainty shoes that should have
been placed on someone truly delicate—which she most certainly was not. Even if that point could be argued, it couldn't
be argued that her shoes were completely inadequate for con-
cealing weapons.

She considered taking a ribbon and tying the sheath to her
leg, but she feared the ribbon would come untied at an inopportune moment and embarrass her. She finally took the knife
and slid it under her pillow. She took a step back, started to
weave a spell of un-noticing over it, then realized what she was
doing.

She'd forgotten, in the excitement, just what she was running from.

It was also a little unsettling to think that instead of looking
for a decent place to stash something, her first instinct was to
look for a decent spell.

She finally plumped her pillow, arranged it so it looked as
it should, then hoped that Mehar's knife would be safe enough
underneath it. She pulled a shawl of some sort of other flimsy,
exceedingly fine stuff around her shoulders, then turned and
faced her doorway—such as it was. She recited a handful of
Weger's strictures, then put her shoulders back and left her
bedchamber.

She looked for Miach but couldn't see him in the passageway. Perhaps he had spent the morning in Sìle's library, then
decided that lunch was in order. She could slip unnoticed to a
spot next to him and convince him that they should change
their minds and go. She had the feeling that staying much
longer would result in finding out things about her past she
didn't want to know and wouldn't be able to deny. Well, more
than she had the night before. Her grandparents certainly
seemed to have no doubt that she was who Nicholas and Miach
said she was.

She paused on the edge of the cloister-like passageway
and had a look at the garden. It was full of noonish winter sun,

but quite empty of a certain archmage, so she turned and started off purposefully back the way she'd come from the night before.

She found, to her extreme discomfort, that everyone she encountered bowed to her. She couldn't manage to do more than stare in consternation at the first few because she had no idea what she should do. Was she to bow in return? Wave them off with an imperious gesture? Turn and flee? After a bit, she simply took to scooting by those she passed before they could begin their bobbing.

Finally, she decided she'd had enough for a bit and ducked into a doorway to rest only to find that the alcove was already occupied. She jumped back and started to blurt out an apology, but before she could, the tall elf standing there made her a low bow.

"There. Now you've been genuflected to by everyone you've seen this morning. I daresay you could retreat to your bed and consider your duty done for the day."

He was teasing her. It reminded her happily of Miach, so she favored him with a smile. "I saw you last night."

"You did, indeed," he agreed. "I'm Sosar, the youngest of Sìle's children, save Sarait. Your uncle, as it happens."

"Oh," she said faintly.

"I know where lunch is," he said. "And your mage."

"Oh," she said quite a bit more enthusiastically. "I'd like both, if you please. Can I hope they're in the same place?"

"Unfortunately not. I understand from my brother the spy that Prince Mochriadhemiach has braved the bowels of my father's library, but I suspect that won't surprise you."

"It doesn't."

"I imagine, as you no doubt do, that we won't see him anytime soon unless we go search for him. And I fear that once you appear at lunch, you won't be released to do that."

"Released?" Morgan said with a frown.

Sosar only smiled. "A poor choice of words. Let me choose others. I fear once you present yourself to the king, he will take you in hand and pepper you with so many questions that you won't have the breath for doing anything but answering them. That will leave you so weary that by the time he toddles off to supper, you'll be too tired to do aught but stumble back to your bed, cast yourself upon it, and pray he eats something that doesn't agree with him so you need not endure the same on the following day."

Morgan almost smiled. "Indeed."

"Indeed," Sosar said pleasantly. "But if it eases you any, let me tell you that last night was the first time in years I've seen my father smile with true happiness. You've given him back something he lost."

Morgan sighed. Miach had been right after all. Perhaps she should just allow Sìle time to ease his heart. It wouldn't vex her overmuch to be polite.

"All right," she said reluctantly. "I'll go eat with the king. But would you do me a favor?"

"Anything."

"Would you go make certain Miach's all right? Just in case I can't escape?" She paused. "I would just go, but I think I will try to be . . . well mannered."

Sosar lifted one eyebrow. "Ah, so it's Miach, is it? Awfully familiar for his being just your escort."

"He's not just my escort," Morgan said in a low voice, "but you could certainly keep that to yourself, couldn't you?"

"I daresay I should," he agreed. "And aye, I will go see to Prince Mochriadhemiach in a bit. I'll make certain he's been fed and that he wasn't required to sleep in the stables. And speaking of stables, I heard that you had a nap in Hearn of Angesand's hayloft."

"Who told you that?" she asked in surprise.

"The horses. They were very impressed."

"You speak their tongue?"

"A little," he conceded. "My father once sent me to buy a breeding pair from Corbair of Angesand." He paused. "He was Hearn's great-great-grandfather, I believe. I asked him if knowing a few words might make the steeds more comfortable."

"Just what a lord of Angesand wants to hear," she said with a smile.

"Aye," Sosar agreed. "He taught me quite a bit, actually, which, as I'm sure you know, is rather unusual. I think he was very pleased indeed that I wanted to learn." He offered her his arm. "Let me see you to the hall and I'll tell you more about it on the way. You know, the horses said you were being hunted."

Morgan stumbled. "Damned dress," she said, stalling for time. She looked up at Sosar, but he was only watching her closely.

"I don't suppose they're lying," he added.

She sighed. "Can you be trusted?"

"I am," he said solemnly, "a vault."

She looked at him seriously. "I'll stick you if you blather these tidings to anyone."

"Hmmm," he said, raising an eyebrow, "I imagine you will. So I will reassure you again that you can trust me. And I'll tell you more. The horses said both you and Prince Mochriad-hemiach bear Scrymgeour Weger's mark. And that the prince didn't kiss you as often during the journey as he would have liked to."

"Those gossiping nags," Morgan spluttered.

Sosar patted her hand resting on his arm. "Go on and tell Uncle Sosar your sorry tale, gel. It will make you feel better."

She shot him another warning look. "Very well, the horses have it aright. We are being hunted. Miach's trying to find out why, or by whom, or by what." She paused. "He thinks our magic draws them, so we've been traveling without."

"Poor lad."

She looked at him gravely. "He spent a month in Gobhann, so he's accustomed to it."

Sosar whistled softly. "Why in the world would he do such a stupid thing?"

"He went inside to fetch me."

"Oops," Sosar said easily. "Sorry."

"No need to apologize," she said. "I thought it was rather stupid at the time as well, though I suppose the training has served him. The entire tale is long, but suffice it to say I fled there because it was the one place I thought he wouldn't follow me. Then when he risked everything to come and get me . . ." She shrugged. "What isn't to love about that sort of man?"

"What indeed," Sosar said kindly. "And the kissing?"

"None of your damned business."

He laughed out loud, then continued on with her until they reached a particular doorway. "I deserved that, of course. Now, here you are, delivered safely to lunch. I'll be about my business quickly, then go see to your lad for you."

"I'm very grateful."

He made her another bow, hesitated, then reached out and tugged on one of her curls. He dropped his hand and smiled. "I used to do just that, you know."

"Do what?"

"Pull on your hair. And you scowled at me when you were six exactly the same way you're scowling now." He smiled, then turned and walked off, humming pleasantly.

Morgan thought she might regain her breath at some point, but she wasn't sure it would be soon. She supposed that perhaps it would be easier if she had somewhere to sit. She put her hand on the door and started to open it.

Brèagha opened the door from the other side, then welcomed her into the dining hall. "Did you sleep well, darling?"

"Very," Morgan said, because it was polite. Actually, she'd had a terrible night. She'd spent most of it reaching for Miach in her sleep and finding that she was very much alone. She would have to tell him as much. It would please him.

"Would you like something to eat?" Brèagha asked with a smile.

"Please," Morgan said.

Brèagha paused. "I think Sìle would like to show you a few things this afternoon. Sarait's things, if you can bear it."

Morgan did her best to swallow, but it wasn't done easily. "As you wish, Your Majesty."

She wondered what in the world she would do when they showed her a picture of Sarait and she found that she didn't resemble her in the least.

Two hours later, she realized that such a thing wasn't going to happen anytime soon. She was standing in Sarait's room, looking at Sarait's portrait. She stared at it for quite some time in silence, then took a deep breath and forced herself to look into the mirror next to the painting.

She and Sarait might well have been twins.

"And here are the rest of the children," Brèagha said, taking Morgan's arm and turning her to look at yet another portrait.

There was Brèagha, sitting on a bench in the garden where Miach had been walking the night before. Held securely on

Brèagha's lap was a young girl of about six. Surrounding the pair were six lads ranging from about ten up to perhaps a score and ten.

Morgan sank down on the bed and stared at the painting. She could hardly believe it, but she knew those lads. She knew the eldest, Keir, because he had pushed her relentlessly to learn more and more spells.

To protect her against their father.

She knew the next eldest, Rùnach, who had shadowed their mother constantly, ever reading ancient, crumbling books full of magic so he might be prepared to aid their mother when necessary. Then had come Brogach, Gille, and Eglach, brothers who had watched grimly as their father's true nature had been revealed, lads who had also been fiercely loyal to their mother.

Last was Ruithneadh, who had burned like a live flame, fierce in his defense of her, guarding her when Keir could not.

Brothers who had loved her.

She had no idea how long she sat looking at that painting with tears streaming down her cheeks and ruining her dress. She supposed she should have said something, but all she could do was look at the lads there and weep for the loss of souls who had loved and cherished her.

"Mhorghain?" Morgan felt her grandmother take her hand. "Darling?"

"I'm fine," Morgan croaked. She looked again at the portrait of Sarait, then looked in the mirror at her own tear-streaked face. Any hope she'd had of denying it was gone.

She was Sarait of Tòrr Dòrainn's daughter.

And Gair's.

"My love, what can I do to help you?"

Morgan looked first at Brèagha, then turned to see who else had seen her come undone. The chamber was empty save they two. Sìle had been the one to insist she come see it, but apparently he'd decided at some point that it was safer to depart unnoticed for higher ground. She would have done the same, but she supposed there was no point. It was difficult to outrun herself.

"Mhorghain?"

Morgan focused on Brèagha with an effort. "Your Majesty?"

"Would you like to lie down?" Brèagha asked, her eyes

clouded with worry. "Perhaps I should stay with you whilst you do."

"I'm fine," Morgan said automatically. "I'm a little overwhelmed, but I'll be fine."

"Of course, darling," Brèagha said with a gentle smile. "I never doubted that. I know this all must come as something of a shock."

Morgan shook her head. "Not entirely. Nicholas—Nicholas of Diarmailt—told me many things. Well, things that Miach hadn't already." She took a deep breath. "I fell apart in his solar a fortnight ago. But Miach was there then . . ."

"Shall I fetch the youngest prince of Neroche?" Brèagha asked softly. "Would that ease you?"

A longing for him rose up so sharply, Morgan caught her breath.

But she pushed the thought aside ruthlessly. He was seeing to the realm. Surely she could see to her own affairs for the day.

"I'm fine," she repeated firmly. "Besides, I've lived all my life I can remember on my own. I can manage this on my own as well."

"Why is it I imagine that wouldn't be what Prince Mochri-adhemiach would suggest?"

"Because he's overprotective."

"He's delightful," Brèagha said, with a smile. "I've always thought him to be so."

Morgan turned to look at her. "Have you indeed?"

"Yes," Brèagha said. "He has managed his responsibilities without allowing them to crush him or embitter him as other young men might have."

Morgan thought that learning Brèagha's opinion about a few things other than her own resemblance to Sarait might be a very good distraction. She looked at her mother's mother and could hardly believe that she wasn't looking at a woman her own age. Brèagha's face was unlined, her hair dark, her fingers slender and smooth. The only things that betrayed her were her eyes. She had seen much, and it showed.

"Mhorghain?"

Morgan focused on her. "Aye, Your Majesty?"

"Grandmother," Brèagha suggested. "I am your grandmother, darling, and we were talking about Prince Mochriadhemiach. I was telling you that I liked him very much. Not, perhaps, that it matters to you."

Morgan smiled. "It matters, but I suspect you know that already."

Brèagha tucked Morgan's hair behind her ear. "Then, since we both seem to find him to our liking and I think you could stand to speak on something perhaps a bit more pleasant than what you've faced so far this morning, I will tell you more. I have known the youngest prince of Neroche, as it happens, since shortly after he was born. His mother, whom I knew very well, would often bring him with her when she came to visit. He has grown into a man who is discreet and responsible, but isn't above a bit of subterfuge—"

"When it comes to spells he shouldn't know?" Morgan interrupted with a smile.

Brèagha laughed softly. "Aye. Sìle has never caught him with his fingers in the pie, as it were, but he roars about it every time he sees him within our borders. Then again, your Miach is only following in his mother's footsteps. She was famous for knowing spells she shouldn't have, but she was more inclined to charm them from her victims than sneak about in their private books." She smiled wistfully. "You would have liked Desdhemar, I think. She was very powerful, of course, and very lovely. And she loved her boys to distraction, especially her youngest. After all, she gave her life for him, didn't she?"

Morgan managed a nod. "I understand she perished fetching him out of Riamh."

Brèagha nodded. "'Tis a pity she didn't survive. She could have eventually left Tor Neroche behind and found some small corner of the Nine Kingdoms to call her own with her beloved Anghmar. But she was older when they wed and had already had enough adventures to fill several lifetimes. I'll tell you of them someday when Miach isn't buried in Sìle's library and can listen too. And," she said, rubbing her hand over Morgan's back, "tales of your love's mother aren't what you need to face today, I fear."

Morgan nodded. "They were a good diversion, though." Then she paused. "My love's mother?"

"Isn't that what he is to you?"

Morgan took a deep breath and looked her grandmother

in the face. "Aye, he is. And I'll not allow Sìle to tell me differently."

"Of course you won't," Brèagha said with a small smile, "though he'll try."

"So Miach said," Morgan admitted. "And just so you know, that is one of the reasons we came. So Miach could ask for Sìle's permission."

Brèagha put her arms around Morgan and hugged her briefly. "The youngest prince of Neroche honors you, as he should. Sìle will say him nay, of course, then you'll do what you must. I will tell you, however, that Desdhemar would have been very pleased with her son's choice. I know I am. And now, before I wax rhapsodic about the charms of your young man, I will go and let you rest. Stay here as long as you like."

"You don't mind?"

Brèagha looked at her in surprise for a moment, then took Morgan's hands in both her own. "I didn't keep this chamber untouched as a shrine, darling; I kept it for you. I always held out hope that you had somehow survived. These things are now yours."

Morgan closed her eyes briefly, then looked at Brèagha. "Thank you."

Brèagha kissed her on both cheeks, then rose. "Of course, darling. And if you want Prince Mochriadhemiach fetched, that can be done."

Morgan nodded and watched her grandmother walk out of the chamber. Then she turned and stared at herself in Sarait's mirror. She almost didn't recognize herself. She looked so much like Sarait, it was almost difficult to decide whom she was looking at. There was a woman in that mirror, dressed in a gown that shimmered white and silver, with bright green eyes and dark hair that had been somehow convinced to hang almost to her waist in sweeping, lovely curls.

There wasn't a speck of mud in sight.

Morgan rose and started to explore before she had to look at herself any longer. She touched the crown that Sìle had left her and remembered that he'd asked her to wear it to dinner because there were new guests he wanted her to meet. She could only imagine and she hoped it wouldn't include long lines of elves whose names she wouldn't remember past the hearing of them.

She continued to pace around the room, touching things on dressers and tables, opening closet doors and dresser drawers. She found a trunk with treasures of a less-than-perfect nature, treasures obviously fashioned by children. There were rocks and pine cones and things carved from wood. She started to look further, but found that she couldn't. She didn't want to find something that she might have made.

Not today.

She closed the lid and rested her hands on its top until she thought she could manage a decent breath.

She could be Mhorghain. Indeed, she could see that she had no choice but to admit that she was Sarait's daughter.

But she didn't have to be Gair's.

She could still be mostly Morgan, live her life mostly by her sword, still comport herself mostly as Weger's apprentice. She could even marry Miach and pretend to be a princess of Tòrr Dòrainn if something at Tor Neroche demanded it. And when that courtly bit of misery was behind her, she could return to just being herself.

She sat down on the edge of the bed and focused on breathing in and out. In time, she thought she might like to lie down, so she did. She stared up at the ceiling of her mother's chamber and let the tears leak out and wet the hair at her temples. She supposed the curl would come out now. She wasn't all that sure she cared.

She closed her eyes. In a few minutes she would get up and look through some of her mother's less private things.

And then she would find the archmage of Neroche and tell him they were leaving.

Twenty-one

Miach stood in Seanagarra's library and wondered if the pounding headache he had came from too many days without sleep, or too many hours spent reading. Surely it hadn't come from all the arguing he'd already done with the fool in front of him. He took a deep breath.

"You've given me several things already," he said, quite reasonably to his mind. "Why not this? What harm can it do?"

The librarian looked down his nose. "I can't imagine His Majesty would be pleased to know I allowed a mage to poke about in the manuscripts kept for him privately."

"Has His Majesty expressly forbidden it?"

"He didn't have to," the other said stiffly. "Your reputation, Prince Mochriadhemiach, is not one that persuades me to trust you with anything important."

Miach didn't often lose his patience. It was a testimony to how desperate he was to satisfy his curiosity that he found his hand on his sword without quite knowing how it had gotten there. He had barely begun to determine how he might explain that when someone leaned on the table to his right.

"Give him what he wants, Leabhrach."

Miach looked to find Sosar, Sìle's youngest, scowling at the librarian.

Leabhrach pulled himself up. "I think not—"

"You think too much," Sosar said bluntly. "Give him exactly what he's asked for and do it now, whilst I'm watching you."

"King Sìle told me to be careful with him," Leabhrach said haughtily, "and even if His Majesty hadn't, I would—"

"Still be a fool," Sosar finished for him. "Oblige our young friend here. Once you've done so, you can scamper straight to my father and snivel out the whole pitiful tale."

Leabhrach looked at them both, then spun on his heel and went to search about in racks of books behind a silken rope. Miach turned to Sosar.

"A friendly face."

Sosar smiled. "So said your lady when I saw her earlier."

"I envy you the pleasure," Miach said.

"No doubt you do," Sosar agreed pleasantly. "She asked me to find you, make sure you were being treated well, and see if you'd eaten. If it eases your mind any, I'll do the same for you."

Miach sighed deeply. "It would ease me, actually. I don't think she's having an easy time of this. Thank you for seeing to what I dare not."

Sosar shrugged. "She always has been my favorite niece. And Sarait was my favorite sister. I think I can't, in good conscience, do anything less. So, to fulfill my promise, I'll ask if you've had anything to eat."

"I'm not sure," Miach admitted.

"Then I'll remedy that first. But before I go, tell me what you're looking for. I'm curious."

Miach considered, then decided there was no reason to be anything but honest. Perhaps he might find aid where he hadn't expected it.

"I want details about Gair's well," he said carefully. He didn't imagine Gair's name was spoken very easily inside Seanagarra's walls, and he wasn't going to be the first to break with tradition. "I'd also like to know about the spells involved in opening that well and perhaps even a bit more about the events of that day." He paused. "And I'd like to know about the talisman your father made for Sarait."

Sosar's mouth fell open. He stared at Miach in astonishment for a moment or two, then shut his mouth and smiled. "My father underestimates you. How did you know about the amulet?"

Miach smiled, relieved to know he'd been right. "I read something at Lismòr about your father giving up his crown for a year in consequence of his labors on it. I assumed he had made something to protect Sarait."

Sosar studied him silently for a moment or two, then smiled. "I'll help you. What did you ask for?"

"The history of your father's reign, volume nine hundred fifty."

"You won't want that," Sosar said cheerfully. "I'll go get you something far more interesting."

Miach watched as Sosar hopped over the desk, then continued on back into forbidden territory. There was a loud squawk, a few minutes of loud arguing, then more squawking. Sosar walked out of the rows of shelves with two books in his hands. He vaulted back over the restraining rope, then handed his finds to Miach.

"Start with these."

Miach accepted them gratefully. "You've saved me time."

"I imagine I have. And I give you permission to threaten Leabhrach with your sword if he becomes feisty. I'll come back with food so you don't starve—and to make sure you haven't been tossed in the dungeon."

Miach smiled deprecatingly. "I suppose it's a concern, isn't it?" He started to walk away, then paused and looked at Morgan's uncle. "Is there anything else you'd like to tell me that I won't read here?"

Sosar leaned back against the table and shrugged. "It is entirely possible that I might know where a few more interesting things are hiding. I suppose it would be impolite to point out that you've never asked for my aid before, wouldn't it?"

"It would be nothing more than I deserve," Miach agreed, "though you'll have to concede that I haven't been rummaging about in your private books, won't you?"

Sosar laughed. "You're shameless, lad. At least your mother paid me a compliment or two before she wrestled spells out of my numb fingers."

"I don't have her charm," Miach admitted. "I just muddle through as best I can."

"How many of my spells did she teach you?" Sosar asked, studying him with a faint smile. "Just out of curiosity."

"More than you would remember giving her."

Sosar blinked, then laughed out loud. "I daresay." He looked at Miach, then laughed again. "Read that business, then I'll see if I can find you other things." He pushed away from the table. "For now, I'll find you something to eat."

"I appreciate your help, Your Highness."

Sosar smiled. "It's Sosar, Prince Mochriadhemiach."

"It's Miach, Sosar."

Sosar extended his hand and shook Miach's. "An ally in the court. What legendary feat will you accomplish next?"

"The Fates are breathlessly awaiting it."

Sosar laughed again, then walked away. "No doubt."

Miach carried his treasures over to a cushioned chair next to a roaring fire, laid his sword on the floor, and sat down. Well, the first thing he would admit was that Sìle's library was by far the most comfortable he'd ever been in. He could only hope the quality of information he would glean would be equally as magnificent.

He sat and opened the first book. It was a detailed court history and he did as Sosar had suggested and skimmed it. It was interesting, but not overly enlightening. He had just flipped past the last page when he looked up to find Sosar walking toward him bearing a tray.

"Strength for your labors," he said, setting it down on the table near Miach's chair.

"Thank you," Miach said, with feeling.

Sosar filched an apple and tossed it up in the air. "My pleasure. And just so you know, Mhorghain has been in Sarait's chamber most of the afternoon."

Miach closed his eyes briefly. "Poor gel."

"Aye," Sosar agreed. "I fear things will only get worse. I heard that my sire is planning a formal ball tomorrow night. I suspect he'll have an elvish prince or two to present to your lady."

"Perfect," Miach muttered.

"I doubt you'll be invited," Sosar continued, his eyes twinkling, "but never fear. I'll go and take copious notes on everything that happens. Every glance, every compliment, every kiss—dutifully recorded for your pleasure."

Miach gave him a baleful look. "Are you being helpful?"

Sosar grinned. "Of course not, but you couldn't expect anything else. Actually, I imagine you'll be too busy reading all the deliciously forbidden things I find for you to think about who might be wooing your lady. I might even find a book or two of spells for you."

"I'd rather dance with your niece."

Sosar straightened and laughed. "You are a besotted pup. Enjoy your reading, Miach. I'll keep you apprised of the madness above."

Miach watched him go, then poured himself wine. He flipped open the cover of the second book. He set his wine down carefully and stared in amazement at what he was holding in his hands.

It was Làidir's private journal.

Miach supposed he really shouldn't be reading it, but it was too great a gift not to. He turned pages gingerly, trying not to pay heed to more than he had to.

And then he saw Gair's name.

He closed his eyes briefly, then began to read.

He was immediately drawn into Làidir's world. However prickly the eldest prince of Tòrr Dòrainn might have been in person, he was, in his writing, rather likeable. He recorded all he saw and felt with an unvarnished honesty that was engrossing.

Miach watched events unfold from Làidir's eyes and saw Gair from an entirely different perspective, the perspective of a man who had been befriended by Gair, then watched him destroy Sarait's life. He read of attempts to take the children away, to take Sarait and the children away, to make a magic that would render Gair powerless. He read with a sickening feeling just how powerful Gair had been—powerful enough to leave the elves of Tòrr Dòrainn believing that they could not stop him.

He watched, with Làidir, as Sìle held Mhorghain in his arms and vowed on his life that he would see Sarait and the children protected. He listened in on conversations between Làidir and Sìle concerning how best to see that done. He watched them finally decide on an amulet that Sarait could claim was a simple gift from her father. He stood at Sìle's elbow over the course of months and read the spells that were used in the amulet's fashioning.

He memorized those, of course, without hesitation.

He read of Sìle's fury at Sarait's refusal to accept his talisman, then his anguish once the fury had dissipated. Làidir had supposed that Sarait had been afraid Gair would sense the amulet's power, then her plan would have been ruined. She had been determined to kill Gair herself and confident she could manage it without help.

Miach took a deep breath, then continued to watch with Làidir as events marched relentlessly on toward their disastrous conclusion. He saw the events of the year Sìle had spent recovering from his magic, watched Sarait visit often and spend most of her time in the library searching for spells to help her. He read them one by one, then sat for a minute and contemplated them.

At first blush, they seemed more than adequate for her purposes. He rubbed his finger over his lips thoughtfully. Truly, Sarait had been powerful. There was no reason she shouldn't have succeeded. He was missing something, obviously.

Perhaps it was the same thing Sarait had missed.

He ignored the chill that ran down his spine at that thought. He continued on with Làidir as Làidir watched Sarait come for a final visit. Sìle pleaded with her to remain. She vowed she could not; she would destroy Gair and free herself and her children. She'd had no choice. Gair had become increasingly irrational and had begun to accuse the children of plotting to steal his magic.

Miach paused and considered that for quite some time. He had wondered, over the past pair of months, why Sarait had allowed her children anywhere near the well. He realized now, as he continued on, that she had feared for their lives.

Besides, her children hadn't been all that young. Morgan had been six, true, but the eldest, Keir, had been a score and eight.

His own age, actually.

He ignored the shiver that crawled up his spine, then turned back to the diary. Once the children had known what Sarait intended, the older lads had insisted they come along, determined to add their magic to their mother's when the time came. As for the younger lads and Morgan, Sarait hadn't dared let them out of her sight, lest Gair make good on his threats.

What a terrible choice. Miach pitied her for finding herself needing to make it.

Sìle raged in such a frenzied fashion after she left that final time that they all despaired of him ever finding his wits again.

Làidir followed to gather tidings. By the time he'd reached the well, Gair, Sarait, and the children were dead. The destruction had been so complete that not even all the bodies had remained. Sarait had been lying next to the well, her hands on it as if she'd been in the middle of a spell when she'd been slain.

Làidir had then found a woman who claimed to have sheltered Keir, but she'd been so terrified of things she wouldn't name that Làidir hadn't managed to pry any but the barest of details from her. She'd said that Keir had indeed come to her, he'd died in her house, then others of Ceangail had come to take him away and cremate him.

Miach looked into the fire. First Keir had died, then he had disappeared, and now he had died again. He wanted to believe there was something to the discrepancies, but he dared not. Contradictions in differing versions of the same tale were legion. It was interesting, but not unusual.

He turned instead to something else that had puzzled him. Why had Gair named himself after a place that hadn't belonged to him, given that his father was from Ainneamh and his mother from Camanaë? Ceangail was not a place travelers nowadays went willingly, for 'twas rumored that there was evil in the forest . . . there . . .

Miach froze.

There was evil in Ceangail.

He sat there for several minutes, stunned by the direction his thoughts were taking him. Was it possible that Gair's well was still geysering, twenty years later? Was *that* what was washing away his spells?

He examined the possibility of that from all angles and decided upon one thing only.

He was an idiot.

A deep shudder went through him. How could he have been so stupid? He rubbed his hands over his face. He should have seen it before. If that evil was still gushing out of that well, it was possible it was trickling down through all the Nine Kingdoms. He had no idea why it had only begun to assault his spells in the fall, but there had to be an answer to that as well.

He turned back to the diary and continued on. Làidir had come home and relayed the tidings to the king. Sìle had turned away and refused to speak further of the entire affair.

Làidir continued on with the events of his own life, but Miach shut the book before he went any further. Those were details he didn't need.

He stared down at the book in lap. The most unsettling thing about what he'd read was seeing in such detail just how badly Sarait had failed. Surely she would have known the spell Gair had intended to use to open the damned well. Nay, something had gone horribly awry.

He drew his hand over his eyes, then set the book aside. It was enough for the day.

He looked around him to see if anyone else was left below and saw a woman sitting across the room from him. She was arrestingly beautiful, with dark hair curling down to her waist, dressed in a lovely, flowing white gown. She wore a crown, but it was slightly askew—

Miach realized with a start that it was Morgan.

He rose to his feet in astonishment, then crossed the room toward her. He went down on one knee in front of her and stared at her because he simply couldn't look away.

He felt a little winded. "Morgan?"

She shoved her crown back atop her head. "Who else?" she said crossly.

"I thought there for a minute that I was dreaming," he said. "You look so . . . well, elvish."

"I feel ridiculous."

"You're absolutely stunning, despite how you might feel." He brought her hand to his mouth. "I'm almost afraid to touch you."

"I'm afraid to move." She pulled him up to sit in the chair next to her. She laced her fingers with his. "This thing is completely impractical. I had to leave Mehar's knife under my pillow because I didn't have a decent place to stash it. I didn't dare put a spell on it," she said unhappily. "I also learned this afternoon that Sìle wants me to begin lessons in Fadaire. I didn't dare tell him what you'd already taught me." She paused. "I don't think that I should have anything to do with that magic right now, do you?"

"Learning the spells wouldn't harm anything," he said, "but I think you shouldn't use them." He reached out to wrap a lock of her curling hair around his finger. "You're very distracting in that gown."

She blew a stray hair out of her eyes. "Am I less distracting in boots?"

He laughed softly. "Nay. I just didn't expect the pleasure of seeing you today. I'm overwhelmed. And your hands are cold—" He stopped suddenly. "You were in Sarait's bedchamber today, weren't you?"

She started to shiver. "It wasn't as disturbing as I thought it would be, but . . ."

"But?"

She took a deep breath. "I look like her."

"Of course you do, my love," he said quietly. He rose and pulled Morgan up with him. "That padded chair over there in front of the fire is large enough for two if we're friendly."

"Will you hold my feet?"

He realized then that tears were rolling down her cheeks. "Of course, Morgan."

She walked with him across the chamber, then waited whilst he sat down. She kicked off her shoes and curled up on his lap. He took her very cold feet in his hands and rubbed them until they weren't quite so chilly. Then he reached up and took off her crown to set it aside. He trailed his fingers through her hair and looked at her gravely.

"Would you like to tell me about it?" he ventured.

She took a deep breath, then nodded. "I saw paintings of Sarait's children."

"And how was that?"

She met his gaze. "I knew them."

"Did you?" he asked gently.

She nodded. "I can't deny what my eyes have seen, but I don't want to believe it." She hesitated, then put her arms around his neck and buried her face in his hair. "I wish I were anywhere but here."

Miach held her as she shook. He didn't think she was weeping, but he couldn't help but think that would have been better than what she was doing.

"You should have sent for me," he said quietly.

She let out a shuddering breath. "Queen Brèagha offered to fetch you, but I thought you might be busy—"

"Morgan!"

A half sob escaped her, then she took a deep breath. She pulled back and pressed her sleeve-covered fists against her eyes for a moment. "I've spent my whole life alone. Now, it seems a strange thing to not be with you." She took her hands away and looked at him. "Isn't that odd? I never expected that when I left Gobhann to come with you."

"I'm so happy you did," he said, taking her face in his hands and wiping her cheeks with his thumbs. "Thank you, my love. And the next time I'm too stupid to sense your distress, send for me."

She managed a faint smile. "It was enough to know you were near, though I cannot deny it was difficult to face alone." She looked at him seriously. "I will give you anything you ask if you'll fly away with me right now."

He combed through her hair with his fingers for a few moments, then met her eyes. "Of course I will go with you," he said. "If that is what you truly want."

She looked at him for several moments in silence, then sighed and put her head on his shoulder. Miach put his arms around her and simply held her until her breathing evened out and deepened. He knew she didn't sleep because she was stroking the side of his hand she held.

He didn't press her for a decision. It was certainly one he couldn't make for her.

He heard the door behind them open, listened to Sosar and Leabhrach argue for a moment, then heard a tray be set down with a bang. Supper had arrived, apparently.

He looked up as Sosar came to a halt in front of them. Sosar had hardly opened his mouth to speak before there was a bellow from behind them.

"What in the *hell* is going on here?"

Sosar was already striding back across the library before Miach could ask him if he would mind seeing to the disturbance.

He didn't bother looking over his shoulder because he could easily hear Làidir and Sosar discuss quite vigorously the fact that Sosar was a liar and Mhorghain was consorting with someone who should have been thrown in the dungeon yesterday.

"Leave them be," Sosar said loudly. "If you have half a thought in that empty head of yours, you'll turn around, make yourself present at table, and keep your mouth shut. And take this bloody, huffing keeper of the books with you. We would like a bit of peace."

"You lied," Làidir repeated incredulously. "You said Mhorghain was indisposed, yet here she is—with *him*! You *lied*."

"Aye, I lied," Sosar said unrepentantly. "I lied and I will again. Mhorghain is tired, heartsick, and in need of comfort. It isn't for you to say where she finds it."

"But—"

"Go!"

Miach listened to Leabhrach and Làidir being shoved out of the room and the door being slammed behind them. He trailed his fingers idly through Morgan's hair and listened to Sosar curse as he apparently looked for a lock. He was soon weaving a spell of closing Miach suspected would take Sìle and Làidir both to undo.

Morgan sighed. She lifted her head and looked at him bleakly. He smiled and smoothed her hair back from her face.

"Stay or go?" he asked quietly.

She took a deep breath. "I do not run."

"Nay, love, you don't."

She closed her eyes briefly. "You have more to do here, don't you?"

"A bit, but I might find those answers elsewhere. Don't stay on my account."

She looked at him, then nodded just the slightest bit. "I'll stay. But I want to remain with you tonight whilst you work."

"I would welcome your company," he said. "I'm sure Sosar's spell will win us peace. And if it doesn't, I have my sword."

She hugged him briefly, then dragged her sleeve across her

eyes and looked up as Sosar sat down across from them. "I don't suppose you brought supper, did you?"

"The finest the kitchens could produce. And, as you heard, I lied through my teeth so you could eat it here and not upstairs. Is there another lad to equal me anywhere?"

Morgan smiled faintly. "I suppose I'll reserve judgment until I've seen what you brought."

Miach watched Sosar fetch a tray laden with food from across the room and set it on another table in front of the fire. He would have given Morgan her own chair, but she seemed content to share with him. He ate, made sure she did as well, then sat back and listened to Sosar relate impossibly unflattering tales of men, dwarves, and elves of Ainneamh who had come to woo the various eligible, elvish misses to be found within Tòrr Dòrainn's borders.

Miach supposed that Morgan might have even laughed at one point. For himself, he was simply happy to have her near. He would have to work eventually, but for the moment, he was content.

"I envy you."

Miach realized that Sosar was speaking to him. "Do you? Why?"

Sosar looked at him evenly. "A beautiful woman who obviously loves you? I should be so fortunate. I don't suppose you have any sisters tucked away in Tor Neroche, do you?"

"You know I don't," Miach said.

"I won't bother asking Mhorghain. It wouldn't do me any good if she had a sister. I suppose 'tis up to me to find myself a bride."

"Why aren't you wed?" Morgan asked.

"I have a sour disposition."

She smiled. "I daresay you don't. You should make a visit to Lismòr. Lord Nicholas is a decent matchmaker."

Miach listened to Morgan and Sosar discuss whether or not Nicholas had any taste when it came to matters of the heart and smiled to himself. If Nicholas could have seen Morgan at the moment, he would have been very relieved. She had faced many, many difficult things and survived.

Well, perhaps that wasn't exactly true. She spoke to Sosar

at length about several things, but she avoided discussing her place as a princess of Sìle's court, she hedged when Sosar asked about her magic, and she completely ignored any tentative references he made to Sarait.

Miach wasn't surprised.

She turned to him, at one point, smiled bleakly, then leaned close and kissed him.

Sosar cleared his throat. "Cards, anyone? Before you nauseate me overmuch with any more of that sort of affection?"

"Miach will lose," Morgan said without hesitation. "He doesn't cheat well."

"But I do," Sosar said, pulling cards out of thin air and shuffling them expertly, "so perhaps you and I will have a game after all."

Miach played only one hand, partly because he preferred to simply watch Morgan and partly because as much as he would have liked to ignore them, his thoughts nagged at him.

He needed to find that well and he would have to go see it without Morgan.

She wouldn't like that.

"Miach?"

He pulled himself back to himself. "Aye?"

"I think we're distracting you," she said quietly. "I don't have to stay—"

"I want you to," he said, putting his arms around her waist.

"I'll stay as well," Sosar said. "It will irritate Làidir no end to know we're safely tucked inside here whilst he remains without, and you know I can't pass up an opportunity to do that."

Miach smiled and closed his eyes. He felt Morgan kiss his cheek, then pull away to sit on the floor between his feet. He heard her talking with Sosar quietly, but soon lost himself in his work.

By the time he finished, Morgan had fallen asleep with her arms around his calf and her head on his knee. He looked at Sosar and found him watching them both with a smile.

"I approve," he said softly.

"A pity yours isn't the approval I need," Miach said with a deep sigh.

"It helps, though, doesn't it?"

"Aye," Miach agreed, "it does."

"Did you find anything interesting today?"

Miach nodded. "Those were handy things you gave me, but I'm sure you knew that already. What else can you find me?"

"I'll see," Sosar said. "I'll meet you here in the morning and we'll have at it. Now, why don't you kiss that girl of ours once more, then let me walk her to her chamber. It will no doubt be what keeps you free of the dungeon and able to peruse more things you shouldn't."

Miach nodded, then put his hand on Morgan's head. She woke immediately, then looked up at him.

"Finished?"

"For tonight," he said. "Let Sosar walk you back. I'll see you at some point tomorrow. For a proper good night, if nothing else."

She nodded, accepted Sosar's help to her feet, and only hesitated just a bit before she accepted her crown that Miach handed her. She leaned over and kissed him.

"Be here tomorrow," she whispered against his mouth.

"I will," he promised.

She put her arm around his neck, hugged him briefly, then walked away before he could say anything else to her. He watched her leave the library, but she didn't turn to look at him again. He looked at the door for quite some time, then leaned his head against the back of the chair and closed his eyes. At least Morgan would be safe whilst he saw to a few more unpleasant matters of business.

He had to find that well—to see if he was mistaken, if nothing else. He had the sinking feeling he wasn't. His spells were being undermined as if a tide washed them away. What better to do that than evil flowing from a well? The sooner he determined whether or not he was right, the better off Neroche's defenses would be.

He only hoped he would be able to find that well before someone else managed to open it fully.

Twenty-two

Three days later, Morgan sat at the high table in Sìle's hall and stared fondly at the lovely eating dagger in front of her. It seemed a shame to sully it with the blood of either of the dolts sitting next to her, eating Sìle's food and generally making nuisances of themselves, but she was tempted. Those fools were Draghail and Buaireil of Ainneamh and they were two of the three lads Sìle had been able to produce on short notice to come court her.

Hence her search for something sharp to disabuse them of that notion.

Her first instinct, when she had been introduced to the elves on either side of her, had been to tell her grandfather to go to hell, that she could choose her own husband, but she supposed Sìle knew that already. Her only avenues of escape had been either to hide with her grandmother and learn deportment or feign interest in court politics so Sìle would go on about it and spare her lectures on the proper sort of man for her.

All of which resulted in her knowing several sets of dance steps and which visiting ambassadors she could safely insult, but not much else.

She had only seen Miach in passing. He was generally with Sosar when she did see him, which eased her mind about how he was being treated, but it didn't ease her heart. She supposed he was doing what he needed to do.

She was fairly certain, though, that he had to be finished with it by now and it was past time for them to be going. She had been polite, memorized all the spells Sìle had pressed upon her, and given him more time and deference than she'd ever intended to. She was, to put it simply, finished.

"So, Princess Mhorghain," the elf on her right said, leaning in very close and almost felling her with his perfume, "I thought you would be interested in the extent of my wealth."

Morgan opened her mouth to tell him she couldn't have cared less, but she was interrupted by her aunt Ciatach pulling her chair out from underneath her.

"Come with me," Ciatach said, catching her by the arm and hauling her to her feet. "Hurry."

Morgan had no idea what was wrong, but if it meant she could escape the table and the buffoons peopling it, she was for it.

She stopped Ciatach just outside the dining hall. "What is it? Is it Miach?"

"Aye."

Dread settled into the pit of her stomach. She ran through corridors with her aunt until they reached a gate that opened onto a field that could have passed for lists in any other place. She slowed to a walk, then came to a complete stop. The lists were being used for swordplay, to be sure. She found that the combatants were two she wouldn't have expected to see there. One was Miach; the other was Cruadal of Duibhreas.

Cruadal had been the first of her potential suitors to arrive. Even if her heart hadn't already been given, she never would have considered him. He made her skin crawl.

She looked out over the field. She supposed one might have said that Miach was fighting him. To her mind, Miach was embarrassing him, but the other man didn't seem to realize it. Cruadal was boasting in a most obnoxious manner that he would most certainly have—

Mhorghain of Tòrr Dòrainn.

"Cruadal challenged Prince Mochriadhemiach a quarter of an hour ago," Ciatach said quietly.

"For me?"

"Aye. Sosar thought you should be here."

Morgan saw Sosar standing off to her left. Sìle was there as well, as was Làidir. Neither her grandfather nor his heir were doing anything besides standing with their arms folded over their chests and identical, inscrutable expressions on their faces.

There would be no aid from that quarter.

Perhaps Sosar would be up for it, if necessary. Morgan thanked her aunt quietly for the escort, then went to stand next to her uncle. She clasped her hands in front of her, under her sleeves where no one would see how white her knuckles were.

Miach was, she had to admit, a spectacular swordsman, but she didn't know enough about Cruadal to speculate on what he would do when he realized his swordplay was not going to win the day for him. He wasn't arrogant in the overly loud, obnoxious way that only bespoke stupidity. He was arrogant in a cold, cruel way that made her want to have a blade in her hand, just in case.

"This is promising," Sosar remarked.

"Do you think so?" she asked, not taking her eyes off the field.

"It says Cruadal thinks our good mage has some claim on you. That alone made my father grind his teeth."

Morgan pursed her lips. "That won't mean much if Miach is dead, will it? Not that he'll lose. As you can see, he earned what he took away from Gobhann."

Sosar smiled. "You, or his mark?"

"Both," she said pointedly.

Sosar only smiled and turned back to his contemplation of the battle in front of him. He frowned suddenly.

"What's he doing?"

Morgan was almost positive Weger had once said the same thing about Miach. She let out her breath slowly. "He's allowing Cruadal to underestimate him. 'Tis his favorite ploy."

"I hope it serves him," Sosar muttered. "Cruadal is famous for his sword skill."

"Surely not," Morgan said in disbelief. "I could best that bumbling oaf with one hand and a broken blade. I think Miach could use a few harsh words on him and send him scampering off in tears." She looked at Sosar assessingly. "I think, uncle, that even you might be able to best him."

Sosar laughed. "Good heavens, Mhorghain, you are harsh."

"Seasoned," she corrected. "Cruadal is cruel but relatively harmless. Miach will have no trouble with him."

"I hope you're right," Sosar said slowly. "I hope so indeed."

Morgan decided there was no reason to try to convince him of anything. He would see in time that she spoke the truth.

She watched, suppressing her yawns, then suddenly found herself quite a bit more awake as Cruadal conjured up a second sword. Morgan knew that Miach wouldn't use magic to do the like and she wished that she'd brought her blade. She could have at least thrown it to him.

Perhaps it wouldn't matter, in the end. Cruadal was not Miach's equal. He would not best him.

Miach threw away any pretense of being less than he was. He fought with a ruthlessness that might have forced even Weger to give a slight nod of approval. As for herself, she found herself a little breathless at the sight of him and she wasn't one to swoon over a man. He was a lethal bit of business clad all in black, and if Cruadal had had any sense, he would have turned tail and fled.

Unfortunately, he seemed not to have any sense. He did, however, have that savage streak that she had sensed in him. Stupid and cruel, but ruthless nonetheless. He used his two swords to their best advantage, then started to weave spells as he fought.

Morgan realized she was chewing on her lips only because she bit down too hard and it hurt. She wiggled her jaw, took a deep breath, and forced herself to relax her hands. Miach would manage what he needed to. He wasn't, as he had once said, a village witch's brat. Searbhe had learned that well enough.

Miach avoided Cruadal's spells, stepped around them, and flat out ignored them. Perhaps he was canny enough at present to avoid the traps Cruadal was setting for him, but Morgan had to concede that there would surely come a time when he could do so no longer.

Sosar was watching the field with a look of astonishment. "Use your magic, you fool!" he shouted at one point.

"Then cover what I do!" Miach shouted back.

"Sosar most certainly will not," Sìle bellowed, his face turning red. "You insolent *boy*, are you ashamed to have anyone know you've been here?"

Morgan shoved past Làidir and ran to stand in front of Sìle. "He's trying to protect me—"

"Nonsense," Sìle huffed. "He's being disrespectful."

"He isn't," Morgan insisted. "There are creatures outside your borders that are hunting us. If Miach uses any magic, he will draw them to us." She put her hands on his crossed arms. "Cruadal will use whatever magic he has to hand without thought, but Miach will not because he wants to protect *me*. If you do not at least hide what he does, you doom him to defeat."

Sìle looked down at her stiffly. "I will not aid him."

"But you won't stop me from doing it, will you, Father?" Sosar said sharply.

Sìle shot his son a murderous look, but said nothing. He merely turned back and looked over Morgan's head at the field where curses mingled with the ring of swords. Morgan slowly and very deliberately turned her back on her grandfather, then walked over to stand next to Sosar.

"Will you help us?" she asked quietly.

"Absolutely."

"Sosar," Sìle warned with a growl.

Sosar ignored him. He spoke several sharp words and made a sweeping gesture with his hand. Morgan watched as a shimmering arc of magic sprang up over Miach and Cruadal. It spread out until it formed a ceiling five score feet in the air, then walls dropped down like curtains to the ground. The entire spell glistened for a moment, then faded until there was only a hint of magic there. It was so beautiful, Morgan had to blink away tears. It seemed almost blasphemous that something so lovely should enclose something so terrible.

Once the wall touched the ground, Miach threw away his sword. Morgan gaped, then stepped forward in surprise. She heard a horrible rending sound and realized, only because Sosar caught her before she fell on her face, that she had stepped on the hem of her dress and ripped it half off. Sosar whispered a spell and the gown was made whole.

"Thank you," Morgan said. "Now let go of me so I can beat some sense into him—"

"Don't," Sosar warned. He kept hold of her arm. "Let him fight as he knows best. And watch through the filter of elven magic. You'll see things you wouldn't otherwise."

She didn't want to leave Miach to his own devices, but she supposed she could trust that he didn't need any aid. She also didn't want to watch, but she was not a fainthearted miss, so she put her shoulders back and contented herself with knowing that Miach was defending her honor.

Cold comfort indeed.

Cruadal threw his swords at Miach. They burst into flame and became barbed as they flew. Miach waved them off and they exploded with the light of a thousand torches. Cruadal changed himself into a snake with half a dozen striking heads with venom dripping from their exposed fangs.

"Disgusting," Sìle snapped.

Morgan didn't comment. She was far too busy gaping. Miach had become a bitter frost that covered the snakes and rendered them slow and useless. The next minute Miach was himself again and he was throwing a human-again Cruadal across the field.

"He should just kill him," Morgan said under her breath.

"He doesn't dare," Làidir said slowly. "Sìle will not forgive murder within his gates."

"And if Cruadal murders Miach?" Morgan said, turning to look up at him. "Then what is left me? Miach's honor to keep me warm for the rest of my days? Will your father do me the courtesy of putting Cruadal's head on a pike outside my door so I'll have something to watch as my heart breaks into thousands of pieces?" She paused and glared at him. "Did you let this proceed?"

He hesitated. "They are grown men, Mhorghain. They know what they're doing—"

"Which they wouldn't be doing if Cruadal hadn't been invited," she said bitterly.

Sìle shifted, but said nothing.

"What was I to do when Cruadal issued the challenge?" Làidir asked her. "Forbid it and cost Prince Mochriadhemiach his pride?"

"Nay, you shouldn't have done anything," Morgan said sharply. "But your father should have listened to me when I told him I wasn't interested in any of the princes he was determined to auction me off to."

Làidir chose, perhaps wisely, to remain silent.

Morgan shot Sìle a glare, which he didn't see, then turned away from the both of them. She found that Sosar was rocking back on his heels, his hands clasped behind his back, whistling softly. She was quite happy for someone else to glare at.

"I think your levity is misplaced," she said curtly.

"You don't actually think Miach will lose, do you?" he said in surprise. "Good heavens, Mhorghain, you have no idea who he truly is."

"I know who he is," she muttered.

"Then instead of wringing your hands like a fretful alewife, why don't you enjoy the spectacle? I can't imagine he has much call for this sort of display at Tor Neroche."

Morgan cursed him, but it didn't ease her any. It was one thing to discuss Miach in a scholarly sort of way and hope for the best; it was another thing entirely to watch him fighting off the ferocious attack of a man with nothing to lose. Perhaps it would have been easier if she'd had anger to keep her warm. Now all she had was the cold terror of fearing that perhaps Miach might stumble, or slip, or falter and she wouldn't have the skill to aid him.

It made her wish she'd paid quite a bit more attention to the spells Sìle had tried to teach her.

Cruadal took shape after shape, each more terrifying than before. Miach exceeded him in each: things with claws; creatures with fangs dripping with blood; huge, wild-eyed men covered with open sores full of maggots.

Sosar made appreciative noises.

Sìle did not.

And then, quite suddenly, in Cruadal's place stood an enormous, misshapen troll. Morgan blinked. She had to stare at it for a moment before she realized what was so shocking about it.

It was the same sort of creature that hunted her and Miach.

Miach stood there just a moment too long, gaping in surprise. The creature snatched him up, bound him with cords of magic, then held him over his head and flung him against the smooth rock wall that bordered the field. Morgan took several steps forward, then stopped still.

Miach no longer hurtled toward the wall. Instead, there was darkness—

Morgan found herself jerked around by Sosar.

"Don't look," he commanded.

"Aye, let her look," Sìle snarled. "Let her see what he is."

Morgan looked up at Sosar, then slowly pulled herself away from him and turned around.

She saw and heard the spells of Olc that Miach wove, spells full of the worst things from her nightmares. The darkness that made up the core of what he'd turned himself into terrified her where she stood, and she was not the object of its wrath. It was full of terrible claws, silver, glittering, all extended toward Cruadal.

Cruadal screamed and fell backward into his own shape. He looked into the darkness and screamed again and again until he was hoarse. Who knew what he saw? Morgan wanted to look away, but she couldn't bring herself to.

"Is this the sort of man you want?" Sìle said, shooting her a furious look. "One who has this sort of darkness in him? I don't suppose he's ever told you that his mother's grandfather was Wehr of Wrekin, has he? Wehr, whose power was greater even than Lothar of Wychweald's? And he's Lothar's cousin, as well! He has more dark magic inside himself than light—"

"Would you rather have him conjure up flowers and twittering birds to defend me with?" Morgan shot back. "I think I would rather have a man who isn't afraid to fight for me, no matter how he goes about it."

Sìle grunted. "More darkness than light. Mark my words."

"Marked and discounted," Morgan said, before she thought better of it.

Sìle shot her a displeased look, then turned back to watch the battle.

Actually, it wasn't a battle for much longer. After only a moment or two more, Cruadal was simply lying on the field, curled in a ball with his hands over his head, whimpering as the darkness loomed over him.

In the space of a heartbeat, the darkness left and in its

place stood Miach with his hands down by his sides, his chest heaving.

"Yield," he demanded.

Cruadal said nothing.

"Yield, you fool!" Miach bellowed.

"I yield," Cruadal said, rolling away suddenly and heaving himself to his feet. He dragged his arm across his face. "Honorless whoreson."

Miach backhanded him and sent him sprawling. "My mother was Desdhemar, queen of Neroche, and she was not a whore." His expression was cold. "Stay away from Mhorghain. I'll kill you if you come near her again."

Cruadal only remained silent.

Miach turned and started to walk off the field, then he stopped in mid-step when he caught sight of her. He bowed his head, dragged his hand through his hair, then went to find his sword. He resheathed it, then turned and came through Sosar's magic. He stopped a pair of paces away from her and bowed to her.

"Your Highness," he said quietly.

He was simply drenched in sweat, his hair was plastered to his head, and his eyes were full of wildness—only this was something entirely different from dragon wildness.

It was not pleasant.

She supposed he didn't come any closer because he feared she would be repulsed or terrified or some other womanly emotion Weger wouldn't have approved of at all.

He sighed and took a step backward.

Morgan threw herself at him. She wrapped her arms around his neck and held on tightly.

"Morgan, I'll sully your gown—" he said, trying to unwrap her arms from around his neck.

"I don't give a damn about the dress," she said.

"Morgan—"

"Damn you, put your arms around me!"

He relented and hugged her tightly. She closed her eyes and held on to him as he shook. She supposed he wouldn't notice, then, that she was trembling far worse than he was. She heard Sìle cursing, Làidir trying to calm him, Sosar offering biting observations about his father's taste in suitors, but she didn't respond to anything. She simply held on to Miach and muttered curses in his ear each time he started to release her.

He surrendered with a sigh.

In time, she felt the darkness begin to leave him as surely as if she'd seen it go. Once he felt more like himself, she released him and sank back down on her heels.

"Thank you for defending my honor," she said quietly.

"I think, my love, that *that* should count as a fair bit of wooing."

She smiled. "I agree wholeheartedly."

He started to say something else, then looked over her head. The next thing Morgan knew, she was standing behind him and he was holding on to her arm so hard to keep her there that she didn't dare move. She did, however, peek around him in time to see Cruadal sauntering over to Sìle, looking as if he'd learned not a bloody thing in the past hour.

"He should have killed me," he said with a yawn. "His kindness will be his undoing." He looked at Miach. "I'll have her yet."

Morgan tried to get around Miach, but he wouldn't release her.

"I told you," Miach said in a voice so cold it made her stop suddenly, "that if you come near her again, I will kill you."

"Will you, indeed?" Cruadal mocked. "Or will you send little Mhorghain out to fight your battles for you? I heard tell she bears Scrymgeour Weger's mark. Did she earn that in his bed—"

Morgan heard the sound of something breaking. She realized, as she saw Cruadal sprawled out unconscious on the ground at Miach's feet, that it had been something—or perhaps several somethings—in his face. Miach turned and fixed Sìle with a steely look.

"If this is the way you'll allow Princess Mhorghain to be treated, you'll excuse me if I escort her elsewhere before luncheon," he said curtly.

Sìle looked down his nose at Cruadal lying senseless at his feet. "I misjudged his character. But I don't believe I misjudged *yours* at all. That was a dreadful display." He looked at his guard. "Kill Cruadal and escort the youngest prince of Neroche to the outer gates."

Morgan pulled her arm away from Miach's hand and moved to stand next to him. "Then I go with him," she said calmly.

"You will not," Sìle said sternly.

She slipped her hand into Miach's. "Throw him out and see, if you like."

Sìle cursed, looked at her, then cursed a bit more.

"I would prefer it if you left Cruadal alive," Miach added. "If you please. I'll see to him in time."

"He'll bear you no fondness," Sìle warned.

"Does anyone?" Miach asked pointedly.

Sìle pursed his lips, then looked at Dionadair. "Do as the mage requests. Now, Mhorghain," Sìle said, turning to her, "come with me. We have business together with a pair of decent lads inside."

"And *I* have business with Prince Mochriadhemiach," she countered. "Business that will not wait."

"But those other lads—"

"Absolutely not," Morgan said sharply. She looked at Sìle. "I apologize for being frank, Grandfather, but I will not be put to market like a mare."

He opened his mouth in surprise, then shut it. He looked at her for several moments in silence before he managed to speak. "What did you call me?" he asked gruffly.

Morgan thought about it, then realized what she had said. If she'd known how much it unbalanced him, she would have done it much sooner. "I appreciate the trouble you've taken to find me a husband, *Grandfather*, but I'm not interested in any of the lads you've shown me. Now, if you'll excuse me, I'm going to cross swords with the prince of Neroche. You may not want to watch."

Sìle looked terribly indecisive, as if he couldn't decide if that were a good thing or not. Perhaps he hoped she would mortally wound Miach and save him the trouble.

He blustered, cursed, then took one of her hands and kissed it. He glared at Miach, barked at Làidir and Sosar to follow him, then walked away.

Morgan watched him go, trailed by the rest of the court who had come to witness the spectacle, then waited until they had all gone inside the gates. Then she looked at Miach.

"Well," she managed.

He gingerly put his arms around her and pulled her to him. "I wish you hadn't seen that. Especially not the last." He paused. "I'm not Gair, Morgan."

"Why would I think you were?"

"Because I lost my temper and used magic I wouldn't have if I'd been thinking clearly. I could have finished that better."

"You finished it, Miach," she said seriously, "and that is what matters. That was an interesting shape Cruadal took at the end, wasn't it?"

"It was," he agreed. "I'm tempted to follow him and see if he'll return to where he learned it."

"I'll come—"

"I wasn't serious," he said quickly. He looked at her. "At least not completely."

She frowned at him. "If you leave me behind, my lord Archmage, you will regret it."

He smiled and bent his head to kiss her carefully. "I'm properly cowed, lady. Go fetch your sword and finish the job. An hour or two spent training will put us both to rights, don't you think?"

"As well as irritating my grandfather no end," she muttered.

Miach laughed and released her. "That is always uppermost in my thoughts. Run on, gel. I'll wait for you here."

Morgan hesitated, then leaned up on her toes and kissed him quickly before she ran back to the palace. She would be grateful indeed for an hour that didn't involve magic, or elvish lords who wore troll shapes they shouldn't have known about, or duels of terrible magic.

Or dance steps, the proper way to address ambassadors from other countries, or how to pour bloody tea, for that matter.

Swords were so much simpler.

It was very late before Miach walked her to her bedchamber. After a proper morning in the lists, the afternoon had been passed pleasantly in her grandmother's private solar thanks to an invitation to come for cards and conversation. Miach had charmed everyone from her grandmother to the serving maids without an effort. Would that her grandfather would have been so won over, but she supposed there were some things better left unwished for.

Miach stopped her in front of her door, then looked down at her seriously. "I need to tell you something."

She felt a little chill settle into her at the seriousness of his tone. "What?"

"I need to make a very brief journey," he said slowly. "Alone."

"I *knew* it," she exclaimed. "Damn you, Miach, I *knew* you were going to go off on your own—"

He wrapped his arms around her and held her tightly. "I won't be gone long. It will no doubt be a useless exercise, which is why your time is better spent here. You won't even notice that I'm gone."

"Is this what being married to you will be like?" she asked, finding herself shivering all of the sudden. "You going off and leaving me behind? Waiting like a helpless woman when I could be being useful with a sword?"

"Morgan, I'm not going into battle. I'll be as invisible as the wind and back before nightfall tomorrow. *Nothing* will happen to me."

"Are you trying to convince me, or yourself?"

He laughed a little. "I'm not going to answer that." He smiled down at her. "Help Sosar find a bit of sword skill while I'm gone. Heaven knows he could use it."

"When did you decide this?" she asked.

"This morning," he said with forced cheerfulness. "Before that business with Cruadal."

He obviously wasn't giving her the entire truth, but perhaps it was pointless to press him on it. There would be times when he would need to be off and doing by himself—though he had damned well better make those times few and far between.

She cursed silently, more because it made her feel better than any anger it released. She wasn't angry. She was cold and discouraged. What she wanted was to find a hayloft and sleep in Miach's arms. She didn't fear her dreams; she hadn't dreamt of Gair since Lismòr. She did, however, dread going in her bedchamber alone.

"At least let me stay with you whilst you see to your spells," she said quietly.

He shook his head. "I'll see to them on the way. If I leave now, I'll be back before supper tomorrow."

"You're going *now*?" she asked incredulously.

"The sooner I go, the sooner I'll be back."

"Miach, I—"

She would have had quite a bit more to say, but he kissed her. In fact, he kissed her long and so well, she had a hard time remembering just what it was she'd wanted to stay. By the time he lifted his head and looked down at her, she could hardly keep her eyes open or keep herself on her feet.

"Wait for me," he whispered.

"Please be careful," she said. "Miach, if anything happened—"

"It won't." He stepped away from her. "I love you."

She could hardly see him for her tears. "Please hurry."

He nodded, then disappeared. Morgan felt a breeze stir her hair, wrap itself around her for a brief moment, then rush away. She stood there for quite some time until the last tree in Sìle's inner garden rustled and was still.

She was tempted to follow, but she'd given her word.

She went inside her chamber to look for another cloak to put on, though she supposed it wouldn't do anything for the chill that settled upon her heart.

She would give him the day, but no more.

If he wasn't back by supper on the morrow, she would go after him.

Twenty-three

❧

Miach wondered, as he flew along as a bitterly cold wind, why he didn't fly that way more often. It was a substantially more difficult change than merely something with wings, and he tended to feel a little scattered whilst he was at it, but it was much faster.

He focused his thoughts with an effort. He had told Morgan that he was simply off following a hunch. Aye, it was a hunch, but it had basis in a terrible reality.

He had found the location of Gair's well.

Simply finding the directions to it had been more difficult than he'd imagined it would be. He and Sosar had spent hour after fruitless hour in the books behind the velvet rope, enduring the screeches of Leabhrach the librarian and the silent, watchful stare of Làidir, who had suddenly taken an inordinate amount of interest in their doings. Miach had pored over maps, over histories, over obscure journals full of travels in unpleasant places. Sosar had done the same, delving through books that even Làidir warned him he shouldn't be reading. They had found it that morning, just after dawn.

But the directions hadn't been in the library.

Miach had been gingerly turning pages in a book on dwarvish travel routes to Durial that some enterprising elf had obviously pilfered at some point when he'd looked up and found Sosar gone. Làidir had shot him a long look, then turned and left the library as well.

Sosar had returned minutes later with a letter in his hands. He'd given it to Miach and said that he'd forgotten all about it until something he'd read just then had jostled his memory.

Miach had opened the letter and almost dropped it.

It was from Sarait.

Sosar had said he'd found it on his bed the morning Sarait and her children had left Seanagarra for the last time to make the long journey to Ceangail. Miach had been surprised to find that the letter hadn't been opened.

"What was the need?" Sosar had asked wearily. "I knew what she planned to do."

Miach had begun to read. He hadn't read but one paragraph before he'd realized what he'd just been given.

Directions to the well and as much of Gair's spell as Sarait had been able to piece together herself.

She warned that it wasn't the complete spell. Gair had been notorious about guarding his magic and extremely stingy with his knowledge. Sarait had suspected that he'd found something useful on one of his journeys to Beinn òrain and she'd included a list of masters she suspected might have helped him.

Sosar had cursed viciously. Miach had joined him. It was better that than to weep over events that were a score of years behind them and couldn't be changed.

But he could change the future.

He blew north until sunrise. Ceangail was on the western slopes of the Sgùrrach Mountains, so it was still in shadow when he reached it. It reminded him somewhat of Riamh, desolate and uninviting. There was a castle there, built on the side of a cliff, hovering over a valley of ruined soil. The keep was unrelentingly grim, devoid of any but the most rudimentary of windows. Miach could only imagine the darkness that dwelt inside.

Poor Sarait. How had she borne such a place, she who had spent all her life in the beauty and luxury that was Seanagarra? He pitied her as he never had before.

He scanned the countryside for landmarks, then saw, even

from a great height, a hint of a path that wound through a forest—a forest that tended to slip away out of his vision if he didn't concentrate on it fully.

Much like the magic that was assaulting his spells.

He would have caught his breath if he'd had breath to catch. So his suspicions had been right. He promised himself a good bout of surprise later. He swirled downward, slipped through the spell that covered the forest, and resumed his proper form on that path. He was immediately assailed by a chill so profound, he shivered in spite of himself.

There was more to that chill than just a forest in shadow.

He was not fainthearted, but even he hesitated. He had spent a year in a dungeon full of horrors meant to drive a man mad and walked in half a dozen other places where Olc reigned supreme and no light was possible, yet he had to force himself to walk forward here.

He saw, as he walked, why it was a man would pass the forest and never take notice of it. It was covered by the most extensive spell of un-noticing he'd ever encountered. Layer upon layer of distraction, illusion, and confusion hung in great tatters from the trees, yet now that he was under it, Miach could see how it was still intact above. A man would trudge past that forest every day of his life and never notice it unless he somehow had the misfortune to accidentally blunder under the eaves of the spell.

Miach wondered if he'd just managed to fall through a hole in it or if his magic had been enough to penetrate it.

He didn't particularly want to examine which it might be.

He continued on, feeling the remains of Gair's spells press in on him more with every step. He finally had to stop and simply breathe for a few minutes. He lifted a part of the spell that blocked his way. It moved easily, so he supposed that he wouldn't have trouble removing the entire thing if he needed to.

Though even having to touch it in any fashion was abhorrent.

He tried to ignore how it fell down through the trees like rancid bits of sunlight. The evil was everywhere, making it difficult to think, difficult to walk, difficult to breathe. Miach stopped thinking about Sarait, Morgan, or any of the rest of them having been anywhere near the place.

He hoped Gair had suffered a bloody great bit before he died.

It took what felt like hours to reach the end of the path, though he supposed it hadn't been that long. He walked out into a glade and had to lean over and stare at the ground to keep from puking.

It was so much worse than he'd thought.

The glade itself was dripping with tentacles of evil that hung down from the sky above. The air was heavy with a stench of rotting things that lay below the surface of the worst of his nightmares. It took him several minutes of desperately sucking in air before he thought he could straighten without heaving.

He managed it, eventually, then dug the heels of his hands into his eyes and blinked away the mist that blinded him. He looked in front of him.

The well was there.

It was actually a rather unassuming thing, perhaps six feet in diameter, and built up from the ground with three feet of rock. Miach would have thought it a simple country well if he hadn't known better.

And if he hadn't been able to see the evil trickling from it still.

He willed his gorge back where it belonged, then walked across the glade. He stood ten feet away from that well and watched as what should have been water but wasn't bubbled up, caught hold of the rock, then clawed its way up and over to drop onto the ground with a distinct *plop*.

Miach watched in astonishment as that evil began to take shape. There was a spell there, just under where that vile, putrid bit of watery substance fell. The spell waited patiently until enough had been gathered, then it shaped that evil into a formless creature that grew, filled in, then straightened.

And became one of the nightmares that had been hunting them.

Miach drove his sword through its heart as it flung itself toward him.

He pulled his sword free and stepped aside as the creature fell to the ground, fortunately quite dead. He walked over to the well, his sword still in his hand, and looked down. The

stench there almost knocked him flat. He looked down and
knew with a sickening bit of certainty that this was what had
been undermining his spells. How the water, if that's what it
could be called, had gotten from Ceangail to the borders of
Neroche was a mystery, but he had the feeling he knew who
was behind it.

He squatted down and looked at the spell in front of him.
He could see the strands of it as easily as if they had been
threads woven there by some untidy spider. The spell was
saturated with a vile magic that was all too familiar. Miach
swallowed his revulsion and sorted through the strands, looking for how it was fashioned and what the purpose was.

It was as all Lothar's spells were, crudely wrought but ef-
fective nonetheless. Miach saw how the creatures were made
from the watery spewings of the well and realized without surprise what they were to do.

Hunt down those with Camanaë magic and kill them.

He caught sight of something just before he stood. He
looked closer, then found himself having to lean quite thoroughly upon his sword.

They were also to hunt down Gair's descendants and carry
them to Riamh.

Miach straightened and resheathed his sword. He supposed
he shouldn't have been surprised by either. Lothar's idea of
sport was to leisurely track down any with but even a hint of
Camanaë in their blood and kill them slowly, if possible. 'Twas
a certainty he wouldn't have wanted any of Gair's descendants
interfering with his plan to rule the Nine Kingdoms.

But he didn't want to think on what Lothar planned to do
with them in his keep.

He closed his eyes briefly. No wonder they had been coming for Morgan. He supposed it also explained why Adhémar
had been hunted on the borders in the fall. Obviously, Lothar
had been somewhere nearby, watching Adhémar huffing and
puffing as he rode the northern border, then helped himself to
the king of Neroche's power simply because he could. Adhémar was too stupid to ever protect his magic, and he had paid
the price as a result. Miach had never, even in his youth, been
that foolish. He might have spent a year in Lothar's dungeon,
but Lothar hadn't been able to touch his power.

He rose and looked at the well itself. Though the cap wasn't completely covering the opening, it had been pulled over almost all the way. That said a great deal about Sarait's power.

But she had failed.

He had planned to see if he couldn't succeed where she had not, and flattered himself that he would manage it, but now he wondered if he had been overconfident.

Well, there was nothing to be done except to try. He wove a spell of concealment over himself and the well, thicker and more impenetrable than Gair's. What he intended to do would render him quite vulnerable, and he had no one to guard his back.

He set spells of ward along the spell of concealment, then added other spells that would incinerate anything that came close to him. He finished by diverting the trickle from the well so it didn't touch the magic waiting there to receive it and mold it into something else.

Once that was done, he set to work. He very carefully wove the first spell that he'd read in Sarait's letter. He threw all his own power behind it and spoke the final word with an additional word of Command attached to it.

The ground trembled beneath his feet, but the cap of the well didn't budge.

He tried the other two spells he'd found in Sarait's letter with exactly the same results. At that point, he put aside what Sarait had used and settled for things of his own making. He spoke other words of Command, he wove complicated changes of essence, he tried to seal the opening with an impenetrable spell of Binding.

The evil oozed through the last spell as if it hadn't been there.

And then his spells of ward began exploding around him.

He tore his attention away from the well and found himself surrounded on all sides by trolls. They couldn't break through his protection, fortunately, and that had apparently driven them mad. They were flinging themselves at his spell, shrieking with rage and fear.

Miach didn't have the luxury of a lengthy contemplation of what to do next. He had the feeling that even if he pulled the entire mountainside down on the well, it wouldn't do anything but bury the evil. It would bubble up eventually. It had to be capped, permanently, but it would take the proper spell.

He refused, absolutely refused, to consider the postscript of Sarait's letter.

Gair uses his own blood in all his spells. I fear that it will take one with Gair's blood to succeed. If I fail . . .

Gair's blood, or enough power. He didn't consider himself particularly arrogant, but he had a fair idea of what he could do. Perhaps Sarait hadn't been able to close the well; with the right spell, he was certain he could. He had to. He could not ask Morgan to do it for him.

Nay, he would look for the spell and see to it himself. But he wouldn't have the luxury of finding that spell if anyone knew he'd been here, poking his nose where he shouldn't be. He removed his spell that diverted that business seeping out from under the well's cap, then changed the dead troll nearby into harmless and unremarkable dirt. He then gathered up all the edges of his spells of protection. One of the trolls slipped under and rushed toward him.

He flung himself up into the air as a bitter wind, destroying his spell and sending it into untraceable oblivion. He sliced through Gair's spell, leaving behind a large contingent of furious demons. He looked down as he floated higher, watching the forest shimmer with its coating of disregard. He left it in the same state he found it. Truly, it was better if no one managed to get themselves lost there.

He turned and blew south again, keeping to the western side of the Sgùrrachs, paying no heed to the updrafts that tore into him and the peaks of the mountains that cut through him. He was heartily sick both in body and mind from what he'd seen. The fact that he now knew what was attacking Neroche and trailing after Morgan didn't ease him any.

It also left him with the uncomfortable feeling that there was still more to it than he was seeing. Lothar would have been pleased to have some new means to wreak havoc, but Miach knew damn well he wouldn't settle for that. If he had found Gair's well, he wouldn't be content with just sitting and watching it trickle. He would be actively seeking to open it fully, using any means at his disposal.

Or any*one*.

And it was only a matter of time, perhaps, before he found
out that there might be someone he could use.

Miach bolted back south.

Two hours later he reached Slighe, the village at the cross-
roads a pair of hours north of Seanagarra. It was notorious
for rough company, quietly disposed-of bodies, and very bad
ale. Miach imagined Làidir had spent more than his share of
time in the taverns there. He couldn't even truly enjoy that as
he should have.

He didn't particularly want to stop there either, but he was
exhausted. Even half an hour of simply sitting would be
enough.

He walked through the muddy streets and pulled disinterest
about him like a cloak. It kept him from being noticed, but it
didn't keep him from noticing who was cursing his way up the
same street.

Searbhe of Riamh.

Miach wasn't sure if he was surprised that Searbhe would
find himself so far from home, distressed that Searbhe was
so close to where Morgan was safely hiding, or terrified that
Searbhe might know where Morgan was.

And *who* she was.

Miach followed him without hesitation. As he did, he considered that evening when Searbhe had attacked Morgan in
Weger's gathering hall. Had it been in retaliation for Morgan's
having thrown him down the stairs, or had there been more to
it? Morgan had been particularly loath to talk about it, which
likely should have given him pause. It wasn't possible that
Searbhe had recognized Morgan as Sarait's daughter, was it?

Perhaps he had good reason to find out the truth of it.

He followed Searbhe into a particularly unpleasant-looking
tavern and took a seat in the corner where he could watch him.

Searbhe sat down near the ale keg and demanded quite
loudly to have his cup filled. Repeatedly.

Miach paid for ale that he left untouched on the table in
front of him. The serving wench didn't approach again, but
he'd planned that. What was the use in being the archmage
of Neroche if he couldn't drape himself in a decent spell of

aversion now and again? A pity he didn't dare use something to silence Searbhe.

Instead, he sat in the darkest corner of the great room and watched Searbhe drink far more ale than he should have. The longer he drank, the more he seemed to think there were actually people in the chamber who gave a damn about what he said.

Miach found that he certainly did.

"She was bloody beautiful," Searbhe said, waving his mug about expansively. "Dark-haired, green-eyed, slender. And that wench could even wield a sword."

Snorts of derision greeted that announcement.

"I lost her outside Angesand," Searbhe said, looking about himself for sympathy, but finding none. "The creatures followed her there, and I followed *them*, but I was too late to capture her."

Miach closed his eyes briefly. He had suspected they wouldn't escape that encounter completely unscathed.

"But now I have a handful of those same creatures listening to *me*. They seek out magic, you know, and *she* has an abundance of it. So does that mage who was with her."

Miach watched as every man in the chamber turned his back on Searbhe. There was one rule in Slighe: no magic was allowed. Obviously, Searbhe hadn't read the sign posted prominently over the bar. He continued to drink, continued to blather on, continued to make others in the chamber extremely uncomfortable.

Miach was equally as uncomfortable, though for different reasons.

It came as no surprise to him that Searbhe was looking for them. Miach imagined that Searbhe had every intention of doing him in if he could. He hesitated to think what Searbhe would do if he actually managed to capture Morgan. It was, however, the knowledge that Searbhe had managed to bend the wills of a few brutes to his own that was unsettling.

They would have to be seen to.

Searbhe demanded more ale, but apparently the barkeep had had enough. Before Searbhe could blurt out any more of what he planned, he'd been taken in hand by a pair of burly lads and hauled to his feet.

"I've got to find her," Searbhe slurred as he was helped toward the door. "Find the wench and I'll find the mage. And if I kill the mage, then *he* will trust me."

Miach could just imagine who *he* was. Searbhe would need to be careful or he would be meeting Smior of Treunnar's fate soon. Lothar was not one to be either trusted or courted. As Nicholas had said, he was capricious.

Miach rose and eased unobtrusively outside. Searbhe was lying in the mud, unmoving. Miach watched him for a few minutes, but the other man made no move to rise. He was breathing, though, so perhaps he would manage to get himself to his feet in time.

Miach stood in the shadows and considered. As tempting as it was to merely drag Searbhe behind the tavern and silence him forever, he just couldn't bring himself to do it. There was always something to be gained from a fool who blurted out all his secrets to anyone who would listen.

At least it didn't sound as if Searbhe knew who Morgan truly was. As far as Searbhe was concerned, Morgan was only a means to Miach himself.

Miach could understand that. He'd humiliated Searbhe more than once. He wondered, absently, if he might somehow use that to his advantage at some point.

He'd barely begun to truly contemplate that when he felt the hair on the back of his neck stand up. He looked about him, but saw nothing suspicious. Even so, he slipped along the front of the tavern slowly, then ducked into a side street and changed himself into a sparrow. Within moments, he was sitting on top of a lamppost, looking down at the street. What he saw almost knocked him off his perch.

Cruadal of Duibhreas was standing in the middle of the street, looking at where Miach had last been.

He knew he shouldn't have been surprised.

Cruadal walked over to Searbhe and hauled him up out of the mud. Cruadal shook him vigorously. Searbhe's head lolled from side to side. Cruadal swore.

"Wake up, you fool!" he shouted.

Searbhe's only answer was to vomit down the front of Cruadal's tunic.

Miach fully expected that Cruadal would fling the other

man away and stomp off in a fury. He did throw him back into the mud, but he didn't walk away. He went to sit on the edge of a horse trough, apparently content to wait for Searbhe to sleep off his malaise.

Miach watched him for quite some time, wondering if Cruadal might lose interest or if he was truly that determined. The elf didn't move, not even when a rather audacious lad bid him be off so his horse could have a drink.

The lad must have seen something that troubled him, for he gulped and backed away without making any more demands.

Miach reconsidered his decision to allow Searbhe to live. If he joined forces with Cruadal, it could spawn a truly unfortunate chain of events. Miach supposed he could rid himself of Searbhe and Cruadal both, true, but it would take killing magic, which would not only be difficult to hide but draining.

And no matter how detestable the fools in front of him were, he simply didn't have it in him to kill them without a fair fight.

Perhaps Cruadal had it aright and his kindness would be his undoing.

Well, as long as it wasn't Morgan's life in trade for it, he would keep his soul—and his kindness—intact.

He supposed, though, that any hope of keeping himself and Morgan hidden would disappear once Searbhe had regained his powers of speech and babbled every bloody thing he knew to Cruadal.

He turned away from renewed thoughts of assassination and wondered how he might turn what would no doubt become an alliance between the men in front of him to his advantage. Searbhe would wake, Cruadal would learn many things he hadn't suspected, then they would travel either to Riamh or to Tòrr Dòrainn.

Unless they could be drawn another way.

What if Searbhe managed to do what he so obviously desired? What if the man had—or thought he had—killed the archmage of Neroche? Searbhe would cease hunting Morgan and likely go back to Riamh and live out his life in boastful bliss.

Cruadal was another tale entirely. Miach suspected that if Cruadal somehow learned that Lothar wanted a descendant of

Gair's to open the well for him, he would run to Riamh as fast as his legs would carry him and attempt a bargain with Lothar himself. It wouldn't go well for him, but he would likely manage to live long enough to tell Lothar who Morgan was. Lothar would then sweep down to Tòrr Dòrainn with every fiend he'd ever created hard on his heels and pound at Sìle's spells until they gave way.

Miach calculated furiously. If he could just give himself a se'nnight's time, long enough to be in and out of Beinn òrain and back to Gair's well. He would shut it, stop the magic, then return to Tòrr Dòrainn to put himself between Morgan and Lothar.

And this time, he *would* keep her safe.

He had a final look at Searbhe, but saw no change in his condition. He flung himself up into the sky and flapped off energetically. He watched behind him, but saw nothing following him. He flew into the nearby forest, then swept up out of it as a strong north wind, tearing south toward Tòrr Dòrainn.

He would spent a few hours in Seanagarra, see to Morgan's protection as best he could, then determine how in the hell he was going to leave her behind and convince her to stay there. She wouldn't agree, but he had no choice. He was not going to subject her to Gair's evil and he wouldn't leave her vulnerable to Lothar's rage.

He would keep her safe, if it meant his own life in trade.

Twenty-four

❧

Morgan walked down the passageway, cursing under her breath. The afternoon had waned and still Miach had not returned. She had spent the morning trying to beat the truth out of Sosar in the lists, but he had proven to be more closed-mouthed than she would have expected, even under such duress. She'd allowed him to go finally, but promised she would hunt him down and have the truth from him if Miach wasn't back by supper.

Supper was about to be served and Miach was nowhere to be found. Unfortunately, she hadn't a clue where to even begin looking for him. And since she didn't have that ability of his to sense her from great distances, she would have to resort to things she could manage such as threatening to slide Mehar's knife into her uncle's belly if he didn't open his mouth and spew out something useful.

She rounded a corner and came to a skidding halt. There were two men standing there, arguing in angry whispers about things Morgan was certain she would find highly instructive if she could just eavesdrop long enough. She jerked herself back behind the corner post, then went so far as to tuck herself into an alcove and push herself back into the darkest corner of it where she couldn't be seen.

She closed her eyes briefly and fought the temptation to sit down. Miach was back safely. She took a deep, unsteady breath. He was, of course, capable of seeing to himself, but just the same . . .

"I don't care where you've been," Sìle said angrily. "How dare you tromp through my halls in your slovenly condition, unwashed, unshaven, looking as if you'd just finished rolling in the mud with the hounds!"

"I apologize," Miach said tightly. "Now, if we might return to what I was trying to discuss with you—"

"I can just imagine what *you* want," Sìle interrupted with a snort.

Morgan wished that her grandfather would, for once, just be quiet. She was desperately curious about where Miach had been and what he'd been doing. She would certainly never learn that if Sìle didn't shut up.

"I want Sarait's amulet."

"You want *what*?" Sìle gasped.

Morgan, for once, agreed with him. Miach wanted what?

"I want the amulet you made for Sarait that cost you a year of your reign," Miach said firmly. "I want it for Mhorghain."

"Never," Sìle spat.

Miach cursed. "Can you not be reasonable? I want it to protect Mhorghain for precisely the same reasons you wanted to protect Sarait—"

"Mhorghain has no need of it. *I* will keep her safe."

Morgan pursed her lips. How conveniently Sìle was forgetting that it was Miach who had saved her from Cruadal the previous morning.

"With all due respect, Your Majesty," Miach said, sounding as if he were holding on to his patience only barely, "you're wrong. You will not be able to. I have seen what hunts your granddaughter. I have set my own spells of ward within your borders—"

"You set *what*!" Sìle roared.

"I didn't do it for you," Miach roared back.

Morgan listened, openmouthed, as they snarled at each other for a full ten minutes before there was anything to listen to besides curses and insults.

It was, she had to admit, rather impressive.

"I did it for Mhorghain," Miach shouted, finally. "For Queen Brèagha, for your sons and daughters, your grandchildren and great-grandchildren."

Sìle was silent.

He was silent for so long, she began to wonder if something had happened to him. Miach wouldn't have slain him, but her grandfather could have shouted himself into a stupor. She eased out of the alcove and peeked very carefully around the corner. Sìle was merely standing there with his arms folded over his chest, glaring at Miach.

Morgan pulled back and waited.

"And I misspoke," Miach continued in a rather more calm tone of voice. "I did it for you as well, Your Grace, because when those creatures that have been hunting your granddaughter come into your lands and your spells fail, mine will hold."

Sìle began to splutter.

"And if mine fail, that amulet you fashioned for Sarait will, I believe, at least keep Mhorghain safe from them."

"Then you acknowledge that my magic is superior," Sìle said huffily.

"You poured a year of your love and fear into that talisman," Miach said. "I only had a pair of hours to use on my spells—"

"How dare you invade my land and pollute it with your magic," Sìle said, though in far less stentorian tones than before. "Wexham, Croxteth—what manner of bilge did you use? Olc?" he finished with a sneer.

"Fadaire," Miach said quietly, "strengthened with Camanaë and a great deal of my own power."

"Fadaire?" Sìle thundered. "And how in the *hell* do you know enough of that—"

"I've been in your private books," Miach shouted back, "and I've spent the past three days and nights memorizing every last bloody spell I could lay my greedy hands on!"

There was a gurgling noise. Morgan had another look, but found it was only Sìle in a towering rage. Miach merely stood there, letting her grandfather rage on. She would have smiled to herself, but Miach's words were starting to sink in.

He'd set spells of protection all around Tòrr Dòrainn. He

wanted an amulet to protect her . . . because he wasn't planning on being there to do it himself.

Damn him to hell, he was going to leave her behind.

"I will not use the spells anywhere else," Miach said quite loudly, then he took a deep breath. "Well, I would if it meant keeping my lady safe. I am, as you well know, discreet. I will not give them to anyone else. And I will not use them in the business I'm about outside your borders."

"And what is that business?" Sìle snapped.

Morgan leaned forward to hear, but found a hand over her mouth and her body pulled backward. She had her assailant on his knees with her thumbs in his eyes before she realized it was Sosar. She released him immediately.

"Sorry," she whispered shortly. "You shouldn't sneak up on me."

"Apparently not," he said, wide-eyed. He struggled to his feet, rubbing the spot on his neck where she'd clutched him on his way to his knees. "What are you doing?"

"I am successfully eavesdropping on the man I am considering marrying because I know he's too bloody stubborn to give me the details on his own." She glared at him. "I don't need any aid in this endeavor."

"Hmmm," he said, but he didn't move.

Morgan shot him another warning look, then turned her attentions back to what had become a rather quiet conversation all of the sudden. She eased closer to the corner of the wall she was hiding behind and breathed silently.

"You'll never manage it. But by all means, go try."

Morgan cursed silently and shot Sosar a look of fury. She'd obviously missed the most useful bits.

"I will go," Miach said tightly, "*after* I watch you give Mhorghain the amulet."

"So you can take her with you and use her whilst she's protected by *my* magic?" Sìle spat. "I don't believe you want it for any other reason."

"And I don't care what you believe. Damn it, Your Grace, I have her best interests at heart! I *will* do whatever is required to *keep* her safe even if that means giving my life in exchange for hers."

Morgan found that tears were running down her cheeks.

She had no idea where Miach planned on going, but it had to be somewhere unpleasant if he didn't want her along. Were the schools of wizardry so dangerous, then?

Sìle was silent a bit longer, then he sighed gustily. "Very well, I will give her the amulet. At a time of my own choosing," he added sternly.

"Tonight."

"I will do it—"

"Tonight," Miach said firmly. "You will allow me to have a final meal with my love and I will watch you hand her that amulet. And then I will go."

Sìle only grunted.

"And a dance," Miach added.

"Absolutely not!"

"And one last thing," Miach continued, as if he hadn't heard Sìle's protests. "When I return, I want Mhorghain's hand."

"I wouldn't waste much thought on *that*," Sìle snarled. "You'll be too dead to wed with her."

"We'll see. For now, I'll be satisfied when Mhorghain has what I want for her. Now, if you'll excuse me, I'll go make myself presentable—"

Morgan shoved past Sosar before he could stop her, then ran back to her chamber. Her maid was sitting on a stool, half asleep.

"I need the finest gown I own," Morgan said quickly. "Perhaps even a crown."

"Of course, Your Highness," the girl said, jumping up immediately. She smiled. "In truth?"

Morgan wondered if she had been so obstinate about matters of grooming before, then decided it wasn't worth wasting time on. She was more than willing to be fussed over at present and perhaps that was what counted.

She didn't say a word at the outrageously elegant dress of deep green velvet the girl put on her. She sat perfectly still as the wench took an inordinate amount of time to see to her hair and settle her crown. It was weaponry. Sìle would think she had accepted her birthright and leave her be. Miach would be so dazzled with her clothes and hair, he wouldn't notice when she followed him from the palace.

She rose, thanked the girl, then walked from her chamber.

She considered several locations, then decided she would start in the garden. Perhaps Miach was working on his spells.

Perhaps he was merely seeking a bit of silence after what he'd just listened to.

And so he was. She stood in the shadows of a path and watched as he paced restlessly under trees that had begun to bud out in preparation for spring in the midst of winter.

Morgan found it quite difficult to take a decent breath. He was dressed in black hose and a blue tunic that made him look so regal, it was all she could do not to drop to her knees and bow her head to him. He wore black boots, apparently shined for the occasion, and a circlet of silver atop his head.

He looked remarkably like a prince.

"He is handsome, isn't he?"

Morgan turned to find her grandmother standing next to her. She managed to swallow. "He is," she said. "Exceptionally."

Brèagha linked arms with her. "You will have beautiful children, love. And powerful ones. If Sìle allows it."

Morgan looked at her seriously. "He will have nothing to say about it. I will wed where I will, Grandmother. Besides, Miach is *not* Gair."

"Mhorghain, darling, you're right. Miach's not Gair. He makes Gair look like a village sorcerer's apprentice and *that* is why Sìle dislikes him so. I have lived centuries and seen mage after mage walk across the world's stage." She smiled. "Prince Mochriadhemiach stands alone before them all."

Morgan felt a little faint. "But he's just Miach."

"Darling, he is so much more than that. Perhaps he doesn't realize fully what he's capable of, but there will come a day when he must." She reached over and touched Morgan's cheek. "You will need to come to terms with that same thing someday as well, darling."

"Oh, I don't know—"

"Mhorghain, you must accept who you are at some point, just as you must accept that if you give yourself to Prince Mochriadhemiach, you cannot change what he is, or what he can do."

Morgan looked at her grandmother. "He would never use his power for ill."

"He wouldn't, which is why you love him. Neither would

you, which is why you are worthy of being his consort." She kissed Morgan on both cheeks. "And you will have beautiful children, which is what this grandmother's heart awaits with pleasure. I'll leave you to fetch him, darling. I imagine he's waiting for you."

Morgan watched her walk away, then turned back to look at Miach. Surely he was just a man with substantial sword skill and a few spells at his disposal. She didn't want to think about what else he might be, or what he might possibly expect of her. It was much easier to limit herself to wondering where he'd gone and why he'd looked as if he'd been to hell and back.

Had he encountered more of those creatures? Had he gone all the way to Riamh? She didn't want to believe the last, but she supposed it was possible. He looked impossibly grave, like a man who had a terrible secret that he knew he would have to keep under difficult circumstances.

She thought she just might not make that easy for him, actually.

Then again, perhaps for the night he could stop being the archmage of Neroche and she could stop being a princess of Tòrr Dòrainn and they could be Miach and Morgan. They could take one night for themselves, one night that would count as a stolen moment of ease and happiness before the real task was faced.

Even Weger wouldn't begrudge them that.

She walked along the path, then stopped under a tree and waited for Miach to turn toward her. He did eventually, walking with his head bowed and his hands clasped behind his back. Then he looked up. He stared at her in astonishment for several moments.

"Morgan?"

She took a deep breath, then walked over to him. She reached up and put her arms around his neck, then pulled his head down and kissed him.

She kissed him for quite a while, truth be told.

He finally tore his mouth away and laughed uneasily. "Have pity on me, woman. I think I've been granted a dance with you tonight and I don't want to embarrass myself by not being able to walk steadily."

She put her hands on his chest and looked up at him. "I love you."

He flinched as if she'd struck him. He took a deep breath, then gathered her close, as if she was a great treasure he wanted to protect.

"Thank you," he whispered against her hair.

"I should have told you sooner," she said. "I'm sorry I didn't." She paused. "I do love you."

"And I love you," he said quietly, "though that seems a poor way to express what I feel for you." He pulled back and fussed manfully with her crown. Then he met her eyes. "Her Highness is exceptionally fetching tonight."

"I'm perpetrating a strategy."

"Well, if your strategy is to leave me on my knees in front of you, begging you to be mine, you've succeeded." He looked at her crown, then back down at her. "Our crowns match, you know."

"I suspect that's my grandmother's doing. She likes you."

"I'm grateful," he said honestly.

"Actually, I think there are quite a few here who like you, your unsavory magelike qualities aside."

He laughed, apparently in spite of himself. "You're teasing me."

"I am." She put her arm around his waist and tugged him back toward the palace. "Come with me, my prince, and let me feed you. I will even dance with you."

"Will you?" he asked in surprise. "I wasn't serious about any of that sort of thing, actually."

She looked up at him. "I am able, you know. It's what I've been doing whilst you were sitting in comfort with your nose buried in a book." She smiled up at him. "I did it for you, so I wouldn't shame you at Tor Neroche."

He stumbled, then had to pause and catch his breath. "Any more of these kinds of revelations? I think I need to get them all over with now so I won't land on my arse in front of your grandfather later."

"Nay," she lied cheerfully, "that's all. Unless you'd care to share any of the delicious gossip you've been gleaning from the books behind the silken rope. Or anything about your recent journey."

"I had a hunch about something unimportant," he said, apparently struggling to find a casual tone. "It turned out to be, um, not what I thought it might be."

She didn't press him. Mochriadhemiach of Neroche might have been many things, but a good liar he was not.

Somehow, she liked that about him.

"Put it aside tonight," she advised. "I want your full attention."

He closed his eyes briefly. "Heaven help me."

"You'll survive it well enough, I imagine. Let's go find supper."

Sìle met them at the door to the dining hall. Before he had his mouth fully open to protest, Morgan shot him a steely look.

"How kind of you to allow Prince Mochriadhemiach to be my escort tonight, my liege," she said, in a tone that told him he would be wise not to gainsay her. "In repayment for his having brought me home to you, of course."

Sìle glared at Miach. "One night, boy," he said sharply. "You'd best enjoy it."

Miach bowed low. "Your generosity, Your Majesty, knows no bounds."

Sìle growled at him, kissed Morgan's hands roughly, then turned and barked for Làidir to vacate his seat. He then rearranged everyone so there were two seats on his right. Morgan stole a look at Miach. He was watching her with a very small smile.

"Very well played, princess," he murmured.

"There's a stricture for it somewhere, I'm sure."

Miach put his hand on the small of her back and guided her toward the table. "It wouldn't surprise me. I suggest we sit before he changes his mind. You sit between us, though."

"Coward."

"Realist," he said dryly.

Morgan sat next to her grandfather and found that if she scooted her chair just the right way, she could hold Miach's hand under the table. She smiled at him, then steeled herself for the lengthy business of supper.

She supposed she ate, but she didn't remember any of it. All she knew was that after almost a se'nnight without Miach sitting next to her, she was undeniably and unreasonably happy to have him there. She looked at him often only to find him each time leaning back in his chair, nursing a goblet of wine, watching her with a small smile.

"Eat," she said.

He shook his head. "A waste of time that could be better spent looking at you."

She squeezed his hand, then set to filling a plate for him. She handed him a fork.

"You'll need your strength."

He sighed lightly, then set to his meal without his customary enthusiasm.

Troubled by a guilty conscience, no doubt.

She did take the opportunity to watch him whilst he was otherwise occupied. He looked tired, which led her to suspect that he had indeed been up for several days doing things he shouldn't have been. She reached up and smoothed his bangs out of his eyes before she thought better of it. He smiled.

"Aye, my love?"

"I've missed you," she said simply. "I missed you today especially. I wished we had been sitting in the library before the fire in that chair that's almost large enough for two. Shall we tomorrow?"

He hesitated, then shook his head before he slipped his hand under her hair and pulled her close. "I love you," he whispered against her ear. "I never want to be without you."

Morgan smiled at the words, but couldn't help but notice that he hadn't answered her question. Perhaps he'd decided that hedging was better than attempting an outright lie. She wondered absently if he'd done the same thing in the fall, but she honestly couldn't remember. She'd been too distracted by her dreams and the way he'd held her hand. Perhaps she would think on it later, when she'd finished with her plans for the night.

Sìle cleared his throat pointedly. Miach smiled at Morgan, then sat back.

"I understand, Your Majesty," he said idly, "that you have a gift for Mhorghain."

The look Sìle shot him should have felled him on the spot. Morgan sincerely hoped they wouldn't begin a battle over her. Sìle finally sighed heavily, then pulled something from a pocket and handed it to her.

"I made this for your mother," he said in a very low voice. He paused for quite some time. "That mage there demanded it for you, though I don't know why. It won't protect you against him."

"I need no protection against him," Morgan said quietly.

"So said your mother."

Morgan turned to face him. "Grandfather, I wish you would cease comparing Miach to Gair. That is not who he is. He did bring me here, after all. I don't imagine he did it for any other reason than to ease your heart."

Sìle grunted. "I daresay."

Morgan pursed her lips at him, then felt Miach take the necklace from her. Morgan watched him examine it and leaned close to see what he was looking at.

It was quite lovely, with a single diamond set in a circle of gold and silver. It was surrounded by all sorts of runes she couldn't decipher. What she could say for certain was that it was simply drenched in power. She could feel it from where she sat.

Miach studied it for another moment or two, then looked at her.

"Hold your hair up, love, if you will."

She did so and shivered as he fastened the chain about her neck. He sat back and looked at it silently for several minutes. Then he met her eyes.

"Pretty," he said casually.

Morgan had no idea what the amulet's true purpose was, but she could feel the magic that had enveloped her the moment it had touched her skin.

Pretty, indeed.

Well, she would discover the truth of it all later. For now, she had more beguiling to do. She took Miach's hand and smiled. "I hear the musicians tuning up. Shall we?"

"Please."

She found as the evening wore on that she was rather glad she'd bothered with the reams of dances her grandmother had wanted her to learn. She was surprised Miach knew them as well, but realized she shouldn't have been. He had no doubt spent his own tortured hours learning courtly comportment.

"You're smiling," he said.

"I'm imagining you in some dreadfully boring session with your dancing master," she admitted.

"Boring, but brief," he assured her. "I learned quickly, so I could pull off my court clothes and go tramp about in the mud."

"I don't doubt it." She smiled at him. "I keep forgetting who you are and where you grew up."

"Obviously, I spent too much time with you at Gobhann," he said wryly.

"And in Hearn's hayloft."

He laughed. "Please let's not talk about that whilst Sìle's nearby. He will hear, then he truly will thrust me outside his gates."

"Are there gates at Seanagarra?" she asked.

"I imagine he'll conjure some up, just for me," Miach said, but he didn't sound particularly worried.

Neither was she, for she knew he had no plans to be there long enough for Sìle to begin to contemplate gates. It didn't matter, though, for neither did she.

She would tell him as much when he tried to leave her at her bedchamber.

The evening was magical. The music was glorious, the wine delicate and sweet, and the dancing actually quite enjoyable. Miach watched her closely, as if he couldn't look at her enough to suit himself. Perhaps he thought to save his memories against a time when she wouldn't be near.

Foolish man.

It was very late when she bid good night to the souls in the hall and walked with Miach out into the passageway.

"It was a perfect evening," she said quietly. "Thank you."

"It was perfect," he agreed, "but you made it so." He put his arm around her shoulders. "Let me walk you to your chamber. You look a little tired."

"I'm exhausted," she said, putting her hand over her mouth to cover her yawn. "Why aren't you sleepy?"

"I was too busy worrying about Sìle possibly flinging a knife at my back," he said ruefully. "That sort of concern tends to drive off weariness."

Morgan put her arm around his waist and leaned her head

on his shoulder. She could have perhaps benefited from that kind of worry. She was so sleepy, she could hardly put one foot in front of the other.

And then she realized, quite suddenly, that it was more than dancing that had made her so. Miach had woven some sort of dastardly spell over her!

He swept her up into his arms and continued to walk.

"Damn you," she spat. "I'll see you repaid, you . . . honorless . . ."

She would have said more, but she was slipping toward blackness and couldn't stop the slide. She felt her bed suddenly beneath her back and Miach's lips on hers.

"I love you," he whispered against her mouth.

"Damn you . . . to . . ."

Blackness descended and she knew no more.

Twenty-five

Miach gently unpinned Morgan's crown and took it off. He removed his own and looked at them together in his hands. Doubting himself wasn't in his nature, but he couldn't help a brief moment of it. It was tempting to undo his spell, tell her to dress in traveling clothes, then fly off with her into the night.

But he couldn't. He had a duty to the realm of Neroche; she did not. That duty would lead him along a very dark road, one Morgan had already been down on the day her family had died. He could not ask her to walk it again.

But he thought it just might kill him to leave her.

He set his jaw and put the crowns down on the table next to her bed. He took off her shoes, then covered her with a blanket. Then he sat down next to her for a few minutes and simply watched her. He looked at the peace that rested on her features and knew he was making the right decision. Perhaps she had seen much of the horrors of battle, but they paled in comparison to the horrors of Gair's well. He simply couldn't subject her to them when he could see to them himself.

He took off his boot, shook Mehar's ring into his hand, then pulled his boot back on. He looked at the ring for several moments, considered leaving it with a note, then discarded the idea. Morgan wouldn't need an explanation.

He set the ring in the midst of the crowns, then rose. He started to leave, but found he couldn't. He leaned over her with a hand on either side of her, then bent and kissed her softly. He pulled back and stared down at her. Who would have thought that sending Adhémar off on a quest to find a wielder for the Sword of Angesand would have resulted in his giving his heart to the woman lying before him?

Or that leaving her was shredding his heart into great, tattered pieces?

He bowed his head. He couldn't ask her to come. He just couldn't.

Besides, he wouldn't be gone long. For all he knew, he would finish his business before she managed to shake off his spell. With any luck at all, she wouldn't have to watch what he would need to do to best Lothar.

He looked at her one last time, then straightened and walked out of her bedchamber before he thought better of his decision.

He jumped a little in surprise to find Sìle leaning against a pillar opposite the door, waiting for him. The king of Tòrr Dòrainn straightened and frowned.

"You're making the right choice, I see."

"I can do nothing less."

Sìle studied him for quite some time in silence, then nodded shortly. "I will do everything in my power to keep her safe."

"And I will return."

Sìle looked down his nose. "You may return, but you will not have the prize you seek."

"I imagine Princess Mhorghain will have something to say about it."

Aye, and that something would be peppered with many, many things he was certain he wouldn't want to hear—*if* she deigned to ever speak to him again.

"She will follow my instructions," Sìle announced.

"My liege," Miach began patiently, "you do not know your granddaughter at all if you think that to be the case. And I warn you, if you force her to choose, you won't like the choice she makes."

Sìle glared at him, but said nothing else.

Miach made the king of Tòrr Dòrainn a low bow, then turned and walked away. It didn't serve him to argue with the king. It served him even less to think about wedding Morgan until he had accomplished what he needed to. The sooner that was done, the sooner he could be about a more pleasant bit of business.

He continued along at a brisk pace, then slowed as he reached his bedchamber. He wondered if this was the night for callers because both Sosar and Làidir were waiting for him in front of his door. He stopped and looked at them in surprise.

"Isn't it a bit late for a visit?" he asked.

"Isn't it a bit unwise to be going off on a quest by yourself?" Sosar asked pointedly.

"Very unwise," Làidir agreed. "Which is why we're here, though my brother refuses to tell me what sort of quest it is you're contemplating."

"Nothing particularly interesting," Miach said.

Sosar gaped at him. "Miach, I sat with you in that library for *three bloody days*."

Làidir frowned fiercely. "I knew I shouldn't have allowed you such free rein."

Sosar shot him a look. "Nitpick later, brother, when we're certain the archmage of Neroche isn't going to go do something stupid and leave us with Mhorghain to comfort for the next thousand years. Now, Miach, give us the details we want before we're forced to beat them from you."

Miach folded his arms over his chest and looked at them both. "Do you two join forces often?"

"Never," Sosar said with a smile. "But tonight, aye, we thought it best. So, save us all time and dispense with trying to hedge your way out of telling us where you're going. In fact, I'll help you. You've been to Gair's well—"

"Has he?" Làidir asked in surprise. He looked at Miach. "Have you?"

Miach decided that perhaps silence was the best course of action.

"You tried to shut it and failed," Sosar continued. "Now, you believe that you'll track down the complete spell, try again, and this time you'll succeed because you have enough power—even though my sister failed using that same logic. How close am I?"

Miach dragged his hands through his hair, then rubbed his face. "And what would you do in my place?" he asked wearily.

"I would ask for aid," Làidir said simply.

"Would you?" Miach asked, turning to look at him. "Would you, the crown prince of Tòrr Dòrainn, actually present yourself at my door and ask *me*, the youngest prince of the house of Neroche, for aid in ridding the kingdom of Tòrr Dòrainn of an evil you thought you should be seeing to yourself?"

Làidir looked at him, openmouthed, then shut his mouth with a snap. "I see your point." He considered for quite some time, then took a deep breath. "I give you my word that if there comes a day when I need your aid, I will bend my knee to you and ask for it. *If* you will ask me now. And," he added with the faintest of smiles, "I don't require bended knee."

It was Miach's turn to gape at him. "Why would you help *me*?"

"Because you love my niece," Làidir said quietly. "And because I've seen what you are made of. I will aid you in whatsoever thing you ask me."

Miach stared at the two elvish princes standing in front of him, men who were centuries older than he was, men whose magic and power ran far back into the reaches of legend, and found himself too surprised to speak.

When will things stop being something other than what I thought they were? Morgan had once asked him.

Death is the final surprise, he'd answered.

He'd been right. He'd just never thought that answer would apply to him.

He took a deep breath, then smiled at Làidir. "I appreciate that, Your Highness. I appreciate it more than I can say. And perhaps there is something you can do for me. I have sent your father into a frenzy by setting my own spells of ward and defense along his borders, but they will hold when his fail. If you want to help me, keep Mhorghain inside those spells. That is what I need from you."

"Sosar can see to Mhorghain," Làidir said without hesitation. "I will come with you and offer my sword, at least. You don't know that you won't need someone to watch your back."

Miach wished he had a scribe such as Adhémar did, some quick-scribbling lad whose only task was to record every word and deed of his life for posterity's sake. Truly, no one would have believed what he'd just heard otherwise.

"Coward," Sosar said, shooting his brother a look. "You just don't want to face Mhorghain when she wakes and finds out what Miach has done." He rubbed his neck absently. "I've felt her anger. I think I would be safer with our young mage here."

Miach shook his head. "You must both keep her here. She cannot be with me whilst I'm seeing to the dirty business of black magic. And believe me when I say that Gair's well is still spewing the very blackest of magic."

"Necessitating at least one companion on your journey," Sosar said pointedly. "Làidir can stay behind to watch after our niece and catch Father's crown if it happens to fall off his head. I, on the other hand, am eager for a tramp through unpleasant territory. Now, shut up and fetch your gear. I'll meet you in the stables."

Miach blew out his breath. "Sosar, nay. A thousand times nay. I must go alone."

Sosar opened his mouth, no doubt to argue, then shut it with a snap. Làidir reached out and put his hand on Miach's shoulder.

"I think this is a mistake, but I can see that you are determined. Short of following you, I suppose we cannot change your mind. What do you need for the journey? What can I give you?"

Miach shook his head with a smile. "A show of support has been more valuable than you know. I'm usually going off accompanied by snorts of derision from my eldest brother."

"Adhémar is an ass," Sosar said promptly. "Làidir, go fill his saddlebags. I'll make certain he's well stocked with spells."

Làidir scowled at him, then turned back to Miach. "I will see to food for your journey. I would send out spies for you, but I imagine you don't plan to be gone long."

"Not if I can help it," Miach agreed.

Làidir looked at him a final time, then sighed and walked away. Miach looked at Sosar.

"Thank you."

Sosar pursed his lips. "Aye, you'll need to thank me in truth after I've kept my niece trapped within these walls. I just want you to admit that you're leaving me with the more difficult task."

Miach managed a smile. "I will concede it without hesitation. You can at least take comfort in knowing that Mhorghain's wrath won't be directed at you." He sighed deeply. "I don't know if she'll forgive me for this one."

"Then why do it?"

"Because the well was worse than you can imagine, and I suppose you can imagine quite a few vile things. There is nothing in the Nine Kingdoms that will convince me to allow her anywhere near it. I'm very sorry Sarait attempted it."

Sosar gaped at him. "And what in the bloody hell do you think *you're* doing to attempt it? Miach, it's suicide!"

"Power is as strong as blood—"

"So said Sarait," Sosar said pointedly.

"I'll find the spell."

"And if you don't?"

"I will. I will find the proper spell if I have to search through every drawer of every corrupt wizard in Beinn òrain. I will shut the well, then return before a se'nnight has passed."

Sosar sighed deeply. "Be careful."

"I'm always careful." He started to turn away, then stopped. He looked at Sosar. "I don't have time to give you the reasons, but I fear there may come a time when Lothar comes looking for Mhorghain. Here."

"Lothar?" Sosar said in surprise.

"'Tis possible. Go behind my spells and place your own there. Have Làidir do the same. I will be back well before Lothar could possibly discover who my lady is, but just in case . . ."

"Very well, Miach," Sosar said grimly. "I'll see it done."

Miach nodded, went inside his luxurious chamber, and changed into his traveling clothes. He quickly wrote Brèagha a brief note of thanks, then gathered his gear and walked back out into the passageway. Sosar walked with him to the stables where Làidir had Fleòd already saddled and filled saddlebags attached.

"Fare you well," Làidir said simply.

Sosar put his hand on Miach's shoulder. "I don't suppose I need to say this, but don't be stupid enough not to send word if you need aid. We would come, if you asked."

He nodded to Sìle's sons, mounted, then rode out of the stables and down the path toward the outer gates.

Then he turned and headed east.

He let his mind lie fallow and only used enough magic to completely cover his tracks and himself. He didn't dare allow himself to think about Morgan, what she would say when she woke, or what she would do. All he could do was trust her uncles and concentrate on the task that lay before him.

It was an hour before dawn when he stopped close to a bend in the river Allt that cut through the plain of Ailean. He dismounted under the trees and made himself a quick breakfast from what Làidir had provided, then pulled what gear he needed off Fleòd's back. He put his hand on the horse's withers.

"Go back to Tòrr Dòrainn," he said quietly. "You'll be safe there."

The horse balked, but Miach pointed west and commanded him to go. The beast backed away, slowly and without enthusiasm. Miach watched him until he'd turned and trotted off up a small rise. The horse refused to go any farther. Miach was tempted to force him, but decided there was no point. Hearn had given the beast its instructions and it would follow them to the death. Perhaps the gelding would bolt when it saw what was to come.

Miach wouldn't have blamed him.

He turned and surveyed the countryside before him. He walked about the place for quite some time, examining it from all angles until he was satisfied that he could carry out the pretense he planned. He found an old tree stump and sat down.

Then he began his magic.

He created an enormous fire in front of him that burned without heat but rose hundreds of feet into the sky. He wrapped his name in the flames so it would be clear to any soul with magic in his blood who had created it.

He sat and watched it burn.

It would be only a matter of time now.

They came at noon.

There were so many of them, they looked like a wave sweeping over the plain from the northwest. He stood and drew his sword, more to give himself something to do than from a desire to use it. Magic would be his weapon, not steel.

He began to lay snares for the faster trolls, spells meant to entrap, then engulf in flame. He waited until the first one reached the first trap.

And he stared in horror as the creature shook it off and continued on.

He realized with a sickening feeling that it was going to take much more than simple spells to counteract what he would face—and that he should have realized that far sooner than he had.

He killed the first troll with a quick and brutal spell of Wexham that fell upon the creature like a hammer. The troll dropped with a hoarse shout, stunned, then shook its head and continued forward on its hands and knees.

Miach swore viciously. He threw another spell of the same sort at another troll, but this one was of Olc. The creature screamed and fell dead. That would have been a relief—for the spell was unsettlingly easy to use—except now he had scores of the creatures to deal with and they were, quite suddenly, hard upon him.

With Searbhe riding on a scruffy steed, leading the charge.

Miach quickly wove the most extensive spell of death he'd ever used. He put his fire behind him, kept his eyes fixed on the creatures rushing at him from the north, and forced himself to speak the words slowly and clearly. He supposed that if he had to, he could leap up into the air and leave them all behind.

In fact, he was beginning to think that might be the best idea.

He had almost finished when Searbhe reached him. Miach leapt up, but Searbhe caught him before he could finish the change and flung him to the ground. Miach cursed and heaved himself to his feet. He continued with the spell of death, fought off Searbhe's clumsy attempts at his own killing magic, then found himself needing his blade after all.

He built a perimeter around himself with a single word, a shield that the creatures could not penetrate, then concentrated on Searbhe. The howls of outrage from Searbhe's companions were terrifying, but Miach forced himself not to heed them. He kept Searbhe at bay and put the finishing touches on his spell. It lacked but a trio of words and then he could be on his way.

Searbhe began to smile. "Go ahead and finish," he goaded. "I only wish I could see your face when you realize all you've killed."

"I'll weave a special dispensation in it so you will," Miach assured him. He did, then opened his mouth to speak the final words—

"Miach, don't!"

Miach whipped around to find Morgan standing just outside his spell. She held the amulet in her hand, though it was still on its chain about her neck. Miach wasn't sure what surprised him more: that she had broken through what he'd used to put her into a dreamless sleep for a se'nnight or that the amulet worked as it should. The trolls avoided her completely. That was a great relief.

Or at least it was until he saw a troll outside his spell change himself into a man.

Or elf, rather.

Miach reached out and jerked Morgan through the spell before Cruadal reached for her, then spun her around so her back was against his. He raised his sword as Cruadal slipped inside his protective net.

"You won't survive the day," Cruadal said in a flat, expressionless voice. "I'll see to that."

Miach didn't waste time arguing. He had stopped himself from killing Cruadal within Sìle's borders and he had shown him mercy in Slighe, but he labored under no such constraints here. He fought against the elf ruthlessly with sword and magic, holding on to the threads of his spell of death and trying to separate Morgan's essence from it at the same time. It wouldn't have been difficult if he hadn't been distracted by the noise the trolls were making and Cruadal's very vile spells. He was very grateful to have Morgan standing at his back so he didn't have to try to fight Searbhe at the same time.

It probably would be what saved his life.

Cruadal tore a hole in his perimeter suddenly, sending trolls rushing in. Miach crushed three trolls with a spell of Olc, but the surge continued. He sealed the rent with a single word, then smashed the hilt of his sword into Cruadal's face, sending him sprawling. He concentrated on the creatures Cruadal had allowed inside, slew them ruthlessly, then spun around to see how Morgan fared.

She leapt aside to avoid Searbhe's thrusting blade. Miach didn't pause to consider, he merely took his sword and plunged it into Searbhe's belly. Searbhe fell forward, grasping for Morgan as he did so. Miach yanked her out of the way, then watched grimly as Searbhe crashed to the ground and was still. He sighed deeply. One less thing hunting them now, at least.

Morgan dragged her sleeve across her forehead. "Don't regret that," she said, panting. "He would have killed you if you hadn't finished him first."

Miach nodded, then flinched as he felt something slam into his back. He caught his breath at the agony of it. Bloody hell, had one of the trolls broken through his spell with a rock? It was a damned large stone, if that were the case. He looked at Morgan and saw an expression of absolute horror on her face. He looked down and realized why.

There was a sword point coming out of his chest.

It was coming out of the front of him because it had gone into the back of him. He realized that he wasn't making much sense, but it wasn't every day that he found himself impaled by a sword he hadn't expected.

"You bloody whoreson," Morgan spat.

Miach looked at her quickly, but realized she wasn't talking to him. She threw herself at someone behind him, then she pulled up short and cursed viciously.

"He's gone," she said, looking around frantically. "Miach, I can't see him anywhere."

Miach didn't have the energy to look. He found himself on his knees without exactly knowing how he had gotten there. He saw Morgan standing over him with her sword bare in her hand. He reached up and put his hand on her lower back. It was excruciating to do even that, so he sank down on his heels.

Then he realized that he couldn't see anything anymore.

He hunched over and sucked in desperately needed breaths. Perhaps he should have taken Làidir up on his offer of aid. He might have avoided a bit of his present distress if he had.

"Sosar, I've lost Cruadal!" Morgan shouted.

"Forget him," Sosar called. "See to Miach!"

Miach would have sighed in relief, but it hurt too much, so he merely crouched there and was enormously grateful for aid that was unlooked-for.

He heard the king of Tòrr Dòrainn wiping out evil with words alone. Làidir and Sosar were doing the same thing. He supposed there were others in the party as well, but he didn't mark them. He felt Morgan's hand on his head.

"I've got to pull the sword out," she said in a low, urgent voice. "It will hurt."

He nodded. He thought he might have made some sort of noise as she carefully pulled the sword free of him. He hoped it hadn't been a scream. He fell over because he simply couldn't keep himself upright any longer. He felt for Morgan's hand.

"I love you," he whispered. "I'm sorry."

"You idiot," she wept. "You fool. You need me, damn you!"

"I know," he wheezed.

"Don't leave me," she pleaded. "Please, Miach. Hold on. I can fix this."

He didn't think so, but he didn't have the heart to tell her as much. He felt her hand on both sides of the wound, on his chest and on his back. He heard her quickly speak a spell of binding. It did nothing. He could still feel his life ebbing away.

She tried a different spell. And another. She started to repeat them one after another, weeping so hard he could scarce understand her.

"I love you," he whispered. "I love you."

"Help!" she shouted. "Someone help me!"

The sounds of battle started to recede a bit. Miach found that pleasing somehow. If he was going to die, he didn't want to have his passing be accompanied by sounds of trolls shrieking. He felt Morgan's hand clasp his and hold on, hard.

"Hang on," she pleaded. "Please, Miach, hold on."

"Try this spell, Granddaughter."

Miach listened to Sìle give her a Fadaire spell of healing. It wouldn't work, of course, but he didn't have the strength to tell Morgan that. He was too close to death, too empty of what he needed to hold his soul in his body. He felt Morgan put her hands on him again, one on his chest, the other on his back, then begin the spell. He felt more pressure. Perhaps Sìle's hands were pressing on top of hers. Well, at least he would slip into the next world with his love's hands on his chest and her words in his ears.

Morgan neared the end of the spell, then Sìle spoke the last word with her.

Miach felt a white-hot magic streak through him.

And then he knew no more.

Twenty-six

❧

Morgan swam through deep waters, struggling to surface and finding it impossible. It was a magical sort of lassitude, much like what she'd fought off that morning. Damn that Miach of Neroche—

She opened her eyes with a start, realizing at once where she was and what had happened.

Miach was dead.

She had come too late.

A black pit opened up suddenly in front of her, the same pit that had caught her when she'd learned her father had killed Nicholas's wife and children. To keep from staring into its fathomless depths, she forced herself to look up at the sky above her. Perhaps if she looked at the clouds wafting lazily above her, she could keep herself from falling endlessly into darkness.

It seemed somehow too cheerful a sky to be shining down on a place of such desperate tragedy. She contemplated the shapes of clouds and wondered absently who would be archmage after Miach. She wondered, with substantially less detachment, how she would manage to draw many more breaths without Miach alive in the same world she inhabited.

She had taken too long to realize that she couldn't unravel his sleeping spell. In desperation, she had finally spoken a word of Opening. It had broken the spell—and opened every drawer, door, and box in her chamber. She had ignored the complaints coming from those in chambers surrounding hers who had likely experienced the same thing, flung herself into her clothes, and bolted down the passageway at a dead run.

She'd made it almost to the great hall before she ran, bodily, into her grandfather. He'd folded his arms over his chest and said four words to her.

The mage, or me.

He'd likely said the same thing to Sarait. Morgan had ignored the chill that had gone down her spine at the thought, then thanked him politely for his hospitality before pushing past him and continuing on her way.

Sosar had been waiting for her in the stables. The only thing she had wanted to hear from him had been directions to where Miach had gone. He'd considered, then sighed and told her that he wasn't exactly sure, but he had the feeling she wouldn't have much trouble finding out.

She had raced out of the stables, turned east, then seen the enormous stream of fire that reached into the sky and announced in runes that even she could decipher that Miach was there.

She'd wanted to kill him.

Her fury had lasted a handful of leagues before something resembling common sense had returned. Miach wouldn't have left her behind because he didn't love her, he would have left her behind because he was an idiot and thought she would be safer out of harm's way.

How unrelentingly unforgiving that decision had to have been for him.

Luath had raced toward the fire without her having asked it of him. Eagles had flown over her head soon after, reaching the scene of the battle just as she did. Those eagles had changed themselves into her grandfather, her uncles, and two score elves with very sharp swords and useful spells. They had fought valiantly, but it hadn't been enough. Not for Miach.

She closed her eyes because she couldn't bear to look up into the sky anymore. Of course, darkness didn't help either. All she could see was Miach standing there with Cruadal's sword sticking out of his chest, all she could hear was the sound it made as she had pulled it from him, all she could feel was his blood on her hands and the way his breathing had grown more shallow every time he had sighed.

She remembered Sìle's hands over hers, the pain of his immeasurable power rushing through her hands and into Miach's chest. If the sword hadn't killed him, that likely had.

She held her hands up where she could see them. They were covered in blood, but other than that they didn't look any different. The only thing that was different was the fact that she was wearing Mehar's ring on the middle finger of her left hand. It had been sitting in the middle of Miach's crown that had been intertwined with hers on her bedside table. It hadn't been placed there by accident, that much she knew.

A pity it was nothing more than a memento now.

She felt next to her with her hands that were still a little scorched and found that her sword and Mehar's knife were lying beside her. She put her hand on the cold steel and struggled to take even breaths. Well, if nothing else, she could return to Melksham and take up her life again as a mercenary. This time she could even fly and avoid having to take a boat. She would fly one last time, then put it all behind her . . .

Except for the fact that turning her back on what she could do wouldn't do anything for the number of monsters that would still come hunt her.

Tears leaked out of her eyes and trailed down her temples to dampen her hair. How could she possibly face the sunrise each day knowing that she would never again share another one with Mochriadhemiach of Neroche? She would never again feel his hand on her hair, hear her name from his lips, watch him smile that grave smile he wore when she suspected he was thinking how much he loved her.

She wept for quite a long time.

The clouds continued to drift by and the sun turned toward the west. Morgan sat up finally, dragged her bloody hands through her hair, then waited until her head stopped spinning before she staggered to her feet. She resheathed her sword and stuck Mehar's knife back down her boot. She would have to face life sooner or later. Perhaps if she got the pain over with quickly, it wouldn't be so terrible. She took a deep breath, then looked around her to get her bearings.

Searbhe was lying quite a distance away from her. She couldn't find Miach, though, which left her a little breathless. Was he so gory, then, that they wouldn't allow her to see him?

She saw her grandfather's elves busily dragging trolls into piles. Sosar and Làidir were bending over to study a corpse lying at their feet. Sìle was standing several feet away, arguing fiercely with a tall, dark-haired man who was covered in blood. Morgan could hardly believe her eyes.

That was Miach.

A sound escaped her. She was sure it hadn't been a pleasant sound, and it had Miach immediately turning to look at her. She ran toward him, but tripped and went sprawling. She found herself caught in strong arms and clutched tightly against a chest that was no longer sporting an enormous hole.

She burst into tears.

It was loud, uncontrollable, and messy weeping, but she couldn't seem to stop herself. She'd never been so completely undone in her entire life.

"I'm all right," Miach said soothingly. "Morgan, I'm all right."

She would have cursed him, but what came out of her mouth was another noise of agony so terrible that it frightened her.

Miach swung her up into his arms and carried her over to a tree stump, away from the field of battle. Morgan felt him sit, settle her more comfortably on his lap, then begin to rock her as if she were a child who needed comfort. She didn't protest.

Losing him had been every bit as awful as she'd feared it would be that afternoon in Hearn's hayloft when she'd first considered it. But having his arms around her, his hand smoothing over her hair, his chest rising and falling against hers with each breath he took—that was even more devastating than having thought she'd lost him. She wondered, absently, if she would ever be able to release him.

She suspected not.

She had no sense of how much time passed as she sat with her arms around his neck, her face pressed against his hair.

When she thought she could open her mouth without shriek-ing, she pulled back and looked at him.

"You idiot," she croaked. "What in the *hell* were you thinking?"

"A worthy sentiment," Sìle put in from behind her.

Morgan heard her grandfather's voice and realized that be-hind her lay the first matter she should address. She shot Miach a warning look. "I need to talk to my grandfather, but don't go. I'm not finished with you."

He only smiled gravely. His eyes were, as it happened, quite full of something that might have passed for tears. "I'm thankful for that," he murmured.

She glared at him, just so he wouldn't think she planned on giving him any flowery sentiments, then pushed herself up off his lap. She turned and threw her arms around her grandfather. "Thank you," she said, unable to fight the catch in her voice. "I would have lost him if I had been alone. Anything I can do to repay you, I will do."

He hesitated only slightly before he returned the embrace. "It was nothing, Mhorghain," he said gruffly.

"You know it wasn't," she said quietly, pulling away and looking at him. "You have given me back my life. I am in your debt."

He looked at her, startled, then looked around her, presum-ably at Miach. He embraced her again, made a few gruff noises, then set her back with an awkward pat on her shoulder. "I'll remember that."

"I imagine you will," Morgan said with a smile. Then she turned and looked at Miach. "I find, however, that I have a very different list of things to say to you."

He only looked up at her, clear-eyed. "I imagine you do."

"Would you like my grandfather to enjoy them with you, or shall I take you off and flay you alive in private?"

He managed a smile. "I'll leave that choice to you. But first perhaps you would care to have my apology."

"Your apology?" she echoed in disbelief. "Why in the *hell* would you bother with that, you treacherous bastard—especially when I have no doubt you'll leave me behind again the first chance you have!"

Sìle grunted and walked away.

Morgan found that her mouth was hanging open. It matched Miach's perfectly. She'd never seen him look quite so startled. She shut her mouth with a snap.

"I meant to say—"

"Precisely that," he said, reaching out and jerking her down onto his lap, "which I deserved." He wrapped his arms around her and held her tightly. "I almost woke you and told you to get dressed and come with me."

"Why didn't you?" she asked, pained.

"Because I cannot take you where I'm going."

"Why not?" she asked in surprise.

He started to speak, then shut his mouth into a grim line and shook his head.

"Do you want me to guess?"

He closed his eyes briefly. "Please don't."

"Do you think I'm afraid?"

He shook his head slowly. "And that is what makes *me* afraid."

She crawled ungracefully off his lap, then wrapped her arms around herself. "I am not going to marry you, Miach, if you're planning on leaving me behind every time you suspect a small bump in the road."

"This is not a small bump, Morgan."

"Tell me what it is and let me decide that for myself."

He looked up at her for a moment or two in silence, then sighed. "I will later. I need to go clean up first."

She watched him heave himself unsteadily to his feet. He swayed, then steadied. She took the hand he offered instead of throwing herself in his arms again, which was what she would rather have been doing. Perhaps he was afraid if she got too close, she would stab him.

She was tempted.

But since he'd just been through that, she supposed it would be cruel to put him through it again. She walked with him silently over to where her grandfather and uncles were studying what was left on the ground.

Làidir looked up as they approached. "I've never seen anything like this."

"Aye, you have," Sosar said. "Remember Cruadal?"

Làidir shot Miach a look. "We didn't find him amongst the dead, you know."

Miach sighed deeply. "I don't imagine you did. I also don't think it will serve us to go look for him. I can almost guarantee he will either remain close to us or run to Riamh. All we can do is keep our eyes open and wait to see which it is." He looked at Sosar. "I'm not certain where he saw the creatures before he arrived in Seanagarra." He started to speak, then shook his head again and said no more.

Morgan decided that perhaps there would come a time later that day when she would draw her sword and pin him against a tree with it and prod a few answers from him.

It was a certainty that she would have no answers from the men in front of her. Miach was exchanging meaningful looks with her uncles, but nothing else useful was being said.

She supposed it would have gone on for the remainder of the afternoon if she'd allowed it. Her only option was to force their hands. She turned and looked at Miach coolly.

"Perhaps instead of looking them over, we should see to the corpses. You and I need to be going soon—"

"Absolutely not!" Sìle roared. "I'll not have it!"

Morgan looked at her grandfather. "It is *my* choice to go with him, Grandfather," she said calmly.

"Which choice you wouldn't have even thought of if this mage here hadn't suggested it to you. I *knew* he wasn't to be trusted." Sìle shot Miach a glare. "And here I was prepared to suffer you—"

"He doesn't want Mhorghain to come with him, Father," Sosar said quietly. "He didn't need to stage this whole battle if his intent was to merely take Mhorghain to the—"

"Sosar!" Miach exclaimed.

Morgan looked at them, knew that Miach had trusted Sosar with details he hadn't been willing to give to her, and couldn't decide if she was furious or if her feelings smarted.

Furious was better.

She strode away before she couldn't stop herself from drawing her sword and doing him in for good this time. She walked down the bank to the lazily flowing river there, then knelt and washed her hands. She washed her face as well and worked on the spatters of blood on her sleeves. Those were hopeless and 'twas Miach's blood anyway, so she let them be. She finally did nothing but kneel there in the mud and watch the water.

She didn't like where she found herself. She was accustomed to leading the charge, not being told to go back to the house and wait whilst the men took care of the truly difficult work. And she simply couldn't face another day where she woke thinking, *knowing* that Miach was dead and she could have prevented it if she had been with him.

It was almost enough to convince her that perhaps she should take Mehar's ring, hand it back to him, and bid him a final farewell.

She heard soft footsteps behind her, but she didn't turn. Miach knelt down next to her and was silent for a minute. She was afraid if she looked at him, she *would* stab him, so she continued to simply look down into the water. She heard him strip off his shirt, then saw out of the corner of her eye that he had leaned forward to wash the blood from his arms and chest.

She didn't think; she merely gave him a hearty shove.

He went rolling into the water. She would have told him that he deserved it, but before she managed to open her mouth and get the words out, she found herself being jerked into the water as well.

The river was deeper than it looked. She resurfaced with a curse, coughing out things she hadn't intended to ingest. She managed to get to her feet only to find Miach unbuckling her swordbelt.

"What are you doing?" she squeaked.

"Ridding you of any potential weapons," he said, reaching down into the water and pulling Mehar's knife free of her boot. He tossed it onto the bank with her sword.

She tried to get past him, but he caught her about the waist and turned her to him.

"Let me go," she snapped.

"Nay."

She scowled up at him. "You're going to leave me behind again, aren't you?"

He sighed deeply and pushed his hair out of his eyes. "Morgan, I will *not* take you any farther on this journey."

"And when was it, my lord Archmage, that I became a help-less woman who is only fit to sit and stitch whilst you're about the business of keeping the realm safe?" she said sharply. "I am part of the Nine Kingdoms too. If I cannot do my part as well as you, then what use am I?"

"Do you have any idea," he said through gritted teeth, "what it would do to me if I lost you?"

"Actually," she said quietly, "I do."

He opened his mouth, then apparently realized what she meant. He suddenly looked quite winded. He looked at her for a long moment in silence, then bent and carefully rested his forehead against hers. "I'm sorry, Morgan, for this morning," he whispered.

"Yet you'll leave me behind again."

He lifted his head. "Aye."

She was rather grateful to be drenched from head to toe. It hid her tears quite nicely. "I am beginning to think you don't want me—"

His eyes widened, then he jerked her against him and cut off her words with his mouth. She tried to protest the tactic, but realized rather quickly that Miach wasn't at all interested in idle chatter. He kissed her until she began to have trouble stay-ing on her feet. He took her hands and put them around his neck, then pulled her hard against him and kissed her quite a bit longer.

Then he suddenly tore his mouth away. "Wash your hair," he said hoarsely. "I'll comb it out for you."

She reached out and took his face in her hands so she could force him to look at her. "I will not let you leave without me. I'll come and guard your back."

He smiled wearily. "Of course, Morgan."

She was vaguely unsatisfied with that answer, but saw that she would have nothing more from him. She rinsed things out of her hair she preferred not to identify, then climbed out of the water and stood on the bank, shivering, while she waited for Miach to finish. He came out of the water dripping, but looking much more like himself. He gathered her blades for her, then took her hand and his ruined tunic and walked with her back to where a fire had been built near the trees. Morgan saw that Sìle's elven army was gone. Only Làidir, Sosar, and

Sìle remained, but Làidir was wearing a cloak and looked ready for travel.

"We've decided," Làidir said, "that one of us needs to return home now. I'll go and take Mhorghain with me."

"Mhorghain isn't going with you," Miach said. He shot Làidir a look. "Let me walk with you a minute so I might give you my final thanks, if you don't mind."

Morgan watched them go off together. She might have enjoyed the sight of them speaking companionably, but she was too busy wondering what they were saying about her. They spoke in low voices for quite some time, then Làidir turned himself into a powerful eagle and soared off into the west.

Sìle sighed.

Morgan watched Miach come back to the fire. He caught a tunic Sosar tossed him and pulled it over his head. He took off his boots, set them down by the fire, then sat down on a stump. He produced a comb from somewhere and looked at her.

"Come and sit, love," he said quietly.

She took off her own boots, set them next to his by the fire, then sat down in front of him. She wanted to ask a score of questions, but she knew she would have no answers. Even Sosar wouldn't meet her eyes. She gave in, for the moment, and closed her eyes as Miach worked on her hair.

"Sosar, you saw to the trolls?" he asked quietly.

"I did. And Father has provided us with a covering here. Lads may walk toward us, but the glamour will confuse them and send them in another direction. We're safe enough."

"Thank you," Miach said quietly.

There was, for quite some time, nothing but the sound of the fire popping and cracking in front of her. She opened her eyes, finally, once Miach had finished working tangles from her hair and was simply trailing his fingers through it. Sosar was watching them with a sad smile on his face. Her grandfather, though, wasn't looking at her; he was watching Miach. She didn't bother to try to decipher what his expression might mean.

"Perhaps we should be on our way," Sosar said casually. "Beinn òrain, Miach?"

"Hmmm," Miach agreed. "In a bit. When Mhorghain's boots are dry."

Morgan knew exactly what he planned because she would have done the same thing. He was going to wait until she'd fallen asleep, then desert her without a backward glance.

Well, there was no sense in not helping him along.

She yawned. "I think I might want a little nap before we go. What do you think, uncle?" she asked, looking at Sosar pointedly.

His eyes widened for a moment, then he suddenly produced a considerable yawn. "I agree. A little rest is just the thing for us."

Sìle said nothing. He merely sat with his feet toward the fire, his arms resting on his knees, looking for all the world like a soldier who had seen so many battles that they had ceased to hold any excitement for him.

Or he would have, if he hadn't looked so much like an elven king, beautiful and terrible.

He wasn't watching her, though; he was watching Miach.

Morgan took Miach's hands that were resting on her shoulders and pulled them forward so she could wrap his arms around her. "Thank you, my love," she said leaning back to kiss his cheek. "I think, though, that I truly do need a rest."

"Of course, Morgan."

She squeezed his arms briefly, then stretched out near the fire. She closed her eyes, let her breathing deepen, then waited for the inevitable to happen.

"You *would* give your life for hers."

"Aye, Your Grace. And I will."

"She will mourn."

"She will be alive to do so."

"All right . . . Miach."

Morgan continued to breathe evenly. She would wait, then follow him before he could leave without her.

Again.

She heard him rise at midnight. She listened to him walk off with a lightness of step she had to admire, then she tapped the top of Sosar's head with her toe.

Sosar lifted his head slowly, looked toward where Miach had gone, then looked at her. "Aye?"

"Where's he going?"

Sosar closed his eyes briefly. "The well."

"Damn him to hell," she whispered fiercely. She rose soundlessly and looked down at her uncle. "I'm going with him."

Sosar reached out and put his hand on her foot. "Take care of him, niece. And yourself."

She nodded, then turned and melted into the shadows. She made it only a few paces into the darkness before she found herself slowing to an uncomfortable stop.

She didn't want to face what was there in front of her mind's eye, but she knew she could avoid it no longer. If Miach tried to shut that well, he would fail. Just as her mother had.

But what if she could help him?

She remembered vividly the feeling of her grandfather's hands over hers. He hadn't repeated the entire spell of healing with her, just the last word. She had felt his power rush into her hands, *through* her hands, into Miach's chest. It had been a blinding flash of magic that had rendered her senseless. But it had accomplished what it had been meant to.

What if she could do that for Miach?

She shivered. It had very little to do with her clothes that were still damp and everything to do with the hard, unflinching realization that she was forced to accept.

She *could* help Miach.

But only if she accepted who she was.

The feeling that washed over her was every bit as unpleasant as the one she'd experienced when Miach had told her about her parentage at Lismòr. She thought, for a moment, that she just might be ill—she who had never shied away from the difficult.

But this was magic, not swordplay, so perhaps she could be forgiven for having to lean against a tree and simply breathe until she was sure she wouldn't retch.

It took far longer than it should have, but she finally found the strength to straighten. She had to take several more deep, fortifying breaths before she could continue on. She walked until she could see Miach near the river. His horse was standing there, saddled and ready. Miach was sitting on a log, bent over a sheaf of paper.

Writing a farewell note, no doubt.

She stopped because she couldn't bring herself to go on any farther. She wrapped her arms around herself. She was cold, suddenly. Cold and frightened.

If she took a step, a full and committed step into Mhorghain of Ceangail's world, there would be no turning back. She could no longer be Morgan of Melksham who loved the way fire danced along her blade and preferred a game of cards where magic was only used to describe how she slipped cards out of her sleeve. If she chose to be Mhorghain, she could no longer be that girl with no past and no responsibilities past the current siege. She could no longer relegate elves and wizard-esses and fierce, beautiful magic to tales told by the fireside at night.

She could also not choose to merely be Mhorghain of Tòrr Dòrainn. She would have to accept that part of her that came from her father as well.

She stood there, terrified by the choice and all it would mean.

Then she took a deep, steadying breath and deliberately shoved aside her fear.

She put her shoulders back. She would do what needed to be done. After all, wasn't that what Weger had taught her? To press on ahead, no matter the cost personally, no matter the danger or peril? To see the job done, then weep later?

So she took a step forward, her first step into the world of elves and elvish magic and a lineage that included souls she'd only heard tell of in legend.

It was very hard, that first step.

But the second was easier, the third easier still. She walked forward slowly, walking into her future, walking toward the man who would shoulder everything alone if she didn't force him to let her be a part of it.

It was easier than watching him walk away from her again.

Though not by much.

Twenty-seven

❧

M iach had had better days.

Almost dying had been the least of the misery, though his chest still ached abominably and he wondered if he would ever truly catch his breath again. He didn't want to admit that the shortness of breath came from more than just the sword that had resided there in his heart earlier. If leaving Morgan the night before had been difficult, this was a thousand times worse. And he was leaving her not safely hidden at Tòrr Dòrainn, but out in the open with only her marginally qualified relatives to guard her.

Unfortunately, he had no other choice.

He had a sheaf of paper in his hand, but he couldn't bring himself to write anything down yet. How could he possibly put into words how much he loved her, how hard it was to leave her, and how greatly he feared he would not return from the business in front of him? It was impossible, so he looked for something else to do to put off the inevitable a bit longer.

He reached for Sarait's letter and read it one more time. It still said all the same things, still implied that only one of Gair's blood could close the well, still left Miach feeling that he could only make the choice he was making at present. He could not subject Morgan to the horror there.

He set the letter aside, considered, then started to write.

My dearest Morgan,

I must go alone on this errand. I'm certain Searbhe and Cruadal were in league together and 'tis now only a matter of time before Cruadal joins forces, even briefly, with Lothar. Once Lothar knows you're alive, he will follow in a rage. He will assume you are with me, so you must not be. Please, Morgan, please go back to Seanagarra with your grandfather and wait for me.

I remain—

"A lying, honorless whoreson," a voice said from behind him, "and that is a slur for *you*, not your honorable dam."

Miach fell off the log he'd been sitting on. He looked up and found Morgan standing over him, glaring at him. He opened his mouth to argue with her, but before he could, she had snatched up not only his letter but Sarait's.

He jumped to his feet. "Morgan, don't—"

She held him away with a stiff arm. Then she looked up at his magelight and called it to her.

It deserted him without hesitation.

He went down on his knees in the mud. "Morgan, I beg you. Please give me back—"

She shot him a look that made him shut his mouth. She pulled him up to his feet and pointed to the log he'd been sitting on. He hesitated, then retreated to sit down on it. There was no point in asking her to stop reading. Not now.

She'd said she would come with him wherever he went, just to guard his back so he could be about whatever business lay before him. He supposed she hadn't considered that the business might be the business of her father's well and that she might be the one doing the shutting of it.

She read his letter, shot him a glare, then crumpled up the sheaf and threw it at him. He would have smiled, but his heart pained him too much for that. He spelled his unfinished letter into oblivion with a quiet word and waited.

Morgan took Sarait's letter in hands that were steady at first, then began to shake. The blood drained from her face as she read. He waited, silent, as she finished. Then she turned the letter over and read the postscript. She looked at the letter in her hands for quite some time before she looked at him.

"Oh," she said quietly.

He leapt up, strode over to her, and pulled her into his arms. He heard Sarait's letter crumple as Morgan threw her arms around his waist and held on to him. Her breath came in gasps.

But she said nothing.

Miach found nothing to say either. He cradled her head against his shoulder, wishing there was some way he could have spared her what she'd just read. He could only say that he'd tried.

Perhaps he shouldn't have.

"I'm so sorry, Morgan," he whispered.

"Was it bad?" she asked. "There at the well?"

"Words are inadequate to describe it."

She let out a shuddering breath. "I don't think I remember much of it."

"You're fortunate, then."

She put her hands on his chest, then pushed away only far enough to look up at him. "And you think she was right?" she asked. "My mother?"

He nodded.

"In my dreams I have seen my father standing there with blood on his hands." Tears were streaming down her face. "It will take someone with his blood to undo what he has done, won't it?"

Miach closed his eyes briefly. "Your mother suspected so."

"Then why in the *hell* do you think *you* can do it without me?"

"I won't accept anything else."

"Even if it costs you your life?"

He took a deep breath. "Aye."

"And the realm?" she asked pointedly. "Are you not the archmage of Neroche? If memory serves, you have a duty to that realm."

"I chose duty over you the last time—"

"So you'll sentence yourself to death this time?" she asked furiously. She pulled out of his arms. "You will take from the realm of Neroche what keeps it safe and you'll take from me what makes my heart whole."

"Morgan—"

She poked his chest with her finger. "Just stay out of my way, damn you to hell. I will find the spell on my own, then close the well on my own."

He looked at her with her tears streaming down her face and couldn't decide if he was grateful for her courage or very, very ill at the thought of what she would face.

He reached for her, wrapped his arms around her, and smiled down at her in spite of the tears he could feel on his own face. "I won't stay out of your way," he said. He had to clear his throat roughly. "I will be in front of you, behind you, with my arms around you as often as I can be until you draw your sword and force me away. If you'll allow it." He paused. "Will you give me that answer now, or later?"

"Here's my answer," she said slowly. "If you leave me behind again, when I find you I will take Mehar's ring and shove it down your throat."

"Fair enough." He smiled in spite of the way his eyes burned. "Now look at what you've reduced me to."

"You do love me, don't you?" she whispered.

"With everything I am and to my very last breath," he said seriously. He smoothed her hair back from her face. "I once told you I could not promise you peace, or safety, or respite from your dreams. I suppose that means I can't promise you freedom from the horrors of the world either, can I?"

"There are some things, my love, that you simply cannot. But I can bear them, if you're there."

He rubbed his eyes with his fingers. "I think that was a term of endearment you used on me."

"Apparently it took an event of this magnitude to wrench it from me."

He pulled her close again and rested his cheek against her hair. He couldn't bear the thought of Morgan anywhere near Gair's well, but he realized he had no choice but to accept that he could not stop her from going there. Not now. She would go alone if he didn't keep her near him. He sighed deeply. "Very well, Morgan," he said quietly. "I concede the battle and the war. I will take you with me."

"I will be a help, not a hindrance."

"That, my love, was never the issue."

"I know," she said. "I just thought you should know."

He pulled back and looked down at her with a smile. "Go fetch your gear, woman, and let's be on our way before we have a pair of chaperons."

"Too late," Sosar said cheerfully from the edge of the trees.

Miach looked over to find not only Sosar but Sìle standing not more than thirty paces away. Sosar was smiling. Sìle was only watching, his expression inscrutable. Miach decided that he might have better luck being reasonable with Morgan's uncle.

"I was hoping for secrecy," he ventured.

"We can be secret," Sosar said. "Well, I can. I'm not sure about my father."

Miach found Morgan looking up at him. He felt her lips on his cheek briefly, then she pulled out of his arms and went to stand before her grandfather. She took his hands.

"I will return to Tòrr Dòrainn," she said quietly. "After Miach and I have finished this, I *will* return. And while Miach and I appreciate the show of support, we will be fine on our own."

The king cleared his throat roughly. "I forced you to choose between us, Mhorghain, and I apologize. I was wrong." He shot Miach a look. "I will come along. I can be discreet. Certainly more so than Sosar who requires all sorts of concessions and comforts."

Miach suspected that Sosar was not the one who would require concessions and comforts, but perhaps he underestimated the old man.

"Well?" Sìle prompted.

Miach found that Morgan and her grandfather both were watching him. He wondered, briefly, if it was possible to travel with those two elves and remain anonymous.

He doubted it.

"I appreciate the offer," he began slowly.

"We'll be ready to go in a moment," Sìle said, turning away before Miach could finish. "Sosar, fetch the horses you called to us earlier. I'll ready the saddlebags."

Miach looked at Morgan. She was smiling.

"You're outnumbered," she said.

"I'm a little queasy at the thought, actually," he said seriously.

"I don't think it will go badly for us. Sosar is prudent. Sìle might heal us both if needed. I'll go get my gear."

He nodded.

"Be here when I return."

Heaven help him, he would. It wasn't wise and it wasn't safe, but if he hadn't meant to share his life with her, he should have left her safely in Gobhann. He watched as she walked through the trees away from him and was extraordinarily glad he hadn't managed to rush off without her.

Though he supposed he hadn't tried very hard, truth be told.

He hoped he wouldn't come to regret that decision.

He wished, four days later, that he'd tried a little harder to leave Sìle and Sosar behind.

He walked through the streets of Beinn òrain near sunset, held Fleòd and Luath's reins in one hand and Morgan's hand with the other, and contemplated the ironies of life. The last time he'd been there, three years ago, he'd been escaping clumsy attempts by Adhémar to find brides for all his younger brothers. He'd fled east on the pretext of keeping current with the masters in Buidseachd. He'd made the required visit, of course, then spent several days just wandering the city and wondering if there would ever come a time when his life might include more than just spells.

He never would have imagined that his life might include Mhorghain of Tòrr Dòrainn.

Or her family.

He watched the king of Tòrr Dòrainn and his youngest son walking in front of him, leading their own horses and trying to pass themselves off as simple travelers. Sosar was succeeding; Sìle was failing miserably—and that in spite of the money they'd spent on fitting him with discreet clothing.

Well, at least they'd come this far without magic. Perhaps people would simply overlook them and they would manage a quick and uneventful stay.

He looked to his right and saw Buidseachd sitting up on the

rocky bluff in the middle of town. He remembered his first sight of the fortress. He'd been walking down the very same street at ten years old, holding his mother's hand. She had elbowed him and told him to look up. He could still remember his absolute astonishment at the sight that greeted him. His mother had laughed at him, hugged him tightly, and told him she loved him.

Miach smiled at the memory, then squeezed Morgan's hand.

"Morgan, look up," he said, nodding to her right.

"I'm fine," she said, putting her head down and continuing on through the press. "I don't like crowds."

"I won't let anyone run over you. Just turn your head a bit and look up." He kept her hand in his and pointed with it in front of her nose toward the castle that stood on the edge of the rocky bluff, high above the rest of the city.

She finally caught sight of it. Her mouth fell open.

He smiled. "I wondered when you'd notice."

"What's that?" she wheezed.

"Buidseachd. The schools of wizardry."

"We aren't going there, are we?" she asked, looking absolutely miserable.

"Not today. Today we'll find proper housing for the horses, then find ourselves the same near the gates of the keep. We'll carry on tomorrow."

She nodded, but said nothing more.

He continued to walk with her, but the tension didn't leave her. "Morgan, what is it?"

"There are so many people," she said grimly. "And we're too conspicuous. Look at those two in front of us. How could anyone mistake them for anything but what they are? Their beauty alone is astonishing."

"As is yours," he said, reaching out to pull her hood up over her face. He did the same for himself, then smiled at her. "We'll be all right. No one will find us here, especially after the sun sets."

"And the men at the school? Won't they recognize you?"

He smiled. "I didn't say we'd pay a visit during the daytime, now, did I?"

She looked at him in surprise, then smiled. "I suppose you didn't."

He squeezed her hand and continued on, but he was more careful than he had been. He sensed nothing unusual, but as Morgan said, there were many people around them.

He found himself slightly more at ease once the horses had been stabled. The stable master was of the highest reputation, and he'd been paid handsomely for their care. The beasts would no doubt have a better time of it than he and his companions would.

He paused at the doorway and looked at his little company. "I think we should see if we can't find a room large enough for the four of us. We'll take turns watching."

Sìle frowned. "And what sort of hovel can I expect?"

Miach smiled. "I'll do my best to provide something slightly above 'hovel,' Your Grace. Then we'll find something to eat."

"I'm starved," Sosar agreed cheerfully. "Lead on, nephew."

"He is *not* your nephew," Sìle said sharply. "Don't raise his hopes unnecessarily." He looked at Miach with a frown. "Where to now, lad?"

"Up the way," Miach said. "There's an inn on this side of the street, the Uneasy Dragon. There is a decent tavern attached to it."

Sosar nodded and put his arm around his father's shoulders. They walked ahead, and Miach followed with Morgan. He looked behind him, just to make certain they weren't being followed, then found himself ploughing into Sìle's back. Sìle cursed, then held out a hand until Miach had steadied himself.

"Your Majesty," a deep voice said in astonishment. "I beg your pardon. I didn't see you."

Miach groaned silently.

"What?" Morgan asked.

He put his arm around her and pulled her close. "Just wait. You'll see."

"And Prince Sosar," another voice said incredulously. "What are you doing here?"

Sosar leaned forward. "We're the escort."

"For whom?"

Sosar stepped aside. Miach sighed and pulled Morgan along with him as he went to present himself to the gaping fools, Turah and Rigaud of Neroche, who were standing in front of Sìle.

"What are you two doing here?" Miach asked.

Turah shut his mouth, then shrugged. "Rigaud was fresh out of purple silks and demanded that I accompany him whilst he was shopping. I didn't want to come, but he was afraid to be on his own—"

A fight ensued. Miach sighed, looked at Morgan, who was gaping at his brawling brothers, then took Sìle's elbow and steered him around the madness. He himself stepped over his brothers, watched Sosar help Morgan step around them, then continued on.

His reprieve didn't last long. His brothers soon caught up with him. Turah slung his arm around Miach's shoulders. "Why is the king of Tòrr Dòrainn following you?"

"Because I want to wed his granddaughter," Miach said calmly. "He doesn't trust me with her."

Rigaud leaned around Turah. "But all his granddaughters are already wed. Even if they weren't, surely none of them has so little wit as to look twice at you." He looked at Morgan. "You're Morgan, aren't you?"

"I am," she agreed.

Turah leapt ahead of them to turn around and walk backward in front of them. "I'm confused," he said, scratching his head.

"Your usual condition," Rigaud said, shoving him out of the way. He looked at Morgan. "If you're just Morgan, and Miach wants to wed King Sìle's granddaughter, then why is he holding your hand?" He frowned. "Who else are you?"

"Mhorghain of Tòrr Dòrainn," she said gravely. "And Ceangail, if you want to be completely accurate."

Miach felt his heart lurch just a bit at the look in her eye as she glanced at him. He squeezed her hand gently, felt her do the same in return, then he watched both his brothers gape at her. Rigaud recovered first.

"Are you Sarait's daughter?" he asked.

"Aye."

"And you're the granddaughter my bumbling brother thinks to wed?" Turah asked, surprised.

"That too," Morgan agreed.

"Then how fortunate that we arrived just in time to save you from that horrible fate," Rigaud said, making her a low bow. He took up the place on her right. "Miach, where are we going?"

"The Uneasy Dragon," Miach began, "but—"

Turah pushed Miach out of the way and presented himself to Morgan on her left. "In this, I agree with Rigaud. You don't want Miach. He's messy, ill-humored, and I think he snores."

Miach would have protested further, but Sosar pushed him aside to catch up with his brothers. Miach found himself standing with Sìle, watching three very handsome lads abscond with the woman he loved.

"Pitiful," Sìle said.

Miach looked at him in surprise. "What?"

"You," Sìle said. "Bested by two empty-headed womanizers. Do you actually think I would give her to you when this is the care you'll take of her?"

"I plan to kill them both at my first opportunity," Miach grumbled. "Perhaps Sosar too. It will look like an accident, I assure you."

"Promising," Sìle said approvingly. "If you manage it, I'll think about permitting you the occasional dance with her."

"I appreciate that, Your Grace."

Sìle hesitated, then he sighed deeply. "I'm well aware that you're humoring me by allowing me to remain with you, Miach. I've had her such a short time." He smiled, and his eyes were rather moist. "I can't bear to lose her as I lost her mother. I just wanted you to know I appreciate the concession."

Miach decided that it was only his vast amounts of self-control that prevented him from tearing up as Morgan's grandfather was doing. He put his hand on the older man's shoulder. "'Tis no concession, Your Majesty. Mhorghain loves you. I wouldn't think to come between you."

"Though you intend to take her away to Tor Neroche," Sìle said pointedly.

Miach smiled. "I'll bring her to Seanagarra often, Your Majesty. If you give me leave to wed her."

Sìle looked at him, then snorted. "You'd damn well better wait for my permission, *boy*, or you'll find yourself loitering in my dungeon. And don't think I can't put you there."

"Of course, Your Grace."

Sìle pursed his lips. "We'd best follow those rapscallions you call brothers before neither of us sees her again. And speaking of revenge on men who take treasures they shouldn't, you should know that *I* plan to kill Nicholas of Diarmailt next time we meet."

Miach smiled. "I imagined you might."

"I don't like mages." He shot Miach a sideways look. "And *you* aren't even a mage king. Just a mage. And a young one, at that."

"Your granddaughter is a mage."

"She isn't. She's an elven princess of rare beauty. You're damned lucky she looks at you at all." He paused. "I suppose she might find someone more suitable."

"I suppose you could hope for that," Miach offered.

Sìle grunted at him, then strode forward and elbowed Rigaud out of the way. Miach continued along behind them, then looked at Turah, who had dropped back to walk next to him.

"She told Rigaud to go to hell," Turah said with wide eyes. "That you'd already claimed her."

"Did she, indeed?" Miach asked with a smile.

"King Sìle said it was not at all decided yet and that Rigaud was even less suitable than you were."

"Unsurprising."

"How in the hell did *you* manage to win her?"

"Dumb luck," Miach said.

"It has to be." Turah started to walk away, then he froze. He turned back to Miach and stared at him in astonishment for a moment or two, then reached over and pushed his hair back from his face.

"Bloody hell," he said faintly. "How'd you get that?"

Miach pulled back from his brother and shook his bangs back down over his forehead. "In the usual way, I imagine."

"I want details."

"I'll think about it—later. But I'll know *now* why you're here."

Turah looked at him, then shook his head. "Oh, nay. I have much more interesting things to do than talk to you."

Miach watched him catch up to Morgan and elbow Sosar out of the way. There was a bit of jostling, but finally Sìle came away with the coveted spot on Morgan's left whilst Turah managed to secure the spot on her right. Rigaud and Sosar followed, chatting about how far they could go in removing Sìle from his place without offending him. Turah, apparently, didn't merit any of that sort of consideration.

Miach followed them and realized, with a start, how pleasant it was to have kin about him—even if two of them were rather removed from his generation. They were on his side, and that counted for a great deal.

Of course, the soul who mattered the most to him was enclosed in their protective circle, that astonishingly resilient, courageous, stubborn woman he loved more than his own life.

She looked over her shoulder, found him with her gaze, then smiled.

"Hell," Turah said in disgust.

Miach smiled and quickened his pace to catch up with them.

Twenty-eight

❧

M organ sat on a bale of hay and watched as Miach checked the horses. Perhaps doing so hadn't been necessary, but it had been a chance to escape all their chaperons and she had agreed to it without hesitation. She supposed Miach wasn't particularly happy with the entourage he seemed to have acquired, but she suspected that entourage couldn't help itself. There was something about Miach that drew others into his circle.

She understood that very well, actually.

She realized that he had stopped with his business and was now leaning back against the stall door, watching her with that small smile she loved so much. Fleòd leaned his head over the stall door and bumped Miach companionably. Miach reached up, stroked the horse's nose, then looked back at her.

"How are you?" he asked with a smile.

"Tired," she admitted. "Very uneasy." That was an understatement, but perhaps she was better off not examining it too closely. "I'm happy to be with you, though."

He crossed over to her and pulled her up. "I will stop telling you how much it worries me—"

The stable door opened. Morgan found herself standing behind Miach and he with his sword drawn in front of her before she thought to move on her own. Miach didn't relax any when the door shut, so she wondered who might have entered.

"Your Majesty," Miach said quietly.

Morgan looked around him to find her grandfather standing just inside the door. She slipped her hand into Miach's left and moved to stand next to him. "My liege?"

Sìle looked at them both for a moment in silence, then turned and opened the stable door.

"Follow me," he said.

Morgan exchanged a quick look with Miach, but he only shrugged and resheathed his sword. He led her out of the barn, shut the door behind him, then followed Sìle down the street. Sìle said nothing, not even to her. Miach surreptitiously loosened his sword in its sheath.

"Miach," she whispered, aghast.

He shot her a look.

"You won't need your sword, lad," Sìle threw over his shoulder.

Morgan felt a little faint. She couldn't imagine that Sìle had plans to do Miach in. He didn't look upset, or angry, or as if he were executing some nefarious plot. He merely walked in front of them silently, looking over his shoulder now and again as if he wanted to make sure they still followed him.

Morgan looked at Miach and saw that he was marking their surroundings. He reached over casually and pulled her hood up over her face, then did the same for himself.

"Your Majesty," he said quietly.

"Eh?" Sìle said, looking back. "Oh." He pulled his own hood up around his face, tucked his hands in his sleeves, and continued on.

Morgan felt Miach squeeze her hand. It didn't comfort her overmuch, but she wasn't particularly fond of surprises, so perhaps nothing would have eased her.

They walked away from the university and through the center of town. Morgan saw two small hills in front of them. One was covered in terraced houses that she could see thanks to the lights that glowed in the windows. The other hill was dark, though she could see the faint outline of trees all the way up to the top.

Sìle led them to the darkened hill and paused at the gate. Morgan listened as he murmured a spell. His glamour sprang up over the place and covered it, much as Sosar's spell had

covered Seanagarra's lists. The gate swung open soundlessly
and Sìle led them inside. The gate shut behind them with a soft
click.

Lights began to glow softly along a path that wound its way
upward into the dark. The light was so mesmerizing that Morgan had difficulty remembering she was supposed to be walking. The light cast itself against the trees above and along
flowerbeds full of roses that shouldn't have been blooming so
soon in the year.

She looked up at Miach, but he only shrugged, appearing
as surprised as she. They followed Sìle up a winding path that
led from the gate below to a bower on the top of the hill. The
trees grew together there, rowan trees that whispered a song of
Fadaire as Sìle walked under them. Light sprang to life in their
branches, werelight that danced and shimmered as if it were
pleased to be of use to the king of the elves and his guests.

Sìle led them into the middle of the bower, then turned and
faced them.

"This is the garden of Gearrannan, which my grandfather
gifted to the city of Beinn òrain in the days when we had dealings with the masters of Buidseachd. I came here often in my
youth, before the world grew unruly and we began to disagree
with the wizards." He looked about him for a moment, then
looked at them with a grave smile. "It was here that I plighted
my troth with Queen Brèagha. Only after a lengthy and strenu-
ous amount of convincing her father, Beusach of An Cèin, that
I might someday hope to be worthy of her," he added, shooting
Miach a look.

Miach managed a nod. "Of course," he said faintly. "Queen
Brèagha is a treasure beyond price."

"As is my granddaughter."

"Aye, Your Grace, she is."

Morgan was almost certain she'd heard Sìle say the word
troth in conjunction with plighting it. He hadn't used it whilst
talking about her or Miach, but she also supposed he wouldn't
have brought them this far just to plunge a sword into Miach's
chest.

Then again, she didn't actually know her grandfather well
enough to know what he would do.

"You do love the youngest prince of Neroche, don't you, Granddaughter?" Sìle asked, turning to her.

"Well, aye, I do," she said, surprised that he would ask without snarling.

He looked at Miach. "And you give me your solemn vow you will protect my Mhorghain with your life?"

"Aye, Your Majesty," Miach said quietly.

"And love her?"

"Aye," Miach said. "With all my heart."

Sìle considered for another very long moment, then nodded. "Very well, then. Kneel, children."

Morgan looked at him in surprise. "Kneel?"

Miach squeezed her hand sharply, so she shut her mouth and decided that perhaps when it came to Sìle of Tòrr Dòrainn, it was just better not to ask too many questions.

"Kneel on his right, Mhorghain."

Morgan did so without comment. She shot Miach a look, but he said nothing. He looked rather overwhelmed, truth be told.

"Your right hand, Mochriadhemiach," he said quietly. "Your left hand, Mhorghain."

Morgan felt Miach stiffen next to her, then he very slowly extended his right arm. Morgan looked at him, but he shook his head very slightly. Morgan shrugged. Some elvish rite, obviously. Well, Miach seemed to know what he was doing, so she would go along with it. She stretched out her left arm.

Sìle took their hands and put them close together with their palms facing the ground. He pulled silver thread out of the air and wrapped it first around Miach's wrist, then around hers. He continued to wind spun silver around their wrists, first Miach's, then hers, until there was no pulling their wrists apart. He then plucked gold thread out of thin air and wove it with the silver. Morgan watched as gold and silver threads bound her wrist together with Miach's, over and over again. She looked quickly at Miach.

He only smiled. "Do you understand what he's saying?"

She shook her head.

"Listen harder."

She looked up at her grandfather and tried to make sense of

his words. She'd thought that perhaps he was simply grousing in his own tongue over the fact that he'd apparently relented and given his permission for her to wed with Miach, then she realized, as she began to understand his words, that she was gravely mistaken.

He was joining them together with a bond that could not be broken.

But that was only the beginning of what he was gifting them. He bound other things upon them: courage, strength, elven magic . . . and his own length of life.

She would have let her jaw drop, but she didn't think it would be a particularly attractive way to plight her troth with the man kneeling next to her.

Or accept the gifts her grandfather was giving them.

Sìle continued to speak, but she lost track of all the things he settled upon them: wisdom, peace, joy, endurance for their labors, steadfastness, children to carry on their magic . . . the list lengthened as the strands continued to wrap around their wrists and join them together.

Finally, Sìle put one hand on Miach's wrist and the other on hers. He spoke a final word and the gold and silver sank painlessly into their flesh, becoming thin spiderwebs that formed themselves into runes.

Sìle took her hand and put it in Miach's. He looked at her with a grave smile.

"These are runes of the house of Neroche, which your lad there will teach you, and runes of the house of Tòrr Dòrainn, which he likely already knows but will accord me the courtesy of teaching to you."

Morgan found that she had absolutely nothing to say. She could only look up at her grandfather in astonished silence.

"You are now betrothed, Mhorghain, to Mochriadhemiach, a prince of Neroche. You are not wed"—he shot Miach a look—"so you will both comport yourselves accordingly. But you are betrothed, and nothing will break this bond." He lifted her to her feet. "He will care for you well. And given that he's always angling for a look at books in my library he shouldn't be reading, I imagine he'll see you home often enough to suit me." He held out a hand to raise Miach to his feet. "You'll come to Seanagarra for the wedding. After you're done with this business."

"Thank you, Your Majesty," Miach said gravely. "I am . . . well, I think I'm speechless."

"I should stay just to enjoy that," Sìle said with a bit of a smile, "but I imagine you'll find your tongue soon enough. I'm sure you two will want to discuss this, so I'll leave you to it."

Morgan let go of Miach's hand and threw her arms around her grandfather's neck. "Thank you," she whispered. "Thank you for the gift I wanted most."

He hugged her tightly for a moment, then pulled away and looked at her with a smile. "You are now in my debt twice, missy. Don't think I'll forget it."

"I'll pay gladly," Morgan said with feeling.

Sìle started to walk away, but Miach turned to him. "Your Majesty?"

Sìle stopped and looked at him. "What is it, lad?"

"Why now?"

Sìle smiled. "Because you died for her and it fair killed her to heal you. That proved to me that your love for each other was strong enough to bear these runes. And you'll need those," he added with a nod at their wrists. "The strength they'll bring. I wouldn't think on that overmuch now, though. If I were you, Miach my boy, I'd spend a few minutes telling my betrothed how damned fortunate I was to have her."

"I will," Miach agreed without hesitation.

Sìle smiled at them both, then turned and started down the hill.

Morgan watched her grandfather go, then looked at Miach. "Will he find the inn, do you think?"

"I hope so," Miach managed. He took a deep breath. "Well."

"Well, indeed," she agreed. She looked up at him. "I don't think I heard any sort of *formal* proposal from you in all that. And I'll also be happy to listen to anything my grandfather suggested you spew out."

He laughed and pulled her into his arms. "Too late for the first, I imagine, though I'll oblige you with the second."

She scowled up at him, but he only laughed again, picked her up and twirled her around. By the time he set her on her feet, she couldn't have cared less if he intended to propose; all she wanted to do was sit down. He wrapped his arms around her and held her close to him.

"Wed me?" he whispered against her ear.

She nodded. "I had best say you aye, hadn't I?"

He pulled back to smile down at her. "I imagine so." He shook his head in wonder. "This is unprecedented. The elves of Tòrr Dòrainn do not wed with mortals. Ever."

"And my mother?"

"Gair wasn't precisely mortal, was he?"

"And you?"

He took a deep breath. "I suppose I'm not precisely mortal now either."

"Because of your ancestors?" she asked.

"Partly, aye, but mostly because your grandfather has, through these runes, gifted me the same length of life that he has. So I suppose it makes me less mortal and more elvish." He shook his head in wonder. "I had hoped he would give me permission to wed you, but I never dreamed that he would go this far."

"How far has he gone?"

He tilted his head. "Did you notice that your grandfather and grandmother bear these, but not all their children?"

Morgan shrugged. "I hadn't thought about it, but I suppose you're right. What does it mean?"

"What it means, Your Highness, is that if something were to happen to Sìle and then to the only other of his line who bears these marks, Làidir, that you would then become the queen of Tòrr Dòrainn."

She swayed. Fortunately, he had hold of her. She looked up at him in shock. "And you would be king," she said slowly.

"I told you this was unprecedented."

She rested her head against his shoulder. "Why us?" she whispered. "Well, I can understand why he would choose you—"

"And I was going to say the same thing," he said with a half laugh. "You are his granddaughter. I am—"

"The man I love—and a very powerful mage," she said. She shivered violently, once, then took a deep breath. "I think it may take me a bit to accustom myself to it."

"I suppose we now have several lifetimes to think about it," he said quietly. "But for now, let's find somewhere to sit."

Morgan nodded, then watched a bench materialize from the sparkling air under the trees. She looked at Miach. "Camanaë?"

"Fadaire," he said, a twinkle in his eye. "Appropriate, don't you think?"

She laughed as she sat down next to him. "It is."

He put his arm around her and pulled her close. Morgan took his right hand and trailed her finger over the runes there, comparing them with hers. They were the mirror of each other, faint gold and silver lines that were beautiful and powerful at the same time. "Teach me just one," she said, looking up at him.

"I'll teach you two." He took her hand and touched the lines that formed a pattern in the precise center of the back of her wrist. "This represents the kingdom of Tòrr Dòrainn. Well, rather the crown of Tòrr Dòrainn and all that entails." He shot her a quick smile. "Pretend I didn't tell you that when Sìle explains it to you. You'll notice whilst yours is on the outer side of your wrist, mine is on the inner." He shot her a quick smile. "Closest to my heart, you see."

"I do see," she murmured.

He turned her wrist over. "And this one," he said, trailing his finger over the one in the precise center of the underside of her wrist, "this one represents the royal lineage of the house of Neroche." He looked at her from under his eyebrows. "Closest to your heart."

She smiled. "I see that as well."

He held her hand up and studied it with a frown for a moment. "I think it depicts my position in that house, though the crown is rather robust. He did it, no doubt, to irritate Adhémar." He brought her hand closer and studied it for another moment. "See here how it is hopelessly intertwined with elven runes of power and might? I think it will take me a year to unravel it all and try to guess the meaning of each thing, then likely several more years to determine how it all fits together."

"I think he approves of us," she said with a smile.

"I daresay he does," Miach agreed.

"There appears to be no going back now," she said casually. "Do you mind?"

"Would the trees tell tales if I showed you what I thought?"

She laughed uneasily. "Is that your answer?"

"Not by half," he said purposefully, slipping one arm behind her back and the other under her knees. He pulled her over onto his lap. "Here's my answer."

Morgan supposed, the next chance she had to think clearly, that she didn't much care what the trees had to say. Well, outside of listening to the song they seemed to have begun just for her and her betrothed.

She suspected they approved as well.

I t was very late before she walked with Miach into the Uneasy Dragon only to find Turah waiting for them at a table in a darkened corner. He rolled his eyes when he saw them.

"Finally," he said. "Where were you?"

"Trying to stay out of trouble," Miach said, dropping down on a bench and pulling Morgan down next to him. "Go be a love and fetch us something to drink."

Morgan watched Turah flick his brother's ear, then wink at her before he rose and walked over to the bar. She leaned back against the wall with Miach's arm around her shoulders. She closed her eyes and smiled.

"Happy?"

She opened her eyes and looked at him. "Very."

"You know, I fully intended to wed you in the chapel at Tor Neroche with all the trappings requisite for an elven princess, but I had assumed I would be doing that only after I'd stolen you out from underneath Sìle's nose. I fear now my concern is how to stop Adhémar from offending everyone in sight when he comes to Seanagarra for the wedding."

"Well, at least all your brothers are not so objectionable," she offered. "And speaking of those brothers, why did these two come to find you, do you think?"

"To be chaperons."

She laughed softly. "I would accuse you of jesting, but I think you might be right—and I think we need them."

"So said the trees as we left Gearrannan. At least they won't be watching now," he said as he tipped her face up and kissed her.

"Oh, hell, is this what I have to look forward to?"

Miach sighed. "Told you so," he said against her mouth.

Morgan smiled into his eyes, then smiled again as he pulled away and thoroughly cursed his brother. Turah pushed two glasses of ale toward them, then sat with an easy smile.

"I promise not to come along on your honeymoon if you manage to wed that lovely maid there, though I'm not convinced she wouldn't prefer me if she thought about it long enough."

"She doesn't need to think about it," Morgan said pleasantly, "though she appreciates the offer."

Miach snorted. "She's being polite. What she really means is cease pestering her or she'll stick you with whatever blade she has to hand. Now, before you tempt her overmuch to do just that, tell me why you're here."

Turah looked about him as if he wanted to assure himself they would have privacy, then he leaned in close and motioned for them to do the same thing.

Morgan looked at Miach's brother and had to admit, objectively, that he was rather easy on the eye himself. He shared Miach's dark hair and blue eyes, though his eyes were a darker blue. She supposed that if she had seen him first, she might have thought him handsome enough.

"She's watching me," Turah said in a loud whisper. He nodded knowingly. "Very promising."

Miach looked at her. "Changed your mind, did you?" he asked with a smile.

She pursed her lips at him. "I will admit the sight of both of you together makes me wonder how any of the serving wenches at Tor Neroche manage to do their work, but nay, I have not changed my mind. But you never suspected I would, did you, my love?"

Miach looked at his brother. "A term of endearment. I must make special note of them."

Turah rolled his eyes. "Be brief, then."

Morgan found herself properly, if not briefly, rewarded for her efforts. Then she held Miach's left hand in both her own and leaned her head on his shoulder as he looked at his brother.

"What's amiss?" he said without preamble.

Turah had a very long drink of ale. He set his cup slowly down on the table, then leaned in again and looked at Miach seriously. "Adhémar was out riding—"

Morgan felt Miach stiffen. "Is he dead?"

"I don't think so—"

"You don't *know*?" Miach said incredulously.

"Would you just let me finish!" Turah exclaimed. He took a deep breath, then leaned closer. "He was out riding with Adaira, along the northern border, with only a pair of guardsmen in tow. He and Adaira were captured and the slain guardsmen left behind."

Morgan lifted her head and looked at Miach. He was gaping at his brother.

"He was captured by *Lothar*?" Miach said, stunned.

"Aye."

"How do you know this?" Miach asked. "What proof have you?"

"Lothar sent back the Sword of Neroche with a message that the king wouldn't be needing it at present."

"Has the mantle fallen on any of you?" Miach asked. "And who sent you, by the way? Does the Sword of Neroche still lack its magic?"

Turah sighed. "To answer your questions in order, nay, the mantle still rests with Adhémar, which is why we know he's still alive. Cathar sent me, as you likely suspected. He's holding things together, but he isn't happy about it. He got your message a fortnight ago, which is how he knew to send us here. We left night before last and flew hard. And for the last, aye, the Sword of Neroche is still naught but ordinary steel."

Morgan watched Miach bow his head. He stared at the table for quite some time in silence, though his hands around hers were warm and steady. If he wrestled with something, he didn't show it.

Then again, this was his duty, to protect the realm.

He finally sighed and sat back. "If the mantle still rests with Adhémar, then you've no need of me yet."

"You'll leave him there?" Turah asked in astonishment.

"I have a duty to protect the realm of Neroche," Miach said grimly, "and the task that Morgan and I must see to is relevant to that duty. If we're successful, I'll come home and rescue the fool. If we fail, then it won't matter where Adhémar is because we'll all be dead and he'll die along with us."

Turah blanched. "What is it you're about?"

"You're better off not knowing. Go home and tell them I'll be there as soon as I can."

Morgan watched Turah stroke his chin. "Perhaps for the safety of the princess of Tòrr Dòrainn, I should take her with me."

"Morgan is happy where she is," Miach said.

"Can't understand *that*," Turah muttered.

"It is a mystery, isn't it?" Miach agreed. "Now, shut up and go home. And *please* take Rigaud with you."

"I'll send Rigaud home," Turah said easily, "but I think I'll stay. You might need me."

Morgan watched Miach start to open his mouth, no doubt to protest, then shut it. He looked at his brother for several moments in silence.

"I'll think about it," he said, finally.

"As if you could tell me what to do," Turah said, winking at Morgan.

"Turah," Miach warned.

Turah laughed. "So you see how it is, Morgan. Adhémar thinks he rules the realm, but in truth 'tis my little brother here who engineers it all. That is why the king of Neroche never sleeps well. I imagine, though, that he'd be damned happy to see you unlock the door of his dungeon, Miach."

"Lothar's dungeon has no door," Miach said grimly, then shook his head. "Let's not speak of that. We'll retreat to our chamber, and I'll let Rigaud think 'tis his brilliant idea to hurry home and save the realm." Miach rose, pulled Morgan up with him, then eased around the table. He put his hand on Turah's shoulder. "I think we'd be glad to have you."

"It helps to have family about when you're embarking on a dangerous quest," Turah agreed. He walked off in front of them. "Besides, it will allow me to be the humble and attentive servant of the lovely princess of Tòrr Dòrainn."

"Turah!"

Turah only laughed at Miach over his shoulder and continued on his way toward the stairs.

* * *

An hour later, Morgan sat by the hearth in the very adequate chamber Miach had found for them and watched a rather intense game of cards in progress.

She thought back to where she'd been but a pair of months earlier: shivering in Weger's gathering chamber, wondering if she would ever again be whole, and studiously avoiding thinking on the fact that what pained her the most was her heart.

And now she found herself in the company of five powerful, stalwart men, not a one of whom was cheating in cards. Well, perhaps Rigaud was. He met her eyes periodically and smiled smugly. She returned the smile because she found herself quite unaccountably content. Who would have thought that she would have relatives of this ilk? A king and a chamber full of princes. It was astonishing.

The prince she was most interested in soon tossed in his cards with a sigh and got up from the table.

"I told you he'd lose," Rigaud said pointedly.

Sosar laughed. "He gave up. I imagine he has more interesting things to do than play cards."

"Not while I'm here he doesn't," Sìle said sternly. "Boy, don't you dare maul my granddaughter, or you'll answer to me."

"Of course, Your Grace," Miach said, sounding completely unintimidated.

Morgan smiled at him as he crossed over to her and pulled her up out of her chair. He sat down, then pulled her onto his lap. He leaned his head back against the chair and sighed deeply.

"I lost on purpose," he remarked.

"I imagined you had." She smiled, then her smile faded. "The tidings about your brother are grave. I am not overfond of him, but I wouldn't wish this current torment on him." She paused. "I don't think he will ever be the same."

"I daresay not," Miach agreed with a sigh. He looked at her casually. "Do you think I'm being cruel?"

She shook her head. "Nay, I think you're only doing what your duty demands. Even if this had been a terrible accident instead of your brother being his ridiculous self, you cannot leave the safety of the realm to pursue what your heart might dictate."

"But I did," he said with a weary smile. "I was willing to risk quite a bit in Gobhann."

"You did what you had to to fetch the one you needed to wield the Sword of Angesand—and to close a certain well—"

"But, Morgan," he interrupted, sounding shocked, "you know I didn't do it for either. Don't you?"

"Of course I do," she said with a grave smile, "but it worked out for the best, didn't it?"

His eyes were suddenly very red. "I swear I never know what's going to come out of your mouth next."

"As many terms of affection as you can possibly bear," she said, leaning forward to kiss him softly. "Thank you for braving Weger's gates."

"I braved them to fetch out the mage's daughter," he said, "but not so I could use her to wield a sword or to close her father's well. I only went in because my heart couldn't survive without her."

"I know. And that's made all the difference," she said. "Just you, loving me for me and waiting for me to find my own way."

He pressed her head against his shoulder. "Don't watch me weep over you yet again," he said gruffly. "It will completely unman me in front of my brothers, and I will *never* live that down."

Having spent an hour or two in the company of those brothers, she could see where he had a point, so she settled comfortably in his arms and allowed him a bit of peace. She watched her grandfather and uncle and Miach's brothers continue to play cards, pulled Miach's arm from behind her back and laid it over her lap. She traced the runes of Neroche and Tòrr Dòrainn that encircled his wrist. They were beautiful, true, but she found that looking at them now, faint in the firelight, caused a flicker of something to spring to life in her heart. It was a fiercely encouraging feeling, as if it had been fire leaping onto the top of the torch at Gobhann when Miach had used the spell of Fadaire.

She couldn't say if she and Miach would be successful. Her mother hadn't been. There was no guarantee that she wouldn't meet the same fate. There was nothing but darkness in front of her and darkness following.

But that flame was stubborn and it was beautiful. Morgan found that just concentrating on it made her feel as if she might have the courage to continue on that path she'd begun when she'd taken her first steps as Mhorghain of Tòrr Dòrainn. She let out a deep sigh, then looked at Miach. He was watching her with a smile.

"Good thoughts?" he asked.

She put her hand over his wrist. "I feel better when I look at these. As if I might actually manage the task set before me."

He took her right hand in his, turned her wrist over and trailed his finger over her skin. He looked up at her. "I might be able to tell you partly why. You're reading your name. Can you see it here?"

Morgan looked to where he was pointing. She couldn't see it, but that didn't mean anything. She had far to go before she would recognize anything her grandfather had written there. She frowned.

"Morgan?" she asked.

"Mhorghain," he corrected. "It is a Camanaë name, you know." He smiled. "It means *hope*."

Tears stung her eyes suddenly. "Truly?"

"Truly," he said. He reached up and tucked a lock of hair behind her ear, then he smiled at her. "It is something you bring wherever you go, Mhorghain."

She looked at him in surprise. "You've never called me that before."

"It seemed appropriate." He took her left hand, kissed the inside of her wrist, then smiled at her. "I think, my love, that hope may be what saves us all."

She merely nodded because her heart would have broken if she'd opened her mouth.

So she put her head on Miach's shoulder and closed her eyes. The darkness would be faced soon enough, but at least she wouldn't face it alone. She would have Miach, his family, her family, and even her mother who lived on in dreams and a single letter.

And she would have hope.

It was enough for now.

For more of Morgan and Miach's adventures,
be sure to read
Princess of the Sword
Available now from Berkley Sensation.

———

Turn the page for a preview of
Lynn Kurland's newest trilogy
set in the Nine Kingdoms

Dreamspinner

Coming January 2013 from
Berkley Sensation!

The pub was as unremarkable as any pub would be on the last day of the week, lit with just the right amount of candlelight reflecting off the dark wood of the floors, tables, and beams in the ceiling. If things were a little more worn than was polite, the wooden paneling sporting more evidence of knives having resided in their soothing embrace than was comforting, and the barmaids more steely eyed than in other places, who could complain? When a pub owner found himself with a pub in the seediest district of Beul, seediest of all cities in Bruadair, he was simply happy to sell his wares in peace.

Aisling slipped inside the door and flattened herself against the wall, in as much shadow as she could find, and forced herself not to gasp for breath. She wasn't sure she had ever run as she had just run, as if her life had depended on it, and she sincerely hoped she would never need to run that way again. She clutched the wood behind her and told herself that there was indeed still an hour before twilight, ample time to decide what she was going to do.

She leaned her head back against the wall, allowed herself several more steadying breaths, then searched through the crowd to see who might be lurking there. It wouldn't have surprised her to find it full of armed guards looking for her.

Fortunately, it was simply full of the usual suspects, lads

and lassies gathered to eat and drink the cheapest fare the kitchen had to offer. It was Beul, after all, and even a full six days of labor didn't provide much in the way of funds to splash out on fancy foodstuffs.

She looked across the large gathering room to the table where her usual companions were wont to hold forth. She was rather relieved, all things considered, to find just her familiar mates there. Or, rather, two of them. A thrill of fear went through her at the thought that any of the other four might have been detained to tell those who might want to find her where she might be found—

She pushed aside the thought as a perfectly ridiculous one. She was one of hundreds of weavers who made up the Guild, and she was the least of those who sat before their rickety looms, turning out reams and reams of dull, grey cloth. No one would come looking for her, not until her precious few hours of weekly liberty were over and she wasn't to be found where she was supposed to be.

No one, perhaps, save someone who might have a vested financial interest in her presenting herself at her loom at dawn on the first day of the following week. Or perhaps two some-ones—

She realized she was wheezing, but she blamed that on smoke in the air. It had nothing to do with having seen, not a quarter hour ago, a very well-dressed man and woman exiting a very fine restaurant, pausing to allow themselves to be admired, then starting toward an exquisitely appointed carriage. She had gaped at them, convinced she was imagining things, only to hear them instruct the driver of that fine carriage to take them im-mediately to the Weaver's Guild. The woman had paused before she'd entered the conveyance, then turned to look over her shoulder as if she felt something untoward looking at her.

Aisling supposed that untoward thing would have been she herself, the woman's daughter.

Her first instinct had been to step forward, but she'd found her way suddenly blocked by a tall, well-dressed gentleman who had paused to ask her directions. If he had thereafter ar-rived safely at his destination, she would have been surprised. She wasn't at all sure she'd said anything that made any sense at all, but who could blame her for her alarm? She had just seen her parents; parents she had been separated from at the tender age of seven and not seen but thrice since.

She had long since been resigned to the knowledge that when they came to visit, it wasn't to take her to tea.

The door next to her opened, startling her so badly she jumped. She put her hand over her heart, nodded to the entering patron, then pushed away from the wall. She still had time to decide what to do, though the sands were falling rapidly through the hourglass. If she returned to the Guild, she would, she was absolutely sure, find that her parents had come not to rescue her from her last possible months of indenture, but to secure another seven years of her labor for which they would take a hefty advance.

But if she didn't return to the Guild it would mean consequences so dire she couldn't think on them without horror.

She walked unsteadily across the common room, then collapsed onto the bench set against the wall, thankful it was in the darkest corner of the pub. Perhaps if she could simply sit and think, a solution would come to her.

She looked at the man across the table from her who was cradling his empty mug between his hands and speaking in a low, angry voice. Quinn was the leader of their little band, primarily because he was the loudest. He was not now a handsome man, nor had he been, she suspected, before he'd spent years brawling over his very loud opinions. He looked at the moment as if he were fully prepared to brawl a bit more with the only other member of their group present, a thin, passably handsome man named Euan.

"You're a fool," Quinn snapped. "How many ways must I say this before you understand what must be done?"

"We've been over this dozens of times, and you're still daft," Euan said calmly. "This is Bruadair, remember? No one gets in or out."

Aisling knew that very well. In fact, not only did no one leave Bruadair, no one left the Guild. She had been granted an afternoon a week to leave the grounds and visit not only the market but the pub where she currently found herself, but that was only because she had proven herself to be so relentlessly trustworthy.

Until an hour ago, of course, when she'd seen her doom

standing there, dressed in clothing so fine she could safely say the fabric had not been woven on any loom she had ever touched.

She saw a cup of ale suddenly in front of her on the table. She looked at Euan quickly, had a wink as her reward, then wondered how she might manage to imbibe any of that unexpected gift with any success at all. She reached for it, but her hands were simply not equal to the task of holding it.

"Bloody hell, Aisling, what ails you?" Euan said, rescuing her cup before she dropped it in her lap.

"Who gives a damn what ails her?" Quinn growled. "Aren't you *listening* to me? We have to do this thing, before 'tis too late."

Aisling couldn't have agreed more. She managed a sip of ale, then relinquished her cup and tucked her hands under her arms to hide their trembling. She shook her head at Euan's questioning look, for what was there to say? *I am considering running away from the Guild, the penalty for which is death.* That was the fate of weavers who fled, when they were found. It was also the fate of those who dared cross Bruadair's borders, though it was rumored there was no finding involved there. Death followed them as if it were Murcach of Dalbyford's finest hounds, relentless and without mercy. If she didn't return to the Guild or, worse still, tried to escape Bruadair altogether—

She wished she had a warmer cloak. Not even the fire could mitigate the chill that ran through her, though she supposed that was perhaps more from the cold hand of terror gripping the back of her neck than it was the draftiness of the pub.

The hard truth was, she had to make a choice between two things that were equally terrible. She could return to the Guild and submit to her parents borrowing against another seven years of her labor just a trio of months before she came of age and could no longer be forced into servitude. They had done it twice before: first when she'd been ten-and-four and easily convinced that her family truly needed the fruits of her labor, and again when she'd been a score-and-one and less than convinced that the pittance she made could possibly make any difference to the very well-dressed couple who had so briskly signed away her freedom.

Or she could flee and most likely find herself submitting to death by any number of unpleasant means.

She put her hand over her eyes and forced herself to breathe normally. She couldn't sit at that bloody loom for another minute, much less another seven years. But the consequences of running away were so terribly dire.

And not just for her.

The Guildmistress had told her very plainly, on that first day when she'd been granted a bit of freedom, that if she didn't return, not only would they hunt her down and force her to pay the ultimate price, they would slay the weaving mistress as well, first, so Aisling would be forced to watch.

The weaving mistress who had taken her on that first horrible, endless day, fed her, soothed her, then put her to bed and told her a heroic tale of daring battles and romance. The weaving mistress who had, in all the years since, taken an especial interest in her, loaning her an endless number of books, telling her an endless number of obscure tales from less obscure kingdoms, finding an ironclad excuse for an extra hour or two now and again for Aisling to come and read to her once her eyes had begun to fail her. It was not exaggerating to say that the weaving mistress had saved her life.

And to repay her with harm . . .

Aisling leaned her head back against the wall and closed her eyes. What she wouldn't have given for a timely rescue. Unfortunately, there was no handsome lad waiting to carry her off to his impossibly lovely castle and keep her safe there, no fierce swordsman to stand between her and those who would harm her, no prince wearing a circlet of silver on his head and carrying untold power in his hands to wield his sword and drive away those who wanted her for nothing more than her ability to endure countless hours of backbreaking labor.

Nay, it was just her, sitting in a darkened pub, wearing worn slippers on her feet and a threadbare cloak, hoping beyond hope that she would see a doorway open up before her where there had been no doorway before.

"You have no concept of what's at stake here, or the things I'm willing to do to ensure success."

Aisling looked at Quinn to find him fixing Euan with an icy stare.

"And just so you know," Quinn continued, "a body might get across the border if they knew how to flee."

"Flee?" Euan repeated with a snort. "How?"

"Traders cross the border all the time," Quinn said.

"Traders who are not of Bruadair," Euan clarified, "else they would be dead within the hour. *And*," he added, cutting Quinn off in midprotest, "even if we could find a man fool enough to test the veracity of that rumor, that doesn't solve the very real problem that one cannot cross the border without a specific scrap of paper."

Quinn pulled something from under his cloak and laid it on the table.

It was a trader's license.

Euan's mouth fell open. "Where did you get that?"

"It doesn't matter," Quinn said. "My solution is to walk across the border in plain sight, then trot off to find aid."

"Against Sglaimir's army?" Euan said, rolling his eyes. "Impossible."

Impossible was better used to describe her own situation. Aisling wondered if the two sitting at the table might have an opinion on what she should do. She cleared her throat.

"I need help—" she began.

"Oh, be quiet," Quinn said, obviously annoyed. "We've no time for your womanly cares."

Aisling was tempted to tell him her cares were slightly more serious than which hat to wear with what pair of shoes, but she supposed if they were talking about the fate of the realm, they wouldn't care—

Guards burst in the front door. Before she could do so much as decide how best to hide under the table, Euan had snatched up the trader's license, taken her by the hand, and was dragging her out the back of the public room. She couldn't believe those guards had come for her, but she wasn't about to take the chance of being wrong.

"Come *on*," Euan whispered fiercely. *"Hurry."*

She didn't have to be convinced. At the very least, she would find a quiet place—truly quiet this time, not the false quiet of a crowd—and come to terms with the choice she would have to make.

The thought of seven more years . . .

She ran with Euan through the kitchens and out the back door. She continued to run down the street with him, because it seemed like the most sensible thing to do.

Until she realized Euan had run them into an entire clutch of city guards.

Euan shoved something into her hands. She looked down at it and realized, to her surprise, that it was the trader's license. She looked up and watched as Euan disappeared into the crowd of black-garbed men brandishing swords. Before she could say anything at all, she had been taken by the arm and pulled away.

By a Guild guard.

"Nay," she gasped, trying to jerk her arm away from him, "I've done nothing!" She fully intended to do something very soon, but he didn't need to know that.

He drew a knife. "If you want me to use this, keep struggling."

She stopped only because it occurred to her suddenly that she might stand a better chance of getting away from him if she feigned acquiescence. After all, it had worked for her countless times in the past.

He looked over his shoulder, cursed succinctly, then resheathed his knife in his belt and dragged her off the main street and down a side street she'd never seen before. The pub wasn't in the nicest part of town, so there were several streets she hadn't dared explore before.

She went with him because he gave her no choice. It occurred to her as they fled that she might manage to dart away if she were moving instead of digging in her heels. That might have been a more appealing proposition if she'd been able to recognize her surroundings, but she didn't. Perhaps the man knew something she didn't about trouble in places she'd never been.

Or perhaps he was merely hurrying to meet someone else who might want to hurry her back to the Guild.

She considered that as she found herself suddenly handed off to none other than the finely dressed gentleman who had blocked her view of her parents. Aisling looked back at the guard, but he had melted into what she realized with alarm had become rather deep shadows. She didn't want to think that her hour had come and gone, but it was difficult to deny.

"Come along now, lass," the man said pleasantly. "No making a fuss. Wouldn't want to draw any attention to ourselves, now, would we?"

Aisling felt as if she were dreaming. She would have pinched herself, but her arm was already throbbing from where the guard had been holding onto her. She trotted along with the fop, because he was as insistent in his own way as both Euan and the guardsman had been.

She continued to hurry with him along streets, past pubs and music halls, until finally her escort had come to a gentle but inexorable halt.

And she was looking into the face of none other than the weaving mistress herself.

Aisling blinked. "Mistress Muinear, what are you—"

Mistress Muinear looked behind Aisling's shoulder, then swore. "You'll have to run."

Aisling looked over her shoulder as well, just to see what else she would have to be running from. To her horror—as if things weren't bad enough as they were—there was the Guild-mistress herself, bearing down on her, her face and her stride full of fury.

Aisling almost went down to her knees then because she knew she was doomed. Another seven years, another enormous chunk of her life spent in a grey, soulless, freezing hall listening to the endless clack of looms—

"I'll see to them," the weaving mistress said. She shoved something into Aisling's hand. "You go through the border."

Aisling looked at her and blinked. "What?"

Mistress Muinear took her by the arms with surprising strength and shook her. "I do not matter," she said, her normally watery blue eyes bright and fierce. "Get yourself across the border, then go do what must be done."

"But—"

The old woman embraced her briefly, then turned her around and pushed her. "Go, whilst there is still time."

Aisling stumbled forward then found herself swept up in a press of men who seemed to be in a great deal of haste. She hastened with them, because they gave her no choice. Within moments, she found herself facing a border guard who seemed unaffected by the shouting she could hear going on behind her.

She looked over her shoulder and could see through the crowd that Guild guards had surrounded the weaving mistress—

"You're Quinn?"

Aisling looked at the border guard. His expression of absolute boredom was visible thanks to the excessive and unpleasant amount of torchlight. She supposed there was good reason for that. It allowed the guards to identify miscreants more easily, no doubt.

"Quinn's wife," Aisling lied, her mouth very dry. "On his business."

"Do you have anything to prove that?"

Aisling realized with a start what he wanted. She looked down at her hands and realized that what she was clutching in one of them was coins Mistress Muinear had given her. She slipped a pair of gold sovereigns into the crease of the trader's license, and handed it back to the guard. Her hands were trembling so badly he had to snatch it before she dropped it. He slid the gold—she could see it glinting warmly in the torchlight— into his sleeve then back down into his glove with the practiced ease of a man who had done the like a time or two before. He shoved the license at her.

"Go on."

She went, because the men crowding in behind her didn't give her any choice.

It was only as she stepped across the border and looked back to see a very thin, red line behind her heels, that she realized just what she'd done.

She had just sentenced herself to death—and not just from the Guild's bright swords.

She agreed with everything Euan had said about leaving Bruadair. It was common knowledge that to cross the border without leave meant death by any of several means, ranging from a long, slow, lingering illness to a sudden collapse. It was said that those of noble blood could come and go as they pleased, but she had never met anyone noble to ask them. And being as it was that she was nothing more than a common young woman of a score and seven, her blood would not save her.

"Well, get on with ye, gel," said a rough voice from behind her. "Or at least out of the way!"

She found herself pushed aside by a burly trader who

apparently was in a hurry to be about his business. She looked to her left. A wagon was receiving its final passengers, having been already loaded with whatever cargo it was carrying.

"Where is that wagon going?" she managed, looking at another man who was moving past her.

"Gairn."

Aisling heard shouts behind her, shouts that made her blood run cold because she recognized the Guildmistress's voice. She turned, because it was what she was accustomed to doing, though she could hardly bring herself to look and see what the woman would do.

The Guildmistress was holding aloft a sword, stained with blood. She looked at Aisling, her gaze making the distance between them seem much shorter than perhaps it was.

She was smiling coldly.

Aisling took a step forward, back over the border, but before her foot touched the ground, she found herself jerked backward.

"Oh, nay, you're not going there," a voice said firmly.

Before she could do so much as squeak, she was pulled out of the torchlight, away from that thin red line that meant the difference between life and death.

The thought was halfway across her mind that Euan had caught her and was helping her to safety when she looked up at the man who was pulling her quickly into the shadows. It was the peddler she occasionally borrowed books from in the market.

She had actually bought a book from him once, a book she had residing in a pocket she had made in her skirts, a book she had paid dearly for and never allowed to leave her person. Why she should find him where he was at the current moment was one of the more baffling things in an evening that had been full of things she hadn't expected.

"But the weaving mistress—" she protested.

"Dead, most likely," he said briskly. "Count yourself lucky you aren't as well."

Aisling let him pull her with him because he didn't give her any choice. The only thing good about that was that at least he was pulling her away from the border, not toward it, though she thought she might want to know where he intended to take her.

He stopped suddenly, shoved a bundle of what felt like clothes into her arms, then took hold of her long braid. She started to ask him what in the hell he was doing when she saw a knife flash in the darkness.

She gaped at him. "You cut off my hair!"

"And if they catch you, they'll cut your throat," he said harshly. "Those are lad's clothes. Go put them on."

They were far out of the light but still within earshot of a great deal of shouting. Aisling decided that whatever else she chose to do, doing that thing as a lad would be much safer than as a woman. She nodded briskly, hid herself behind an enormous boulder, and changed into the clothes the peddler had given her. She didn't care about their condition.

She took her book from her hidden pocket and shoved it into the waistband of her trousers. She pulled her tunic over them then pulled a cloak around her shoulders. She retrieved her clothes successfully only after having dropped them several times. Her hands were trembling again, too fiercely for her to stop them.

She came out from behind the boulder and walked back on legs that were so unsteady beneath her, she felt as if she were floating. She stopped and looked at the peddler, who was watching the border closely. He turned his head to look at her, then reached down and picked up a pack. He took her old clothes from her, then pushed the pack into her arms. It was so heavy she almost dropped it.

"What's this?" she managed.

"Your new life," he said, taking her by the arm and pulling her along with him. "There's a carriage half a mile down the road, waiting."

She looked at him in surprise. "Why?"

"Because I paid them to," he said impatiently.

"A carriage—"

"Get in it and don't get out until it stops."

She blinked. "But—"

"There's gold in that pack. Find an assassin. Save Bruadair."

She shook her head, but that didn't clear away the persistent sensation she had of having wandered into a terrible dream. Less than an hour ago—perhaps it had been longer, she honestly couldn't tell—she had been looking in the window of a shop and admiring a cloak that, whilst grey, had at least been cut handsomely. Now she stood outside the border of her country, dressed as a lad, knowing that her flight had meant death for the one person in the world she cared about—and knowing further that her flight would spell her own end.

"Save Bruadair?" she repeated, finding herself completely unable to understand how she was to go from merely wanting to save herself to needing to save her country.

He swore at her. "You're dead right now, don't you know? You crossed the border."

She knew it, of course, but she hadn't wanted to face it. "I didn't have any choice—"

"Of course you did," he said briskly. "You could have chosen to crawl back to that miserable guild and spend the rest of your days trapped in a life of endless drudgery. But you chose freedom."

"I didn't choose anything," she protested.

"Didn't you?"

She chose to ignore the implications of what he'd said. She looked at the ground, because it was safer that way. "What does that matter if I've sentenced myself to death?"

He put his hand under her chin, lifted her face up, and looked at her with absolutely no expression on his face. "You haven't. There is a way to save yourself."

She pulled away from his hand, sure she'd heard him wrong. "How?"

"It won't be easy, or pleasant," he warned. "The usurper who currently sits the throne must be overthrown before he destroys every last bit of— Well, that isn't important. What *is* important is that the rightful king take his place. This is not a task for an army, for Sglaimir will see them and slay them before they can touch him. A mage will not manage it either, for his magic will be sensed before he reaches the palace walls."

"Mages?" she echoed, trying to laugh. She thought it had sounded more like a gasp of terror than anything else, but she perhaps wasn't the best one to judge. "I don't believe in mages."

He blew out his breath in frustration. "Seek out an assassin, then, one who will dethrone the king for the glory of it—or as much gold as we've been able to muster." He looked at her seriously. "You have three se'nnights. The bargain must be struck before midnight of the last day or your life will be the forfeit."

She couldn't keep from blinking. "How do you know—"

"Because I know," he said curtly. "Bloody hell, wench, have you no idea—Nay, you don't." He shook his head sharply. "The details aren't important. You have been granted the gift of a fortnight and a half. Complete your quest and your life will then be yours."

She started to speak, then shut her mouth around her protests. "But quests should be left to heroes." She might have been a common weaver, but she was very well-read in subjects ranging from the movements of stars to the movements of men. It took a certain set of skills to embark on any sort of serious heroic business.

"You were all that was available at the time. And you know where to go."

She felt her mouth go dry. "Do I?"

"Did I sell you that book for naught?"

"Which book?"

"The only book you own!"

She put her hand over her belly before she thought better of it. There, in the waist of her trousers, was the book she had paid for with half of all the meager coins she'd managed to accumulate over the years doing odd things about the Guild. *The Strictures of Scrymgeour Weger* was the title. Just looking at the cover had fair burned her eyes. She had fetched the purchase price and paid it without hesitation, because whilst she wasn't a good weaver, she could recognize Fate when it was staring her in the face.

She couldn't quite bring herself to think about the things she had read inside that very worn leather cover.

The peddler put his hand suddenly on her shoulder and turned her away from the border. "Run. The carriage is waiting, but it won't wait forever. Find a solution to what you've left behind here while you're still alive."

Her mouth was very dry. "But I know nothing about wars or rulers or—"

"Then every book you ever were given by the mistress of

the loom over all the years she had you at her elbow was completely wasted."

"But I am nobody," she protested. It sounded more like the
pleading of a child than the protestations of a woman, but she
was, she could freely admit, not at her best at present. "I am no
one of consequence, without friend or family or any gifts—"

"Then no one will miss you when you're gone," he said
shortly, looking over his shoulder and cursing. He turned back
to her and put a heavy hand on her shoulder. "There is no one
else, Aisling, no one but you. I suggest you go south."

South.

The word echoed in her head like a great bell that had been
rung just once in an immense canyon. South. There were many
things in the south, many places to lose herself. Scrymgeour
Weger lived in the south, on an island, or so it was rumored.
Though she didn't suppose he would have an army at his
disposal.

But he might be able to tell her where to find someone who
could do what needed to be done.

"Tell no one of your errand or of your homeland."

She looked at the peddler. "Not even the mercenary?"

He shook his head. "Have him meet me at Taigh Hall three
months from today."

"And you think he will come?" she managed.

"He will, if he wants the rest of his money." He gestured to
the pack. "The first half of his incentive is in there. He can
name his price for the rest when the deed is done. Now, go.
The sands have already begun to fall. Three se'nnights, Aisling, and no longer."

She turned and peered into the darkness, looking for her
means of escape.

And as she looked, she felt her breath begin to come in
gasps. The fate of her land, a land that had hosted her birth and
now would be the reason for her death, was in her hands.

She turned back to the peddler.

He was gone.

Guards shouted in the distance. Aisling didn't wait to see
what the fuss was about. She simply turned and ran into the
darkness.

South.